THESE WICKED TRUTHS

THESE WICKED TRUTHS

THESE WICKED LIES, BOOK 2

MIRANDA JOY

SPELLBOUND SOULS

To anyone on a journey of self-discovery, this one's for you.
Don't worry about finding yourself—create yourself.

CONTENT WARNING

Please be advised that this book is intended for mature audiences, and reader discretion is advised. Content warnings include, but are not limited to: references to abuse, physical violence, death, vulgarity, descriptive sex including MFM polyamorous relations, suicide, murder, anxiety/panic disorder, familial trauma, and more.

As always, take steps to protect yourself and your own mental health. If you are someone who struggles, I'm sending you extra love and support. You're not alone.

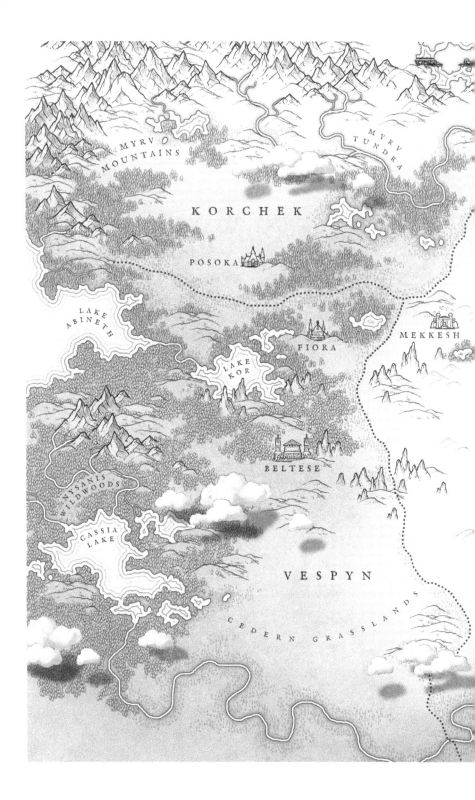

PROLOGUE

AIFE

I hum to myself—a new song Lex played for me on piano this morning—filled with excitement about my two favorite people meeting: my fated and my sister.

My feet carry me mindlessly to the secluded two-story cottage nestled among cheery sunflowers. My little oasis. Sunshine gilds the entire property, highlighting the teal blue house. It's breathtaking. Teal and gold, my two favorite colors.

The air is full of earthy, woodsy, and floral scents. I inhale greedily through my nose, letting the familiar smells soften my body.

I haven't seen Invidia for a while, since before I kissed Lex at the falls. And finally, she's back. She gets to meet my fated. I wanted them to meet here, at my beloved cottage, rather than at my new apartment in Nevaris. I'm not ready to share our secret slice of the world with my sister yet.

As I cut through the yard and move around the side of the house, a sweat breaks out on the back of my neck beneath my curtain of hair. I'm running late, but Lex is always on time. Surely he's already here.

When I enter the garden in the backyard, I pause, detecting voices. A veritable forest of fruit trees, flowers, and vegetable plants block my view, but the voices are unmistakable: Lex and Invidia. I navigate around the vibrant pink plum blossoms, heading straight toward the lone weeping willow.

The branches of the willow cascade down around the trunk like hair as they tickle the ground. I peer beyond the brittle leaves and spy Lex and Invidia standing on the other side.

What are they doing so deep in the garden? And why are they speaking in such hushed tones?

Lex's back is to me, so I can't see his expression, but Invidia's lips move rapidly as she speaks. Even from this distance, I can see how red and flushed her cheeks are. I drift forward, desperate to hear what she's saying.

They've never met before, so what could they possibly be speaking about with such vigor?

The moment her eyes lock onto mine, they widen, and she shakes her head. The scarlet coloring in her cheeks fades into a pale, ashy sheen. Her cheeks begin to hollow out, and her face shrivels in on itself—becoming a desiccated layer of textured wrinkles, as if she's a discarded letter being scrunched within an invisible fist.

She drops to her knees, her body contorted with pain, paralyzed by an unseen force.

No.

Not an unseen force.

Magic.

The power of a vyogra. More specifically, of the god of war.

Of Lex.

My fated. I bolt toward them, a scream ripping from my throat, but it's too late. Invidia's eyes stare up at me from beneath the willow where she's fallen, her thinned lips perpetually paused in a small O of shock.

It mirrors my own reaction.

Pain lances through my chest as I force myself to tear my gaze from her, to face the man responsible. His impossibly green eyes stare back at me with cool indifference; there's not a fleck of remorse or sorrow there—only a glint of wrath, a promise of vengeance. I don't have time or energy to contemplate it. It doesn't matter.

I thought I knew pain, but this...this is too much.

How can this be the same man who kissed me tenderly beneath the falls? Who writes songs for me on the piano? Who sings me to sleep with nothing but adoration in his eyes? How is this the same man who filled my new apartment with my favorite books and scented oils to surprise me?

I already knew of his reputation—his ability to cut down enemies without a single flex of his finger—but Invidia was not an enemy.

A sob escapes my mouth, and I shake my head at him. "Invidia—" My voice cracks.

Lex adjusts the collar of his black button-up shirt before stepping toward me. "Aife, luv."

His cadence is normal, as if everything is okay, but his dark presence is a stain against the colorful, flowery background.

My body kicks into flight mode, and I bolt from the garden.

CHAPTER ONE

ASTRID

There's always an awkward lull after murdering someone.

The hallway is silent, save for the pulsing thud of my heartbeat echoing inside my skull.

A metallic scent, mixed with sweat and a hint of lemon, washes over me. My stomach roils, but I keep my face impassive.

Lex's harbingers stand muttering around Enira's lifeless body. I whirl away, keeping them at my back and facing Dash instead.

His lips twist in discomfort, his cheeks losing their normal tan color. Downed guards lay in motionless heaps on the floor around him, courtesy of the impulsive unleashing of my vygora power.

A hysterical laugh tickles my throat. It's a ridiculous scene— all of us here in this disgustingly gaudy palace together. Dash posturing with his messy hair and scuffed boots amidst perfectly spotless, gleaming floors and marble pillars. Lex standing in his all-black ensemble, contrasting with the colorless ivory aesthetic. Me with my internal chaos burning bright and loud against a backdrop of bone-chilling silence.

None of us belong here.

We're all damaged, woefully flawed people who were born into chaotic, messy lives. No matter how high these domed ceilings reach, how thick and sturdy these statuesque pillars stand, or how long these serpentine hallways stretch, this palace will never be enough to contain us.

Or our layers upon layers of lies.

They pile atop each other, sticking together. Pulling back one layer rips and tugs at the next, until the entire stack unravels into a sticky mess of half-truths and misconstrued messages.

The only one who fit inside the walls of this horrifyingly sterile palace was Enira. And now, in a beautiful twist of irony, she's bleeding out like a sacrificial lamb. Her blood is the color these marble halls lacked.

I was her *vessel* for so long. Now *she* is *my* vessel. Her blood is my paint, and I am the artist spilling it across an unblemished canvas.

It may have been a bit rash for me to take Enira's life, but there is no place in this world for such a vile, abusive woman. I was propelled by the need to avenge my fated, protect my friends. Nobody harms the people I care about and lives to tell the story.

Which leads me to my incredibly hypocritical dilemma regarding Lex: *he* also murdered someone very dear to me.

I shouldn't have kissed Lex like that, but I needed to—one last time. I don't have any memories of kissing him, and if I never get those memories back, I needed to know how it felt.

I wanted to see if it would settle the desire burning inside of me.

That kiss was for Aife and what she lost. It was for Astrid and what she can never have.

The line is thin between love and hate. Their edges blend together until they are virtually indistinguishable from one another.

Lex reaches for me as I step back, away from the heat of his body. His fingers brush the skin of my wrist, but when I recoil, his arm goes limp at his side.

I scrutinize his face, taking in those piercing eyes and frowning lips—lips so soft, made to fit against my own. Behind him, the harbingers, standing in a pool of Enira's blood, quietly debate whether to clean up the mess or leave it.

Although I can't see him, Dash's judgment burns into me from behind. *His* betrayal feels minor compared to Lex's.

"Aife, luv." Lex's lazy, confident drawl makes my stomach twirl. "*Astrid*," he says when I don't reply.

His tender tone, his willingness to address me by the name I identify with, stills the turbulence in my stomach. My jaw softens, and my hands relax at my sides. But I'm dissociating with both names—both lives. Neither feels like *me*, and it confuses the hell out of me.

"No." My voice is confident, despite the insecurities plaguing me. I retreat, shaking my head at Lex. "I shouldn't have kissed you. That was a mistake."

"Nothing between us is ever a mistake."

"Letting you out of the pit certainly was."

"You don't mean that." His eyes flick down to where blood creeps across the floor, settling around his dark boots. "Enira's gone. You're safe. Let's get you cleaned up. We can talk."

Glancing down at myself, I notice the copper-red splatters on my clothes and bare arms. I squeeze my eyes shut, as if I can focus hard enough to will this nightmare away.

"Leave her be, bastard," Dash says as he strides up behind me. He's either a brave man or a fool for challenging Lex. "You've done enough damage here. Take your friends and get out of here."

"Stay out of this, *boy*," Lex snarls.

"She's clearly in shock. You think *talking* with you is going to help her right now? It won't help shit!"

Frowning, I glance at Dash. He clenches his fists, glaring murderously at Lex. Both men have hurt me, but I don't want them destroying each other.

"Stop," I mumble wearily. "I can't do this. Just leave me alone, please. And leave each other alone."

Spinning around, I leave them behind and flee down the corridor. As I pass the fallen guards, I slow to confirm their chests still rise and fall beneath their leathers. I didn't kill them. That's a relief.

Tears prick my eyes as I continue to replay the memory of Lex and Invidia in my mind. It's like a gnat I can't swat away.

Lex and I are fated. I am Aife. Somewhere deep down, I have the memories of an entire lifetime inside of me. But I have more questions than answers now.

Despite the deep loathing I experienced when I relived the memory of him killing my sister, I have built new feelings for him...as Astrid. There has to be more to the story. I don't know what could have possibly justified him taking my sister's life, but there has to be something I'm missing. Lex isn't me—he isn't impulsive.

He is always in control.

It doesn't seem fitting that he would murder my sister on a whim within minutes of meeting her. He didn't seem impassioned in my memory.

I don't remember having a sister, but my adoration of and respect for her was strikingly evident in the memory. It's clear I loved her, and I was shocked by his actions then, just as I am now.

"Astrid, wait." Sighing, I turn to see Dash jogging toward me, alone. His boots slap against the marble, echoing eerily in the grand hallway.

I shouldn't stop and wait for him to catch up, but I do. A

strangled sound, half sigh and half groan, rips through me. "I don't want to talk to you right now."

"No—it's—"

"I need to get out of here." The air is heavy, stifling.

"Please don't go, Astrid." His voice cracks as he repeats my name. He scrubs his face with a hand, exhaling loudly. Warm brown eyes sweep over me in concern.

Regret thickens my throat as I take in the droop of his shoulders. Damn him for taking up space inside of my soul.

It's impossible to carve him or Lex out of my heart simply because I *want* to, but I need to try. Breaking free from Enira is like escaping an abusive relationship—I need time alone to think and heal.

"I'm sorry for reacting poorly about...this. About you. I'm sorry for not being honest before...and for everything I've done to make you doubt *us*, but it's not what you think."

"I meant what I said. This is not what's important right now."

"It might not be important, but you are. *You* are important to me." He unbuttons the top few buttons of his shirt, yanking it down over his shoulder and brandishing the tattoo on his bicep. "I told you before, I promised Ayana I would love fiercely," he says, referencing his first love, the woman he failed to protect. "I can't walk away once I've let someone in. And you're the first person I've let in since her. I'm not perfect, but I truly care about you—"

"For the love of the goddess, stop! After everything I went through with Enira's lies, after all your deception, you have the gall to try and *guilt* me into returning your affections?"

"I am not trying to manipulate you into feeling something for me. We have a connection. We were building something real before *Lexyll* came into the picture."

"This has nothing to do with Lex, and this is exactly why I can't do this with you. Please, go. Leave me alone. Don't make me ask again."

My mouth goes dry, and my hands ball into fists at my sides. Anger churns in the pit of my stomach, and I have to work to keep it down. Keep it from erupting.

Dash isn't entirely wrong. If Lex had never stepped into the picture, maybe I could've fallen for him. But now I remember how intense love can be.

How love with Lex is.

Everyone always talks about how falling in love is the most magical feeling in the world, but no one ever mentions how it feels when you stop falling—when you career into the ground at full speed. The force might not shatter bones, but it ruptures hearts.

I'm not sure I could ever feel about Dash how I once did about Lex, and I'm not sure I even *want* to. But then again, maybe Dash will never feel for me the same way he did for Ayana. Maybe that's what makes love so special: it's unique every time.

It also has the potential to crush you uniquely every time.

While I stand there, contemplating what it is I feel for Dash, he steps toward me. I don't move away when he reaches up to run his thumb over my lips. His eyes bounce around my face, as if he's desperate to memorize every line, every angle.

"I'm not going anywhere." He shakes his head. "I'm staying here. For Hakran. For you. And when you're ready, I'll be here."

I shake my head vigorously. "This is the *last* thing I want to focus on right now."

Lex's face flashes in my mind. My head grows light, and my palms get clammy. Warning bells go off inside me, but then I remember that Lex and I can never be together. I don't stop Dash when he begins to slowly lean in toward me.

At the last second, before his lips meet mine, his expression changes, and I nearly stumble when he pulls back suddenly.

"I'm not Lexyll. I'll never intentionally harm you. Which is why—"

"You know nothing about him," I hiss. Is Dash using his mind reading? "Nor do you know anything about what he has or hasn't done."

"No, but his barriers slipped. I heard it—his thoughts. He has no regrets about what he did."

I knew it! He *is* invading my mind. "How dare you! Stay the fuck out of his head and mine."

"Why do you stick up for him? Protect him? He's hurt you before; he'll hurt you again. He's not a good guy."

"You know what's funny to me?" I ask, shoving a finger into his broad chest. "Neither are you, Dash."

He shakes his head as his mouth forms into a tight line. "I never meant to—"

"Of course you didn't *mean* to. No one ever *means* to!" My hands practically vibrate at my sides, and my head spins with the day's events. I can barely get a grasp on myself, let alone those around me. It's all too much—Dash's desperation to connect, the memory of Lex's betrayal, Ilona, my best friend in the world, bolting from me like a frightened animal.

"I do *not* have the mental capacity for this right now."

He puts his hands up in a placating gesture. "For what it's worth, I'm sorry for everything." His soft brown eyes flicker with sorrow, and I squirm beneath his gaze.

I truly don't have the energy to discuss the petty problems between us. I still don't know if he used me to get Hakran's throne, but it's the least of my issues at the moment, albeit something I will need to address at some point.

"If you ever cared about me, please, let me walk away."

He hesitates, and his mouth opens as if he has more to say, but then he nods and stuffs his hands into his pockets.

As I walk away from him, he whispers, "I'll be here when you get back, Astrid."

Not *if*, but *when*.

His words follow me down the hallway like a ghost.

I'm halfway to Ilona's room when I pause. She seemed genuinely stunned when she saw what I did to Enira. I've put her through so much. Maybe she needs time to heal, just as I do.

Staying here isn't an option. But there's nowhere for me to go. Nowhere that feels like *home* anymore. And I don't know where the cottage from my memory—*my* cottage—is.

The only place that comes to mind that seems safe, accessible, and isolated enough is the apartment in Nevaris. Hopefully Lex and his pals are wise enough to leave me be, but the prospect of solitude is worth taking the chance.

So, with a heavy heart, I leave Ilona and the palace behind.

For now.

CHAPTER TWO

LEX

I'm not sure how much time has passed since I watched Aife retreat down the hallway. Or since *Dashiel Dargan* darted after her.

Following them was a great temptation, but I know Aife well, so I remain stationary.

After Enira's death, when Aife looked at me, she finally *saw* me. There was a glimmer of recognition in those oceanic eyes of hers. And when she kissed me, the dormant piece of my heart pumped back to life.

I let her go because I know she is en route back to me.

I let her go because she needs me to. Not for forever, but for right now. Going after her would be purely selfish.

That logic doesn't stop my ribcage from clutching my lungs in a vise grip. It never gets easier watching her walk away. I'm constantly fighting for this woman in silence, and I anxiously anticipate the day she allows me to speak my truth to her.

But I won't do it before she's ready.

The real challenge is allowing the boy-king to follow her. He isn't unscathed because of my empathy or goodwill. No. I leave him unharmed because it would crush Aife if I hurt him.

The boy might be immune to the powers of myndoxes and vygoras, but my power worked on him in the throne room after

Aife and I power-shared.

Our power worked on him.

Together, Aife and I are truly an unstoppable force. And when she realizes that, our lives together can resume. I pity those who will oppose us. People like her scheming, predatory sister, Invidia.

Worse than Enira, that one.

I know all too well the sting of familial betrayal.

"We shouldn't leave her body here," Lo mutters, glancing down at Enira.

I'd rather not leave the body of a newly deceased goddess behind. Although we are spared from dying of natural causes, gods are not immune to death entirely. And after we take our final breath, our magic seeps from our bodies and goes back into the earth to be recycled. It doesn't happen immediately. It takes time. Placing the body in nature—such as the ocean or a forest—without man-made materials around to dampen the flow of magic, helps it to be recycled more quickly.

I give Lo a sharp nod, and she and Sora unsheathe their swords.

I don't blink as they take turns hacking into Enira with enough force to sever her limbs. It's easier to dismember the body and pack it up than to travel with a full corpse in tow.

We can toss her in the jungle. Feed the animals that reside there.

A speck of blood flies up, splattering on my cheek. Absent-mindedly, I use my thumb to brush it away.

Choosing a white theme for the palace was foolish. Everyone knows darker colors are best for hiding bloodstains.

Then again, perhaps the designer hadn't planned for such a bloodbath to take place in these halls.

The designer was Enira, after all. Although the palace had the same structure and layout when I arrived, it certainly did not gleam with wealth and power as it does now.

Lo remains impassive throughout the task, but the sharp angles of Sora's brassy face demonstrate his fierce anger as he takes out his internalized rage on Enira's corpse. Thick, corded muscles flex and strain against his tight long-sleeve turtleneck.

I let him continue because his intensity harms no one, but we need to have a talk before this fury spills over into other areas of his life.

"Stay close," I tell Callan. "We will do all we can to protect her. But, Callan?" I wait a beat before continuing. "Give her space. She will only lash out if we interfere." It isn't that I want to keep things from Aife. She's simply too stubborn to listen or accept anything she doesn't learn on her own.

Callan tightens his grip on the pommel of his sheathed sword. His normally-animated face is solemn as he nods, understanding the implication of the words I don't say: *Don't let her out of your sight.*

He stalks off in the direction Aife and Dash headed earlier. His figure shimmers, becoming more faint with each step, until he is no longer visible. Everything—from his golden hair, casual clothes, and black leather boots, to his steel sword—is now transparent.

Sora might be the quiet one of the group, the one people fear most, the shadow, but it's Callan, my second harbinger—second only to Lo—who can be truly unseen and unheard. He and Lo have the ability to disappear completely. Unlike a shadow, whose form and darkness can be witnessed, they can slip into full invisibility.

They are neither humans nor gods.

They are angelli.

Beings from beyond our realm. Sora is the most menacing harbinger, but it's my two pleasant-looking allies, with kind eyes and soft smiles, that our enemies should fear. Both Lo and Callan hail from another world, and they have powers beyond what this realm has seen.

They are my secret weapons.

Aife is safe with Callan watching over her.

A second later, the newly crowned boy-king comes into sight, heading down the hallway toward us. A few steps in and he jolts to a stop. His mouth and eyes open so wide it's comical.

"What the actual *fuck*!" he says. Then he gags.

I can't help the smile that crosses my lips as Dashiel bends at the waist, retching all over the floor.

"What kind of guardsman are you that you can't stomach a little blood?" I ask. Pathetic.

If only Aife could see this. Perhaps she'd be less inclined to kiss him after seeing him spew his supper all over his boots.

The thought of her kissing him is enough to wipe the smirk from my lips.

"That is not a *little* blood. That is…excessive. There is something very wrong with you." He scrubs his face with a hand.

Peering over my shoulder, I notice that Lo and Sora have finished cutting up Enira's body. They're covered in gore and the rusty color of blood. They've wrapped Enira's body parts in her skirts, using the fabric as a sack of sorts to move them.

Along with the stench of vomit, the metallic scent of blood taints the air. It's something I've become desensitized to over the last few hundred years. I've become desensitized to many things, thanks to being left to rot in my own filth in the pit for so long.

"Actually…Lo?" I ask. She pauses. "Dump the body, but

bring the head back to Nevaris."

I rather enjoy displaying the trophies of my conquered enemies in my den.

When I turn back to Dashiel, I catch him wiping his mouth with the hem of his shirt. His eyes are wild as he stares at me. He's clearly trying hard not to take in the scene behind me.

I chuckle to myself as I brush past him. To my harbingers, I say, "Let's go home."

CHAPTER THREE

DASH
Three Months Later

The surly bastard glares at me as he leans against the limestone wall, his eyes narrowing into nothing more than dark slashes on his mean mug, perfectly accented by his equally sharp brows.

I bark a laugh, wondering what the hell is up his ass. "If you're trying to intimidate me, it's not working." I thought we'd moved past this. My mental guard is down, allowing his thoughts to filter from his head into mine via my myndox power.

No wonder Lex calls you a boy, Sora thinks. *No king I've met acts so immature.*

"What? Since I have a sense of humor, I'm *immature*?" I smirk. "Not all of us have a stick shoved up our ass."

His scowl deepens, but he doesn't gift me with a reply. He's just pissed about me putting hot sauce in his scrambled eggs this morning. For such a spicy man, he has zero tolerance for spicy food.

I chuckle, and he continues to shoot daggers at me with his eyes. "Sorry—I'm not trying to *egg* you on, I swear." I snort at my pun, and he grunts.

He's been here on and off for three months now, at Lexyll's behest, helping me scour the island for information regarding Astrid's missing memories. My responsibilities as Hakran's king are utterly time-consuming, so his assistance has been necessary.

Unfortunately, we've discovered very little.

The pranks on Sora are a humorous reprieve and a delightful distraction. I discovered early on that he's perpetually pissed off, which makes him the perfect person to play practical jokes on.

Any second now, my commander will arrive and we can all officially debrief and call it a day. Not that I have much to share. It was another disappointing day with no answers gleaned. Based on what I've already sifted through in Sora's brain, he hasn't discovered anything useful either.

We are due to plan a trip to Stellaris though. Since we've failed to gain any insight into Enira's motivations or find out how to restore Astrid's memories, our next step is to speak with Cedrik, the healer. He left Hakran, traveling to the palace in Cerulea with my parents months ago, and he's the only one we haven't pressed for answers yet. Now that Sora and I have combed through the entire island, it's time to switch tactics. Cedrik *has* to know something—even if his memories are technically missing still.

As far as we know, Ilona, Cedrik, and Astrid were the only people whose memories didn't fully return after Enira's death. Our theory is that since they were the closest to Enira, they were likely affected on a deeper level than the rest of the villagers.

If it weren't for Sora's help in pursuing answers about Enira, I wouldn't have agreed to host him in Hakran. I don't trust any of Lexyll's associates. Especially not the muscled-up grump in front of me posing as a diplomat.

I snort. Sora the *diplomat*.

He's useful, honestly, but he lacks humor.

Neither Sora nor I attempt to converse, opting to observe each other in silence as we wait for my commander's arrival.

My mind spins with ideas for my next prank. I could find a milk snake—or better, a tree boa—and slip it into his bath...

I shake off the thought with a sly grin.

Fire orbs—small, glowing balls of fire contained by glass— illuminate the room from overhead. I stand over the table in the subterranean war room, countless sheets of paper spread out before me. Some of the papers cover training techniques while some highlight plans for economic stimulation. Behind me, the corkboard on the stone wall is covered with documents detailing trade routes, ocean currents, and blueprints for new boats.

The new ships will be expensive, but they will also be much better equipped to navigate the brutal Hakranian waters on this side of the Insipid Sea. The waters *are* difficult to navigate here, but with some proper training—and sturdier ships—the task will not be impossible for the Hakranian warriors.

Enira put much effort into cutting Hakran off, and now I'm putting in double the effort to reconnect the island with the continent of Thysia. Hakran and Stellaris might have their sandy beaches and turquoise waters in common, but the natural resources in each region differ substantially, which offers a perfect opportunity for trade. Hakran has the potential to thrive on export, with its rare fruits and considerable limestone and quartz deposits.

Enira purposefully kept the Hakranians weak and impoverished, forcing the people to become reliant on her. There's no reason the island should be as poor as it is.

With the storm season behind us, the humidity has let up significantly, but the air still carries a bit more heat than I'm used to this time of year. Down here, below ground, is the coolest part of the entire palace.

The war room is situated above the pit, adjacent to the training rooms. With its dark stone walls, concrete floors, steel table, and lack of comforts, it's almost like an artificial cave, out of place when compared to the endless marble above. Here, wars are discussed and decisions are made. It's the brain of the palace in some ways.

If it were any darker or dirtier, or made of silenxstone instead of limestone, it would be reminiscent of the pit.

I shudder at the thought of that place, of the stone that mutes magic. Part of me empathizes with Lexyll, for being subjected to that damned place. A much, much bigger part of me feels sorry for Astrid, for being caught up in everyone's manipulation.

My heart doubles in tempo at the thought of her smooth, olive skin, her stormy eyes—fuck, they remind me so much of the waters back home—and her soft lips. I wish I had known the truth about her earlier—that she's the woman of my dreams. If I had predicted I'd fall for her, I would've found another way to break Enira's hold. A way that didn't require deceiving her.

I would've told her all my secrets earlier. Now, as each day passes and distance continues to separate us, the weight of my secrets grows heavier.

If only I wasn't so damn busy with my new duties as Hakran's king, I could do much more. Maybe then I wouldn't need Lexyll and Sora's help. Regardless of what Astrid thinks, I did not want this position. I had truly thought I was helping *her* assume her mother's throne.

It never occurred to me that Astrid might be a goddess. We had no clue who she was.

I miss her so much it hurts.

I almost snort aloud at the thought of Enira pretending to be Astrid's mother. The games that woman played were in an entirely other realm of fucked up. Then again, the goddess of deception was known to toy with others for her own selfish entertainment.

My father viewed the gods as nefarious creatures. Enira's

behavior certainly lined up with that outlook.

I run a hand through my shaggy hair, glancing at Sora. The guy continues to stare at me like I shit in his boot or something. I give him a rude finger and turn my back to him, leaning against the carved stone table. Whatever thoughts are going through his head aren't relevant at the moment, so I block them out. His observations and judgments don't bother me. It's been a learning curve, us becoming *allies*, but here we are.

And, yes, this is us being friendly.

We've come a long way.

Sora's weak mental barriers allowed me to learn that Lexyll has instructed him not to harm me. Otherwise, Sora would have surely carved me up in retaliation for my pranks by now.

The door creaks open. Like the pit, the war room is protected—only accessible by me, my commander, and Ilona, who serves as my advisor. I thought it'd be a pain in the ass to gain access to these protected places after Enira's death, but etheryn magic is painfully intelligent. The spelled doors sensed the shift in rule, automatically knowing who to give access to, without any fuss at all.

It's as if the magic is sentient, living in the walls, listening to our secrets, knowing all.

A flurry of dark curls rushes into view in my peripheral vision. The bitter scent of coffee fills my nose—a welcome invader—as a mug of black liquid is thrust into my hands.

"Dash."

"Fatima." I offer my commander a smile, and she returns it briefly before raising a brow at the man-shaped shadow lurking in the corner of the room. "Finally."

I lower my mental barriers, allowing her voice to flood my mind.

Are you two getting along today?

I shrug in response.

You two pick a date to set sail yet?

"Nope," I answer aloud. "We waited for you."

Sora grunts in response to our secretive half-mindspeak. Like I care.

Better get your shit together beforehand. If you can't stand Sora, how are you going to tolerate Lexyll?

She isn't wrong. The prospect of sailing to Stellaris with Lexyll is already grating on my nerves. It'll be the longest trip of my life.

I give my commander a cheeky grin. "We haven't agreed on *who* is sailing yet."

We've discussed it casually. Of course I want to go—to see my family. And according to Sora's thoughts, Lexyll is feeling like he's not doing enough to help Astrid.

Which means he will likely sail with us.

Hopefully Cedrik knows something and the trip will be worthwhile. Granted, seeing my family is always worthwhile, but I'd like it to be a fruitful journey for Astrid too. Not that she has any idea what we're doing. The stubborn woman has been holed up for months. I'm sure she's going stir-crazy, but I would bet she's refusing to see us just to make a statement.

Fatima gives me a brittle smile.

I wish her sister could see her now. She's awe-inspiring in her leathers, and I'm proud to witness her wearing the uniform with such confidence. The guards no longer wear those ridiculous face covers, so everyone can see my commander in all of her glory.

Fatima is a longtime family friend. I appointed her as Hakran's commander immediately after ascending to the throne. She's a well-rounded warrior with unmatched combat skills, a keen sense of observation, and wily intelligence. She and I battled it out to become Zale's bodyguard back in Stellaris when we were teens.

I *barely* beat her for the spot.

Above all, it's Fatima's unwavering loyalty that makes her a true asset. Her older sister, Ayana, was my first love, and I owe it to Ayana to look out for her. Not that she needs it. Fatima trains harder than anyone I've ever met, which is how she rose through the ranks so quickly despite being a few years younger than me. She doesn't *need* anyone to look after her. If anything, the girl does the looking after.

Through everything, Fatima has stuck by my side as a friend. We've bonded over our guilt; she blames *herself* for Ayana's death. If anyone is guilty for failing to protect Ayana, it's me. But at least there's comfort in knowing Fatima doesn't blame me.

My free hand balls into a fist at my side as I pound my coffee down to the dregs and slam the mug on the table.

Thank the goddess for Fatima. It's a relief not to be stuck with any of Hakran's previous commanders. I can't say I wept when Astrid rid the earth of Commander Jamell.

Astrid.

My beautiful, dark, avenging goddess.

Her love slipped through my grip like sand through my fingers.

"Dashiel?" Fatima waves a hand in front of my face, her wide, molten brown eyes observing me carefully. "Wherever you went off to, I need you to rein it in and come back."

"Just thinking about how good that coffee was," I lie. "Thanks."

"You were thinking about *her*," Fatima says softly.

A scoff from behind has me whirling around on my heel. I almost forgot about Sora, who's lingering like a bad smell.

"Something funny, curmudgeon?"

He simply blinks at me, but his thoughts flick through my mind. *Just take the whore. She doesn't deserve Lex. She will never be on his level.*

Something snaps inside me, bringing forth a darkness long forgotten.

I charge at him, gripping him by the neck, and slam him into the stone wall.

"Dashiel," Fatima scolds, her voice tight with warning. "This isn't you. Let him go."

I ignore her, tightening my hold on his throat. He sputters, and in my peripheral view, there is a flash of orange-red. Glancing down, I realize flames are licking his hands.

"The hell?" I release my grip, jumping backward. Fatima moves closer, getting in between us. Instead of charging the guy on my behalf, like I'd expect my commander to do, she reaches for one of his flaming fists.

The flames die out, and he snubs her outstretched hand, crossing his arms and stuffing his hands in his armpits.

"Aethyn," Fatima says quietly. "Fire aethyn."

We exchange glances, my eyes wide with surprise. That's new information.

Turning back to Sora, I scan his body. He's shorter than me by a few inches, but bulkier. Built like a tree stump, bitter as a boar.

"It's incredibly uncouth to refer to a woman in such a derogatory manner. You talk about her—think about her—like that again, and we will share more than words."

I really, really don't care for violence, despite my history as a guard. Frankly, it's exhausting.

Fatima sighs. "We're all on the same side." *I don't trust him either, but he* is *loyal to Lexyll. And Lexyll is loyal to Astrid. You need to keep your cool if she really means that much to you. Do it for her. Sora's been helpful.*

"I know," I say.

And maybe stop intentionally angering him? The hot sauce thing was cruel.

I stifle a laugh, fighting the curve in my lips as I nod at Fatima.

Before we debrief, there's something you need to know. We received word from your brother today. You might want to have a look. She stands tall and unrolls a piece of parchment she had tucked beneath her arm. *It's not good. Aethyn workers are disappearing from Cerulea. Word on the street is that it's the empress of Vespyn. It's...unexpected to say the least. The message is short. Not much detail.*

Rubbing my forehead, I try to contemplate what that could possibly mean for Zale. For Stellaris. My home country.

Cerulea, the capital of Stellaris, is where the palace is. It's where I grew up. Vespyn is a neighboring country, much larger in size to Stellaris, but deeper inland. It's known for its scenic landscapes, wildlife, and agriculture. It's normally a quiet country. Other than occasional issues regarding trade, there's rarely any notable activity on our borders.

Vespyn and Stellaris are not the only countries in Thysia, but they are by far the most powerful. Why would the empress of Vespyn, a peaceful country, our ally, start a conflict with Stellaris?

I snag the letter from Fatima, reading it over twice.

My heart pangs with sorrow for my brother.

Zale is doing his best, but without Emman's guidance, with Joccelyn's grief paralysis, and with Fatima and me gone, he's probably struggling. His normally impeccable handwriting is sloppy, as if he was rushed or perhaps writing the missive with a trembling hand. The letter is short—merely half a page. Unusual, considering his letters to me are normally a few pages long.

I'll bet my left nut he's afraid.

Stellaris is a much bigger country than Hakran, and I can only imagine how difficult it is as a new ruler, based on my own experiences lately.

"Stellaris is preparing for war," I say. It's not a question, and based on the glint of fear in Fatima's eye, she surmises the same. She's equally as concerned about our home country.

We don't have to discuss this in front of him. Fatima's eyes dart to Sora and back to me.

He's a fucking spy, sent here to eavesdrop and prod me for information—there's no sense in even *trying* to keep it secret from him.

An idea strikes me.

"This is good timing," I murmur. "We were planning a trip to Stellaris soon anyway."

Lexyll, God of *War*, can help us.

It's that bastard's specialty, after all.

"Shit." I groan, running my fingers through my hair before shifting my gaze to Sora, who continues to watch us like the predator he is. "We need you to get a message to Lexyll. We need his help."

His voice flits through my mind: *I'm not your dog. And we don't care about your political issues.*

"You might not, but Lexyll will certainly be interested in hearing of *war*." It's in his nature—it's his job—to care.

Sora merely narrows his eyes at me, lips tight and unyielding.

The harbinger is utterly infuriating. I'm tempted to tell him to speak, but then he'll certainly accuse me of treating him like a dog.

"We need to get a message to Lexyll, *please*." I add the pleasantry for good measure.

"What's in it for me?" he says.

So he can talk, after all. "Job security?"

He blinks, clearly unamused by my joke. "No."

"How about I don't tell Lexyll what you really think of his fated?" Sora's thoughts pissed *me* off enough to incite a violent rage, and I'm a much more forgiving guy. I can't imagine Lexyll would let it go as easily.

The threat seems to do the trick, and Sora exhales heavily. "Fine."

My tone is even as I say, "We can debrief later tonight. First, return to Nevaris. Tell Lexyll that war is coming and we need his help."

I'd love to darken his door myself, but I still don't know how to get there. Fatima and I have scoured the entire island. We can travel from coast to coast within a day's time, and we've seen almost everything Hakran has to offer, but we still haven't found out how Sora travels between villages so quickly.

He can get to Lex quickly, get an answer, and get back to us in time for dinner.

I'm certain Lex will at least hear us out. The conflict involves Stellaris, where Cedrik is currently located. And I know he badly wants to interrogate the healer for potential answers about Enira and Astrid, so a threat to the healer is a threat to him personally.

Plus, I'm sure his balls ache for a chance to fight.

He's the god of fucking war.

There's no way he'll decline.

But if he does, I might know of a way to persuade him otherwise.

Once Sora exits the room, I turn to Fatima. "What do you

know about invoking gods?"

Her eyes widen. She opens her mouth to speak, pauses, and then closes it with a heavy sigh and a shake of her head.

If she doesn't have the information I seek, I know of a certain redheaded reader who can find out more.

CHAPTER FOUR

LEX

After a particularly tiresome day of training with Callan's legion-two soldiers at the main compound, tucked in the meadow just north of Nevaris, I want nothing more than an oversized glass of whiskey and a cold shower to settle my sore muscles.

Instead, as soon as I step foot into Harmony House, Lo informs me Sora is back from Hakran. He's been staying there for the last few months, only returning to Nevaris if he has particularly useful information regarding Aife and her memories.

The shower and whiskey must wait.

I stride through the foyer, past the ornate iron staircase, under the loft, and into the wide-open living room. When I stop in front of the expanse of windows, I sigh. The view of the frozen lake inspires a sense of tranquility.

Precisely why I love my lake house.

Hanging a right, I open the sliding doors that separate the enclosed den from the rest of the house. Sora stands there, his dark eyes narrowed into slits.

The fireplace against the far wall has a lively fire crackling in it, casting a lazy orange glow around the room. All the uncomfortable furniture is in here—high-backed chairs, stiff sofas—as well as fancy paintings of random shit like cows and flowers that offer no aesthetic appeal. The dull decor and lack of cozy furniture is a methodical choice meant to dissuade undesired guests from prolonging their visits.

It used to be where we took care of business, before I warded Nevaris and stopped inviting outsiders to the village. While I was *away*, the harbingers started conducting business beyond Nevaris. Never at home. Never again.

My gaze immediately falls on the vitrine against the wall behind Sora, adjacent to the fireplace. A dozen heads sit on display, pale and preserved, their eyes shut for eternity. Reminders of who I am and what happens to those who challenge me.

A quick glance at Enira's headful of thick, dark hair and frozen frowning lips brings a glimmer of pride.

That trophy technically belongs to Aife.

Sora shifts his weight, and the motion catches my attention. Him being in here means he wants to converse in private, away from the other two harbingers.

"What happened tonight?" I ask. I flex my hand at my side, knuckles aching from sparring with Callan and his top legionnaires in today's instructionals.

Sora moves closer to the fire, peering into it. Brilliant light dances across his stoic face. Everything about his appearance is normally sharp and angry—the brows that cut straight lines above each eye, the harsh blue-black color of his hair, his thin lips that press tight together—but right now, he looks lost. Sad.

When I first met Sora as a boy, he had a much softer face. But years of self-hatred have hardened him. It's not his features that make him terrifying but how he wears them, as though he purposely shapes them into a mask meant to repel.

"I almost let it out." His voice is flat.

My eyes flicker between him and the fireplace, and I instantly understand why he's so distraught. "You have control, Sora. You have nothing to fear."

He turns to me, and his nostrils flare. "I don't fear it. I *loathe* it."

"I know."

"I don't want it." He glances at his hands, turning them over and inspecting them with disgust, as if they're traitors. They begin to shake, and he continues muttering to himself, "I don't want it. I don't want it."

"Look at me, Sora." I keep my expression cool and raise my voice until it's demanding, booming off the walls. "I said look at me!"

It snaps him out of his spiraling, and he glances up at me, the tension in his features subsiding as he tucks his hands into his pockets and out of sight.

"Where are you right now?"

"In Nevaris. Harmony House."

I nod. "Yes, and who are you?"

"Sora Kai Kahale."

"*What* are you?" I say with a raised voice again.

"Warrior. Spy. Third Harbinger of Death, to Lexyll, God of War."

"And what else?"

"Fire aethyn," he says, his voice wavering slightly on the last syllable.

"Fire aethyn," I repeat. "You own your power; your power does not own you."

His usual bad-tempered expression returns to his face, and I know he's back with me now. With one last glance at the fire, he steps away from it, turning to address me face to face.

I don't bother asking if he's okay—not anymore. He doesn't need me to ask in order to know I care. Simply being here with him, remaining patient and forgiving, providing work for him—it's enough. I learned long ago that Sora doesn't appreciate comfort and affection. At least not in the standard way most people do.

They see a man who lives in the shadows, who spits venom and breathes fire. I see a scared little boy who experienced a nightmare and lived to tell the tale. Though years have passed since that damage was inflicted, he is still a terrified child trapped in a vicious cycle of relieving those traumas.

He's different, and I understand that. I respect that. I care for him because of that, not in spite of it.

His eyes drop to the floor, and he releases a heavy sigh before speaking. "I need to apologize for disrespecting your fated this evening."

I freeze, fury building. "Oh?"

His voice is tight. "I was intending to rile up the boy-king. I referred to her as a whore."

I snarl at him, surging forward. "I will not allow you to speak about my fated like that. Not in front of me, not behind my back, not ever."

We have an honesty policy—my harbingers and I—but his admission still pisses me off.

Sora grunts. His brown eyes, so dark they're almost black, hone in on me. He doesn't look away, and I appreciate that about him, even though I don't appreciate what he said about Aife.

I take a deep breath, allowing my rage to settle before stepping back.

"Lex, she makes you weak."

"That is not your place to judge. Nor is it your place to condemn her."

"Heard," he says. His jaw clenches as he tugs mindlessly at the cloth around his neck. It's much too hot in here for a turtle-neck, but he refuses to wear anything else. He's covering the mark Aife left on him.

A mark he refuses to forgive, much to my dismay.

As much as I want to brutalize anyone who speaks ill of Aife, I know Sora does not mean it. He's the same struggling boy I met long ago. It softens the disrespect, but only slightly.

If it were anyone else, they'd be lying in a pool of blood on my floor right now.

"That is not why I returned from Hakran though."

That piques my attention. My body tightens, and I draw up to my full height as I peer at Sora with open interest, willing him to continue.

"We aren't done with the previous conversation," I warn. "But go on."

He nods, remorse flickering across his features. "The boy-king received word from his brother."

"And?"

"He requests your assistance. Stellaris is facing new threats from Vespyn."

My brows rise. The lower-level spies from my legions haven't heard any chatter in the wind regarding this. It comes as a total surprise. "Vespyn?"

"Aethyns are going missing."

"They think it's the Vespynians?" That strikes me as odd. Vespyn is a peaceful, pious country.

"Yes."

It's brave of the boy-king to assume I'll help. But he isn't wrong. It's in my nature.

Stepping foot on Stellari land with ill intent is an act of war. And considering I have my own business to take care of in Stellaris—seeking out Enira's old healer for information—this is also a personal matter.

I would have liked to speak with the healer earlier, but I was patiently waiting for Aife to come around, so she could join us on the mainland. Especially considering her old home is there. I have plenty of my own tasks occupying my time, anyway. Plus, with Sora and Dashiel scouring Hakran, we weren't exactly rushing to speak with the healer.

Until now.

My heart skips a beat as I mull over the words. When I finally speak, my tone is lethal. "Have Lo prepare the first and second legions. You will be staying in Nevaris."

"Don't you think it'd be better if I go with—"

"Do not question my decisions," I hiss. I grip the chair tighter, until the wood finally cracks. Sora is struggling because he has been away from home for so long. Despite the traumatic memories associated with Nevaris, it's his safe space. I've already put his mental health at risk by having him be gone for such an extended period of time. I refuse to watch him regress further.

"Nevaris needs a harbinger," I say. *And you need Nevaris.* "We will station Lo in Hakran, and should the situation… escalate, she will be on standby with her legion. Callan will accompany me to the mainland."

Callan and Lo can communicate across seas—realms even—and will act as our communication line.

"Heard." He stands ramrod straight, acknowledging me with proper respect this time.

Sora is perfectly capable of overseeing Nevaris with the third legion during my absence.

Despite his struggles, I trust him wholly. His admission tonight only solidifies that further. I might not like his attitude, but I respect that he can admit when he's wrong.

I grip Sora's broad shoulder and rest my forehead against his.

"We will avoid war if we can, but we must be prepared."

It seems we are sailing to Stellaris sooner than anticipated.

This is what we train for. This is when we *thrive*. As much as I despise the humans' politics, this is my job, after all.

At least with Nevaris, I have a little sliver of untouched land, a protected sanctuary to help those who can't help themselves. Something peaceful amidst the eons of conflict.

Sora heads to the door.

"Sora?" I grit my teeth, a set of teal eyes flashing through my mind. "Send Callan to retrieve Aife."

I've given her enough time and space.

CHAPTER FIVE

ASTRID

Despite the premature winter chill settling over Nevaris, a thin sheen of sweat covers my body. I lie back on my too-firm mattress, staring at the pitched ceiling and exposed wooden beam as I shake off the nightmare I just woke up from, in which *I* was the villain.

In my dream, I used my vygora power to take the lives of dozens of faceless guards and servants in Hakran's palace, absorbing their lives without a hint of remorse. A trail of bodies was left in my wake, tainting the otherwise pristine marble flooring. Then I did the same to Ilona, Dash, and Lex as they pleaded for me not to.

A twisted, horrifying facsimile of my last memory with them.

Afterward, in my dream, I sat amidst the strewn bodies, alone. Utterly, soul-crushingly alone. When I cried, I choked on my own tears and drowned.

It's likely a metaphor for my current circumstance. Ever since I took Enira's life, I've been plagued by a recurring stream of bad dreams. They're less about her death and more about the betrayal I faced from her, Dash, and Lex—that and my fractured relationship with Ilona. I've somehow managed to avoid speaking with any of them since I left, falling into a new routine in Nevaris.

A lonely routine.

When I left Hakran, I had nowhere to go. The cottage in my single restored memory called to me, but I still don't know where it's located. Instead, I ended up in the only place I could think of—the apartment in Nevaris. Even though it's in the heart of the village, it's more peaceful than the palace ever was.

I have space and privacy to rest and think. The villagers leave me alone, save for the occasional visit from Fara, who lives below.

Tonight, the nightmare lingers in my mind. My hands tremble as I work to steady my breathing. Normally I can shake off the dreams and brush them aside, but this time the despair it implanted lingers. I may not have killed my friends, but metaphorically speaking, I killed our friendships.

Time and space have revealed to me the truth: only I am responsible for the loneliness drowning me.

In a way, my nightmare demonstrated something profoundly true. I *am* the villain in my life.

The brick-mantled fireplace crackles on the wall opposite my bed. The pop of logs reminds me to ask Fara for more wood next time I see her. Locals chop wood and store it in sheds around town for anyone to use as needed, and she's been kind enough to ensure I'm well stocked.

A book clatters to the floor as I shake out my left arm, trying to regain feeling there. It's half numb, half tingly from poor circulation. It's no surprise I fell asleep reading, again, considering it's all I do these days. I've read almost every book on the shelves at this point.

After a while, devouring romance novels is like eating too much chocolate—sweet and satisfying at first, until the ache sets in.

A blunt *bang* sounds from the other side of the room. I jolt at the noise, swinging my feet over the side of the bed.

I tilt my head, listening for another noise, but when nothing comes, my shoulders loosen. It was probably the wind. Or the old pipes settling.

From where I sit in bed, the entire apartment is visible. It's shaped like a long rectangle, with a beamed A-frame ceiling and a mixture of exposed brick and wood. A blend of natural and man-made materials. My full-sized bed doubles as a sofa, and there's a bookshelf on the wall to my left. On the other side of the room sits an unused dining table with chairs for four, placed beneath the window wall that overlooks Main Street and the lake beyond.

The kitchen is in the middle, separating the space into three distinct parts—bedroom, kitchen, dining room—despite the open layout.

Overhead, skylights offset the slanted ceilings, making the apartment appear larger and brighter in the daytime. Right now, nothing but a bleak darkness exists beyond the sturdy glass panes.

I listen for the sound I heard before. A small part of me hoped it *was* a knock, but no one is coming for me. If they were going to, they would've come by now.

I'm not sure Dash and Ilona even know how to get to Nevaris. Hell, even I couldn't pinpoint the village on a map. The magical tunnel could have taken me anywhere. And Lex? Well, he's been smart enough to leave me in peace after our explosive *reunion*.

Lo and Callan poked around during the first few weeks, until I threatened to leave Nevaris if they didn't back off. It's already bad enough that everyone knows where I am. I wanted to run away entirely, leave everything and get a start fresh with no Astrid or Aife to haunt me, but there was nowhere to go.

Even Fara is wise enough to let me come to her on my own terms. And when she does leave small gifts—like strudel, blankets, winter jackets, or my favorite floral-scented bath oils—she leaves them outside my door. She doesn't intrude or invite herself in, which I appreciate.

I've succeeded in pushing everyone away. And I thought it was what I wanted.

"Ugh." I put my face in my hands, cringing at my unrealistic expectations. It's been three months, and I miss my friends tremendously, but I've refused to admit my mistakes and make the first move.

I ran like a coward, and I continue to hide like one.

Because running and hiding are easier than facing my problems.

I miss Ilona.

Though I only have one memory of Invidia, my real sister, it sparked a weird nostalgia inside of me. I miss her as much as anyone else. My love and loss linger like phantom pains.

As much as I hate to admit it, I miss Dash too. His motives were questionable, his actions were less than desirable, and his expression of love was overwhelming, but I was unfairly harsh toward him.

He gave me his heart, and I crushed it in my fist.

Even though I got caught in the crossfire of political manipulation, I know Dash wants to do right by Hakran, which is all I wanted too. Love might be the wrong word, but a strong fondness for him took root inside of me, threatening to blossom into something more.

I've stopped watering it, but it still blooms there in the dark. Deep down, I think I ruined our chances of being *more* on purpose. I overreacted, choosing not to trust him, because of my own fears.

How could I give away a heart that doesn't fully belong to *me*? Because that kiss with Lex...

It changed everything.

Kissing him gave me the gift of confirmation. I truly had a life in this world as Aife, and that life is still a part of me. My soul is tied to him. Worse, my soul begs for his. I'm split in half: one side of me craves Lex's touch, his lips, his electrifying presence. The other side despises him.

Love and hate are both emotions of passion, of obsession. When I'm not plagued by thoughts of vengeance and plotting ways to destroy Lex, I'm lost in daydreams of losing myself to his touch.

Loneliness is the worst kind of torture, and losing the people you care for is like having a piece of your heart die.

Sighing, I stretch my arms overhead and trudge to the bookshelf. One bare foot slaps against the wood, having freed itself from my sock in my sleep.

Snagging one of the books I've already read twice—a deliciously sinful story about two pirates—I flop back down onto my bed. Rummaging through the sheets, I find my rogue sock and pull it back on. Sinking into the mattress's dip and cuddling into the knitted blankets, I flip through the worn pages, looking for the dirtiest chapter.

Not only is my heart lonely, but so is my body. I miss intimacy, human touch. I've never gone this long without it. Dash once commented on my notoriety concerning taking guards to bed, and he wasn't wrong. I enjoy pleasure. It's one of life's most beautiful offerings.

Slipping a hand beneath the waistband of my pajama pants, I relax my legs open into a more comfortable position as my eyes skim the words on the page.

Something awfully similar to a cough echoes from somewhere in the room, and I freeze. My blood turns to ice. A *thud* sounds again, and I jerk upright, freeing my hand from my pants.

"Who's there?" I throw the book down, my eyes frantically scanning the apartment.

One of the chairs on the other side of the room tips over, thundering to the floor with a loud *crash*. At the same time, I hear a manly "Whoaaaaa" ring through the space.

Air near the table shimmers, and Callan appears, splayed out face down on the ground. He climbs to his feet, rubbing his neck sheepishly. His cheeks are flushed.

"Callan?" My mouth drops open, and my own cheeks heat up. "What—did you—are you—"

"Aife. Bruisebringer, kicker of shins. It's been a while."

"Where the hell did you just come from?" My brows rise into my hairline as I process the scene. Callan materialized out of thin air. Was he invisible? Right as I was about to— "Ew! You were *watching* me?"

"No!" He raises his hands in a placating gesture. "Well, yes, but no. It's not what you think. I wasn't going to let you...you know. I got stuck in here."

"Stuck?"

"Yes. I wanted to talk with you, but then I realized I'd probably frighten you. So then, I was waiting for you to leave so I could sneak out the door. I have invisibility, not the ability to walk through walls. And if I opened your door on my own, well, that would've freaked you out. I was actually waiting for Lo to—" *Knock. Knock. Knock.* "Ah. There she is. Late, yet somehow on time."

"Invisible?" I mutter to myself. "*Invisibility?*"

I scurry to the door. For a second I pause, wondering if I want to open it. Opening this door means opening myself up to whoever is out there. I could ignore the knocking, wait things out, and find my solitude again. Except that nightmare sits heavily on my chest, and I don't want to be alone anymore.

Not only that, but Callan is already here. Maybe it's time to face my problems instead of running.

I fling the door open, and a flurry of snow whooshes in. Callan stands out of sight, against the wall to my right. I shiver at the nip in the air, gritting my teeth as I scan the woman before me. Lo appears surprised, as if she hadn't expected me to answer.

Her dark, slanted eyes fill with anticipation.

"Hey, Aife," she says, shifting her weight. Her eyes dart past me, silently searching the room.

The apartment is a mess. Books are scattered on the floor around the bed. Ilona would scold me for my poor treatment of the spines—I may have cracked more than a few. Wrinkled clothes are strewn around. Dishes sit unwashed in the sink, and I probably look like a disaster. At least it smells nice and floral, thanks to all the herbs and oils wafting up from the two lower levels.

I run my hands down the front of my sweater, still not quite used to the scratchy wool on my skin. Hakran's clothing is much more my style—lighter and airier—but the Nevarian clothing is more appropriate for the cold climate. It's less attractive, but crucial for protection from the elements. Not that I've cared much about my appearance lately. I'm lucky if I put on a clean outfit these days.

Considering the current circumstance, I'm glad I'm dressed at all.

I turn to Lo, eyeing her skeptically.

They're up to something, of course. These are two of Lex's three harbingers. His friends. They live at Harmony House with him and work for him, which means *he* likely sent them.

Great.

Lo's pale cheeks are stained pink from the cold. She steps toward me awkwardly, then stops, as if she's fighting the urge to hug me. Thankfully, her hands are occupied with a glass jug of golden-brown liquid and a basket, so I don't have to subject myself to an awkward embrace. Her pale braids trail down her back, shining with a collection of snowflakes.

My fingers begin to go numb as icy air continues to pour in, and I shiver.

"I wanted to stop by and offer some—"

"Your ruse is blown. Just come in. It's cold." I step back, waving her in. Her breath hitches, as if she hadn't expected me to let her in. "Your partner in crime is here. As I'm sure you know."

She frowns, muttering to herself. "Damn it, Callan."

Lo stomps her boots out on the landing before stepping over the threshold. Callan moves into sight with a smile, reaching for Lo's jug. "Let me help."

She jerks away from him. "No."

"You gals are a stubborn bunch. Just accept the help, Lo."

Kicking the door shut, I shiver and impatiently wait for the heat to warm my flesh back up.

"I don't need help carrying things because I have a vagina," she says, exasperated. "You want to help? Don't get yourself into sticky situations."

"It's not because of your...gross, Lo." His face distorts with disgust. "Please don't mention your vagina ever again. Even if you were Lex, I'd offer to help."

She tosses a braid over her shoulder and scrutinizes me. "How have you been?"

"Fine," I say warily.

Her eyes narrow and her lips purse, as if she sees through my half-truth. "Good."

"Well, since we're all here," Callan says, "and you brought snacks, let's have an intervention."

"Callan," Lo says through gritted teeth. "That wasn't the plan."

He shrugs a shoulder. "Now it is." He jerks a thumb toward me. "We're all here."

"Intervention?" I ask, balking.

Lo at least has the decency to avert her eyes in embarrassment as she cautiously glances around my apartment. She and Callan tower over me—they're both around the same height—but where Callan's flamboyant personality takes up space, Lo's lithe body slinks around with an understated, cat-like grace.

"Fara sent these up. She said you know how much better they are warm." Lo hands me a basket of Fara's strudel, and the decadent apple-cinnamon scent wafts up, causing my mouth to water. She glares at Callan. "Someone interrupted our date."

"Explains why you're so late." Callan's brows rise. "I thought you two stopped seeing each other."

She ignores him, holding the jug up. "I also brought cider."

I mumble a thanks, reluctantly accepting the basket and jug. I step aside to deposit it on the kitchen counter while they shuck off their coats and hang them beside the door. Lo pulls off her hat and shakes out her braids. Her thin lips pull into a smile, and I can't help but soften at the kindness in her eyes.

As she slips out of her boots she adds, "It's *hard* cider."

"Thank the goddess," I mutter. *That* I'll gladly take. Especially since they're getting comfortable. Though their intrusion doesn't bother me as much as I thought it might.

"Is our presence so unbearable you must rely on liquor to get you through?" Callan asks. Lo shakes her head at him and sighs.

He glances at her, then back to me. "Oh, stop. I didn't mean it as a slight. We worry about you, Aife. That's all."

"We agreed not to harass her," Lo hisses at him through gritted teeth.

Callan laughs, gracing us with a brilliant smile, and it loosens something inside of me. "It's an intervention; it's kind of impossible not to bring up the thing we are *intervening* about."

"I barely drink. What are you talking about?" I ask, bewildered. I purchase one bottle of wine a week from the market. Surely that doesn't constitute a drinking problem. And how would they even know how much I drink?

"This intervention is not about alcohol," Callan says, rubbing his jaw. "It's about the self-isolation. We're concerned about you."

"Okay, can we back up and talk about the invisibility thing?" They're way too nonchalant about this. "I'm a bit shocked you're both here, first of all. Second—*invisibility?*"

Callan glances at Lo, who scoffs. "Your mess, your explanation, buddy."

"Okay, well, it wasn't like that. I came to check on you, like I do sometimes. But I normally don't come in. Like I said, opening doors and moving stuff around defeats the purpose of being invisible and going undetected. Anyway, I caught you just as you were entering your apartment, so I snuck in through the door behind you, not realizing I'd basically be locked in here all day. I didn't really think it through. But trust me, I was not trying to watch you pleasure your—"

"Callan!" I groan, burying my face in my hand. "For the love of the goddess."

Lo claps her hands together. "Callan, take the strudel to the table and set up a game of Squids—the cards are tucked in the basket."

"Demanding, Lady Lo!" Callan snags a strudel and stuffs it half in his mouth, letting it dangle. He leaves a trail of crumbs as he finds a seat at the wooden table beneath the oversized window.

I shake my head while Lo pours us some cider.

Naturally, I'm tempted to use my power and sift through their emotions, but then I remember the wards preventing outsiders from using magic. They're meant to keep the residents safe; I don't blame Lex for keeping them up.

But it's been months since I've felt the tickle of vygora energy coming to life inside of me. My magic is a big part of who I am, and not using it only enhances my loneliness.

Sometimes my palms tingle and my skin itches from the inside out, like my power is desperately begging to be released. I almost miss the bacchanals simply because they gave me the opportunity to use my ability. I don't miss hurting people, but I miss feeling powerful.

"How can he become invisible?" I ask Lo, still caught up on that. "I've never heard of that power before. Is he an etheryn of some sort?" Of the four types of magic—myndox, vygora, aethyn, and etheryn—I know the least about etheryn. I wouldn't be entirely surprised if invisibility was in their repertoire.

"We're not human," she says, biting her lip. "We're not even from this realm."

Now *that* throws me off. "Then what are you?" *Please don't say you're gods too.*

"Angelli."

"Ang—what? I've never heard of that. Did I know this? Before?"

She hesitates. "Yes. We were friends, Aife. All of us. You knew all about our pasts."

My chest aches at her words. "Is Callan telling the truth? Was it an accident tonight?"

She chuckles, then says softly, "Unfortunately, yes. You and Callan were closer than anyone, you know. He means well, but he worries incessantly."

That eases a bit of the violation I felt at Callan's surprise appearance. "Can you become invisible too?"

She nods. "But I swear I don't use it to cross boundaries. At least not with you or my other friends." She cocks her head, brows drawn together in a pensive expression. "It's a helpful tactic when infiltrating enemy territory to gather—never mind." Chuckling, she waves a hand in the air. "No work talk."

After a moment of silence, she frowns. "Speaking of boundaries, if you want us to go, we will. I came to rescue Callan, but I really did bring the cider for you. I was hoping we could catch up. Maybe intervention is the wrong word, but we're worried about you, Aife."

I hesitate, wondering if I should throw them out or let them stay. It's strange hearing my *true* name roll off their lips so casually. It's stranger yet that I naturally respond to the name after being *Astrid* for what seems like my whole life.

But really, I've never been Astrid. That was a name given to me by Enira—an enemy.

It's not fitting anymore. Maybe it never was.

To make my identity crisis worse, the nightmare I had creeps back into my brain, and I shudder.

Taking a chance on *Aife* and her old friends, I whisper, "Stay."

CHAPTER SIX

ASTRID

Pulling a chair out, I sit across from Callan, leaving the spot on my left open for Lo. She places a mug of cider in front of each of us. The aroma is sweet, with a bitter bite to it.

"I'm good, Lo," Callan says. "Thanks though. I'm sure one of you beautiful ladies will enjoy it for me." He winks at me.

"Such a flirt." She shakes her head, undeterred, as she pulls his mug back toward her. "Bea would be disappointed to know you've turned down her specialty cider."

Beatrice, the old farmer who lost her husband a while back, sells eggs and milk down on Main Street most mornings. She's a nosey thing, always staring at me unabashedly with a hint of judgment in her eyes. Anytime I make a purchase from her, she insists on telling me how grateful she is that the goddess returned Lex to Nevaris, no thanks to me. Whatever that means.

Once, I even gathered the courage to visit the local library in the town center. But as soon as I saw Beatrice's hawk eyes following me to the romance section, I scurried back to the safety of my apartment. I have no intention of going back. From what I glimpsed, the selection was sorely lacking anyways.

The old woman is fond of everyone except me, it seems. I think she blames me for Lex leaving in the first place.

"I'm not refusing her cider." He leans his chair back so it's balancing precariously on two legs. "You of all people know how much I love it, but I need to keep a clear head for tomorrow. In case Lex needs—" At Lex's name, a jolt of energy shoots through my body. Even though it's accompanied by fury, I'm desperate to hear more. Callan plants the chair back on the floor with a *thump* and leans forward. His eyes crinkle at the corner, and he frowns.

Lo grunts before taking a big swig of cider, but no one talks.

"You can say his name." I sigh. "You don't have to censor yourselves." In an attempt to convince them I am indeed doing fine, I take a big inhale and ask, "How is he...*Lex*?"

Callan shrugs before grabbing Lo's mug from her hands and taking a swig. She stares at him with her mouth agape. "He's a little rough around the edges lately. But as long as he's not Sora-level cranky, I'm not too worried."

Lo snags her cup back from Callan's hands, gesturing at the full mug that sits in front of him, the one she initially poured for him. "I thought you couldn't have any?"

He flashes his charming, crooked grin at her. "I only wanted a sip."

"You have your own," Lo says pointedly while he laughs.

"I didn't want to waste a whole cup for one teensy sip."

"Seriously? I've already poured it, Callan. You're wasting it by *not* drinking it."

It's borderline hilarious that these supposed warriors, leaders of legions, harbingers of death, argue like siblings over a mug of cider. I might've laughed if I wasn't consumed with thoughts about my fated.

"So, what is Lex up to tonight anyway?" I ask.

"He had some business to attend to," Lo says, her gaze

darting away. "Sora too. They send their regards."

My brow scrunches.

"It's probably for the best, honestly." Callan takes the words right out of my mouth. He keeps his eyes on the deck of cards as he flicks through it. "But"—he glances at Lo—"you should know that they've been searching for answers about your memories."

They? "Lex *and* Sora?" I frown. Sora has made it clear he hates me.

"Yup. Well, Sora is working under Lex's orders."

I clear my throat. "Have they…found anything?"

"Nothing too helpful, yet. They discovered Enira was harnessing wild magic from the storms, but it's all etheryn magic—elemental. So far, it doesn't seem connected to your missing memories. Lex and Dash were talking about a trip to the mainland to find Cedrik and pick his brain about—"

"Lex and Dash?" I ask incredulously. "As in the only *Lexyll* and *Dashiel* I know?"

Callan grins. "Yeah."

"A lot has changed in the last few months, Aife," Lo adds.

"Lex and Dash are friends?" This is more unbelievable than the invisibility thing.

"Absolutely not." Callan laughs. "Those two hate each other more than ever."

"But they're communicating? Why?"

"For you," Lo says.

Callan stops shuffling, giving me a careful look.

Squirming uncomfortably under their scrutiny, I snag my mug to distract myself from the tension. Taking a sip of the cider, I grunt with approval. When the spicy cinnamon-and-apple taste washes over my taste buds, I widen my eyes in surprise. "This is good. *Really* good."

"You missed the Autumn Festival," Lo says with a pout. "It was a few weeks after you arrived. It's the one time a year Bea makes her cider, and Fara makes the flakiest pie I've ever tasted. We kept the cider frozen for you all this time so you could have some. It might be the last jug in town." She shakes a finger at Callan. "Which is why this guy is getting on my nerves by pretending he doesn't want any. I give it ten minutes before he caves and chugs his whole mug."

"If he doesn't drink it, I gladly will."

"Oh, trust me. He won't let it go to waste. Just like he didn't let the pie go to waste." She crosses her arms.

"Well, er—" Callan's cheek's turn pink.

"He ate the pie I was saving for you."

"It was going to go bad! No offense, Aife, but pie only lasts so long. Even when it's frozen."

At this, I finally laugh. He tries to apologize, but I wave it off. "I'm perfectly happy with strudel."

The tension slowly bleeds out of the room as Callan begins dealing the cards. He places eight cards facedown in front of each person, and he and Lo teach me how to play a game called Squids.

While we play, Lo and I discuss the Autumn Festival and how the locals head over the hill to the apple orchards to harvest the fruit at its prime. It's a week-long event, and the villagers host a variety of challenges and games for kids and adults alike. The way Lo tells stories about the local families warms my chest. I'm saddened I missed out on the events.

It sounds unlike anything we ever had in Hakran. Briefly, I wonder if Dash will be the kind of leader to host fairs for his village and create a tight-knit community.

It surprises me that Lex runs such a family-oriented village, considering he's so formal and restrained—not at all how I'd picture a *family* man.

It goes to show how little I truly know about him.

According to Lo, seasonal fairs are a big thing in Nevaris. And the Snowfall Festival is right around the corner.

"...and there are snowman-building contests, snowball fights, and a window-painting contest! You..." Lo's voice reaches a high, excited pitch before fading away, and an awkward silence fills the air.

"I what?"

She hesitates, her eyes flicking toward my oversized window, then back to my face. "You won that contest. Before you..."

"A window-decorating contest?"

"Yes." She smiles softly. "Your first Snowfall Festival was right after you bought the apartment. You went all out, painting the window with a frosty forest scene."

"Wait—I can paint?"

Callan chuckles. "Nope."

"Not really," Lo says at the same time. "You were pretty awful, actually. But you were so excited to show Nevaris how much you appreciate their heritage that the judges couldn't not vote for you. You won."

"So it was a pity win." I frown, unable to imagine myself painting anything, especially not for a contest. What kind of murdering goddess partakes in such trivial events?

"No. You won because you put the most effort in and your hard work was recognized."

"It is possible the rest of the villagers were afraid of you so they let you win," Callan says. He jerks, and there's a loud *thump* as his knee hits the underside of the table. "Ow! What the hell, Lo? I was kidding. She knows I'm kidding. What is with you two and kicking shins?"

"Can I ask you something?" I say, ignoring their shenanigans.

"Technically you just did," Callan says, rubbing his knee.

I roll my eyes, even though I secretly find his humor comforting. His charm and good-natured personality remind me a little of Dash. Except Dash is more arrogant and vulgar, whereas Callan has more of an endearing, forthright appeal. I can't help but think the two would get along well.

It makes me miss Dash even more.

"How long have we known each other?" I ask, gesturing between the three of us.

Lo's brows pinch together, and a pained look crosses her face. She and Callan exchange glances.

Finally, Callan speaks up. "We've known each other for quite a few years. Way before Enira sunk her claws into you and stole you away." His mouth pulls into a frown. It's strange seeing anything other than a smile on his lips. "You and Lex met through me."

"It was hard when Lex forbade us from looking for you," Lo adds with a whisper.

I try to conjure an image of Callan, Lo, and me spending time together, but I fail. Did we drink tea and chat about books like Ilona and I used to? That's more of Ilona's thing than mine, so I doubt it.

There's a tug in my skull, a memory—but it's out of reach.

"I don't remember any of that," I murmur. The ghost of our friendship lingers though, and deep down I know we *were* close. My self-reproach grows. "I'm sorry," I whisper. "For...pushing you guys away."

"Nothing to be sorry for," Lo says. "We all agreed to give you space and time to work things out for yourself, without us pressuring you. A few months is nothing in the grand scheme of our lives."

"*I* told them they're doing you a disservice by keeping so much from you, just so you know." Callan reaches forward and ruffles my hair with a big paw. Lo chuckles into her mug as she sips her cider. "But Lo's right, you can be a touch emotional at times."

My cheeks heat with embarrassment at being called out, at being around people who seem to know me better than I know them. If they weren't good people, they could've used that against me. They could've tried to mold my story to fit their own agenda. Lex said something before about not wanting to influence my memories…

Now it makes sense why Lex has given me space; he not only knew I needed it, but he also respected me enough to give it to me. He could've wielded the truth over me like a powerful weapon, but it would've made our relationship unbalanced and dishonest.

He wants what's between us to be honest. He wants us to be equals.

My stomach drops.

How could someone who seems to care so deeply for me take away my sister like that?

He loathes Dash and surely wanted Enira dead, yet when he had them both within reach, he never struck. Not only is he an extremely powerful vygora, he's a warrior. Surely there were a thousand ways he could've killed them. But he's too controlled, too methodical to lash out because of his emotions—the opposite of me, actually.

Thinking about Lex starts to drag me under. Callan and Lo's presence is forcing me to think about the life I don't remember.

"Why did you two come? Why show up here randomly, *three*

whole months after I carved everyone out of my life?"

Lo shoots an inquisitive look at Callan, and he raises his eyebrows. Irritation spreads inside of me in response to their silence, like a poison coursing through my veins.

"It was an accident," Callan says. "I was checking on you and got stuck—"

"No. Why stay? Why do this 'intervention' now?" I say, putting *intervention* in air quotes.

"Because it's time," Callan finally says.

I scowl at them, chugging the rest of my cider before slamming my mug down.

He sheepishly rubs the back of his neck. "Fara said she hadn't seen you in a while, so we wanted to make sure you're all right."

"She sends up oils and clothes often enough." And snacks. And other goodies.

"Actually—" Lo shoves her tongue in her cheek, looking anywhere but me.

I narrow my eyes. "Actually what?"

"Well, those were from Lex," she coughs out. "The frankincense oil. Eucalyptus salts. The winter coat. The wool socks—"

"Lex—" I pause. The revelation only confuses me further. "Forget it. You came to check on me and make sure that, what? That I'm cleaning my apartment and washing my hair?" My scowl deepens at the thought of Fara keeping tabs on me. Of her pretending to send me gifts when they were really from Lex. "My hair's washed, my dishes are not. There's your update. You can go now."

Lo tightens her lips. "We came to check that *you* are okay." Her voice rises slightly at the end, her eyes shining with anger. "How long do you think we're going to stay away and watch while you waste away up here alone?" She waves her hand around at the space.

"As long as I want. It's not your—"

"No." She shoves away from the table, the chair screeching on the hardwood floor, before she stands and slams her hands down on the table, causing the mugs to rattle. She leans toward me, her voice low, at odds with the angry pink blotches coloring her cheeks. "You're shutting down again, right here in front of us. You're about to push us away, *again*. That's not how this works. You have people in Hakran wondering if you're okay. People in Nevaris worrying about you. No matter how betrayed you feel, how alone you *think* you are, you're not. Everyone hurts someone at some point. Get over it, Aife! Get yourself together. Don't you remember what happened last time you pulled this sh—"

"Of course I don't fucking remember!" I yell, matching her aggravated tone. I'm ready to kick them both out. I stand, crossing my arms angrily in front of my chest. Letting them stay was an awful idea.

Her face morphs, anger melting away into sorrow, as she realizes what she said.

"Hey, hey, hey," Callan says, gripping Lo gently by the shoulders and pulling her away from the table. "I got this. Take a walk."

She sighs, slapping his hands away and slipping her boots and jacket on. "This is exactly why I said no to this little *intervention* idea before, Callan. Bad idea."

"It's okay. Everything is fine." He flashes her a grin. "I'll see you back at the house."

Lo composes herself, not sparing me another glance before heading out into the flurry.

Cold air wafts over me as the door slams behind her. I shiver, wrapping my arms around myself.

"Is she always that dramatic?" I ask as Callan makes his way back to the table.

"*Lo?* You think *she* is the dramatic one?" His lips quirk. "You managed to make Lo lose her cool. *Loisia.*" Unable to hold his mirth back any longer, he releases a wheezing laugh. When he doubles over in his chair and grips his side like he's in pain, I can't help but snort with my own humor. "The way you manage to undo even the calmest people is a talent." He takes his seat across from me, eyeing Lo's abandoned mug before snagging it and taking a big gulp, finishing it off. "That talent, my friend, is far more dangerous than the magic running through your veins."

His words sink like lead into the pit of my stomach. He might be onto something. I've seen Lex, Dash, and Ilona all lose their cool around me. I've known Ilona the longest—well, I *remember* knowing her the longest—and she's never been as angry as she was the last few times I saw her.

Ilona almost cursed at me, for goddess's sake.

Obviously I am the common factor.

"If I piss everyone off so much, how about you all just leave me alone then? I don't need any of you," I lie, clenching my teeth and crossing my arms.

"Aife," he says. I reluctantly meet his eyes. Instead of pity or judgment, all I see is kindness. "You might not need us, but did you ever think that maybe *we* need *you?*"

Shaking my head, I refute the notion.

"For one, if we didn't care about you so much, you wouldn't have the ability to piss us off."

"Maybe it's a vygora thing."

"Trust me, it's not." His grin fades, and his face becomes somber. "Lo isn't wrong though."

"I don't owe anyone anything."

"You don't. But the woman I know—Astrid, Aife, or whatever you want to call yourself—is fiercely loyal. She wouldn't cast everyone aside because things got hard or confusing."

"Things didn't get *confusing*, Callan," I snap. "I've been betrayed by everyone in my life. I don't trust anyone." *Not even myself*, I want to add. *Especially not myself*.

"Betrayed, huh? Last time I checked, *I* didn't do anything to betray you. Neither did Lo."

"You know what I mean."

"No, I really don't." He interlaces his fingers on the tabletop, leaning forward until he's only about a foot away. In the orange glow of the fire orbs, his hazel eyes appear more brown than green. "I'm going to give it to you straight. You think Dashiel betrayed you, and I get it, I do, but his actions kept you safe. His intent was not to harm you. In fact, thanks to him, you are *free*. Lex is free. Hakran is free. Dashiel has done nothing but great things for Hakran, an island you supposedly care about." He grabs his own mug and takes a sip. "From what I've heard about your friend Ilona, *you* betrayed her, not the other way around. *You* ran. Not her. *You*."

I grunt in response, not knowing what to say as I process the truth of his words. It's something I've contemplated many times over the past few months—my actions and reactions to everything that happened and how I could've done things differently.

"And with Lex," he says with a heavy sigh, "you only have a single memory. How reliable is that memory really?"

Shaking my head, I work to keep my composure. "He killed my sister, Callan. I don't need any other information. Nothing will change that."

"You're being too stubborn to see past what you want to

see." He leans down to snag a book from one of the precarious stacks beside the table. He holds it up, showing me the short summary on the back cover. His eyes sparkle with good-natured humor as he shakes it at me. "The synopsis never tells the full story." He opens the book and starts flipping through the pages. "It only offers a sneak peek, and it leaves out quite a bit. Your imagination will fill in the blanks until you read the full story and discover what really happens." He sets the book down between us. "With the amount you read, you'd think you'd have learned that lesson by now."

All I can do is stare at him.

"Just talk to him," Callan says, leaning back into his chair.

"No." It's petty, I know, but I can't stop the defiant word from slipping out. I've gone back and forth with myself for weeks; I'm torn between seeking revenge for the loss of my sister—inflicting the same pain on Lex that he bestowed upon me—or embracing forgiveness and being the better person. But I don't think I can.

Callan and I sit there in silence for a bit, and I stare at the oversized window, catching my reflection in the glass. It's dark now. The sun has fully set, concealing the village center and the lake beyond.

I thought Lo and Callan's visit would be a good distraction from that awful nightmare. Instead, it turned into an Astrid-bashing extravaganza, and now I'm spinning in a whirlpool of self-pity. Somehow they've both managed to make me feel guilty and ashamed tonight.

"You're not this person," Callan says, breaking the silence.

"You don't know who I am. *I* don't even know who I am."

"You're caught up on the wrong things. You aren't a name, or a label, or even your memories." He stands up and crosses over to me, gently placing his hand on my heart. "This beats the same no matter what you call yourself. Let your actions, your choices, be the defining factor for who you are. Be who you *want* to be, Aife." He removes his hand and steps back.

Without waiting for a reply, he heads to the door and begins lacing up his boots. I chew on my lip and try not to let the tears fall. His words have struck a chord deep inside of me.

"And, Aife?" he asks.

"Yeah?" My voice is quiet, hollow.

"If you're waiting for anyone to come save you, you'll be waiting forever."

I bristle. "What do you mean?"

"You told Lex you wanted to be left alone. He's respecting your boundaries, and he's ensuring others do the same. The villagers are afraid you'll kick their ass if they show up here. Honestly, I'm surprised you haven't kicked *my* ass yet."

He opens the door, and I brace myself for the rush of cold air. The bitter sting of fresh snow invades the space, carrying a fresh, piney scent with it.

My skin pebbles, and I wrap my arms around my midsection. The cider coursing through my bloodstream softens the sting of winter, but barely.

"Hey, Callan?"

"Yeah?" He looks over his shoulder, one foot out the door, waiting for me to speak.

"Thanks." His words haven't fully sunk in yet, but the message behind them is already simmering beneath my bones.

He gives me that beautiful smile of his, showcasing the small, endearing gap in his front teeth. "It's better than Lo's 'get over it' speech, huh?" I nod, and his smile grows. "In case you need the reminder, you're a *goddess*, Aife." With that, he shuts the door behind him, leaving me alone to stare at the cards and the cider still resting on the table before me. I'm numb from his words, wondering what the hell just happened.

Their visit made one thing very clear: that bad dream I had about being truly, utterly alone? It's more than a nightmare—it's my biggest fear—and if I continue down this path, I'll be the only one to blame for turning that nightmare into reality.

CHAPTER SEVEN

DASH

It's been a busy day. After Sora left this morning to seek Lex's aid, I met with Ilona to inform her about our trip to Stellaris. Then I listened to grievances from the villagers, trained with Fatima, and finished mapping out the new trade routes. Sora has been running back and forth between Hakran and Nevaris making preparations for the journey all day. Now, Fatima and I need to update Ilona on Lex's agreement to aid us and see if she has found out anything about the invocations.

Fatima and I enter the library, a solemn silence stalking us.

I command my other guards to remain in the hallway, then slide the doors closed behind me.

"Good evening, King Dashiel," Ilona says with a salute. Her feet are curled up beneath her in an oversized armchair, a thick book opened on her lap and a mug of tea beside her on the table. She smiles sweetly at my commander. "Hi, Fatima."

A hint of color invades Ilona's cheeks when Fatima plops down in the chair beside her.

It's always baffled me how much the library reminds me of home, with its mismatched area rugs, colorful books, and carved bookshelves. So unlike Enira. I'd heard she was responsible for rebuilding and redecorating the palace when she assumed the throne, but I never understood why she left the library so...*ugly*, in her terms. I don't think it's ugly; I find it comforting.

Except those worn wingback chairs—they can go. Based on how they sag and groan every time Ilona shifts, they've outlived their use.

Fatima returns Ilona's greeting, then sighs. "Are you ready for the journey tomorrow?"

Ilona jolts up. "Of course I am. Sora's back? He confirmed? We're really leaving tomorrow?"

I nod. He made it to Hakran and back already. He missed dinner, which I'm sure was intentional, considering the *egg*cident at breakfast.

"Are you *sure* you want to come?" I ask.

Ilona snaps her book shut and narrows her eyes at me. Ever since Astrid left, she's been slightly more defiant, but I'm proud of her for it. There is something admirable about a woman with a backbone.

"I'm not going to be held back *again*. I might not be a warrior like you or Fatima, but it doesn't mean I'm useless or delicate. I *am* your advisor, after all."

She has a point. I couldn't think of anyone more trustworthy, caring, or knowledgeable to fill the position. I expected her to be nervous, but she jumped in with ease and has been a sounding board for countless issues over the last few months.

And of course, she and Fatima get along swimmingly.

"I had not intended to imply you were useless, Ilona. I had simply meant the journey will be long, arduous. Lexyll will be aboard the same cramped ship as us. Are you sure seeing Zale is worth a two-week journey?" Three days there, three days back, not to mention the week—minimum—we'll be in Stellaris.

"I've told you ten times now, yes, it is." Her tone is softer now, but her cheeks darken with frustration, and her brows draw together. "Zale will need a friend now more than ever."

Fatima looks from her to me, smirking. She loves it when the sweet, soft-spoken redhead stands up to me.

Ilona and Zale have been writing to one another, growing closer in their friendship. As soon as we discussed our plans to visit Stellaris earlier, she immediately volunteered for the trip.

I had never intended to hold her back. I never thought her weak, or a liability, like she so vocally accused me of. I had only meant that she needn't feel obligated to take such a turbulent trip simply to uphold her word to Zale. He would understand.

"Then it's agreed," I say, nodding at her.

"It's *been* agreed," she replies. "For hours."

Fatima clears her throat, adopting a serious expression. "I should really be accompanying you on this journey."

"I refuse to leave Hakran unattended. You must be here in my absence."

"Hakran will be fine. There are plenty of Stellari guards around, and despite the hiccups, the people are pleased with your rule so far. We run practically no risk of resistance—or invasion, for that matter."

"No."

She rubs her forehead in annoyance. "I think I could really help—"

"Plus, you weren't trained as a sailor."

"Neither was I," Ilona chimes in, looking from Fatima to me, confused.

"I'm an aethyn, Dash," Fatima says. "I can manipulate all four elements. I can start a fire for food. I can control the wind in the sails. I can ensure the waves—"

"You can't do that all at once," I mutter.

She throws her hands up in frustration. "For the love of the goddess, Dash."

I run my hand through my hair. "Fine," I concede. "Come."

I worry about leaving Hakran in the hands of anyone else, but Fatima will undoubtedly be an asset on the journey. And Hakran is fairly self-

sufficient, especially with Enira's hold on the minds of the people broken.

Fatima pumps her fist in the air and gives me a smug grin. "You know what they say: 'The enemy of my enemy is my friend.'" She crosses her legs, sitting back in the chair as she steals glances at Ilona. "Right now, Lexyll has the opportunity to be our friend."

"I wouldn't go that far, Fatima." I hold up a hand, shaking my head at the notion. "The trip is planned to last no more than two weeks total. But it could take longer depending on how quickly Lexyll ends the war."

"I've done a lot of reading on him," Ilona whispers, lifting the book on her lap to reveal the title: *Myths & Legends: Gods and Goddesses Who Roam*. "Did you know he's fought in some of the most prominent wars throughout history? Even one in another realm! Hundreds of years ago, the War of Realms. Legend says etheryns were responsible for opening portals to other realms." She pauses. "Hmm, I wonder if those portals still exist. Anyway, Lexyll allegedly sided with humans in a realm called Dovenak and forced thousands of magical beings off their land."

I grit my teeth. Of course I've heard of the War of Realms. All the guards in Stellaris know of Lexyll, God of War, and how he *saved* our world from extremely powerful invaders who were equipped with their own unusual magic. It was one of the many stories we were told during training—at least before Ayana died and the stories of the lesser gods were prohibited.

Hearing the myths and legends as a young boy is one thing—they're stories meant to act as lessons or warnings, or to keep morale alive—but meeting one of the gods from those stories is another. The myths about the god of war and his ability to knock out entire armies with his power don't impress me.

Character does.

And the god of war has poor character.

I used to admire Lexyll. But that was back when he was a myth, not a flesh-and-bones man who stole my woman.

Astrid deserves better than a man who cuts down others remorselessly, a man with no empathy in his heart.

"What does it say about the goddess of death?" I ask Ilona.

"Not much." Her emerald eyes widen imperceptibly before darting toward the floor. "She and Enira are mentioned briefly in various books, but the stories are always vague, discussing their powers and not much else. And they're mentioned by title, not by name. Lexyll seems to be one of the most popular gods. There are a few other gods and goddesses mentioned that seem quite popular. Do you think they're still around?"

My lungs constrict. *I hope not.* "It's likely, all things considered."

Fatima gives me a sharp, knowing look.

One particular god comes to mind—one I know little about. I'm tempted to ask if *he* appears in any of the books, but I don't want to bring it up in front of Fatima. I'll do my own private research another time.

Fatima stifles a yawn, leaning toward Ilona to glance at the book she's flipping through.

"How about Osiris, God of the Underworld? They call him the fallen deity, the amoral."

"The fallen—" I pause, rubbing my jaw. "He's Sama's

opposite in every way." Where Sama is all that is good and pure, Osiris is darkness and destruction.

"Sama," Ilona muses. "Also known as the mother, our creator, the original goddess. The goddess of the sky.

"Apparently Osiris refused to assist the humans, claiming he was better than them. He wanted to rule them—not help them. So Sama used her last dredges of magic to cast him to the Underworld, a realm where the dead rest, to rule over souls. Apparently he— Sorry, never mind." Ilona bites her lip, and her eyes shoot downward. "I'm rambling again. Astrid used to tease me about it. I miss that, to be honest. I miss *her*."

Me too. "You two will make up."

"I know." Her eyes water, and I immediately regret saying anything. Fatima jumps up and perches on the edge of Ilona's armrest, tucking Ilona into her side in a comforting hug.

"Dash is right. And it sounds like she's done this before."

"Yeah, but not for this long. It's been three months. Last time it was only three days. It's all my fault."

"It's not." *It's mine*, I want to add, but I know that's wrong too. "It's no one's fault. Except maybe Enira's for playing with everyone. Astrid went through her own trauma. I'm sure being alone is her way of processing it."

"Why can't you ask Lexyll to let us see her?"

"I have. The bastard refuses. He said she's alive, healthy, but that she still requests her space. We have to respect her." At least she isn't talking to Lexyll either, according to what I've heard in Sora's thoughts.

The mood in the room turns somber, so I take the opportunity to inquire about what I really came here for. "Did you find what I asked?"

Ilona frowns. "About the gods' invocations?" She stands,

snagging a book from a pile beside her chair. "It's pretty vague. It basically says that the gods were created by Sama to assist the humans, and when invoked properly, without malice, the gods could not refuse."

"Does it say *how* exactly to invoke them?"

"Well, yes, but may I ask why you need to know that? You're not planning on invoking Astrid or something, are you? You'd tell us, right? After everything, that doesn't seem wise."

I look her in the eye, saying sincerely, "I do not plan on *ever* invoking Astrid. I swear to you, Ilona."

"Okay," she says skeptically. She glances at Fatima, who nods. "Here." She points to the page, beckoning me over to read it.

There on the page are the exact words I need to say to invoke a god. The question is whether or not it will work. I suppose I'll find out soon enough.

"Thank you, Ilona. Best advisor ever."

She giggles at this, and then the three of us move on to discussing our strategy for the trip.

Fatima and I leave the library's soulful kaleidoscope of color, entering the bleak hallway. We trek down the main hallway, following it as it curves into the royal wing. As we approach my room—the same one I've been staying in since my initial visit to Hakran—she reaches out and places a hand on my arm. Glancing over her shoulder, she eyes the guard stationed at my door, and when she notices he is Stellari, she relaxes a bit. There were some tensions between the Stellari and Hakranian guards at first, but everyone integrated fairly well once it became obvious our goal was to protect the island. I can't help but notice Fatima is still wary of anyone not from Stellaris, however.

She looks like she wants to speak, but she waits until we step into my room and I close the door behind us before saying anything.

We head over to the sofa on the far side of the room. Even after all these months, my room is fairly bare. It's dim, decorated in muted shades of gray, with ornate details carved into the ceiling and bedframe. It's nicer than half the palace, but still not my style.

It's not home.

"I won't tell you what to do, Dash, but I don't think it's a good idea to threaten Sora," she says, referring to my outburst earlier. Her dark brown eyes flash in warning.

"He had it coming."

"I don't know exactly what he said—or *thought*—but you can't let him get to you."

I sigh, stroking the thin layer of stubble on my chin. It wasn't even *what* Sora called Astrid that pissed me off; it's what he represents, who he works for.

"I can't get her out of my head," I say.

"I know this isn't easy for you." Fatima reaches for my hand and gives it a squeeze. "I haven't seen you this torn up about anything…not since my sister died."

Ashamed, I can't meet her eyes. Ayana died because of my negligence. I should've never left her alone that day. It only took a few minutes, and when I came back, it was too late. I found her soaking in a tub of crimson water, a bloodied blade discarded on the tile beside her. I wasn't there for her, and she took her own life.

I still remember the *drip, drip, drip* as the last bit of blood drained from her veins. I could've stopped it. I should've been there.

"I've told you a thousand times to stop blaming yourself," Fatima says. "It's not your—"

"But it *is* my fault. It was my job to protect her. To—"

"No. It was not *your* job to protect her. No one knew the extent of what she was going through, and there's no way we could've. You couldn't be with her every second of every day. You couldn't control every aspect of her life. Just like you can't control Astrid's. You should love fiercely, as you do, Dash, but you also have to give the people you love room to breathe and exist. You need to trust that they'll be okay."

"But they're not always okay," I whisper. Pulling Ayana out of the bathtub and laying her on the floor as I tried desperately to staunch the bleeding, to give her chest compressions and resuscitate her, was traumatizing. Both her body and the water were still warm, but it was too late.

She had seemed so happy. I didn't know she'd been struggling so deeply.

I didn't know.

Her last words to me were, *"Love is the currency of life. It's the true magic of our world, because the more you give, the more you shall receive. Make sure you spend freely, and you will enter your grave a rich man, Dashiel."*

I never expected that to be the last time she spoke to me, but I remember her words—they're permanently carved into my skull—because of how powerfully she delivered the message before we parted ways that day.

It was as if she spoke them with purpose. As if she knew that—

No.

"I should've prevented it," I whisper. "I should've stopped her. I'm a myndox, for fuck's sake. If I would've just listened in, I would've known what she was planning. I could've stopped it. It *is* entirely my fault."

I grab a fistful of my hair, tears blurring my vision.

"Dashiel Dargan!" Fatima yells. I blink away the moisture, staring at her in defeat. "I hate it when you make me yell at you, but goddess above, you are so stubborn! You need to *stop* blaming yourself for what happened to Ayana. You didn't listen to her thoughts because you *respected* her, as you should have. I miss my sister terribly, and there's not a day that goes by where I don't think about her. I wish *I* would've done more. We all do! I wish I would've known what she was struggling with, but that's the thing, Dash; we didn't know. She didn't tell anyone how much she was struggling. She hid it well. She hid it behind smiles and laughs and too-long hugs. We were there as much as we could've been for her, and you can't go back in time to fix anything. If she saw you blaming yourself and harboring this pain, she would be so brokenhearted. She wanted you to live and love, Dash. She wanted that for you, and you know it."

A tear slides down Fatima's cheek before she sniffles and wipes it away. "I love you like a brother, as I have for many years, but I thought you were done blaming yourself. Clearly whatever you're going through with Astrid is dredging up old pain. And it's not only hurting you, it's hurting those around you too."

"I'm sorry." My voice cracks. "Every day I worry that Astrid will follow the route Ayana did and that I won't be able to stop it."

"Astrid is *not* Ayana. And you're not yourself. I need you back. I need your stupid sense of humor and cringey jokes. I want the Dash that laughs and smiles and makes everyone around him feel better, just by being near them. More than that, I need you as a leader. You're a king now. The people need you to act like one. Own up, and work your shit out with Astrid. Stop making excuses."

I lean my head against the sofa, rubbing my eyes as I process her words. "It's going to be a long couple of weeks, Fatima."

I run a hand through my overgrown hair. I had meant to ask Ilona to cut it tonight, but I got distracted. My mind has been all over the place lately, and frankly, I don't give a shit about how unkempt I might look. "I won't be able to speak to her until we're back. How am I supposed to hold onto my sanity on a ship, next to her fated lover, and during a *war*?"

"They may be fated, but you and I both know that doesn't necessarily mean anything. It only means their magic is a match, but if *your* hearts are a match, that trumps all. Don't give up simply because you're intimidated by the man."

"I'm not intimidated by him," I lie.

"Sure. I believe you." She smiles, but it's forced. "Maybe if you two can get along, you can learn to share."

My eyes narrow as I pin her with an irritated look. She knows I've shared women with Zale before, but that was different. Neither of us were *in love* with the women.

"If it came down to it, would you rather lose her entirely? Or would you rather share her with another man who loves her?"

I grunt, scrubbing my face with my hands, not wanting to admit to her that I've already decided I'd never make Astrid choose, even if that means sharing her. "I am not having this conversation with you."

"The old Dash loved these kinds of conversations."

"I told you, this is different. *She's* different."

"Then she's worth fighting for." Fatima gives me a genuine smile this time as she repeats her sister's words to me. "Love is the currency of life. It's the true magic of our world. Spend freely."

Sadness creeps into her features, and I draw her in for a hug. She releases me first, assuming a stoic stance as she opens the door, glancing down the hallway, before she steps out.

"Just wait until you set your sights on some poor woman," I

tell her. "I can't wait to interfere."

"Now *that* I won't tolerate." We both laugh. When the humor fades, she says, "I know you don't want to hear this either, but try to be patient with Sora. You might dislike him too much to notice, but behind all that sneering and brutish behavior, he harbors real pain. You don't know what he's gone through."

I wish she wouldn't say things like that. I try hard not to care, but she's right. And the more I think about it, the more I realize I need to have empathy for him.

Sighing, I nod.

Fatima knows how to get to me.

CHAPTER EIGHT

ASTRID

Callan's words hit me hard tonight, just like the cider did. Thanks to his and Lo's intrusion, I've gained the confidence to face Lex and figure out how to get my life back. I'm not as angry about them showing up as I might've been a few months ago—hell, even a few days ago. But the nightmare I had left me vulnerable and raw, and it allowed me to see a new perspective on things.

Tonight, I'll confront Lex.

Tomorrow, I'll visit Dash and Ilona.

Or maybe that's the cider talking.

Snow falls around me, blanketing Nevaris in a thin white layer as I stomp my way toward Harmony House. The rhythmic crunching of my footsteps is a lullaby, attempting—and failing—to guide me toward tranquility. The serene nightscape around me does little to calm my erratic heartbeat.

Everyone is resting indoors for the evening, enjoying the first snowstorm of the season from their windows, keeping warm beside their fireplaces or beneath their blankets, rather than experiencing the brutal chill firsthand.

The faint scent of pine, mingled with a hint of cinnamon, carries through the fresh air, burning my throat with each breath.

A few posted fire orbs illuminate the way through the village, allowing me to make out the faint outline of the stacked houses on my left. They're built into the hillside in a collage of wood, steeply angled roofs, and overhanging balconies.

Single-story houses lie along the shore of the lake on my right. The dim light allows me to catch glimpses of the docks between the houses. All the boats have been pulled out of the icy water for the season and are stored in the small marina at the other edge of town.

Even with the numbing cold, Nevaris is cozy.

Once I hit the fork in the path on the outskirts of the village, I go right, toward Harmony House. The other path, the one that carves up through the dark thicket of pine and cedar trees, eventually ends at the apple orchards.

I press on, passing the silent farms and snow-kissed evergreen trees, not pausing until I come upon the stone bridge leading across the lake to Harmony House.

"Dammit," I mumble to myself as I squint through the falling snowflakes.

I haven't been here in months. Not since before Enira's death. Then, I was in awe of the house, the way it appears to float. But now, with the lake frozen and the snow falling, it's almost impossible to see where the bridge ends and the lake begins. One wrong move could send me plunging into the icy depths. I doubt the new layer ice is thick enough to support my weight, with this being the first big freeze of the year.

Luckily, I can make out a trail of fast-fading footprints leading toward the house. I scurry along the slippery stone bridge as fast I can without losing my footing and huff with relief once I've made it across safely.

By the time I'm standing before Harmony House, my heart is ready to burst from my chest. At this hour, the house is a daunting collection of harsh shadows, sharp angles, and looming spires reaching up into the night sky. The large windows are illuminated from within, but the interior of the house is hidden behind curtains.

Similar to my apartment, it's constructed of brick and dark wood. Its classic, muted shades blend into the night. Last time I was here, it appeared inviting. Now, it's ominous—spooky even.

Apprehension creeps down my spine, and I take a deep breath to compose myself. For a few minutes, I stand in front of the imposing front door, staring, not knowing whether I should knock or simply enter. I didn't knock the last few times I visited.

Finally, I raise my knuckles to the door and rap a few times. My hands hurt from the cold, and I curse myself for not putting gloves on before I left. I bring my hands to my mouth, exhaling heavily on them, using my breath to warm the red, raw skin.

When the door creaks open, I audibly suck in a breath at the sight of the literal *god* standing before me. I might not remember exactly what the title means yet, but dammit, every inch of him looks how I imagine a god would. He's so beautiful that he's almost painful to behold. His chiseled jaw and cheekbones are accentuated by full brows and plump lips—a perfect harmony of harsh and soft features. The vibrant green of his eyes, darker near the pupils and brighter around the edges, is almost haunting against his rich olive skin and thick, dark hair.

He's a man of contradictions, and his appearance is no different. Every inch of his face calls to me, sparks my attraction to him.

Lex's body goes still. "Aife."

A gravitational pull draws us toward one another, as if he's the moon and I'm the tide. Everything else fades away. For a moment, my hatred no longer exists, and I'm struck with a keen sense of longing.

No matter how far apart we are, I can never seem to get him

out of my mind. And now that we are finally near one another, the air is heavy with danger and desire.

His piercing gaze locks onto mine, and despite the temperature, my frozen hands grow clammy.

"Lexyll." I square my shoulders and incline my head, feigning a greater confidence than I currently have.

"Hello, luv." My stomach tightens at the term of endearment.

He stands with the door open wide, letting the soft light and warm air leak out. Behind him, from somewhere in the house, a tranquil tune plays. Snowflakes begin to collect on his dark hair, and our breaths come out in steady white puffs. His green eyes don't waver from my face, and I shiver. He's put on quite a bit of muscle over the last few months, and his skin has lost its pallor. He's looking healthier and stronger than when I last saw him—nothing like the pale, sickly man I found in the pit.

The memory of him in that place is a punch to the lungs.

We stand there for a moment, neither of us moving.

"It's a little cold for a staring contest, no?" Callan asks, appearing over Lex's shoulder, shattering the fragile moment. "Let the girl in before she freezes to death, Lex." He winks a hazel eye at me and mouths, "Proud of you."

Silently, Lex steps to the side, his face unreadable as he scans me from head to toe.

I enter the house, and he shuts the door behind me as I stomp my boots on the entrance mat before bending to slip them off. The house smells woody, earthy. The dark hardwoods glimmer, as if they've been freshly polished. Everything about Harmony House is smooth and gleaming. It's a perfectly curated, unblemished space.

Sparkly silver, red, and green tinsel is wrapped around the carved iron railing that guards the staircase and the loft overhead. It makes for a stunning focal point. Vaulted, beamed ceilings extend to the second story, making it seem like one giant space despite the division of tiers.

I scan the wide open space behind Lex. The first floor alone could fit five of my apartments.

The entire back wall of the house is made of glass, though it's dark and reflective at this hour. Various seating areas marked by aesthetically appealing area rugs and classic, clean furniture are purposefully placed.

The house is delightfully warm, courtesy of the gigantic pale-brick fireplace snapping and sputtering in the sitting area. A few closed doors line the wall to the right, between the fireplace and kitchen, which is barely visible from where I stand.

To the left of the main floor is an arched entryway, leading to where Lex's piano sits.

Once I finish shedding my winter layers, I turn to the man responsible for the majority of my pain and confusion. The single memory I have as *Aife* comes crashing into me, and my chest squeezes so tightly that I almost can't breathe.

Despite my agreement with myself to stop acting impulsively, I allow myself this one time to give in to my fury. My hand whips out and collides with Lex's cheek in a loud *smack*. My palm, still half-numb from the cold, tingles with the impact.

"Well, that's my cue," Callan says awkwardly as he shuffles away. "I think I have something to do over there."

Lex never removes his eyes from mine, and I swear, the man didn't move a centimeter when I slapped him. He didn't even blink. In truth, he seems tired, like he did when I found him in the pit. His appearance is neat and clean, nothing like how it was during his imprisonment, but he's missing his usual spark. His eyes are hollow, tortured almost.

He's not a man born of this earth but a man carved by an

artist familiar with painful beauty. His lashes frame his eyes as if intentionally placing them on display. The contrast of bright eyes and pure black hair is awe-inducing.

My stomach clenches. I ache to reach out and trace the angles of his stubbled jaw, to apologize for slapping him. But I can't. I'm a traitor to my dead sister with these feelings.

"I suppose I deserved that," Lex says, tilting his head to the side as he watches me carefully.

"You murdered my sister." My voice cracks, but I keep my head held high.

His throat works as he swallows, and he nods softly, but nothing changes in his expression. I wait for an apology, an excuse, a flicker of remorse, something to spark the guilt inside of me again, to help the side of me that longs for him to win, but when nothing comes, I ball my hands at my sides, incensed.

"And you've had Fara watching me." At his lack of response, my loathing returns. "You've had her *spying* on me and reporting back to you. You sent your minions to check on me with some ridiculous intervention—which, by the way, wasn't even an intervention as much as it was them shitting on me for my choices. Which isn't any of your business."

"I assure you, I was wholly unaware of any...intervening." His lips twitch.

"Don't smirk at me." I surge toward him, planting my hands on his muscular chest and shoving him. At that, the spark blazes to life in his eyes like it was never gone in the first place. My stomach flutters at the sight. "This isn't funny."

"I'm not laughing. But I am pleased to see you back to your brilliant self."

"Me being enraged at you for *murdering* my sister is not something I'd consider brilliant."

"You are always exceptional, Aife, luv. Especially when you stand up for yourself. This is much better than your self-wallowing, and something I would absolutely consider brilliant." He slowly adjusts the cuffs of his sleeves, rolling them up to showcase his muscular forearms.

A growl tears from my throat as I rear my arm back, ready to strike his face again. His hand flies out, catching mine at the last second.

"You infuriate me, Lexyll!" When I yank my hand from his, he doesn't fight me but moves forward until my back hits the door. My body buzzes at his proximity.

He leans in, his warm breath tickling the shell of my ear as he says, "And you are a vicious thing tonight."

Goose bumps decorate my arms, and I grit my teeth, battling against my unwelcome attraction to him. It doesn't help that his heady, musky scent invades my nostrils, enticing me further.

"Stay the hell out of my personal space." Coming here was a stupid idea. I plant my hands on his chest, shoving him away. "I don't want you anywhere near me."

"Fascinating." His ethereal face glows, his eyes trailing down my body before snapping to my face with a glint of interest. "Your feelings say otherwise."

"Don't you dare use your power on me, you ass." I thought myndoxes were the most annoying of all, but vygoras might win that title now, thanks to Lex.

A shadow flickers across his face. "You are doing an abysmal job of keeping your barriers up."

"If you respected me, then you'd stay out on your own. I wouldn't need to keep my barriers up."

"Do you truly believe others will *respect* you enough to leave you be?" He chuckles darkly. "You think they won't use their powers to invade your mind, or your feelings, and do much, much worse? Because they *will* try, and if you let them, they will succeed."

"Who will?"

"We gods have many enemies, luv."

"And what? You think you'll teach me some kind of lesson by invading my personal space and referencing some obscure adversaries?" I spin toward the door, not bothering with my boots or coat in my stubborn, irrational anger. "I shouldn't have come."

Right as I open the door, Lex's hand flashes out and slams it shut, sandwiching me between him and the door. His firm body presses into my backside. My traitorous heart spasms at the contact.

"No," he whispers in my ear. I whirl around to face him as he once again enters my personal space. "*You* might not remember who your enemies are, but all of your enemies certainly remember you. If word gets out about your...*condition*, it could be a precarious situation."

"It would help if you stopped being so—so damn vague and aloof." He stares down at me, our warm breaths mingling. My gaze flicks to his lips, then back to his jade eyes. "Give me something useful for once, Lex. Something real."

"You want something real? Your enemies aren't the only ones who remember you. *I* remember everything about you—about us." I open my mouth to speak, but he continues: "I remember how you act tough to try and keep others away because you're afraid of letting them in. I remember how you roll your eyes when something bothers you—not because you're annoyed but because you don't know how to properly articulate your feelings and it frustrates you. The way you fall asleep reading, gripping your books so tight that I fear the pages will rip as I pry them from your fingers. It's an entire technique—a careful extraction, really." His pupils dilate as he lowers his voice. "And I remember the way your lips fall open when I touch you. How you give a soft gasp when I angle my fingers inside of you and hit that little spot—"

Smack.

My hand lands in the same place as before. Once again, he doesn't even flinch at the impact. I inspect my stinging hand, almost expecting his sharp cheekbones to have sliced my flesh. My chest heaves rapidly; there's no hiding the effect his words have on me.

"Didn't I warn you that some men like violence, luv?" He chuckles. "What is that—three times now that you've hit me since entering my home?"

I quiver with rage at his nonchalance. I'm not some toy he can play with, break, and cast aside. And luckily, I have more fight left in me. I came to say my piece and take out the anger I've been sitting on for months.

Closing my eyes, I focus on pulling his energy toward me. It's an impulse of wrath and desperation. I'm not expecting anything to happen—because of the wards in place—but when a rush of his life force surges through me, I gasp, and my eyes fly open at the delightful turn of events.

He can touch me all he wants, try to subdue me, but I'll suck his life force right out of his skin. He won't harm me in return, not truly—I somehow know that deep in my bones—but he's mistaken if he thinks I won't harm him.

As I begin drawing his energy out, my wrists shimmer at our point of contact, and a wave of pleasure washes over me. At first, he appears shocked. Then his eyes darken with lust. His tongue darts out to wet his lips.

Lips that beg to be kissed.

A moan escapes me as Lex presses into me, and I feel him harden between us. My hips shoot forward, and I rub against him as I continue to draw his energy out. Energy absorption always feels good—for me and for whomever is on the other end—but with *him* it's extremely erotic.

Nothing else matters but his touch.

"Naughty," he says with a gleam in his eye. Suddenly, the glowing between us grows brighter, and the pleasure intensifies. I spiral into unfathomed territory as I realize he's pulling my energy toward him, too, as I continue to tug on his. It's a constant cycle of pure, delicious gratification.

"You are nothing to me." My words come out breathy. I reach up and run my hands through his hair. I grab a fistful of his long, dark locks and jerk his head back aggressively.

His response is a wicked smile. "I love it when you're rough with me."

"You truly are a masochist," I whisper, pulling his hair harder.

As we continue to trade energy, I writhe against his hard length. The friction is undeniably hot. I trail kisses across his jaw before nibbling at his ear. He responds with a shudder, and it gives me a sense of satisfaction. When I bite down on his lobe, he groans and grips my ass in both hands, pulling me closer.

I want to hurt him.

I want to please him.

And I think I can do both at the same time.

I bite his shoulder next, hard enough to draw blood, and he growls. "You will *always* be mine." He shifts us, bringing his mouth to my neck and nibbling there in return. I moan, lost in the sensation.

"Touch me," I beg desperately. All of my logic has dissipated.

I'm a prisoner to my lust.

"I *am* touching you, luv." I can feel his smile against my neck.

"No," I say, pulling one of his hands away from my hair and placing it between my legs. "Touch me here."

"Demanding." His fingers explore the aching area between my legs. Even with the material between us, his touch intoxicates me. "Is this what you want?"

I reach between us and palm him through his pants. He's rock hard, more than ready to give me what we both want. When he groans at my touch, I can't help the satisfaction that rises.

"Yes," I whisper. His name escapes my lips as I pant.

It feels so good, *too* good, and I can't think about anything but him. The cycle of pleasure, enhanced by our powers, quickly brings me to the precipice. The pressure builds deep in my core, and I grip him by the shirt, pulling his lips to mine as he works me closer to orgasm. His tongue forces its way into my mouth, and I return the favor as we lose ourselves. He kisses me like he's a drowning man and I'm his only source of oxygen.

Right as I'm on the brink of exploding, he pulls away, cutting the cord on our power-sharing. It's as if someone flicked the lights on, waking me from a deep slumber. It leaves me with the worst ache between my legs.

I try to steady my erratic breathing. "Unbelievable, Lex."

He rubs a hand over his jaw, acting as if he's entirely unbothered by putting an end to whatever was happening between us.

"Well, that was unexpected...and hot," Callan says, and my cheeks heat with embarrassment as I distance myself from Lex. The golden-haired harbinger stands in the foyer with a sandwich in his hand.

"What the hell, Callan!" I say, scrambling to fix my hair.

"I thought I should check on you two, make sure you're not

killing each other." He shrugs, then takes a bite of his sandwich like what he just witnessed was the most normal thing in the world. "If you wanted privacy, there are better options than the foyer." He juts a thumb over his shoulder toward the kitchen. "I could see everything."

Lex ignores his friend in favor of gaping at me with a cool expression. His shirt hangs untucked and is halfway open, the top few buttons missing, and his shoulder-length hair is a ruffled mess, having come loose from the low bun it was in. A pale blue celestite stone rests against his collarbone, dangling from a thin black cord. It matches the stone on the cord around my neck, tucked into my shirt. A link between us should we ever need one another.

Quickly, I avert my eyes, not wanting to process what it means that we both kept them on.

This man is a cruel sonofabitch, but seeing him come undone by my hand is the sexiest thing in the world.

A feral grin grows on his face as he leans in to whisper in my ear, "He can watch all he wants, but you will always be *mine*." His lips brush my ear, planting a soft kiss there.

My cheeks burn with mortification as he pulls away to adjust himself.

Lo appears in the loft overhead, leaning over the railing and looking down at Lex and me, then at Callan, then back at me.

"Hey," she calls down, appearing puzzled, her voice carrying through the house. "Aife came."

"No, but she almost did," Callan replies through a mouthful of food.

Lo makes a choking sound, like she's trying to stifle a laugh. She turns and heads out of sight. "There are plenty of rooms with doors, you know!"

"That's what I said!" Callan replies.

"What the hell, Callan." I shrink into myself, wanting to get away from this entire interaction.

"It's true." He shrugs again before finishing his sandwich and jogging up the stairs to Lo.

I've been out of the apartment for less than thirty minutes, and things aren't working out in my favor. But as much as I hate Lex, I can't deny how he exhilarates me.

Too bad he murdered my sister.

CHAPTER NINE

LEX

Aife's stubbornness is unparalleled. I never back down from a battle, but she is the one person on this planet who could obliterate me. Not because I'd let her, but because she is truly a worthy opponent.

She is the *only* worthy opponent.

She is still the same beautiful, infuriating, whirlwind of a woman I fell in love with.

A roaring sound fills my ears as I continue to stare at her, battling the need coursing through my veins. I want nothing more than to ravish her. To ruin her. To let Callan watch. It takes everything in me to stop myself from ravaging her. A weaker man wouldn't have been able to pull back, but I pride myself on my strength. I respect her too much to take her like this, while she's confused about her feelings for me.

I tried to stay away, to give her patience and distance, to let her remember our history on her own terms, but I am losing the fight.

I wasn't lying when I said our status as fated doesn't impose upon our free will. It doesn't mean anything other than that our magic is a match. We are able to freely power-share, to allow our magic to mingle and become an unstoppable force. It does not mean she will never find love beyond me. Hell, it does not even mean she is destined to love me...as I very well know.

Still, I fell in love with her before I kissed her under the falls and discovered our truth.

I would let that woman shatter my kneecaps for one more second of those lips.

She might be a goddess by birth and blood, but it's those soft lips, the confidence in those sharp, teal eyes, and that violent yet loving heart of hers that truly make her a goddess.

I deserve her hatred. Every single stinking ounce of it, but now that I've tasted her lips again, I'm not backing down.

"We'll be upstairs," Callan says, leading Lo toward the loft.

I grunt a response, unable to pry my attention away from Aife. Her short hair is divine; it puts the soft curves of her neck and collarbone on display. When her lips form into a fucking smirk, it almost ruins me completely. I suppress the urge to get on my knees and beg her for one more touch.

And I don't get on my knees for *anyone*.

I may be immortal, but I swear to the goddess this woman has the power to send me to a grave.

The day she found me in that putrid cell deep beneath Enira's false marble palace, I thought she remembered me. I thought she'd come for me. When I heard them calling her *Astrid*, the *princess*, I realized Enira had won.

She may have won the battle, but she hasn't won the war.

That's *my* specialty.

I owe it to Aife to do everything I can to restore her memory. Even if it means working with the ever-infuriating Dashiel Dargan.

I adjust my shirt as best as I can and push the long, dark strands of hair out of my face.

"I'm glad you came tonight," I say. "We need to talk."

She rolls her eyes at me. "Fine."

Those pouty lips, still swollen from my kisses, threaten to

distract me. Talk about the greatest temptation. Her tongue darts out to wet her lips, and my eyes track the movement greedily. Her scent fills my nostrils. She always smells divine—it's the same blend of oils she bathed with years ago.

Slowly, I drag my eyes back up to those keen eyes of hers, willing my lust to stand down.

"You're still wearing my celestite necklace," I muse, a smile tugging at my lips. After all this time, she still wears it.

She glances down at her chest and stuffs the necklace back into the collar of her shirt before scoffing at me. "It doesn't mean anything. I just like the color."

"Of course." I wonder if she noticed I was wearing my matching necklace too. She must know I'll always come when she calls. All it would take is for her to rub it.

"What did you want to talk about?" She juts out a hip, resting her hand there.

"Sora has been in Hakran," I say, getting straight to the heart of it. "A—"

"I swear to the goddess, Lexyll, if you hurt Dash, you *will* regret it!"

My jaw twitches in response to her outburst. I had assumed she was done with *lover boy*. "*Dashiel* is fine." I try not to make a face as I say his name, careful to keep my expression neutral.

She purses her lips, narrowing her eyes at me, and my gut tightens unexpectedly at the revelation that she still cares for him. It chafes me that she's clearly willing to look past his transgressions but not mine.

"I did not harm the boy," I say through gritted teeth. "Quite the contrary. We are…in an alliance, I suppose one could say."

She snorts a laugh, crossing her arms and arching a sharp brow. "Guess Callan was right," she mutters. "You and Dash?"

I cock my head to the side, straightening my shirt. "Yes. Dashiel and me." Her eyes bulge. "However—"

"Wait," she says before I can continue. "How is Hakran? Is Dash...doing right by the people? Is he okay? And what about Ilona?" Her eyes flash with concern.

My lips tighten into a frown. Striding past her, I make my way toward the curved staircase, gripping the iron railing solely to keep from grabbing her instead. I begin ascending to the loft. Mostly because I can't bear to face her when she answers my next question. "You still care for the boy who hurt you?"

I hear the patter of her little socked feet on the wooden stairs behind me, and I know she's rushing to catch up with me.

"First of all, that isn't any of your business," she calls from behind me. I feel her heat mere inches away from my back as she closes the gap between us. "Second of all, if I can get over *our* past enough to hold a civil conversation without slitting your throat, then I can put my irritation with Dash on hold long enough to ensure he's all right. And third of all, stop with the condescension."

I smirk at her threat, grateful she can't see me. Beyond the promise of violence, her true heart shows. She *is* trying to get over our past. She cares about the boy because that is who she is. When we met all those years ago, her fiery personality attracted me and her power intrigued me, but it was the kindness she held in her heart, despite being the *deathbringer*, that caused me to fall so hard.

Smoothing my shirt down with one hand, I glide across the beige saxony carpet to the oversized leather sofa facing the stairs. Two sofas and a couple of plush chairs, with a low table between them, take up the center. Off to the left is a wet bar, and next to it is a small hallway leading to the turret, which serves as a library.

Grabbing a decanter and glass from the wet bar, I make my way back to the couches and carefully place the glass on one of the coasters on the table. I sink into the buttery soft leather with a sigh. To my left, Callan and Lo share a matching armchair meant for one. The two of them are practically inseparable, due to their angelli bond.

Aife bypasses the couch, stepping up to the thinly carved railing and gazing down onto the first floor.

The first time I brought her here, she was all giggles and awe, taking in the space with wide eyes and flushed cheeks. For someone who chose a small cottage and an even smaller apartment as her primary residences, she seemed to revel in the grandiosity of Harmony House.

The memory squeezes my heart, and I rub my chest absent-mindedly.

I step up to Aife, caging her in my arms as I grip the railing on either side of her. Leaning forward, I inhale the soft, spicy-floral scent of her hair. Her backside presses into me, and I have the strong urge to wrap my fist around her long dark locks. It's enough for me to grow hard.

"Lexyll," she teasingly admonishes as she wiggles, pressing into me further.

"Yes, luv?"

"I'm trying to admire the view."

"So am I," I say, looking down at her. She glances up with wide, ocean-blue eyes, and I know she's impressed by the view. The house was designed to almost seem as if it is floating. It's almost level with the water, with only a thin strip of grass and wildflowers separating the structure from the lake. We're all alone in the center of the lake.

"It makes me feel so small," she whispers, jerking her chin toward the mountains. They're grassy during this season, reaching up into the skies. Lazy clouds shroud the peaks, slowly rolling past. Whenever the sun finally pokes through, the rays sparkle off the smooth lake.

I plant a kiss on the top of her head, resting my chin there. "I'm surprised Callan and Loisia haven't brought you here before."

"Actually—" She makes a small choking noise, and her body tightens. "I didn't want to intrude."

"You could never intrude, luv."

Her muscles relax. "Yeah, you say that now because I'm here with you.*" She has a way of making the most innocent phrases sound seductive, and her words make my stomach knot. It's a strange thing, a sensation I've never experienced in all of my years on this earth. "I never realized how…"*

"Yes? Do go on."

"How normal it is here. How snug and warm it is. I see it now. This is more than work or an obligation—it's family." She glances up at me and grins before rolling her eyes and wrinkling her nose. "Even Sora fits in with you all."

I lean in to kiss her on the forehead, and the front door slams open. Chatter fills the space, echoing off the tall ceilings as Loisia and Callan bicker about something.

Impeccable timing, those two. I groan in Aife's ear.

"Come. Before they spot us." I grab her hand and lead her down the hallway to my bedroom at the far end of the house, where we will find privacy.

Those are the moments I want Aife to remember—the small, insignificant ones.

I try to imagine how the house must look from Aife's eyes now, without our memories. It's gorgeous, with its tall ceilings, carved wooden beams, and seasonal silvery tinsel accents. But I wonder if she still finds it as warm and cozy, or if it was our love that made it homey for her.

That's certainly what made it special for me. Without love and family, a house is no more than walls and a ceiling. And as much as I try to create a home here, it seems that there is always a threat to my love, my family. At times, being a god is more of a burden than a gift, and being responsible for so many— the people of Nevaris, my harbingers, my legions—means I have little time to myself.

I established Nevaris as a sanctuary for all those who need a safe space. Magic or not. Human or not. From our realm or another. It doesn't matter. After experiencing the brutalities of war and seeing so many innocent eyes go dim, I built Nevaris as my promise to protect.

Like Aife, I destroy. I maim. I kill. It's who we are. We were designed to serve the humans. Though I can't force humans to find their peace, I can cut conflict short. I can offer a sliver of rest and security to those who need it most, here in Nevaris.

Protecting the people, training the legionnaires, and scouring the seven realms for refugees is a time-consuming job. It leaves little time for helping Aife the way I desire, and for *that*, I harbor a touch of resentment.

Aife plops down in the chair to my right, across from Callan and Lo. My fingers itch to reach for the whiskey decanter, to fill a glass and throw it back. I'm desperate to chase a buzz and muddle the too-clear image of the woman beside me.

It's painful remembering her while she has no recollection of me. Of us.

"We have much to discuss tonight," I say. Callan and Lo nod in unison.

Aife grimaces. "I've had enough of the whole intervention thing."

"Aife, luv, this is not an intervention." I shoot a glare at Callan. "It was never my intention for Callan to corner you in such a manner. He was simply meant to fetch you."

"You mean *stalk* me?"

Callan's cheeks turn pink, and I slowly blink at him before addressing Aife. "First, you shall be pleased to know the boy-king is absolutely fine." She scowls at my nickname for Dashiel, but I ignore her reaction. "Dare I say, he appears to make a decent leader. The redheaded gal is fine as well."

"Ilona? What has she— She's okay?" Her words come out rushed. She scoots to the edge of her seat, desperate for more. "You can't just throw those bits in there and glaze over them."

"Yes. Ilona is fine."

She chews her bottom lip. I'm tempted to reach out and pry it from her teeth, but I fist my hands on my lap and refrain. I'm battling to remain composed, but she is too. I can tell she wants to ask more, but she won't. Instead, she sits up straighter, narrowing her eyes at me. She's sparing her pride, refusing to rely on me for intel, settling for the bare minimum instead.

For her, this isn't a friendly visit. Funny, considering she was writhing on my hand a few minutes earlier. She's probably denying she feels anything for me.

If she is, she's lying to herself.

So stubborn, this woman.

CHAPTER TEN

ASTRID

I sink into the suave, dark-brown chair, trying not to admire the house as we chat. It's just as gorgeous as the last time I was here months ago, but I didn't slow down to take it all in then. It's like an extravagant cabin, perfectly suited for wintertime in Nevaris. I'm grateful for the enormous fire crackling in the fireplace. My body is used to the balmy heat of Hakran, so the frigid temperatures here in Nevaris have been difficult to acclimate to.

The festive winter decorations—tinsel, pine wreaths, and poinsettias—that have been placed strategically around the room bring a spark of joy to my soul.

A soft instrumental tune continues to play in the background—a recording of some sort, no doubt. I wonder if Lex still fills the house with his beautiful music. The way his fingers danced over the piano keys last time I was here was enchanting. The way he belted out the vocals with such passion tickled my ovaries.

Lo watches me curiously as Callan rests precariously on the armrest beside her. He finishes his sandwich with slow bites, relishing the simple meal. When a few crumbs sprinkle onto Lo's lap, she scrunches her face and makes a disgusted noise.

"Gross, Cal." She uses the back of her hand to brush the

crumbs onto the floor. "You're a mess. I'm not cleaning up after you again."

"Sorry," he says bashfully. "I'll send for Ana."

Ana.

The name brings a wave of bitterness to my mouth, and I purse my lips.

Ana has been around?

After she was naked in front of Lex?

Lex certainly doesn't belong to me—I've made that clear with how I've pushed him away—but my gut aches with a weird, unwarranted jealousy.

"She's our housekeeper," Lo says softly, apparently picking up on my distress. "And Callan's ex. Not Lex's."

Avoiding eye contact with everyone, I nod and pick at a hangnail.

My thoughts and questions continue to spiral—picturing Lex with Ana—until eventually Enira's disgusting words pop up out of nowhere: Does your lover even belong to you anymore either? Or did I ruin him for you?

My ears ring, and my hands vibrate at the thought of that vile woman touching Lex while he was imprisoned in the silenxstone. The thought of her forcing herself on him sickens me.

"Are you all right?" Lo asks, her brow pulling into a frown.

"Yeah, I'm—" I turn to Lex. With a thick swallow, I ask the question weighing heavily on my mind. "Lex, I need to know. Did—did Enira hurt you?" Silence settles in the air, and I hold my breath as I wait for him to answer.

His jaw tightens. "That is a question I would expect from someone who cares."

I fiddle with my pants, embarrassed I've shown weakness by asking. "Never mind. I shouldn't have asked."

He leans back in his chair, crossing a leg over his knee. "No. She did not touch me."

An exhale leaves me in a whoosh. I'm immensely relieved he wasn't violated. Though my hands still shake with rage at the mere thought of Enira's words—of her taunts. She was the goddess of deception, after all. I can only imagine how many lives she ruined, how many people she deceived.

At least she's dead now.

"She never put her hands on me. If she had been close enough to touch, I would've snapped her slender neck." A shadow crosses his face.

I don't miss the way Callan's face shutters, too, a line forming in his forehead as he stares ahead into the empty space above us. Lo watches him with concern, resting a reassuring hand on his knee. Her touch shakes him out of whatever dark place he went. His expression relaxes, and he smiles sweetly at her.

I wonder if it's an extreme loyalty that brings Callan second-hand pain, or if my question elicited a memory of something else, something from his own past.

I squeeze my eyes shut, mentally cursing myself for being so blunt with such a sensitive topic. It was easy being arrogant and ruthless when I was in Enira's circle. It was encouraged, applauded. But I don't want to be like that anymore—I don't want to be like her.

"Thank the goddess you're back, Lex," Lo murmurs. "We needed you. Nevaris needed its leader."

Catching Callan's eye, I give him an apologetic look, and he smiles at me, though it doesn't quite reach his eyes. Lo watches him closely, and when she pats him again, he relaxes into her touch, and his eyes finally crinkle at the corners with a true smile.

They said we were friends for years. Maybe once upon a time

I could read them as well as they can read each other.

"I want my memories back," I tell the trio, cutting into the silence once again. I'm sick of hiding.

"Finally," Lo says. Her tone is soft, understanding. Gone is the rage I saw in my apartment, as if it never existed. Her lips turn up in a soft smile. "Sorry for pushing you earlier, but we ran out of time to wait for you to figure it out."

Callan and I trade glances, and I say, "I think Callan's tactic worked a little better than your aggression."

Callan throws his head back with a hearty laugh, and Lo chuckles. I can't help the smile that graces my lips.

"What do you mean you ran out of time?" I ask.

"We're leaving for Stellaris." Lex's deep voice sends a tremble down my spine, snapping me out of the lighthearted moment, and my body shifts toward him of its own accord. He commands attention without even trying. Confidence and power radiate off him the same way a full moon radiates light in the night sky. "It's clear the answers we seek about your memories are not in Hakran."

Even when I discovered him in the pit, without knowing who he was, I was drawn to him. It's more than the fated thing though, because Callan, Lo, and even the villagers watch Lex with awe and reverence, as if they all worship the ground he walks on.

It's simply a Lex thing.

"I'm surprised you want me to remember." I hold his gaze, showing him that he doesn't affect me at all. Even though it's a lie. "Aren't you afraid of what I'll recall?"

"You already remember the worst of me. Why not remember the best?"

I roll my eyes and lean back into the chair, crossing my arms. "So it's all about you? You think I'll come crawling back to you if I remember the good parts?"

"You are impossible." His eyes sparkle with delight. He enjoys it when I challenge him. "It doesn't matter what I want, Aife. You should know that by now. What matters is what you want."

"Does what I want truly matter to you?" I say, my voice going up an octave. My cheeks heat with anger.

Callan clears his throat, his attention jumping between me and Lex. "You know, you two are arguing just to argue at this point." Lo nods enthusiastically.

Lex shoots him a glare before allowing his eyes to slowly drag over my body. His gaze strips me bare. "You haven't changed a bit, and I will always want what you want. I will always want you."

"I will never want you," I spit. The image of him sucking the life force out of Invidia burns in my brain.

Lex walks to the bar, bringing a decanter of whiskey back. He offers me a drink, which I decline, given what almost happened last time I drank whiskey with him. With a knowingly smug look, he fills one of the empty glasses with the amber liquid, swirling it around and then sipping it carefully with his eyes glued to mine. He drinks his whiskey the same way he does everything else—with calculated control. A hint of danger lingers in his piercing eyes as he observes all the small details around him.

Lex is a master at schooling his expression, never letting anyone peer beneath the impassive mask he wears so well. But his irritation reveals itself in the way his jaw clenches after he sips his liquor.

The front door bangs shut below, snapping me out of whatever weird moment Lex and I were having. The smell of soot, of something singed, fills my nose as Sora bursts into sight at the top of the stairs a moment later.

Sora is unreadable, a continuous cloud of disdain. He's dressed in fitted black pants—so tight they're like a second skin—and a snug turtleneck. Muscles bulge from beneath his clothing. He normally moves like a silent shadow, despite his bulky size.

I think back to the scar I spied on his neck. Callan said I did that to him. Perhaps Sora has good reason to despise me, but I assume I also had good reason for attacking him to begin with. Now that's a memory I would like to recall.

Callan smiles at Sora, who simply grunts.

Lex cocks his head. "That was fast. I take it he's agreed to leave tomorrow?"

"The boy-king says, 'When the tide is highest,'" Sora says through clenched teeth.

I cross my arms and snort. They all appear around the same age—mid-twenties to early thirties—well, maybe except for the god. But Dash is no more a boy than Sora.

Lex sips his beverage, appearing uninterested.

Sora's eyes flit to me, then back to his boss. "What is she doing here?"

"Seriously?" I scoff at him, and the words bubble up inside of me, overflowing before I can stop them. "You are so petty."

"You have been hiding for months, coward." Sora's voice is hard as stone, snarky. "Any—" Before he can finish that sentence, his eyes flare open and his hands grip his head. He drops to his knees in silent anguish.

Lex rises, squeezing his glass so tightly that it shatters. Brown liquid splashes onto his shirt, and blood trickles from the fresh cuts in his hand, mingling with the whiskey as it drips onto the hardwood flooring below.

"What. Did. I. Tell. You?" Lex's tone sends a flare of warning up my spine. Callan and Lo wear tense expressions as we watch the scene unfold. "You do not speak to her in that manner."

Sora rests on his knees before Lex, paralyzed with pain as the life force slowly drains from him. His face pales, and his eyes begin to lose their shine. Right before they glaze over entirely, his body jerks, and he inhales a massive breath, visibly released from Lex's vygora hold.

"Sorry," Sora mutters, rising to a stand and shaking off the near-death experience.

My body freezes at Lex's reaction to Sora. His harbinger. His friend. If he can treat one of his friends so callously, it's no wonder he was morally fine with murdering my sister—someone he didn't even know. Maybe I've gotten him all wrong.

"I am not the one who requires an apology." Lex strides over to the wet bar and grabs a fresh glass before sitting back on the sofa and pouring another drink, like nothing happened. The only proof that he lost his cool is the blood trickling down his wrist and the dark stain surrounded by crushed glass on the beige carpet. "Twice now I've warned you. There will not be a third time."

Lex catches me eyeing the mess and leisurely wipes his blood on his slacks. The dark color of his clothing conveniently conceals it.

His eyes sparkle with humor, his lips turning up slightly as he raises the glass to his mouth.

Where the hell was this methodical savagery when Enira was jerking me around back in Hakran?

Sora apologizes—to me this time, his dark eyes narrowing into slits. Callan and Lo silently excuse themselves, hustling down the stairs to the main floor, with Sora at their heels.

I'm unable to peel my eyes from Lex. "What the hell was that?"

"Sora knows better than to speak ill of my—you."

"I knew you had issues, dammit, but where the hell did that aggression come from? Where was it when you left the pit?" Sure, I witnessed a glint of danger in those gorgeous green eyes the day I rescued him from the pit, but this is different. It's as if he was holding back before, but now, he isn't restricting himself any longer.

"It was always there, luv."

"Uh, I never saw you lash out like that."

"Didn't you though?" His face darkens despite the smile playing at the corner of his lips.

A flash of him downing everyone in the throne room pops into my head.

"But now that you are starting to recall just how much you love the violence, the thrill, I am finding it less necessary to subdue myself in your presence. I am glad you are remembering yourself, Aife."

His words send a zing of excitement through me, but I don't let it show. He's wrong. I don't like the violence or the aggression. No. Internally, I'm working hard to be a better person. More like Ilona. Or Dash. Or even Callan or Lo. Kinder, patient, more socially aware.

Less like Enira...or Lex.

"Wrong," I mutter. "I prefer kindness."

His lips twitch, the corners of his eyes wrinkling. "You can have a kind heart and still appreciate the beauty in brutal justice. The two are not mutually exclusive."

I grunt, not wanting to argue with him. "Where did you go that day, when you ran out into the storm after I transferred energy to you?" It was so odd. He disappeared into the night, only to reappear in the throne room right before I snapped. I never figured out what he was doing when he left.

His tongue darts out, wetting his lips as he hesitates before speaking. "The transference...it sparked something in me. It was temptation. It was too much. After being in the pit for so long, I needed air to clear my mind, to regain my control and think rationally."

Even when he snaps, like he did with Sora, he has this terrifying calm about him.

"You're always controlled," I say.

"Not when it comes to you."

My breath hitches as his features soften. He lets his mask fall for a brief moment, letting me witness the adoration in his eyes. And then, just like that, he slips the mask back on.

"Why did you come back for me?" I whisper.

"I was never going to leave you in that damned place."

"Yet you were a bit of a bastard."

He chuckles. "I don't deny it. Though I do recall apologizing for riling you up."

I held a dagger to his throat in Dash's room, right after he knocked everyone out. It was the first time Lex apologized for pissing me off. Despite his arrogance and unpredictability, he seemed genuine.

"How long were you down there anyway? A few weeks? Months?"

"Aife..." The room goes silent. "Much longer than that."

"How long?"

"Almost seventeen years."

I stop breathing. My head buzzes.

Years.

Seventeen years.

And he was okay without me never fully understanding the extent of what he went through for me.

I soften, pity filling my heart. I look up at him and sigh.

"Lex," I whisper. I cannot fathom the fact that he was in that dank pit for seventeen years. That I was with Enira for that long. The implication of his words shifts my perspective.

My heart aches for Lex and the years he lost. He wasted away in the bowels of the palace while I danced, two flights above, on marble floors with golden sunlight raining down on me. While I tangled in my sheets with countless, nameless lovers.

I can't meet his eyes.

I could've had it much worse with Enira. She stole my memories and wrapped her fist around my remaining freedoms, but she let me have a life. Even in death, the woman continues to confuse and anger me.

Callan was right. Surely there is more to the story with Invidia and Lex. But I'm not ready to dive into that yet. It's still a fresh wound, and I'd like to hold onto this fleeting moment of peace between us for a little longer.

CHAPTER ELEVEN

LEX

After a few generous glasses of my favorite barrel-aged whiskey, my head barely buzzes. It takes a tremendous amount of liquor to have an effect these days, and I almost wish it were easier to drown my sorrows in drink to escape the emotional turmoil Aife stirs up inside of me. The only thing that captivates me more than her fierce stubbornness is the way her eyes soften and her voice lowers as she questions me about the events in Hakran.

She's concerned. She cares.

After a few minutes of sitting in easy silence, she finally speaks again.

"I don't know how I feel about you and Dash working together. Or whatever it is you're doing. I swear, if you do anything to harm him, you'll regret it." The harsh, matter-of-fact tone returns to her voice, a reminder that she truly despises me.

It's enough to settle my lustful urges toward her.

I clear my throat. "As I was saying before we got sidetracked, Dashiel and I have gleaned new information." Her brow scrunches, and I clarify. "He has been sifting through the minds of Hakran's guards."

Only Aife, the harbingers, Dashiel's family, and I know that he can read minds, making him an utterly superior spy. I'd consider recruiting him as a harbinger—he could be a stronger asset than Sora, even—except for the small fact that he's been inside the love of my life.

There are very few things I refuse to look past, and that one is at the top of my list.

If he wasn't so useful—and I suppose if Aife didn't care for him so deeply *still*—I'd have strung him up by his innards by now. I *must* keep my wrath under control and my violent urges at bay if I want to be with her again. It was my cavalier disposal of someone she cared for that put us at odds in the first place.

"What did you find out?" Her eyes shine with interest.

"Sora was right about Enira storing up an external source of magic. We've confirmed she was harnessing wild magic from the storms."

Aife blinks slowly. Then her eyebrows rise. After a long moment, she nods. "She always disappeared during the storms. *Always.* I knew something was off." She rubs her temples. "How do we break the hold? Where is this stored magic?"

There's no mistaking the excitement in her voice. No one wants her to regain her memories more than I do.

"That's where we have hit a bit of a snag." I sigh, clenching my jaw. "The wild magic is purely aethyn in nature. She has caves filled with it. It's likely she was attempting to absorb and use the magic herself."

"How is that even possible?"

"Callan is better with explaining the details. But there's a natural stone, the opposite of silenxstone, called vimstone. It's rare, and it's known to absorb magic. These caves are filled to the brim with vimstone, which attracts the magic from the storms. I visited Hakran and used my vygora powers to read the energy of the caves. I only picked up elemental magic. The same energy from the storms. There was no myndox or vyogra magic stored in the caves."

"I don't understand. Why capture the magic at all then? What's the point of all that aethyn magic?"

"If Enira were a better person, I'd say she was trying to protect the island by diverting energy, creating a system that absorbs the worst of the storm's impact. In theory, the vimstone acts as a conductor and draws the bulk of the magic out, protecting the island."

"But Enira wasn't a good person."

"Precisely. Which leads me to believe she was harnessing magic for her own use. Sora and Dashiel learned she was confiding in the healer, but apparently he is no longer on the island. He also visited the caves prior to leaving, which is curious."

"Why did you send Sora of all people?" she mutters. "I can't imagine the Hakranians responding well to his brash attitude."

I smirk. "He is skilled in the art of torture." Her eyes widen. "Between Dashiel's myndox power and Sora's...*creative* extraction techniques, there isn't a single piece of information that slips by us."

"Okay, but you think *Cedrik* has something to do with all of this?" She frowns. "He wouldn't willingly help Enira." She pauses, deep in contemplation. "He feared her though. She could've conned him into helping. I think he might be in Stellaris. Apparently he and Joccelyn were friends long ago."

"Yes," I say. "He is on the mainland. He was deeply ensnared in Enira's web of lies. Even if he doesn't realize it, he may know more about Enira's intentions and perhaps any other locations she might have stored magic. At the very least, he's familiar with extracting magic to use in his healing tonics and potions. I imagine the process with the vimstone and wild magic is similar."

Aife nods. "His insights could be valuable."

"Precisely. There's a chance he could know what Enira was doing with the magic, if it's somehow tied to your missing memories. Meanwhile, we have people scouring the island and poring over old books for any insights." And if anyone with information refuses to oblige, I have plenty of other extraction methods.

"Aren't *you* super old? Wouldn't you know just as much as the books?"

"I am unfamiliar with this practice of magic harvesting and harnessing." I pretend to inspect my nails, attempting to project an air of nonchalance as I say, "But perhaps *you* have insights, considering you're the true elder here."

"Wha—no!" Her face pales as she's reminded that she's not the twenty-something she remembers herself to be, and I can't help the chuckle that breaks free from my throat. "How old?"

"Old enough." I wink at her, and she scoffs, clearly unsettled by the bit about her age.

"You are infuriating."

"As are you, luv." We stare at each other for a beat, a thick tension hanging between us. Sadness flashes in Aife's face, shifting to something darker, and I surmise she's remembering again what I did to Invidia. When I try to draw her emotions toward me, I'm pleased to see she has her barriers in place this time.

After a moment, I say, "As you heard, we're leaving for Stellaris tomorrow. My goal is to find answers about your memories, but there's a—"

"Who's *we*?"

"Me. Callan. Dashiel." Pausing, I school my expression and decide to casually extend an invitation. "You?"

My fingers drum a rhythm on the side of my leg, unable to

stay still.

She smirks. She fucking *smirks* at me. "Are you nervous because you're afraid of my answer? Or because you're afraid of *me*?"

I grip my whiskey glass, using it as a shield as I sip slowly and contemplate my answer. "Both," I finally say, deciding to be honest.

Her smile grows. "Good. And you'd better believe I'm coming to Stellaris whether or not you invite me along."

Our eyes lock, and I nod, my body relaxing. "Rest up tonight. Prepare to set sail. When we arrive, we'll be facing—"

"Sail?" Her face twists in confusion. "There isn't a tunnel that goes there? Like the one connecting Hakran and Nevaris?"

Oh.

She doesn't remember. The single etheryn-created tunnel she's referring to connects more than just Hakran and Nevaris. It connects countries and cities all over our realm, even stretching as far as the other realms. It works more like a portal than a tunnel, mimicking the old gateways that were abundant when etheryns were more common.

Some of the old gateways likely still exist, but unless one knows where to look, they won't find them.

An old etheryn friend of mine, Katerina, created the Nevaris tunnel long ago. She died in the process—giving every ounce of her magic and soul to power it. Her sacrifice has allowed my harbingers and legions to move freely through the realms, on our own terms. It connects locations by intent. I share this fact with few people, not wanting to relinquish the power of travel or put Nevaris at risk.

Etheryns like Katerina, known for their mystical abilities, are rare. And even if they were more commonplace, they would likely not share their power with others. It's quite taxing. Not only is it dangerous to them physically, but manipulating space, time, and ether can have serious consequences for the world at large.

Between the dangers associated with their power and the massacre that culled their numbers centuries ago, I wouldn't be surprised if they are actually common but simply choose to stay out of sight and remain quiet about their abilities.

Using the Nevaris tunnel to get to Stellaris is as simple as *wanting* to end up there. Picturing the location in the mind's eye is sufficient. But with Dashiel and his associates tagging along, I can't take the risk. Using the tunnel would mean revealing a well-kept secret with a potential enemy. Though I'm cordial with Dashiel for Aife's sake, I do not trust him.

I'll protect Nevaris at all costs.

"We're sailing," I confirm. I'm not sure how to explain the tunnel to Aife right now, so I settle for deflection, though I hate the guilt that surfaces.

Standing, I adjust my collar and swipe a hand across my tense jaw, reminding myself to relax. "Would you care to spend the night?"

"Absolutely not." She stands, her mouth in a tight line.

She treads past me, purposely going out of her way to knock into me with her shoulder.

Chuckling, I follow her down the stairs to the front door. She slips into her wool jacket—the one I sent for her—and puts her boots back on.

I notice she doesn't have gloves, and I frown.

"Frostbite happens quicker than you think, luv." I reach for my coat that's hanging beside the front door. There's a pair of gloves in one of the pockets. I pull them out, handing them to Aife. She bites her lip, eyeing them suspiciously before slowly accepting them and slipping them on.

"Thanks," she mutters.

The tension settles over us like a thick fog. I take the opportunity to use my vygora power and draw her emotions toward me.

Her barriers are down, once again. With a sigh, I rub my brow. I only use my power on her to check if she's being safe, *not* to spy on her innermost feelings. Before I can cut the invisible cord of energy between us, a wave of longing nearly crushes me. She craves me as deeply as I crave her. But what prevents me from reaching out and pulling her to me are her overwhelming feelings of anger, disgust, and deep sorrow. Bitter loathing. All directed at me.

It's a reminder of why I can't push her. Why I need to respect her and give her space.

"Keep your barriers up," I growl, my tone harsher than I intended.

She scowls, hurling a collection of expletives toward me. Ignoring the profanity, I grit my teeth and turn away, not wanting to witness her irritation. She doesn't trust me. She won't listen to me when I nag her to keep her barriers in place. And I also know she won't willingly let me protect her. But if she won't keep her barriers up, I won't sit idle and accept that.

I won't leave her unprotected.

Nevaris has wards in place—courtesy not of the gods or humans or even angelli, but of another being sought out by Callan after I was imprisoned by Enira. The wards stifle the magic of outsiders and protect those who live here.

Aife found a loophole earlier and was able to bypass them through our power-sharing, the same way I was able to use my power on Dash in the throne room—but soon we will be outside these protections. We are not the only gods who roam, and there are plenty of others with immense power who abide only by their own morals.

Like my late brother.

Aife slams the door as she leaves, snapping me from my thoughts. The chandelier overhead swings aggressively with the force.

Massaging my temples, I try to relax.

Callan appears at my side a moment later. "She'll come around."

I grunt in response as he shimmies into his coat and stuffs his messy blond hair into a hat. "Her barriers are down," I tell him.

His normally animated face is solemn as he nods, understanding the implication: *Don't let her out of your sight.*

The angelli have an enviable array of abilities—from invisibility to telepathy among their own kind. They can even fly using their powerful golden wings, which stay hidden away when not in use, invisible to the world.

If it were me, if I had wings, I would fly everywhere as a show of power and superiority. The angelli cousins would never do that though. They're far too humble.

Angelli always come in bonded pairs—similar to the fated pairs we have in this realm, except their bonds are specific to angelli only, and they are entirely platonic, often occurring between family members such as Lo and Callan.

I met them hundreds of years ago, when I assisted with the War of Realms. It was a time when gods were often called upon, and refusing to aid was not an option. We had purpose; we were revered.

After the War of Realms had been raging for a hundred years, there was a king—a tyrant, rather—who invoked me. I found myself assisting humans in another realm, pushing back against magical beings until the land was left entirely mortal and no beings with a drop of magic stood on the land.

It wasn't my own personal desires that found me fighting on that side. It was my duty to assist.

I chopped down the resistance with ease, having no patience for drawn-out battles. After the fighting began to subside and the humans faced imminent victory—thanks to the help of my legions and me—I came across two young people in the woods.

They looked to be no more than fifteen. The boy had wavy golden hair and big brown eyes. The girl had hair the color of snow and sharp, upturned eyes a slightly darker shade of brown.

The girl was hunched over on the ground, wails of agony ripping from her lungs. The boy noticed me and immediately balled his hands into fists. He stood to face me.

"If you touch her, I will end you," he said.

"Do you know who I am?" I asked.

The scent of sulfur and rot filled the air, another reminder of the loss and destruction that had taken place over the last few weeks. Despite the plumes of smoke on the horizon, the fallen trees, and the blood and bones littering the ground for miles, the boy stood tall and sure.

Internally, I smiled at his backbone.

He cooly informed me he didn't care.

The boy's face turned burgundy with anger, and when I glanced over his shoulder, I noticed the girl had wings. Rather, she had one stunning wing decorated with brilliant flaxen feathers, gleaming as if they were gold-plated. A smattering of red disturbed the otherwise serene features of her wing.

Blood gushed from a gash where a second wing should've stemmed from her back. The flesh was jagged, as if the wing had been ripped from her body right from the base—cartilage and all.

The boy stepped to the side, trying and failing to block the girl from my sight. Though he was about a foot shorter than me, he tried his best to stand menacingly, staring at me without an ounce of fear.

Me.

The god of war.

The man who had likely ended the lives of his friends that night without a second thought. The man who could have ended the two of them in a flash.

But something in the rigid set to their shoulders and their fierce expressions tugged at me. They regarded me with boldness and dignity, clearly broken and in pain but refusing to admit defeat, their heads held high.

When I glanced back at the girl, she was gazing fiercely at me, gritting her teeth to fight the pain. In between breathless wails, she managed to scream, "You...leave him...alone!"

My chest tightened. My instinct was not to kill them. It was to protect them. To give them a chance to thrive and be the warriors they clearly were meant to be.

Without hesitation, I used my vygora power to take just enough life force to render them unconscious for the journey back to Nevaris.

Lo and Callan woke up at Harmony House, healed and cleaned. The girl's wing regrew slowly and painfully. I expected resistance from them. I thought they'd give me hell for taking them from their homeland. Instead, they pledged their loyalty to me for sparing them. I had known little about angelli beforehand, hadn't realized that bonded pairs dedicate their life to serving a charge of their choice, and when they choose someone, it's irrevocable.

Their family is not determined by blood. It is created. It is found.

Once angelli reach full maturity, their bodies stop aging, granting them similar immortality to the gods. Fitting that we should be stuck together for eternity.

I am far too much of a bastard to deserve their loyalty, but it's something I will never take for granted. We've become a family—the three of us plus Sora—though he didn't join us until much later. Each of my harbingers heads one of my three legions. And though to many people we are no more than a myth, a whisper carried by the wind, we are fearsome.

To outside eyes, Sora is the treasured harbinger—due to his aethyn blood and ability to wield fire—but it's my two angelli allies with kind eyes and soft smiles that our enemies should fear.

Aife is safe with Callan looking over her; that I'm sure of.

I refill my glass and head into the round sunroom just off the main space, where my grand piano sits. The room's circular build and domed ceiling make for beautiful acoustics. I place my cup on a sunflower-shaped coaster—a gift from Aife. The glossy black wood of the piano glistens beneath the overhead orb lights.

Sitting on the padded bench, I take a big swig of whiskey and crack my knuckles. I'll give myself a moment to sift through my thoughts, and then I'll turn them off, letting the music carry me away.

Many things are weighing on my mind. Walking into a potential war is never a small matter. And we must find a way to return Aife's memories. I need to prepare her, protect her. I need to do *more* to retrieve her memories.

I agreed to help Dashiel, even though his timing is utterly poor. I have many pressing obligations I've needed to tend to since returning to Nevaris. Lo, Callan, and Sora did what they could to keep the legions in top shape, and Nevaris has been safe, but they have all been sitting stagnant, waiting for my leadership to

resume. Waiting for me to guide them. There have been countless
conflicts throughout the realms that could've ended more quickly
with my intervention. There have been many innocent deaths that
could've been avoided too, had we been there to offer refuge. But
my harbingers aren't as familiar with the realms as I am, which
leaves them at a disadvantage. And beyond that, it was too dangerous for my legions to head to battle without me. Though their
might is fearsome, *my* power provides the ultimate defense. If
they'd gone on their own, many of our own warriors might have
been lost without my vygora magic as protection.

Instead, they were stationary. Waiting for a leader who might
never return.

Waiting for *me*.

No longer invoked as I once was in the past, I now help by
choice.

I've been working overtime with my harbingers to ensure that
never happens again—teaching them all I can about the realms,
taking them to significant places within the universe so they can
travel the portals with intent. So they don't have to rely on me to
maneuver the realms.

We've been working on defense, training the legions not to
depend on my presence or my power in battle. It put them at an
extreme disadvantage to rely wholly on offensive techniques.

Part of me thinks it's time to take on another harbinger,
promote someone to work alongside me to train a defensive
legion. But there *is* no one else worthy. No one I trust with the
safety of my people.

"Hey, Lex?" Lo calls from somewhere in the house.

Her quick footfalls become louder as she draws closer. When
she steps into sight, her gaze wanders over my piano, then falls
on me. "Oh." A smile graces her lips. "It's not important. I'm

sorry to interrupt."

She leaves as quickly as she came, understanding that when I'm at the piano, I'm not to be disturbed. It's my time to decompress. To let out my feelings on the instrument.

Abiding my own *rule*, for lack of a better term, I close my mind to the issues plaguing me most. My fingers stretch as they reach their preferred placement—aching to warm up with the lullaby I wrote for Aife. They graze the cool ivories in a featherlight caress. My bruised knuckles, stained by today's training, stare back at me.

My feet find the pedals, and my eyes drift closed.

At first, I'm stiff as I move through the motions. The tune sounds fine, but it's missing something.

Soul.

As my joints loosen up and the day's worries fade away, I begin to lose myself. The chords reverberate through my bones, and my soul sings in response. My fingers dance across the keys with a mind of their own. The music slowly changes. The melody captures a piece of my heart and carries it through Harmony House, transforming it into the *home* I always craved.

CHAPTER TWELVE

DASH

A clean lemon scent fills my nose as I stride with several of my guards through the main hallway toward the royal wing. It's a quiet night, save for the clacking of our boots. All of the day's pressing issues have been solved, and the villagers have gone back to town for the evening.

The village is situated a few miles from the palace, on the east side of the island. The town is a hodgepodge of poorly-constructed and badly-maintained buildings, so any storm has the potential to wipe out multiple homes in one fell swoop.

Meanwhile, the palace sits above sea level, away from the flood zone, amongst the jungle trees. Made of marble and stone, it's a well-fortified structure.

How the Hakranians survived this long is a goddess-damn mystery.

I scrub at my brow, heaving a sigh.

I've done my best to turn things around and ease the worries of the Hakranians, but it's impossible to please everyone. Many people are hesitant to trust me, given everything they've gone through with Enira. I can't say I blame them, but I can say it's been nothing short of a migraine.

Sora confirmed that Lexyll and his crew will arrive early

tomorrow to properly discuss the trip. I'm confident the invocation will be successful, which means tomorrow night, when the tide is highest, we will set sail to Stellaris.

At this point, it's obvious I will not enjoy a restful sleep tonight. Exhaustion has always been familiar to me, but it's been a more prominent feature in my life since assuming Hakran's throne. I can't imagine Astrid would've ever enjoyed such a job. It doesn't allow me as much freedom as I once enjoyed. I'm constantly tethered to my work, tasked with solving problems that touch the lives of my villagers while also having to sift through the opinions of the many advisors around me.

The irony is that she thinks I've become king to betray her, when in fact I've done it to spare her. The people are quite outspoken in their disdain for Astrid, and she would have met much more resistance than I did had she assumed Enira's throne.

Fatima sidles up to my side, her curls bouncing with each step. "Relax, Dash." She keeps her voice low so the guards in formation around us can't hear. "Everything will be okay."

"That's not my concern." With the god of war on our side, shitty character and all, the Vespynians don't stand a chance. "We have Lexyll."

Though it still doesn't make sense *why* they'd invade my country when we've had decades of peace.

"Are you sure it'll be a good idea to try and invoke a god?" she asks, not the tiniest bit out of breath despite us hustling down the hallway.

My hands tremble at my sides, and I clench and unclench my fists, trying to will them to stop. I can't believe I plan to use an archaic invocation to call on a god. To call on the *god of war*. I'll be shocked if it works, dead if it doesn't. I'm also highly concerned about how Astrid will react when she finds out.

Because she *will* find out.

"There aren't any other options."

Fatima grunts. "I'm sure he'll help without you tethering him to you with some ancient magic."

"The invocation isn't only meant to bind us for his *help*. It's meant to protect me from him. Protect my family." I'm not stupid enough to think Lexyll and I are truly allies. We might be working alongside one another for Astrid's sake, but I don't trust that he wouldn't slit my throat in my sleep—especially if he discovers my father's vendetta against his kind.

The ancient practice of invoking gods was a mere myth until Ilona found a reference to it in the books. It was rumored to have been used by humans hundreds of years ago—before they stopped *needing* the gods' magic. Before they stopped believing in and worshiping them. It was a way to call on the gods for safety and assistance.

The War of Realms apparently raged for a century without resolution, until Lexyll was finally invoked by King Hamilton. Then the war was swiftly ended.

"What if it doesn't work? Then what? I can't imagine he'll take kindly to you attempting to manipulate him. Or what if it *does* work? What will you do after it ends?"

"Problems for another day, Fatima."

"You're being impulsive and reckless. You don't mess with the gods, Dash. You of all people should know this."

"This is different."

"Either way, you risk making the situation worse."

I stop, holding out an arm to stop her.

"My father is still warm in his grave. My mother is a shell of herself. She's trapped in her mourning. Zale is overwhelmed and alone. Hakran has no other leader besides me. If something happens to me, it doesn't only affect me, Fatima. I'm invoking Lexyll to protect me, to protect those I care about. They don't need to lose me too. We don't need a damned drawn-out war on our land."

Her face softens. "I understand that, but I still don't agree with the invocation. You don't need it."

"It's not your decision to make."

"Maybe not, but as your friend, I'm warning you that you're making a mistake."

"Right now, you're *not* my friend. You're my commander. You work for me."

She scoffs. "If all of this power"—she waves her arms around—"is going to your head, then consider me done. I don't work for tyrants, *Dash*."

"What I'm doing is the opposite of tyranny, *Fatima*. You of all people should understand that. I'm not my father."

Fatima's mouth drops open, and she glares at me. "Dashiel Dargan, how dare you speak of him that way! Emman was a *good* man."

Her admonishment hits home. After a years-long battle with an invisible illness, he's finally at rest.

Emman *was* a good man. He was one of the best parents a guy could ask for. Joccelyn and Emman took me in and loved me like their own. They raised me to be the proud man I am today. They taught me many invaluable lessons, one of those being that too much of anything is terrible.

Too many sweets make you sick. Too much training fatigues you. Too much magic is destructive.

The only thing they said you could never have too much of is love. Just like Ayana, like most Stellari natives, they lived by the rule that you can never give or receive enough love.

But the gods and goddesses? As the humans stopped believing in them, stopped calling on them, the gods ceased to have a purpose. Over the centuries, they became bored. Too much power and too much boredom is a deadly combination, and humans are the ones who pay the price.

According to my parents, the gods have too much of many things: magic, life, power, boredom.

But the one thing that they don't have enough of?

Love.

I've always believed my parents: the gods are cruel, incapable of love. Especially after Ayana's death.

But after falling in love with a goddess, I can no longer blindly follow my parents' teachings.

Astrid *is* capable of love. I've experienced it—I *know* she feels something for me. I see the way she looks out for Ilona. I witnessed that passionate kiss between her and Lexyll. And even Lexyll himself, as much as I hate him, loves Astrid fiercely.

I agree that the world *should* be purged of cruelty and unmitigated power, but not the way Emman believed. Killing all the gods and goddesses for merely wielding a title is genocide. So, yes, my father's order to hunt the gods and goddesses was an act of tyranny. I might've believed in that mission prior to coming to Hakran, but if he was still here, we would no longer be in agreement about it.

I never understood that until I fell for Astrid. And I won't dare fight my feelings for her, because I know in my heart that she is good.

I worry about how she might react when she hears the truth about my family though. I never had a chance to tell her about my past, but I planned to. I *want* her to know everything.

"Your father had intentions of bringing peace to the world,"

Fatima continues. Internally I groan, wanting to be done with this conversation. "He only wanted to prevent others like Enira from hurting innocents."

"Enira is not the standard of goddesses, and you know it. Astrid is nothing like her."

"Do we know that though? For certain?" We stop and face each other. Fatima crosses her arms, giving me a disappointed look. "Just make sure you're not making decisions with your dick, dammit. Your family—your country—they come first. Think of Ayana. What would *she* think of you right now?"

My chest squeezes. There's a reason my father went on the trajectory he did. There's a reason why Fatima thinks my loving a goddess would be guilt-inducing.

But Ayana wasn't one to hold grudges.

"First, don't mention my dick again," I mutter. "Second, Ayana would be proud. I'm following her last wishes." *To forgive and to love freely.*

Astrid had nothing to do with Ayana's death. I feel zero guilt for loving her.

Instantly, Fatima's face smooths out, her lips opening a fraction as she takes in the earnestness in my expression. She's the only other person I know who takes her sister's words as seriously as I do.

"A *goddess*, Dash, seriously?" Fatima admonishes, shaking her head.

"Please, Fatima, for fuck's sake. Let it go." We have this conversation about once a day, and it's exhausting. One second she's telling me it's worth it to be patient, to wait for Astrid, and the next she's judging me for the same relationship she encourages.

It's as if she's torn between her heart and her head. Between logic and love.

This time Fatima acknowledges my request and shuts her mouth. I know she's disappointed in me, but I also know she will come around. As fierce as she is, she's much like her sister—loyal to the core. I'm honoring Ayana's last wishes, no matter who I love, and Fatima knows I'm right.

Even still, she struggles to understand why I'd go against my late father's agenda to eradicate the gods and goddesses from our realm.

After seeing what Enira is capable of, it's understandable that she would expect me to be more driven than ever to seek vengeance—to purge the land of these cruel beings.

That is truly what we came here to do, after all: stop Enira, the goddess of deception. Of course we knew all along who she was. But we did *not* know who Astrid was.

In an attempt to please everyone and protect them, I've weaved myself into a web of lies.

And I've caught my friends in it like flies.

CHAPTER THIRTEEN

ASTRID

Callan comes to retrieve me in the morning. I've dressed in warm layers, with a lighter, airer Hakranian outfit underneath so I can shed clothes as needed when we arrive in the warmer island climate. I'll be carrying nothing other than a single knapsack with a few items.

"Lex told me to remind you to bring some books." Callan smiles, and his eyes crinkle adorably at the corners. He gestures toward my bookshelf, refusing to move until I oblige. I catch a whiff of his leathery cinnamon scent, and it reminds me of strudel.

Rolling my eyes, I grab a few titles without looking. I'm careful as I place them in my knapsack, not wanting to bend the covers any more than I already have. "We'll be too busy for me to read."

"He knew you'd say something like that, and he said, 'We'll be on a ship for days, and she'll get bored.'" Callan mimics Lex's voice, and I chuckle. "I'm just delivering the message. Don't stab the delivery boy."

"It's 'Don't shoot the messenger,'" I say.

"That's what I said." He winks.

When we leave the apartment, I don't worry about locking the door behind me. Nevaris is truly a safe place, and all the villagers know one another. There's no crime, and it seems like nothing bad ever happens here. I wonder if it's because of the wards Lex put up.

Last night, I was able to break through the wards and use my power on him. The memory of us combining our magic makes me giddy. My body hums at the thought, my dormant power waking up and begging to be let free.

Callan and I make our way down the stairs and onto the street. The sun is barely starting to peek out from behind the mountains, but the snow is no longer falling, so I take that as a good omen. The morning light glistens off the fresh layer of powder, making it look like a blanket of white diamonds. There's something soothing about how quiet Nevaris is. As we crunch through the snow, our breaths fogging into the air, I revel in the peace and tranquility.

The air is crisp, and it reminds me of the first bite of an apple.

"Where are Lex and Lo?" I don't bother asking about Sora. I hope he isn't accompanying us on the journey.

"Near the docks. They're waiting for us."

Main Street leads us directly to the docks. Most of the accumulated snow is gone—having been intentionally cleared away. Only a light dusting remains, barely concealing the stones of the street beneath.

It would have taken multiple people quite some time to clear it. Some of the townsfolk must've gotten up early to do it.

I ask Callan about it as we pass the shops. All the windows are dark, as if everyone is closed for the day. I frown. I thought they opened with the sun.

"Sora," Callan says with a sly look.

"What? By himself?"

"Yup."

"How?"

"He melted it." I'm about to push him for a clearer answer, but as we venture past the village center, I notice a crowd of people on the outskirts of town, down by the docks at the base of the mountain. Indecipherable chatter reaches my ears as the people excitedly talk amongst themselves.

"What's going on?" I ask. Callan chuckles beside me, and as we draw nearer, I realize the ground around the crowd is littered with flowers. I spy roses, tulips, and more. "What are they doing?"

"It's a send-off ceremony. The villagers toss flowers at those who are leaving as a way to express their affection and wish them good fortune and safe travels."

I remember all the flowers in Harmony House after Lex returned from the pit. "They do that when people return too?"

"Yes. In that case, it's still a sign of affection, but also gratitude for a safe return."

"Where did they get all the flowers from?" I know it's barely winter, and Nevaris just had its first snowfall, but the ground is definitely frozen, covered in about a foot of snow.

Callan jerks his chin toward a figure standing at the edge of the crowd. I recognize her long dark braids and the basket looped around her arm.

"Fara?" I ask.

"She's an earth aethyn. She has a greenhouse in the back of her shop."

"I've never seen a greenhouse and I live above her, Callan."

"It's not a literal greenhouse. It's just what we call it because, well, flowers grow there." He shakes his head with humor, and his golden hair falls into his eyes. He shoves the stray strands into his hat. "She doesn't need sun, or air, or water, really, just a space to make things grow. She's marvelous."

I raise my brows, interested in this new piece of information. "It explains how she creates fresh scents for her shop year-round."

Callan lowers his voice, leaning in to whisper in my ear. "I have her make me a cinnamon-scented oil. It smells so good."

"No wonder you smell like strudel." My shoulders shake with laughter. "I had no clue she was an aethyn."

"You're going to lose it when I tell you Sora's a fire aethyn then."

"No wa—" I pause, letting it sink in. "Yes way. *That's* how he melted the snow."

"Yup."

"Fitting for the broody sonofabitch."

"Yeah, that fiery asshole!" Callan says with enthusiasm.

I snort. "I thought you two were friends."

"Oh, we are. I love the kid. He's got issues, but don't we all?"

I laugh a little too loudly. I'm overly giddy from Callan's companionship and nervous about going back to Hakran.

"How are they able to use their magic here though?"

"Sora and Fara are both Nevaris-born. The wards protect the residents from outside magic, but anyone born here can use theirs." He pauses. "And we harbingers and legionnaires can. We have loyalty tattoos pledging our allegiance to Lex."

I whip my head toward him. "Tattoos?"

He grins. "I'd show ya, but it's a little too cold to take my clothes off."

"Callan," I admonish.

"Plus Lex might kill me." He winks. "Kidding. It's on my ribcage—a shield the size of my first. Magic ink, put simply. Knows intention. It allows us to use our magic within Nevaris only if our intent is to protect and not harm."

That's astonishing. Surely I used to know all this already, but it's shocking to hear.

Tattoos made of magic?

A few other thoughts swim through my mind: if I wasn't born here, where *was* I born? How did Sora end up as a harbinger for Lex?

But before I can ask anything, we're spotted by several people in the crowd, and the chatter increases. Once we reach the edge of the group, we're pelted by handfuls of petals. Small flowers in various colors rain down around us.

A sunflower lands at my feet, and my laughter dies out as a weird sense of nostalgia slams into me. *My favorite flower.*

I flash back to my quaint cottage where my sister was killed.

A wave of nausea overtakes me. I plaster a fake smile on my face, not wanting to ruin the send-off ceremony. These people all seem so kind. The last thing I want to do is cause them distress.

Fara says something to Callan and me, but I can barely make it out over all the conversations and laughter floating around us.

"Ready, luv?" Lex's deep voice caresses my ear, and I jump, startled at his sudden appearance.

His presence calms my nerves, grounding me, which is surprising, all things considered.

I glance up at the snow-capped mountains and gulp. The tunnel is in the smaller mountain, about halfway up the summit. But still, it's icy and steep. My neck prickles.

We move away from the crowd and step onto the path leading up the mountain.

To my pleasure, Sora doesn't appear to be joining us. Lo and Callan take the lead as I bring up the rear with Lex. I try to purposely slow my pace, to get him to pass me, but he slows down too, insistent on walking beside me.

In my irritation, I change tactics, picking up my pace in an attempt to shake him off. When my foot comes down on a patch of ice and I lose my balance, my heart jolts.

"Ahhhh!" My arms shoot out, flailing around as I fight to regain my footing without any luck. A strong hand snags my arm before I can fall backward, and I'm pulled into Lex's chest.

I groan as our bodies collide. Even with all the layers of clothing between us, I can feel the hard muscles of his warm body pressed up against mine. I fight to catch my breath, unnerved. When I inhale deeply, I catch a whiff of his woodsy scent and grow lightheaded for a second.

He pulls back, a twinkle in his eye. "Did you just...sniff me?"

"What? No!" I scoff, trying to pull away from his grip altogether, only to slip again. He yanks me back to his chest and wraps his arms around my body.

As he continues to hold me tight, he tilts his head down to whisper in my ear, "You seem to have a thing for that, luv."

My traitorous stomach flip-flops with excitement.

I grit my teeth, irritated that he has the gall to call me out. I wasn't *intentionally* sniffing him; he just happens to smell good. Instead of telling him that, I say in a neutral tone, "Maybe I'm just glad you don't smell like you did in the pit."

"Admit it, you find me irresistible." His breath tickles the shell of my ear, and I squirm as I become aroused.

"Never." It comes out weak and breathless.

"I don't believe that for a second. Look at the way you're clinging onto me." I can practically hear the smile in his voice, but when I rip away from him, his expression doesn't give anything away.

"Stop doing that."

"Doing what?" He cocks an eyebrow.

"Touching me. Whispering in my ear. Being all—"

"Irresistible?" he offers.

I roll my eyes, resuming my ascent now that I've finally regained my footing. For the rest of the way up, neither of us speak. He walks behind me, guiding me gently with his hands on my waist so I don't lose my balance again. I work to clear the fog from my brain, to think clearly, but all I can focus on is his touch. His fingers feel as if they're burning through my layers, branding the skin beneath.

When we get to the top of the mountain, he releases me and I spin around to face him. I'm feeling things I shouldn't for this man, and it's bothering me. I don't know whether to give in to my attraction to him or loathe him for murdering my sister. I hate only having pieces of the truth and not being able to trust my own feelings. Not that I plan for anything to happen between us, but I also hadn't planned for anything to happen between us when I sought him out yesterday at Harmony House.

At this point, he's right. I *do* find him utterly, infuriatingly irresistible.

Goddess save me.

We arrive at the entrance to the tunnel—a curved door with splintered wooden planks and rusted hinges—and I halt.

"Lex," I say. He pauses, his back going ramrod straight. He nods to the harbingers, indicating they should go ahead, and I wait until they enter the tunnel. "I want the truth. About Invidia."

If there's anything I've learned, it is that it's easy to misinterpret information or mistrust my own mind. It's easy to react irrationally.

Plus, Callan's book synopsis analogy struck a chord yesterday. And if there's anything I've discovered from reading, it's that I loathe the miscommunication trope. It's irritating.

So I stare at Lex, my chest rising and falling with my anxious breathing. We need to talk this out.

"Tell me why you killed my sister."

CHAPTER FOURTEEN

LEX

My pulse doubles at her words, and my lungs squeeze with terror—foreign and unwelcome. I wasn't sure *when* she was going to ask me about Invidia.

If she was going to ask at all.

I clear my throat, adjusting my gloves to avoid answering immediately.

Despite the distance between them, Aife and Invidia communicated often via letters. Invidia was Aife's confidant, her friend, her biggest supporter...or so Aife thought.

That day, I went to Aife's house expecting to meet the cheery, kindhearted lass I had heard all about.

I hadn't expected to come face to face with the woman I had been hunting. The one marked as a traitor to Nevaris. The one responsible for putting my safe haven on Enira's radar.

For weeks, strange things had been happening in the village. Families suddenly forgot about their loved ones. Shopkeepers failed to open their storefronts. Vendors no longer lined Main Street with their tents and wares. Fishermen failed to show up at the docks.

It was as if a sort of amnesia had swept through Nevaris. More and more villagers began to forget themselves and their lives, without any explanation.

As if that wasn't bad enough, some of the villagers also started experiencing out-of-character outbursts. Mothers turned on their kin. Farmers slaughtered their animals. The peaceful village, heretofore filled with birdsong and the chatter of smalltalk, had morphed into something nefarious. It had fallen into chaos.

I knew there was another god at play; I just wasn't sure *who* was capable of such a feat or why they were targeting the village.

Even more concerning, how had they found it?

We'd never needed wards before then.

Sora had kept to the shadows for months, listening for whispers that could reveal information. He scoured Nevaris for any indication of what was going on. It didn't surprise me when he quickly uncovered the truth. He's incredibly resourceful, more intelligent than most. He followed a lead one night and returned with no recollection of what he'd discovered that evening—his mind was empty like the minds of the villagers—but he clutched a paper in his fist.

Wisely, he'd had the forethought to sketch the profiles of two women he'd overheard that night. He worried that whatever was overtaking the villagers could potentially affect him as well. As it did.

His artistic skills were an unexpected asset. The charcoal rendering showcased two women I had never seen before: one with pitch-black eyes and an eerie smile and one with a distinguishing birthmark above her lip.

My harbingers quietly searched the globe for the two women but had no luck.

Much to my chagrin, when I headed to Aife's cottage a few weeks later, expecting to find the love of my life and her sister, my eyes latched onto a woman I sought for treason.

A break from poor luck?

Or *worse* luck?

Invidia was the mystery woman with the prominent birthmark from Sora's sketch. She was somehow linked to the disruption in Nevaris.

Aife had recently told me her sister resided in the deep south of Thysia and had never been to Nevaris. Aife wouldn't lie to me, which meant her sister had lied to her. And, hoping to spare her from the boring tasks of my job, I had never shown Aife the sketch. The village is home to more than two thousand. It was, and still is, my job to protect them all. Invidia knew who I was to the village *and* who I was to Aife. Still, she betrayed us all with her clandestine meetings with an enemy.

An enemy who threatened the peace of our home.

I still remember the day perfectly.

I've finally found her. But there's little relief. This complicates things.

The same hardened expression I wear into battle slides onto my face, and I push aside all emotion as I make my way toward my new enemy. In the blink of an eye, I am no longer Lex. Now, I am upholding my duty as God of War, protector of Nevaris. My steps morph into the march of a warrior. But this time, for the first time ever, a heaviness forms inside me as I step closer to the sunflowers. It unsettles me.

My eyes sweep the perimeter discreetly.

In battle, I strike first and ask questions later. I never give my enemies pause, but this is different. This involves Aife. I owe it to her to give her sister a chance to explain.

I step into the garden. The wall of sunflowers surrounds us like a private room. The air is light, carrying with it the scent of plum blossoms and spring.

I stay alert but focused, honed in on the woman before me. She could easily be described as beautiful—with curves similar to Aife's and the same teal-colored eyes—but where Aife's gaze is warm and inviting, Invidia's is cold, calculating. Her hair is a shade lighter, thinner, her features more feline.

"I wondered when we would finally meet, Warmonger," she says with a smug grin. She reaches out to trace a yellow petal with her finger as she steps forward, her hips swaying seductively.

My eyes don't stray from hers. "'Warmonger' implies that I encourage war. Despite my title, I do not strive to incite violence." I finish it.

"What a shame." She stops about a foot away from me, tilting her head appreciatively as she looks me up and down. "My sister chose well. She failed to mention those luscious lashes and that kissable pout."

A part of me burns to confront her about her meetings with the dark-eyed woman. Invidia is a vygora, which means the mysterious woman must be the one responsible for altering the villagers' memories and actions. Likely a myndox.

Finding out her sister is somehow tied up in the mystery will only cause Aife pain.

"Whatever you're contemplating. Don't. For Aife," I warn, my love for her winning out. I keep my mental barriers up, protecting myself from anything Invidia might try with her power. I have no weapons on me, but I do not need them. I am skilled enough to take down my enemies without weapons and without magic, should she have barriers in place too.

The same fingers that dance gracefully on the piano are also skilled in the music of maiming.

I'm wise enough not to underestimate the woman in front of me, but I'm confident enough that I could protect myself if she were to strike.

Invidia scoffs. "Aife, Aife, Aife. Not everything is about Aife." *The bitterness in her voice flares like a cruel warning.*

Invidia is the goddess of envy. Though I do not know her on a personal level, I find her jealousy terribly cliché. A god's title is symbolic of their role among humans. The titles indicate the sector of humanity observed and ruled, but they do not define us.

Aife is the goddess of death, but she aids villagers in finding their end peacefully when it's time. She gives life to heal those whose time isn't up yet. As the god of war, I aid in battle when called upon but do not willingly cause conflict. It would be poor form to assume Invidia is consumed by envy due to her title, especially when Aife has never mentioned it as being an issue before.

Assuming the gods wield the traits of their titles is a dangerous way of thinking, reminiscent of the egotistical fallen deity Osiris. Look where that got him: long gone.

"This isn't you, Invidia." *My words are confident, and I am not sure if I'm trying to convince her or me. This cannot be the sister Aife loves so fiercely, the woman she speaks so fondly on a daily basis. The dark-eyed stranger must have done something to alter her personality, as she did the villagers.*

Despite that hope, my warrior brain treats the scenario like a battle, and I quickly calculate all angles.

"You know nothing about me," *she says. Her smile disappears.* "But we could change that. Join us. Enira and me." *Invidia's body language and slicing words are purposeful, wielded like weapons.*

Enira.

The dark-eyed woman?

"I don't know what you are up to, Invidia, but it's going

to destroy your sister. I won't let that happen." I make sure the threat in my tone is unmistakable.

"Join us, Warmonger. Stop depriving yourself of your true nature. You are a god, after all. Stop bowing to the humans. You are not their slave, and you do not need to live by their rules." She steps closer. Suddenly the gap between us is gone. She runs the palm of her hand over my chest. As soon as her other hand disappears into the pocket of her slacks, I realize this show of seduction—or whatever it is—is a distraction. A failure of a distraction, but I am careful not to let on that I know what she is doing. Sure enough, as she slowly removes her hand, I catch a glint of metal in the corner of my eye. "I am a lot more fun than Aife is."

"Last chance to rethink your actions, Invidia," I growl.

"She will get you killed, you know. She will get all of us killed."

My jaw tics, but I don't respond. It's nonsense she's spewing.

"My sister is the link between us and the Underworld. She will be the end of the gods and goddesses—she'll put us all in a grave. We can work together to keep that from happening. Join us."

"I'll put you in a grave long before you ever get near her." Fury rises in me. There's still a chance Enira has Invidia under her thumb, but if she's a risk to Aife's life, I refuse to wait and find out.

"You can either join us, or you can join Aife in the grave."

She steps forward, poised to stab me in the gut, but I'm faster. It's her threat to Aife that dissolves any resolve I had left. Rage seeps from my pores as I unleash the full brunt of my power. I don't hold back as my body hums with energy and every nerve comes to life. My focus latches on to the traitorous woman before me, drawing out her life force. The air around us pulses as her life oozes out of her. Her mouth parts, and her smug expression gives way to one of concern.

Whatever she and this Enira woman are up to, whoever implanted this silly belief that Aife is some kind of threat, I will find out the truth. They shall all lose their lives. I will stop at nothing to protect my fated.

A small sound comes from Invidia's throat, and her eyes widen as I continue to tug at the invisible threads between us with full force, pulling out her vital energy and housing it in my body. Surely she realized I won't waste my time on petty banter. Her face contorts, shifting into a thing of nightmares, but I refuse to let up. Her life force pulses through the air around us, an invisible entity that most are unaware of but one that I can feel with every fiber of my being as it enters my skin.

I hold her stare as I continue to drain her without remorse. There's a pleasure in receiving so much powerful life force. Surely Aife can use this extra energy to aid those who need it. It's what she does: recycle life-force energy. Her power is beautiful. Versatile.

As Deathbringer, she takes the lives of those who don't deserve to live, those who have committed great crimes against humanity, then gives that energy to those in need. Those who deserve a second chance. She also assists with the villagers' natural deaths, using the pleasurable sensation that both parties experience during absorption to ensure they pass pain-free and filled with peace.

Some view death as tragic, unfortunate, but it is a natural part of our existence, a necessity.

So, no, I have no regrets.

Invidia's life force floods my veins. Soon Aife can absorb it from me and transfer it to someone who needs it. Someone much more deserving. Invidia's eyes flicker over my right shoulder before she collapses onto the grass in a lifeless pile. Sweet relief flows through me.

A scream shatters the air, and when I turn, my heart freezes. Aife, standing at the edge of the wall of sunflowers, stares in horror at her sister's body. The cheery blue house and the sunny day make for an ironic setting, a sick contrast to the moment unfolding before us.

Aife looks like a dream—a sweet, beautiful dream—but the look of horror marring her face is something from a nightmare. Her eyes are wide, her mouth open in disbelief.

If Invidia wasn't already dead at my feet, I'd murder her again for putting her sister through this.

Whoever this Enira is, she is next. I shall bestow the same fate upon her.

I adjust the collar of my shirt and step toward the love of my life, unsure of how to break the news of her sister's betrayal.

"Aife, luv," I say. Wordlessly, she turns and flees from the garden.

The memory enrages me all over again, and I hesitate, not sure how to explain this to Aife. The explanation would have been hard enough at the time, but now, she has no context. There's no trust between us. No history.

As my eyes roam over her face and I catch the pain lingering there, I realize I can't tell her everything. Not yet. She might not remember her sister now, but when her memories return and she recalls how much she looked up to Invidia, the truth will destroy her.

Invidia doesn't deserve to be protected, but Aife does. She's been hurt enough. I can at least spare her this pain. I don't want to ruin the love she carries, somewhere deep inside of her, for her sister.

I understand all too well the pain of a sibling's betrayal—the pain of losing them.

Since I prefer not to lie, I tell her *a* truth. "I killed her because she was a threat, and it's my job to neutralize threats."

Aife pauses, her brows pulling together as if she expects me to clarify. I stroll past her, my leisurely steps a contrast to the rapid rhythm of my heart.

Aife might never forgive me, but at least now she can carry the love for her dead sister without the sting of familial treachery. My mouth goes dry, and my jaw tightens at the memory of my own kin—how my brother metaphorically stabbed me in the gut.

Aife doesn't need to experience that.

I will carry that pain for us.

For now, all I can do is help her retrieve her memories and accompany her friends into battle. It won't make up for the past, but it might help bring her back to life, give her a future so she can give that same gift to others. She has already proved she doesn't need me, not the same way I need her.

My sweet angel of death.

CHAPTER FIFTEEN

ASTRID

Lex's words haunt me as I stomp through the tunnel. The two harbingers put enough distance between us that it's like Lex and I are alone. We say nothing, the thumping of our boots echoing throughout the tunnel.

It takes everything in me not to turn around and unleash my rage on him. The only reason I don't give in to the urge is because keeping my mouth shut and refusing to give him anything is likely more of a punishment than raging on him would be.

He would like it if I lashed out.

He stays silent throughout the journey too.

Finally, I spare a quick glance over my shoulder. I'm expecting to find him entirely unruffled by our conversation, but when we lock eyes, I catch what almost looks like regret on his infuriatingly handsome face.

I whip back around, crossing my arms and continuing forward.

"Aife," he murmurs. "Wait."

His fingers skim my elbow, but I jerk away. "Don't you dare touch me. Don't talk to me. I hate you." *And I hate that I want a reason not to hate you.*

I'm being petulant, wiping away the progress I made these

last few months, but I can't help it. He unravels my carefully stitched self-control.

The rest of the journey to Hakran continues on in strained silence.

When we emerge from the tunnels, a weight lifts from my shoulders. Ironic, considering the air is heavier here. I've missed Hakran's warm, humid air, the way it fills my lungs with salty, fruity goodness. Even the fresh scent of decaying bark and soil is comforting.

When I was in Hakran, I missed Nevaris. Now that I've been in Nevaris for so long, I find myself longing for Hakran. It's as if a piece of my heart belongs to both places, which is peculiar, considering neither is my home.

I wonder where my little blue cottage is, if perhaps it holds more answers about my past.

A rustling behind me catches my attention, and I turn my head to see Lex shedding his coat and scarf. I wordlessly let my gaze roam his body like a hungry predator. He's dressed in a fitted silk shirt and trousers that display his strong thighs. Not exactly tropical-island attire, but then again, Lex doesn't seem like the type to own shorts.

My eyebrows rise in delight at how well he fills out his clothes. I can't imagine I'd ever get sick of such a view.

When his eyes lift to mine, I freeze. My cheeks warm. His lips tilt up at the corners, and my heartbeat picks up its pace.

Callan pops out from a thicket of vines, holding a kumquat. His abrupt arrival shatters the moment.

"What the hell, Callan!" I clutch my chest, giving him a dirty look as he bites into the fruit and juice squirts out, dribbling down his chin. "Don't scare me like that. Where is Lo?"

He chuckles, jerking his head toward the overgrowth behind

him. "She had to relieve herself."

"That's not a good idea," I say. Many of the dangerous animals—like snakes, spiders, and frogs—blend in with the ferns and lianas. The thicker parts of the jungle, where we currently are, are teeming with them.

A few seconds later, a feminine scream filters through the trees. A handful of birds scatter overhead, and my heart stutters in my chest.

Callan's fruit thuds to the ground. He swiftly unsheathes his sword from the leather scabbard on his back with a slick *clink*. I've never seen a sword quite like it. The cross guard is bone white, carved into the shape of gleaming feathers. A fierce expression slides onto his face as he shifts into warrior mode. He wields his weapon artfully, slicing through the twisted liana vines in search of Lo.

Once Callan clears some of the overgrowth, we see her immediately.

She charges at us, yanking her leggings up and stumbling ungracefully. "There!" she screams. "There's a beast!"

Callan turns, ready to attack, while Lo unsheathes her own sword—a twin to Callan's. Lex steps in front of me, dual talon blades in his hands. He must've had them hidden beneath his clothing.

"Where?" Callan says in a serious tone, all business.

"There!" Lo points the tip of her blade upward, toward one of the trees in the lower canopy. A soft, feathery set of wings unfurls from her back, sending a blast of air my way. My bangs tickle my forehead. Her wings stretch wide around her, the bright white almost blinding to behold. They're nearly identical to the wings on their swords.

I open my mouth to speak, but it comes out as a squeak.

"You have wings," I point out lamely.

"Put those away," Callan scolds. "We can't fly here."

"Fly?" I repeat, stunned.

"Nervous reaction, asshat. Involuntary." With a whoosh of air, Lo's wings fold away, disappearing entirely. I peer over her shoulder, wondering where the hell they went.

"Umm, okay. You have wings. You can fly. This is all very normal," I mutter. I exhale heavily, shaking my head. I set my sights on the creature Lo is panicking about.

On one of the branches sits a furry brown animal with a white face and dark eyes. Its limbs wrap around a branch as it slowly chews on a palm leaf.

"For the love of the goddess." I roll my eyes, pushing Lex's arms down to get him to relax. "Put the weapons away."

Lo's face is beet red as she stares at the animal, then looks back at us. Callan resheathes his weapon, and Lex's blades retract into their small black handles with the push of a button. He tucks them inside his waistband.

"It's a sloth, Lo. It's fine," I tell her. I can't help the laugh that escapes. The two men start chuckling too, and Lo's eyes darken with fury. She grips her sword until her knuckles turn white. "It's really, really fine. They're harmless. They don't like people much, but they won't attack you for simply peeing in their territory."

Finally, Lo sheathes her blade and grunts.

"I can't believe you have fucking wings," I mutter.

"I can't believe she unfurled them," Callan says, clapping Lo on the shoulder. "It's a total faux pas for an angelli to let their wings out involuntarily like that. Kind of like when a dog gets scared and pees itself."

I snort, and Callan covers his mouth as he laughs.

"Whatever, Cal."

"The First Harbinger of Lexyll, God of War. A fearsome, indomitable warrior. Petrified of...sloths!" The pitch of Callan's voice gets higher at the end as if he's battling to hold in his laughter, and Lo looks ready to punch him in the face.

Lex simply sighs, as if he's used to this nonsense. "It's understandable to be terrified of unknown animals in unfamiliar territory, Callan, especially when one's trousers are down. It's quite a vulnerable position." I swear I catch a hint of humor on his face. "I am sure you'd have fared no better had you been in her position."

"Let's go. We're running late," Lo mumbles, pushing ahead of us, clearly embarrassed by the whole scenario.

"At least it wasn't a snake," I call after her, to which she replies with a thumbs-up over her shoulder. "And at least you didn't pee yourself!"

Her thumbs-up quickly turns into a middle finger.

Callan howls with laughter. My eyes lock with Lex's. An unwelcome wave of longing surges through me. My humor fades, and I scowl at him. His face returns to its normal apathetic state, and he strides ahead.

Every few steps, we encounter more and more low-hanging branches and vines. Lex holds them aside, allowing me to pass before scurrying ahead of me and resuming the lead.

"So has she never seen a sloth before?" I whisper once Lo is out of earshot.

"She's only been to Hakran once, luv," Lex says, sidling up beside me. I glance up at him, the air sparking between us when we make eye contact. I rip my eyes from him, focusing on Callan instead.

"I was talking to Callan," I grumble. "I thought you've all been frequenting Hakran."

Callan shakes his head. "No. Only Sora's been here. We had other duties back home, unfortunately."

I never thought about what Lex and the trio do outside of helping me, and I suppose it makes sense that they have actual duties to fulfill. It says a lot that Lex was willing to spare his harbingers, and so much time and energy, to help me.

"Thanks," I mumble as Lex holds back a particularly thorny bramble.

My arm brushes his, and my chest tightens at the proximity. I quickly pull away from him, as if he's poison to the touch. I'd rather feel the thorns than him. They hurt less.

The rest of the trek through the jungle is fairly unremarkable, but I catch myself glancing at Lex out of the corner of my eye the entire way.

Months of sitting around, with no horseback riding, swimming, or training, has definitely taken a toll on my physical state. By the time we emerge from the jungle at the edge of the palace courtyard, I'm sweating and tired, and my brain hurts from trying to figure out Lex's motivations for killing Invidia. It's impossible to do with no context though.

The sprawling marble structure sprouts up like a mirage. It's a ritzy, grandiose building that stands in stark contrast to the vibrant blues and greens of the Hakranian sky and jungle. It's like a life-sucking fungus contaminating the serenity of the island.

Although Lex's abode also screams wealth and power, it does so with an understated elegance. At least the architecture of Harmony House matches that of the rest of Nevaris. Lex's house and the homes in the village stand together—Nevaris isn't purposefully divided like Hakran. The villagers here live in shoddy, poorly constructed homes that stand on stilts down by the east coast. The grandeur of the palace is frankly disgusting in comparison.

The sun reflects off the pale stone harshly, and I have to squint to make it out. The novelty of returning has worn off a bit, giving way to trepidation. I don't know how I'm going to face anyone, especially when I'm not sure how to act. As much as I needed the past few months alone to find my sanity, I do regret leaving Hakran behind.

We approach a half dozen guards standing between the parallel pillars at the palace's front entrance. They are dressed in traditional brown-and-black Hakranian warrior leathers, but they aren't wearing the signature masks to conceal their faces. I'm not surprised Dash did away with that part of the uniform.

The guards acknowledge us with sharp eyes and pursed lips. Two of them—a man and woman—swing open the heavy, arched doors, and the entire group accompanies us inside.

None of the guards bow their heads to me, or even greet me as I pass. And based on the fact that all six guards are choosing to escort our small group of four, it's safe to say I no longer hold the same power here as I once did. Honestly, it's relieving. I can't imagine what it must be like for Dash. In this moment, I realize how grateful I am that he took that burden off my shoulders.

I'm the kind of woman who cries when she's sad, yells when she's mad, and runs away and hides when she's scared. I feel immensely. I have anxiety and panic attacks, and I'm inconsistent. The last thing I want to worry about is stifling myself for others. The more I've thought about it, the more I realize that ruling would be an extreme burden.

The guards lead us through the foyer and main wing. The

palace looks exactly the same as it did when I left. The waxed floors are so shiny that I can practically see my reflection in them. When we get to the throne room, a chill crawls up my spine.

We pause outside the ornately carved gold-and-white double doors, and I swallow the ball in my throat. At least it's just Dash on the other side. I will never be Enira's vessel again. I will never hide beneath the veyl and cower like a spineless weakling before anyone ever again.

One of the guards flings the doors open with a dramatic flourish and gestures for us to enter. The room is exactly how I remember it, with its soaring ceilings and intricately carved columns. I used to think this space was opulent, magnificent and imposing, but now, it simply seems sad. Cold. Dull. It's no fault of Dash's; it's the way Enira left it.

My eyes wander to the onyx dais, expecting to see the new king himself atop the midnight-colored throne, but it sits empty. The steps I've knelt on so many times, bowing my head beneath the veyl before Enira, seem so innocent now. Without Enira atop the throne, it is not nearly as haunting.

It is merely a chair carved of rock.

Quite a few guards are posted around the room, and I scan them, instinctually searching for a set of honey-brown eyes and a mischievous grin.

Lex's gaze burns into me, but I ignore him, continuing to seek out Dash.

A moment later, I see him. He's dressed in a white button-up shirt and brown suspenders. His leather boots are scuffed. His hair has grown out slightly. It now curls around his ears, emphasizing his boyish charm. There's an unpretentious air about him, and I find it comforting.

Of course he's not on the throne. He doesn't need a crown or a regal outfit to look like a king. His presence is plenty enough.

The guards around him—Hakranian and Stellari both, I notice—all watch him with reverence. Men and women alike. They give him their unwavering attention as he speaks, and when he finishes, they bow their heads deeply and unhurriedly in a show of respect unlike anything they've given Enira...or me.

It's striking. Zale might be the brother who was groomed to rule; he might be tidy, regal, and composed, but it doesn't take away from the fact that his brother, the warrior, is a leader in his own right.

I wait for him to glance our way, but he doesn't. He resumes speaking, taking the time to look each guard in the face as he does. He manages to address each person in the group of twenty or so as if he's speaking directly to each one.

Even from across the room, there's no mistaking the tightness in his lips. As we step closer, I notice new stress lines running across his forehead and dark spots under his eyes.

Most notably missing is his usual swagger.

It hits me how much I doubted Dash. He meant it when he said he never wanted this. Based on his casual outfit and grim, detached expression, I can tell the role is weighing on him. Even when he was my bodyguard, chasing me around the island around the clock and working to free his family and defeat Enira, he never looked this exhausted.

The man I know is meant for adventure, not the cage of sovereignty, of diplomacy.

My heart longs to see the smirk that's missing from his face, his carefree humor. Right now, he's all seriousness and direction. My anger at him has mostly subsided, replaced with anger at myself for being so cruel to him.

I drag my eyes away from him and accidentally catch the gaze of the woman next to him. With her ebony skin and tightly coiled curls, she's painfully gorgeous. The guard leathers she dons only add to her feminine beauty.

She narrows her eyes at me, not in a cruel way but in a contemplative way. Her head tilts slightly as she holds my stare, neither one of us backing down.

A frown creeps onto my face as I realize she looks an awful lot like the woman I saw sneaking out of Dash's room a while back: *Fatima.*

I'm not positive it's her—it was too dim that night for me to fully make out her features—but she has the same tall, lean build and curly hair.

My stomach twists, and for a second I feel as if I'm going to be sick. Dash said she was a Vannyk family friend, but it looks more like she's *his* friend—if that's all she is. She helped us bring down Enira by creating a storm to distract the guard, using her four-pronged aethyn power, and I should be grateful to her for her help...but I can't help the jealousy rising in me.

She's here.

With Dash.

Not in Stellaris with the Vannyks.

"This is a mistake," I whisper to Lex without looking at him. I turn to leave, to at least get away from this throne room, away from all these people who feel too close and too far away all at once.

Lex's hand flashes out and loosely wraps around my wrist to stop me. "No." The word comes out as a soft plea rather than a command, but I shrug him off anyway.

"How dare you tell me what to do." I grit my teeth, rushing out the door before Dash can finish his speech and spot me.

My heart compresses at the sight of Dash ruling Hakran with

Fatima at his side.

The worst part of all is that Ilona is probably near, but I don't know where our friendship stands.

That's on me, though, and it's time to apologize to her.

Making my way through the main hallway, I cross through the gleaming foyer and navigate around pillars until I reach the parlor's sliding doors. The place where I first officially met Dash and the Vannyks. I smile at the thought.

Tugging the doors open, I enter, finding the couches empty. A guard tries to follow me in, but I turn to him with a stern look.

"I need a minute. Please." He stares at me for a moment before finally nodding and backing away. He doesn't shut the doors all the way, leaving them half-open, but at least I have a moment of privacy. I'm grateful for that.

I need to cool down before I see Ilona. The last thing she deserves is for me to show up and immediately start emotionally dumping on her. I've been working on not doing that, and I want to show her that I'm trying to be better.

I hang my head and rub my brow, heaving a heavy sigh. "I need to leave. What am I doing here?" I mutter to myself.

"I'm wondering the same thing," a smooth, feminine voice says. Boots clack across the floor, and I turn to see the curly-haired woman approaching me. There's no aggression in her demeanor, nothing that implies she's a jealous lover confronting another woman, nothing indicating she's a threat. "I didn't mean to sneak up on you," she says.

"You didn't."

I use my power to assess her emotions. After neglecting my

magic for so long, it seems strange to use it. As soon as I focus on the pulsing thread of energy between us, to draw her emotions in, I almost sigh in relief. It comes back with ease, like it's the most natural thing in the world.

It's like oiling a set of creaky old hinges, bringing them back to life with a renewed fluidity.

The first of her emotions to crash into me is grief. It's as if something is gnawing at her from the inside out, and it takes every ounce of energy to keep it inside, to smother it deep down and try to ignore the constant pain of its sharp teeth. It's so palpable that I question if I've ever felt true grief in my life. I've certainly never felt anything like *this* before.

With a gasp, I quickly withdraw my powers, cutting off our connection before I can get a read on anything else.

"You read emotions, right?" the woman asks, arching a brow. The way she asks indicates she knows the answer, but I nod anyway. "Well, did you discover what you expected?" She tilts her head, staring at me curiously from beneath her thick, curled lashes.

There's no venom in her tone, but I have an urge to apologize. I don't know if it's because of how long it's been since I read someone's emotions or because of how potent her feelings were, but my cheeks heat.

It's almost unbelievable that this calm, poised woman in front of me feels such great pain, yet none of it is visible externally.

"No," I whisper.

"You look like you're ready to either attack me or run for your life." I simply shrug. She scrutinizes me again from head to toe. "You are exactly what I imagined and nothing like I imagined all at once. It's perplexing."

"You're Fatima."

"I am." She pauses. "And you're...short for a goddess."

"Dash never mentioned you," I say. It comes out a bit meaner than I had intended, my jealousy peeking through.

She chuckles sarcastically. "Meanwhile, whenever we're not discussing Hakran, *all* we talk about is you." She lowers her voice, like she's telling me a secret. "He thinks about you a lot."

"I'd worry if my lover constantly thought about another person." It's petty and bitter, and I feel ugly saying it, but I can't help it.

Her mouth drops open, and she looks genuinely stunned for a second before she laughs so hard she snorts. Her head tilts back, and her curls bounce with the motion. But she full-on *laughs* at me without holding back. "Are you serious right now?"

Now it's my turn to look shocked, but I have no words for her. I don't know what I had intended with the barb, but I thought for sure my words would piss her off.

She steps forward, resting her hand on my shoulder like we're old friends. But there's a warning in her eyes. "We are clearly not on the same page here." I'm too confused to shake away her hand, and instead I stand there awkwardly until she removes her hand herself. The fake smile doesn't fade from her face. "I am not Dash's *lover*. I am, however, an old friend who cares about him. And as his commander, it's my job to watch out for him."

That explains why she was by his side.

She stands up straight and squares her shoulders. "I grew up with Dash and Zale. Our parents were friends and employees of the palace. Dash dated my sister, Ayana."

His first love.

I nod, slowly fitting together the pieces she's giving me.

"He said he told you about her," she says, observing me carefully. "Anyway, that's not what I want to talk to you about.

Why did it look like you were about to run away? Again?"

I clench my teeth, not wanting to discuss anything about Dash and me, or any of my other concerns, with this stranger. "That really isn't any of your business."

"Like I said, it's my job to look out for Dash, but if you want to make this complicated, go ahead. I don't back down from confrontation."

"I am not in the mood for confrontation. I just don't feel like doing this." I gesture between the two of us. "Whatever *this* is."

"This is us having a conversation." Sneering at me, she crosses her arms. "Or me trying, at least. That's all. And I'm giving you the choice to have a conversation with me as Fatima Abelli or a conversation with me as *Commander* Abelli, your choice."

An image of Commander Jamell—a man I thought was a friend—fills my mind, and I'm grateful that Dash has Fatima on his side. It's unfair to be mad at her for caring about him. He deserves a friend like her.

The tension between us is thick, palpable, all of the previous humor gone. I sigh, biting my lip before answering. "I'm not trying to be hostile. This—being here—is hard for me."

"You're not the only one going through a hard time."

"I know."

"Do you? Then why were you trying to leave?" I open my mouth to reply, but she continues: "Don't try to fool me. I saw that look in your eye and the way you bolted out the door. I came to find you before you run away again."

"Why does it matter to you?"

"I've seen Dash suffer enough after my sister passed, and now I'm seeing him suffer in a whole new way over losing you. You owe the man a conversation."

I swear my heart skips a beat, and like a teenage girl, I almost beg her for more details about what he's been saying about me. "Then why didn't he come talk to me?"

She scoffs, shaking her head. Her curls bounce around her face. "The man is hurting. He's hurting hard. *You* wounded him. Deeply."

My cheeks flood with red-hot embarrassment. "I—"

She raises a hand to stop me from talking. "Look, don't explain it to me. I've heard what happened to you from Ilona. Goddess knows I wouldn't have handled it any better. I'm simply saying the guy is hurting. Talk to him. Mend things with him. I don't care if you get back together as lovers or friends or decide to let each other go entirely. I just ask that you don't leave things unfinished. Not like this. He doesn't deserve it."

Ilona has opened up to Fatima? That hurts almost as much as hearing that Dash is in pain. "I guess I left things pretty bad with him…and Ilona," I add, waiting to see if she says anything more about my estranged friend.

"You did. I won't lie to you. You hurt a lot of people, but I can say that you also have a lot of people who still care for you."

A sarcastic chuckle escapes me. "I've been alone for three months. No one came for me."

Her features harden, and for a second I'm almost afraid of the transformation in her expression. "Girl, if you don't stop the pity party and open your eyes, I will smack some sense into you. Everyone left you alone because it's what *you* wanted. You could've come back at any time, but you didn't. Stop playing games and communicate. Dash and Lexyll hate each other, but guess what? They are standing in the same room right this second, without murdering each other, to discuss an alliance they created to get *your* memories back. Ilona ended things with Marnie because she chose *your* friendship, even though you weren't even

THESE WICKED TRUTHS   159

around to be there for her. She knew you two would find your way, and that's how important you are to her. Look, it is not my place to discuss others, but I just need to make my point here. Wake up and stop moping around. Dash looks out for you in more ways than you will ever understand."

Her rebuke shakes me to my core. It's the second time in two days I've had an intervention of sorts. It seems everyone who cares about me is keen on sending their friends to talk sense into me.

"I'm not here to bully you, but if you don't have good intentions, give him closure so he can move on, and leave his good heart alone."

"I don't have any intention of making things worse," I mutter.

"You gods *always* make things worse."

I sigh. "I'm not even— I'm just Astrid," I say exasperatedly. I don't *feel* like Aife, like a goddess. But on the other hand, the name *Astrid* fits like a shoe that's a size too small.

"Fine." She pauses, her features softening slightly. "If Dash and Ilona like you, well, I suppose I ought to give you a chance too." She steps forward, planting a kiss on each cheek—the traditional Stellari greeting. "It's nice to officially meet you, Astrid. I'm Fatima."

I notice that even after all that, she introduced herself simply as Fatima, not as *Commander Abelli*. It seems meaningful. Like perhaps we could form a friendship.

But I'm still not sure if I hate her or like her yet.

"Now you need to go and talk to Dash."

I suck in a large breath. "I know. I will."

"I mean it, Astrid. He's going to need you after what happened."

Before I can ask her what she means by that, she has disappeared from the room in a few quick strides.

CHAPTER SIXTEEN

LEX

I ever-so-patiently wait for the boy-king to finish whatever *encouraging* speech he's giving to the guards around him. He doesn't look my way once, but his guards' eyes continuously flicker toward me—some out of curiosity, some in warning. There are several who regard me with fear. Good.

Annoyance builds the longer he drones on. I don't care to listen in, and my feet itch to turn out the door and ensure Aife hasn't left.

I know her. When things get tough or messy, she runs. After seeing Dashiel, her face became clouded over with a look I recognize—regret. She's probably trying to abandon us right at this moment. And Dashiel, none the wiser, continues to prattle on like we have all day.

Callan followed her out without needing my order to do so, and surprisingly, so did the Hakranian commander. I trust they'll ensure nothing happens to her, and if she does choose to leave, well, Callan will accompany her back to Nevaris. I'm not foolish enough to think I can stop Aife when she makes up her mind to do something.

My fingers tap impatiently against my thigh.

Dashiel finishes his speech, dismisses the guards, and glances my way. Immediately, his mouth morphs into a scowl, and his brows sink low. I'm sure it's a mirror image of my own expression. Clearly our feelings for one another are mutual.

I break our stare-off to nod at Lo, a silent command for her to give me space. Most of the guards give me a wide berth, scurrying by without looking at me. It gives me a sick sense of satisfaction. It's clear my reputation precedes me.

If I were anywhere else, I'd be irritated that people always choose to see the worst in me. But here, it's almost like a battle won.

I plaster on a smug, patronizing grin as Dashiel approaches. He crosses his arms, his nostrils flaring. Neither of us speaks for a moment.

"War?" I draw the word out, raising an eyebrow in an invitation for him to elaborate.

"Your favorite, no?"

I pierce him with a steely look. "This is an utterly unexpected conflict." I exhale sharply. "If this is a game, or a trap of some sort, I do hope you know it will not end well for you."

His eyes narrow. "The last thing I'd want to do is play a game with *you*. I'm not Enira."

"No? I recall that you enjoy manipulating others and toying with their emotions." I grit my teeth, wishing I had a glass of whiskey right about now. It might make this interaction a touch less painful.

I want nothing more than to punch him in the throat for making my woman cry. And for being intimate with her? I'd love nothing more than to rip off his—

"Cocky, aren't you?" he says. "At least I didn't kill her sister."

Externally, I am the epitome of calm and collected, but internally, I flinch at his words. Of course he knows what happened.

He's a mind-reading myndox, and most people have shitty barriers, loose lips, or both.

Sama knows Sora is one of the former.

"Watch it, *boy*," I snarl at him, stepping up until we're chest to chest. "You might be immune to most myndox and vygora power, but not *all* power." I took him down easily, very easily, the last time we were in the throne room together. Granted, it was because Aife and I had power-shared. I'm not sure I *could* take him down with my power alone.

"I deal with your minion on my property, but that's as far as I go. If you want to step foot on my ship, you'll back the fuck down, Lexyll."

It's an empty threat—we both know it. *He* sent for *me*.

"If you want to see Aife again, you have no choice but to let me on your ship."

"You don't get to decide whether or not I see *Astrid* again."

I step back and adjust the cuffs of my shirt as if I have no cares in the world. "Is that so, lad? You might have tasted her once or twice, enjoyed her for a few short days, but she belongs to me. She is *my* fated."

"You're a bastard." Dashiel shakes his head.

My lips curve into a sharp smile. "Have fun playing king, because that is as high as you will ever rise. You will never be a god. You will never be immortal, or powerful, or worthy. You will never deserve her like *I* do. You—"

Crack.

His fist collides with my nose in a flash. I spit blood at his feet, grabbing him by the neck. There's an audible gasp behind me.

"You just punched a god, Dash!" a feminine voice screams at the same time I hear Callan yell, "What the hell, man?!" Their voices resound through the room like thunder, and I turn to see my two harbingers standing beside Dashiel's curly-haired commander.

Releasing the boy, I step back. Fury rings through me, loud and clear. Rage boils in my veins until it threatens to bubble over. I'm unwilling to irreparably harm Dashiel and risk alienating Aife, but I also no longer care to fully contain my power, so I let it out.

They need to understand what I am made of.

Who I am.

In one quick burst, my power explodes free from me, clawing its way into everybody in the room, ripping out enough life force to knock them to their knees.

The guards go down.

The commander.

Lo.

Callan.

Even Dashiel drops—thanks to the small power-sharing session I had with Aife last night.

Their energy surges into me, flooding my veins with sweet relief. A smug smile works its way onto my lips.

"Lex...*don't*," Callan chokes out. His eyes flash with a plea as he struggles to stay conscious.

His appeal snaps me back to the moment, and I exercise my self-control in a well-practiced move by cutting the cord on my power before anyone loses consciousness.

The room fills with gasps and coughs, roars of outrage. But nobody moves toward me. The guards remain firmly planted around Dashiel, shooting terrified glances my way.

"Dash!" The commander is the first to her feet, wobbling as she surges toward the boy. Once at his side, she watches me with pure hatred.

I growl, irritated that *Dashiel* manages to piss me off as much as I do him. Being around Aife's *lover* makes it hard to breathe, impossible to think.

"This is treason," Fatima hisses, squaring her shoulders and glowering at me. "You gods think you're above it—above us—but you're not. You'll be humbled one day."

I ignore her posturing and focus on the boy-king.

"Don't fuck with me, Dargan." I adjust my shirt, smooth my hair back, and stride toward the door. "And clean this mess up, eh?" I infuse my voice with as much arrogance and disdain as possible while giving the command, as if I'm not the one leaving a trail of blood on the pristine floors.

My harbingers jump to their feet as I pass them, but I keep moving. I won't stop walking until I get to the resident healer. I'll need someone to repair my broken nose.

If only they could work their magic on my mistakes too.

CHAPTER SEVENTEEN

ASTRID

After Fatima leaves, I spend a few minutes reflecting on her words.

It's time to stop running from my problems.

I race through the hallways to find my best friend. As I step up to Ilona's door, I glance across the hallway at my old room, wondering if it has remained unchanged.

I rap on her door, shifting my weight nervously from side to side.

"Hold on." There's a thump, then a shuffling noise from the other side. "I'm coming!"

The door opens, and my heart swells at the sight of Ilona's sweet, freckled face. Her curly hair is tied back, and she's wearing a pale green dress. When she sees me, she gasps and drops the bag she was holding. It crashes to the ground as her eyes widen.

"Hi, Ilona." I offer her a hesitant smile, unsure of how angry with me she is.

"Astrid," she whispers. Tears well in her soulful eyes.

I chew on my bottom lip, and we stare at each other for a beat.

"Hey, Lonnie."

She shakes her head, shoulders slumping. "I can't believe you left me here."

"Sorry," I mutter. My gaze sinks to the floor. "I needed space."

"You didn't have to *leave* to get it."

Neither of us moves for a second, until finally, she flings her arms around my neck. "I am so mad at you. But good goddess, I've missed you so much."

I don't hesitate as I squeeze her back fiercely. "I missed you to the moon and back, Ilona Marielle Palmetta."

She pulls away, trying to force a scowl at my usage of her full name, but her lips twitch and she chuckles, tears streaking down her cheeks. "I'm so glad you're back."

I was petrified that she would send me away and tell me we were through, with no hope of reconciliation.

Her emerald eyes sparkle with affection, and she leads me across the room to a seat on the edge of her bed. Her bedside table is cluttered with empty mugs, and stacks of books around the room threaten to teeter over. The mess resembles my apartment in Nevaris, and I almost chuckle. There's a round burgundy stain at the edge of her fluffy, snow-white carpet. I exhale sharply.

"What the hell?" I point at the stain on her beloved carpet, expecting her to rant about whatever happened.

Instead, she just squeaks and gives me a shrug. "I spilled my wine. It's only a rug."

My eyes widen. "Who are you and what have you done with my Ilona?"

She wraps her arms around me in an awkward side hug, and her shoulders shake with giggles. "It's me. I'm here. And I can't believe *you* are here. I missed you so much. You'd better start talking. You owe me that much, Astrid."

My brows rise at her command, but I oblige, desperate to open up to an old friend.

We spend the next hour catching up, and I'm grateful no one comes to disturb us. There's a lingering tension around us, a hint of awkwardness, like we're strangers yet sisters at the same time.

"I-I didn't know how to process everything," I explain. "Enira's deception. Lex being my fated, my sister and her death. My reality. Dash's suffocating affections." I sigh and shake my head. "I needed to get away and figure things out without everyone pressuring me. No offense."

"None taken." She smiles, but it doesn't quite reach her eyes. "It *is* a lot. I can't imagine what it must've been like from your position."

"There was more to it too." I take a deep breath, preparing myself to *talk* through my emotions rather than lashing out. "I was feeling very...unstable before I left. Everything with Dash's botched power-sharing and using my power to take Gi—" I pause, clearing my throat. "...Gianna and Chancy's lives was just...too much." My chest tightens, and I squeeze my eyes shut briefly. "I was afraid I'd lash out, lose control of my power. I thought everyone would be safer if I went away for a while."

Ilona frowns, and a rogue tear slides down her cheek.

"I think I have my emotions under control though. It's a work in progress, at least. I'm trying to be more intentional instead of impulsive."

"Astrid, you're not your anxiety. You were never alone."

"I know that now."

"How's the emotional control working out for you?" she asks softly.

"Not so bad, but it could be better." I tell her about Callan showing up, seeing Lex and losing myself to him temporarily, about his admission. But I also express the internal conflict I have about Lex and how *not* having my memories only makes it that much more confusing.

I'm eager for answers, now that I've gotten out of my head and back into reality.

"I'm proud of you for talking it out instead of having a break-down. I can't imagine it's easy." She squeezes my hand. "We all struggle with ourselves and our mental health at times, Astrid. You're learning from your mistakes, and you're growing. You're making an effort instead of making excuses, and that means everything. Just stop running from me."

I pick at her purple duvet as I smile at her. I'm grateful she understands me and accepts me for who I am.

"Have you talked to Dash yet?"

"Nope. I talked to Fatima though. She seems…kind of bitchy."

Ilona reaches out to gently shove my shoulder. "Yeah, well, so are you."

"Ilona!" My mouth curves into a shocked smile.

Her cheeks redden. "I'm sorry. I shouldn't have said that." A hand flies to her mouth.

"Don't apologize. It's the truth." I nudge her foot with my own.

Ilona picks at a loose thread on her blanket. "She's tough. But she really is nice, you know. In fact, it's been really nice around Hakran in general lately with her and Dash in charge. Ever since Marnie and I—" Her face falls, and she glances away before continuing. "I've had a hard time without you here, and Fatima and Dash have been there for me. Even with their duties to the throne and the people, they've made time for me. Fatima fetches my tea most nights and sits with me, even though she doesn't like tea or books herself."

"She doesn't like books?" The tea, I understand. It's not my absolute favorite either, but who doesn't like books?

Ilona shakes her head, giggling. "She spends most of her day reading and writing international correspondence. She says the last thing she wants to do is stare at more words. Apparently being the commander is more boring than she expected."

"I guess I can understand that. But it's a good thing there isn't much action, right?"

"Yes, but with the war, that won't last long. Especially—"

"War? What war?" I realize I interrupted her, so I groan apologetically. "Sorry. I really didn't mean to interrupt. I'm... I promise I'm working on it. But *war*?"

Her nose scrunches. "Stellaris and Vespyn are on the verge of war. I thought you knew. I figured that's why you came."

"No one told me anything about a war. I was tagging along to Stellaris to see Cedrik and pester him about our missing memories."

Lex is *really* pissing me off today. How could he neglect to inform me of a whole fucking war?

"About that." Ilona squirms uncomfortably, toying with her hands on her lap. "There's something I have to tell you. But first, I'm sorry for not being a good friend before. It's just—I don't know... And Enira. And my dreams. And you..." She pulls away a bit, staring at me with concern.

I'm puzzled by her rambling. "*You* were never not a good friend."

Ilona shakes her head, and a few curls tumble down around her face. "I should have never pushed you away. You're my best friend."

"And you're mine, but you looked downright disgusted with me the last time I saw you a few months ago." When she saw me use my power to down Dash's guards, she looked as if she'd be ill. I've never seen her dart away so fast. "I thought you hated me for who I am—*what* I am. And I know you have every reason to, but I really, really hope you don't, Lonnie. I don't know what I'd do without you."

"No. It's not that," she says, fiddling with her skirt. Her eyes drop to the floor. "I don't know how to explain it."

I frown, still confused.

"When I saw you in the hallway, with Lex and Dash and Enira the night of her death..." She hesitates, but her eyes shift up and lock onto mine. "Actually, let me start over. Remember at the beach bacchanal, when I said I had dreamt of Enira and her manipulation?"

"Yes." She had mentioned it on a few occasions. It was the catalyst for me finding out the truth.

"Well, I've had other weird dreams since then. I *know* they're only dreams, but they feel so real. They're different. Messages almost."

"Go on."

"I thought for sure you were going to say, '*It was just a dream, Ilona,*'" she mimics in a nasally voice.

"I do not sound like that!" I playfully nudge her shoulder as we both chuckle. She isn't wrong though. I *did* almost say that. Marnie was right all those months ago when she told me I need to be a better friend to Ilona. One way I can do that is by listening to her and taking her seriously. "What's going on with these weird dreams?"

"Well, sometimes my dreams come true. Like, in real life. Usually, it's little things. Mundane things that could be mere coincidence. But I dreamt of you killing Enira before you did. When I rounded that corner and saw you standing there, with all the guards strewn about and Dash so frazzled, it was like my dream."

When I nod, she continues. "*That's* why I ran. I had already seen everything in my dream once before. No offense, but you slitting Enira's throat was disturbing." Her face pales. "I didn't want to see it again. When I got to you, it was all so eerily familiar. Even though my dream was more abstract and disconnected, I knew what was going to happen. It was like I saw the future. But this wasn't the first time."

My eyes go wide. "What the hell, Ilona?"

"I know! I'm so sorry for leaving like that and making you think I was upset with you."

"I don't care about that. I mean 'what the hell' as in, why didn't you tell me?"

"You've been so busy...and I know you left because you needed to. I just didn't want to burden you."

Guilt squeezes my stomach.

I grab her hand. "You will never, ever be a burden to me. You are more than a friend. You are my only family, my sister, and I will always love you and be there for you." The word *sister* makes me feel funny. Not because it doesn't apply to Ilona but because of the fact I *had* a sister. A fact that's familiar and foreign at the same time.

"I love you too, A." She squeezes my hand, her eyes shining with moisture.

"Okay, but back to the dream thing. How often are you having ones like that?"

"Not often." She glances away. "It's probably nothing. Just weird, you know?"

I scrutinize her, waiting for her to go on. But she continues to avoid eye contact. "Yeah," I agree, concern growing in the pit of my stomach. "Probably just a coincidence."

When she meets my eye and offers a smile, I realize she doesn't want to talk about it. At least not right now.

Maybe they were only dreams—weirdly realistic, coincidental dreams. I can understand how unsettling that might have been for her.

Either way, we'll talk about it when she's ready.

"You know how that memory returned when I killed Enira?" I ask, and at the same time Ilona says, "I need to tell you something."

We pause, chuckling.

"You first," she rushes to say, her eyes darting away uncomfortably again.

I narrow my eyes but shrug in agreement. "Okay. Well, I saw a house. I need your help finding it."

"A house?" She perks up at this.

"Well, it's a cottage, rather. One that belonged to me. I remember it, in a sense. I feel connected to it. But the problem is that I don't remember *where* it is."

"What do you remember about this cottage?"

"It's blue. Teal, actually."

She grins. "Fitting."

"There were a lot of sunflowers around it." I pause, thinking about the details of the house. "There was a tree I've never seen before. At least not that I remember. It's not from Hakran or Nevaris, anyway."

"What did it look like?"

"I know it was called a weeping willow. It was a tall, thick tree with these weird branches and leaves that sagged down around it toward the ground. Kind of like an umbrella with a curtain of leaves."

"That is a very…odd but specific description. Okay, good.

Go on."

"The gardens around the cottage were expansive, but what I remember most besides the weeping willow were the pink blossoms. Plum blossoms, I think they're called."

"Come." Ilona grabs my hand and practically drags me out of her room.

"You know where it is?"

"No. But I know how we can find out."

Less than twenty minutes later, we stand undisturbed in the library.

Beneath our feet, the tattered carpet is a welcome reprieve from the gaudy marble flooring found in the rest of the palace. The room stretches like a long rectangle, with thousands of worn spines decorating the extensive shelves on either side of us.

Enira wasn't a fan of books, and she loathed the library. I had thought she built the entire palace for herself, but the library stands in such contradistinction to the rest of the palace that it's almost as if it belonged to someone else.

"What did you want to tell me?" I ask Ilona as we navigate through the rows of towering bookshelves. We turn left, then right, through the bookish labyrinth.

"It's—we probably don't have much time before boarding the ship. We can do this first and talk on the boat. If that's okay?"

"Sure." Unease settles in my stomach.

"The cottage sounds lovely from how you described it," she says. "Besides the whole dead-sister thing." A split-second later, she gasps, her hand flying up to her mouth. "Oh gosh, oh gosh. I'm sorry. I didn't mean that."

A pang of sadness radiates through me. I've killed plenty of people living with Enira, yet death is never *not* shocking.

"Tell me about your house again?" Ilona asks.

I oblige, describing how the property was flourishing with vegetable plants and wildflowers. Rolling hills framed the tree-lined property. There was a small, murky lake off to the side. More brown-green than blue or clear, but teeming with life. If I close my eyes, I swear I can hear the croak of bullfrogs and the vespa deer lapping the water.

I sigh, accepting an aged encyclopedia from Ilona and sifting through it. I'm not sure what exactly we're looking for, but I scan the various images on the pages while Ilona does the same beside me.

Luckily, I don't have to search for long.

"Here," Ilona says. She plops her book down onto one of the high-top tables near the end of the aisle. She points to a colorful page in the thick reference book. "Plum blossoms are native to Vespyn. In Thysia."

"No way."

"Yes, apparently it's the only country they're found in."

I groan. "Isn't that who Stellaris is going to war with?"

She pats my hand sympathetically. "Unfortunately, yes." She points to a hand-drawn map in her book. "Good news is that it's pretty close to Stellaris."

"I remember absolutely nothing about geography beyond Hakran."

She clears her throat and straightens her back, ready to let that booksmart brain shine. "Thysia—or as we like to call it, the continent—is home to a handful of countries. Stellaris is the closest country to us, on the east coast of Thysia, and it hugs practically the entire coast of the Insipid Sea. Northwest of Stellaris is Korchek, the only country in Thysia that determines leadership based on the votes of their people. They keep to themselves and stay out of political affairs usually. Vespyn is in the middle of the continent, south of Korchek and west of Stellaris. The three countries share borders. Then to the west of Vespyn is—"

"It doesn't matter," I say. "Sorry, Ilona. I didn't mean to cut you short. I really only need to know about Vespyn, not the entire continent."

"It's okay," she says sheepishly. "I could've gone on all day."

"You are an absolute wealth of information."

Her cheeks flush. "I mean, this is the stuff I read about while you read your...you know."

"Deliciously smutty books?"

"Yes." She nibbles her lower lip, averting her gaze. I have half a mind to keep teasing her, but it's not the right time for that.

"What else do you know about Vespyn specifically?"

"It's a very expansive and very pious country. Lots of protected lands. It's an empire rather than a kingdom like Hakran or Stellaris. The last accounts I read stated the empire was ruled by Her Imperial Majesty, Rania Haruka, Empress of Vespyn. But I doubt she's still in charge."

I blink slowly at Ilona, impressed by her knowledge. I knew she was intelligent, but seeing her put that knowledge to use is incredible. "What happened to Rania?"

Ilona shrugs, slamming the plant-identification book shut. "The only books we have on Vespyn are quite outdated. She was very old when they were written. It's safe to assume she's passed away at this point."

"Any kin?" I ask. "I mean, assuming that's how the throne is passed down?"

"That's the thing. It isn't a hereditary monarch. The new

ruler is appointed by the previous ruler. It's kept quiet until the day they ascend."

"Interesting," I mutter. "In my memory, my cottage was isolated. I didn't see any other houses nearby, let alone a palace. It was quaint. I only remember the gardens and the trees around it, like I told you."

"Makes sense, considering how large the country is."

Ilona scurries over to the shelf, scouring it intently for a few minutes before pulling a faded book loose. A plume of dust rises, and she coughs as she thumps the book down on the table between us. After reading the table of contents, she thumbs through the pages gently.

"Here," she says, pointing at an image of thin trees with vibrant pink petals—the same ones from my memory. "I knew plum blossoms were native to Vespyn, but according to this, they're found in the northern region. That narrows it down to Fiora, a territory in the northeast of Vespyn."

I hum at her, trying to remember all the information she's throwing at me. I'm going to forget this, I'm sure of it.

"It's a less densely populated region north of the capital, and it's known for its abundant wildlife and serene nature."

"Okay. So you're telling me that based on the description of my one single memory, you can determine exactly what region of Vespyn my cottage is in?"

"Yes." She frowns. "I told you, the type of tree you saw is only found in Fiora due to the winter temperatures hovering around but not falling below freezing, and with plenty of sunshine and warm sum—" She pauses. "That was a rhetorical question, wasn't it?"

"Yes." I wrap my arms around Ilona, giving her a big hug. "You are so beautiful and intelligent and kind and wonderful, and

I love you so much."

"Whoa, you're smothering me with your affections, A." She giggles.

"I'm just grateful for you. Especially after I thought I lost you."

"Oh gosh, you will *never* lose me."

My stomach churns. Enira once said I killed Ilona's mother. Though neither of us have spoken of it, it's something that surely haunts both of us. I fear that gaining my memories will also result in a confirmation that I did the unforgivable.

And then I *will* lose Ilona forever.

I hold her a little closer, scared to let go, until she squirms and pulls away, chuckling. "So, I take it we need to figure out how to get to Vespyn once we get to Thysia."

"Or we can simply find a way to get to the mainland on our own. I have no desire to sail for *days* with Lex and Dash. Or rely on them for any more help right now. It sounds like a bloodbath waiting to happen."

"Or the best time of your life." She winks.

"Ilona." I groan. "You've been hanging out with Dash too much. You know how I can tell?"

"How?" She grins.

"Your sense of humor has become as abysmal as his."

"Oh, you love it though!"

"That is *exactly* something Dash would say. I propose we ditch the men and their war shit. Head to my apartment in Nevaris and come up with a plan. We can sneak out before they realize we're missing."

"You should really talk to Dash first."

Her sentiments echo Fatima's. I avert my gaze. "I'm not sure that's a good idea."

"Please? At least hear him out."

"Fine." I roll my eyes, curious as to why she's pressuring me into seeing him. "Go get ready to leave, and I'll talk to him first."

"Good thing I'm already packed," she says. "I just need to grab my bag."

I slam the old book shut and grab Ilona's hand. Then we weave through the shelves, hustling toward the exit.

CHAPTER EIGHTEEN

DASH

I clench and unclench my fist, distracted by the pain blossoming across my knuckles. I'm holed up in my room to cool down. My body practically quivers as I pace my bedroom. I snag the cloth bag of ice sitting on the side table and press it against my injured hand. I hiss at the sting, but this should at least quell the swelling.

I'll wait to see the palace healer until right before we leave. I don't want to risk running into Lexyll again. Plus, it's only a minor injury. Mostly inconvenient.

There's a knock on my door.

I grunt. "Yes?"

From outside comes a sharp intake of breath.

After an extended pause, the visitor says, "Oh. You *are* in there."

My heart nearly stops. The voice is as smooth as honey—a voice I haven't heard in months.

Tossing the ice down onto the bedside table, I stride to the door and fling it open.

The sight of her familiar round face and wide eyes nearly steals my breath.

"I didn't expect to see *you*, sweetheart," I say like an idiot. Old habits, I guess. I've run dry of all wit, having lost the charm I normally pride myself on. I've thought about what I'd say to her a thousand times, but my lips freeze. We can only stare at one another. "You look well."

My knuckles continue to throb.

"Don't lie." She rolls her eyes, and I grin at the familiar quirk. "I'm pale and weak."

"*Beautiful*, like always. Your beauty is beyond your external layer, Astrid."

"You look...like you've had better times."

"It's been rough."

She chews on her bottom lip, crossing her arms like a protective shield as she scrutinizes me. She seems as nervous as I am about this reunion.

Her eyes flick to my hand. "Heard you punched Lex." She almost sounds impressed.

Opening the door wider, I step to the side to let her in, but she doesn't budge.

"No." She shakes her head, grabbing my good hand and pulling me out into the hallway. "You're going to the healer. Now."

I'll be damned if her bossy tone doesn't turn me on. "Yes, ma'am," I mutter. I shoot her a smirk, my resolve quickly disintegrating. Fuck it, let Lexyll see us.

Shutting the door behind us, I nod at one of the guards passing by. He returns the gesture with a warm smile.

"They like you around here, huh?" Astrid asks curiously.

I chuckle. "Hopefully more than Enira."

"Anyone is better than her."

We fall silent, and Astrid peers around the hallway as if she's taking it all in for the first time. I wonder if she's surprised to learn I haven't changed a thing since she left—it's still tacky, obscenely decorated with gilded chandeliers and gold-and-marble posts.

Not my style at all.

Nothing like the warm colors and the comforting aromas of spices back home. Somehow even the smell of the Hakranian palace is boring—too *clean*.

We walk down the hallway, toward the main foyer. As we near the closed throne room doors, Astrid pauses. She extends her arms and gestures around the hallway. "You got what you wanted after all."

I chuckle. "I never wanted any of this, sweetheart."

"Could've fooled me."

I reach for her arm. "Astrid—I only want the best for you and Hakran."

"It's not up to you to decide what is best for *me*."

"You're right. It's not. But I'm not too proud to apologize for my mistakes. I'm sorry. Truly sorry, Astrid, okay? I only want you to be happy."

"Life isn't about being *happy*, Dash. We have responsibilities, obligations. You of all people should know that."

"*Fuck*, you are stubborn, woman." I sigh and run a hand over my face. "That doesn't mean you can't uphold your duties *and* live a life worth enjoying."

"It's impossible to enjoy my life when I don't even *remember* it."

Goddess above, she's having a pity party. It's infuriating and heartbreaking at the same time. "You are here, and you are breathing. That counts for *everything*. That is a life worth living."

"I am not Ayana. I'm sorry for your loss, Dashiel Dargan, but stop comparing me to your first love."

What the hell is she— "This isn't about *her*."

"Your entire philosophy on love and life revolves around her.

You cannot project that onto me or expect me to be like her."

"No, it's—"

"Because seriously, Dash—"

"ASTRID!" I yell. I didn't want to raise my voice at her, but I need her to pause and listen. "I'm not talking about her." My throat clogs up. "My *father* died."

Her face crumples. "Oh, shit," she whispers. She reaches for me, then drops her hand dejectedly. "I had no idea."

"We knew it was coming, but it still hurts." My voice cracks as I admit it aloud.

"That's why Ilona desperately wanted me to talk to you," she mutters. "I'm sorry. I had no idea."

Her cheeks burn red, and I lean forward to kiss her forehead. "Don't be sorry. I'm not good at talking about this. Saying it out loud makes it real—too real."

"I'm sorry for leaving you, Dash," she whispers.

"Don't be. I get it."

"No." She curses under her breath, looking at me with wide eyes. "I should've been there for you."

Hope doubles in my chest when she steps forward, placing a hand on my jaw. Her sweet, feminine scent hits my nose. I could use my power and listen to her thoughts, but that's not fair to her. I have no right, no need, to invade her like that.

Instead, without overthinking it or talking myself out of it, I take a gamble like any normal man missing his lover would.

I reach down, cupping her face tenderly, and press my lips to hers. It's much more reserved than I want, but it's because I don't want to push too fast or scare her away.

For a moment, she just stands there, her soft lips limp as I kiss her. Then, she moves with me, kissing me back. It's soft and sweet, and I know at that moment I haven't lost her.

There's still hope for us.

Embarrassingly enough, I feel myself hardening at her simple touch. These months without pleasure—without Astrid—have left my skin incredibly sensitive. I trail kisses along her jaw and brush my lips across her cheek before pulling away to address her. "I missed yo—"

Slap.

My head jerks to the side, my cheek stinging with the impact.

"That's for punching Lex," she says.

Talk about a boner killer.

Glancing around, I'm relieved to see there are no lingering guards. They've wisely given me some space. No one was here to witness me get my ass handed to me. My ego is intact.

"I guess I deserved that."

"You did. And if you feel fine enough to punch Lex and try and hump me, I don't feel bad about slapping you." She crosses her arms, looking more like the ferocious woman I know and love so dearly. It brings a smile to my lips. "Stop smirking."

"*Hump* you? Really?" When she narrows her eyes at me, I only smile bigger. "I think you need a lesson in what humping is, if you think that's what I was doing."

She chokes out a laugh, and I draw her in for a hug, crushing her to my chest. She squirms, fighting it with the lamest struggle I've ever seen, before giving in with a sigh and hugging me back. I kiss the top of her head, relishing the feel of her soft body pressed against mine.

I've missed this.

"I still care about you," she says softly. "I never stopped."

"Only *you* would slap me, then tell me you care about me," I murmur, chuckling into her hair.

"There are a thousand things I wish I had done differently,

Dash, like not running away, or coming back sooner. But I made mistakes. We all did. I don't want to dwell on them. You help me want to be a better person, so I'm taking a piece of advice from you and Ayana, and I'm choosing love. Let's forget about all the mistakes we made and move forward. Can we do that?"

There's a thick knot in my throat, but I swallow around it. "Yes."

"Good. I don't think we can start where we left off, but I'd like to be there for you. I'd like to be friends."

Friends.

The word echoes in my head, haunting me. But before I have a chance to protest the label, she leans forward and plants a soft kiss on my lips.

We stand there for a few more minutes, simply embracing one another. I'm devastated that my country's war is responsible for bringing us together like this, but I'm grateful that Astrid is here for me.

"I met Fatima," she says when we break apart. "She seems… nice."

I chuckle. "She means well." I don't know what the hell Fatima said to Astrid, but my guess is that it was probably direct and sharp around the edges.

"I know." She smiles. "I'm glad that you've had a friend around."

"She's a very different type of *friend* than you are." I wink.

Her eyes narrow. "She'd better be."

I groan, running a hand through my hair.

Friends.

I want more than that.

"I fucked up so many things, Astrid. I wish I could have a redo with you. It's all I thought about these past few months. You will never be just a friend to me."

"I'm not saying that's all we will ever be, but I'm also not promising you more. I need time. We both hurt each other, ruined our trust in one another."

"I was only trying to protect you."

"Protect me? You tried to keep me small. You used me to attain your own goals, and then you cast me aside the moment you learned who I truly was."

"No." I shake my head, wondering how we got here, so far apart after being so close. "You misunderstood. Yes, I was in shock about you being...a fucking *goddess*." I swallow, pausing before I continue. "But I had only meant that *hurting the people you care about* isn't you."

"Oh that's—"

"You want to know how I know I'm right?" I step closer, tenderly brushing away the bangs that have fallen in front of her glistening eyes. "Because you ran away and hid for three months. No one saw you or spoke to you. You pushed everyone away. Look at you. You're gorgeous as always, but you look pale and weak. I bet you haven't been outside exploring, haven't been training, haven't been horseback riding. You ran because you were ashamed. A woman confident in herself and her actions wouldn't hide."

Sora's thoughts have already confirmed these suspicions. According to his mental insight, Astrid rarely leaves the apartment in Nevaris. She's been shut off from everyone, and she's probably been lonely like me.

She stands there, her jaw tight. I notice the moment my words hit her the way I intend, because she shudders and relaxes her body. "You're right. Is that what you want to hear? You're right."

"It's not about being right or wrong. It's about us fixing things and moving forward. I don't want to be *just friends*."

"I don't know how we—" Tears well in her eyes, and damn, it stings. "You should hate me."

I lower my tone, hoping to reassure her rather than rile her up any further. "Sweetheart, I could never hate you. Why would you think that?"

"Because of what I did…how I left things." Her cheeks flush with embarrassment, and I assume she's referring to how she challenged me, then scorned me by kissing Lexyll before disappearing.

I run a hand over my face, groaning at her, hating the memory of them grinding against one another. It was a blade to the gut.

"That fucking hurt—I won't lie—but I could never hate you. After everything you'd been through…" I pause, but she only blinks at me, waiting for me to continue. "You deserved time to recover, heal, and explore all options. I would've given you that time, even if it meant—" I curse under my breath, hating what I'm about to say but needing her to understand the truth. "Even if it meant being with *him*." I just didn't want her to push me away. I wanted to be there for her. She was cruel to me, but I probably deserved it after making her question everything. It's my fault she doubted me, doubted us.

"Astrid, I lo—"

"Don't say it." She peers up at me with those big eyes. "You've said that before. But it's too soon. We barely even know each other, Dash."

"If you wait for a certain amount of time to pass before loving someone, you might miss your chance forever," I murmur. People fear love because it's a dangerous risk. They're afraid of being used or hurt or abandoned. They wait to allow themselves to love because they're assessing the risks. I interlace my fingers with hers. "I choose to face my fear and embrace love."

I choose to accept every aspect of her nature—the good, the bad, and everything in between—and I choose to be there for her, knowing she has the power to hurt me.

My hand automatically flies to the tattoo on my bicep. "Ayana left me. She was sick, struggling, and I couldn't save her." It gutted me. I'm not ready to tell Astrid the whole story yet. "I never once regretted loving her. The only thing I regret was not loving her harder." Astrid blinks slowly, sympathy written all over her face. Some people fight their feelings. They try to slow their descent as they fall. But if crashing is inevitable, why waste energy fighting it? Enjoy the fall. "Life is too short and too unpredictable to try and control the uncontrollable. So, no. I don't think it's too soon."

She smiles softly. "Who knew you were such a romantic, Dashiel Dargan? It's gross." I chuckle as she reaches up and tenderly cups my cheek. "I'm sorry for hitting you."

"I'm sorry for hitting Lexyll."

"Don't be. He deserved it." Her smile fades into a frown. "But that's unlike you. You're not a violent man. What's gotten into you? Punching people? Yelling? Where are the jokes and smirks I love so dearly?"

I offer her a sad smile, and my chest tightens at her words. "It's— I've lost too many people I love. I can't lose you too."

She squeezes her eyes shut. "Oh, Dash. I know." My hand nervously dives into my wavy hair. "What can I do to help?"

"You being here helps. More than you'll ever know. My mother is taking it hard, but Cedrik is with her. Zale says he has her on something that's supposed to help with the grief, but it's been a month and a half."

The prospect of Astrid returning to Stellaris with me sends a thrill through me, but it also brings me guilt. At least I don't have to fear for her safety. With Emman gone—may my father rest with Sama—and Zale in power, Stellaris should be safe for her. At least Cerulea should be, since it's a forward-thinking city. I'll keep her away from the more reactionary rural communities.

With Lex and me, she'll have nothing to worry about.

Our eyes connect, and we simply stand there, studying each other. Something comfortable passes between us. After some time, her shoulders relax and she steps back into my body, planting a chaste kiss on my cheek.

"I wish I could promise you that it will be okay, Dash."

I shudder beneath her lips.

"I missed you," I whisper, tugging her to me in a hug. "So much."

"Me too, Dash." Her breath tickles my chest as my fingers play with her hair.

CHAPTER NINETEEN

ASTRID

What starts as a simple hug blossoms into a burning desire. Intimacy has never been our problem.

I've always used my sexuality as an outlet. Living in the palace, I had plenty of handsome guards to enjoy. One of the things I admired about Enira—maybe the *only* thing—was that she embraced her sexuality and allowed me to do the same.

Perhaps it's my nature as a goddess, as a vygora, that makes me crave touch so deeply.

After months without the touch of another, I've been lonely.

The timing might not be perfect, but if I'm heading back to Nevaris with Ilona, I'm going to enjoy Dash first. Sex with someone you have a genuine connection with is a thousand times better than unattached sex. It's messier but more satisfying.

"Astrid," he mutters into my hair as he cradles me.

I sigh, my body molding to his.

Feeling brave, reignited by the heat of his body against mine, I trail kisses along his neck. He shudders, hardening almost instantly. My eyes flick down to his bulge, and I give him a coy look.

Voices echo down the hallway, sobering me up from my lust enough to grip his hand and tug him to the side of the hallway. He winces, and I glance down at his bloodied knuckles.

I frown, holding up his hand to inspect the injury. "We should really go see the healer."

"Now?" His eyes twinkle with mischief. "Hell no. Your lips are healing me just fine."

"If you insist," I whisper, tugging him along.

A smug grin appears on his face. "My bedroom is the other way, sweetheart."

Giving him a coquettish smile, I push open the heavy doors of the throne room, giddy to discover it sits empty, free of peering eyes and open ears.

"Astrid." His tone holds a light warning as I lead him to the onyx throne.

"Sit," I order. Anyone could walk in, at any time, and the idea of that gives me a rush of adrenaline.

Without hesitation, he obeys my command. As I kneel between his legs, he tenses up.

"Astrid—"

"Shhh." I lean forward, planting my hands on his thighs.

He gently grasps my wrists. "I don't want you to be a distraction. You're more than that for me."

This is not a sacrifice or a favor. This is selfish. "I *need* this, Dash. Please."

He groans, swiping a hand over his face. "I'm a weak man. I can't say no to you."

"You are a good, good man, Dashiel Dargan. I should've trusted you."

Seeing him, talking with him, has confirmed what I have come to believe about him over the last few months. He never meant to hurt me with his manipulations. It's in his blood and bones to protect, and that's what he thought he was doing. He was loving me the way he knows how.

He's right—we're not promised another minute or another day, so why fight the things that feel good? Being with Dash has always felt natural yet exciting. We've both been drawn to one another since we met. And now, seeing how much he's hurting, I want nothing more than to be there for him emotionally and physically.

My heart pounds furiously, lust bringing a wave of heat to my core. I want to make him feel good and forget the pain he's in. I want to gift him my physical affection, to show him I forgive him. That I understand him. That the feelings I've had for him are still there.

It's my turn to show him affection the way I'm able.

And in return? I'll receive the pleasure I so desperately crave.

He releases my wrists from his grip. I lean forward and plant my hands on his chest. "Relax," I tell him. Then I sit back on my heels and work his belt buckle. Our breathing grows heavy. The clanking of his belt echoes off the high, arched ceiling.

"Fuck, if this is your definition of *friends*, I'll like friendship plenty." When I search his amber eyes, he stares down at me with pure reverence. "You on your knees before me is the most stunning sight I've ever seen," he says breathlessly. I reach up to free him from his pants, but once again, he stops me. "But this is all wrong."

I flinch at his words, but before I can overthink it, he rises from the throne. He pulls me to my feet and, with ease, picks me up by my waist and deposits *me* on the throne.

"Any man worth his salt knows a queen kneels for no one." He assumes the position I was in a moment ago, kneeling between my legs. "This is more like it."

"But I'm not a qu—" My mouth stops moving as his fingers curl around my waistband, tugging my pants down. I lift my hips, allowing him to slide them off. He discards them off to the side, and I keep my legs squeezed together. "Oh," I say breathlessly.

His fingers gently prod my knees apart. "Open your legs for me, sweetheart."

Hesitantly, I inch my knees open. He gently presses me open until I'm spread completely before him. He groans, lifting a fist to his mouth and biting his knuckle. "*Fuck.*"

I shudder at the cool breeze on my intimate parts and at his words. Here, on the throne, spread out before Dash, I feel powerful. Erotic. And more turned on than ever.

"You are my goddess, Astrid," he says. "Let me worship you." Then he leans forward, trailing kisses up my inner thigh. When he reaches my center, his tongue flicks out and teases my clit. My hips buck at the sensation, chasing his mouth for more. "Stay."

His strong hands press into my thighs, keeping me spread open and holding me down at the same time. His tongue flicks out, lapping at my bundle of nerves. "Does this feel good?"

"Mm-hmm," I mutter. "But this means nothing, Dash. I just need to c—"

"How about this?" This time, his entire mouth descends on me, encompassing my clit. He makes a soft humming noise, and it vibrates my most intimate parts. It's unlike anything I've felt before.

"Dash," I moan. My eyes roll back in my head, and my hips surge forward of their own accord as he hums and sucks on me. When he adds a finger, carefully working me in tandem with his mouth, a fire builds inside of me. His soft, warm lips offset the cold, hard stone beneath my bare skin.

He pulls back to look at me, his mouth and chin shining with my juices. "Will you do me a favor, sweetheart?"

"Anything," I say in a rush, desperate for him to get back to work so I can find my release. "What do you need?"

He gently presses two fingers into me, curving them, and I move in sync with them. He watches his fingers entering me, releasing a guttural sound. "Come on my face. I need to taste your pleasure."

My pussy throbs at his command, tightening around his fingers. Without another word, he plants his mouth back on my sensitive bits. I grip his hair in both fists, directing him toward a rhythm that edges me closer to release.

"Right there, Dash. Please don't stop." My head tilts back against the onyx as my hips thrust upward and I fuck his face. A creaking noise echoes from across the room, and my eyes fly open.

Dash doesn't stop, clearly not having heard the door open.

My eyes meet Lex's as he slips into the room. Even from this distance, I can see the lethal rage practically vibrating off his body. He grips the doorframe so tightly that it cracks under the pressure of his grip. The sound thunders through the room. Dash pulls back.

"No," I tell him, pushing his head back down before he can see the intruder. "Finish me. I'm so close."

My core tightens as my impending orgasm builds. I hold Lex's eyes the entire time, my body heated with arousal. From him watching. From knowing I'm inflicting pain on him in my own sort of cruel vengeance.

I don't belong to you.

Just as the marble begins to crumble beneath Lex's grip, I shatter, screaming Dash's name as I ride out the waves of delicious pleasure. My eyes flutter shut, and I pant as the surge of ecstasy subsides.

When I steady my heart rate and open my eyes, Lex is

prowling toward us with a terrifying calm. Dash stands, using the back of his hand to wipe my arousal off his mouth.

Quickly, I grab my pants and yank them on, my legs still slick with moisture. I jump in front of Dash.

"Lex," I warn. But he's not looking at me. His fiery eyes lock onto Dash's, and I swear one of them twitches. His features tighten, but he doesn't speak. Terror courses through me, and for the first time, I truly fear Lex.

"Like the show?" Dash asks smugly, stepping up beside me.

"Dash," I hiss in warning.

"Give me one good reason why I shouldn't gut you where you stand, *boy*."

Dash smirks. "Because it's obvious you enjoyed what you saw."

I'm confused until I follow Dash's gaze to below Lex's waist-band, where his dark pants tent. My brows rise.

Lex doesn't respond, nor does he make an attempt to conceal his massive erection. Instead, he narrows his gaze at Dash, who drops to his knees onto the stone with a gasp.

Dash groans, clutching his head. His shoulders begin to droop, and he struggles to stay upright. His eyes widen in panic.

Just like Invidia's did before she—

"Lex!" I scream, running to Dash's side. "Stop! Leave him the fuck alone!"

My sharp words bounce off the walls of the room, piercing my eardrums. Lex instantly goes rigid, and Dash's body jerks as he's disconnected from the power absorption.

I grab Dash's face, forcing his eyes to meet mine. "Are you okay?"

His forehead wrinkles, and he nods. "I'm fine," he mutters. "But he—you power-shared with him?" The hurt in Dash's voice pinches my chest. He refuses to meet my eyes, and it crushes me.

Lex shouldn't have been able to use his power on Dash... but we did power-share yesterday, briefly, when I visited him at Harmony House.

"It's not what you think," I whisper.

But it doesn't matter. I don't have to justify anything. Instead of allowing the regret or embarrassment to seep in, I jump to my feet.

My rage is directed at Lex as I charge his way. My hands ball into fists at my side, and my vision goes spotty.

"How fucking dare you," I say through gritted teeth.

He steps forward, trailing his fingers down my arm. It glows gold in his wake, and immediately I'm swarmed by the decadent sensation of our power-sharing. His other hand reaches up, and his fingers curl around my neck. Not enough to hurt, but just enough to incite a thrill.

"Get your hands off her," Dash growls.

Lex ignores him, leaning in toward my ear. I practically whimper at the way his warm breath caresses my lobe, the way our power mingles beneath my skin, the way his hand grips my throat. Danger and lust radiate from him, causing adrenaline to course through me.

"No one is skilled in pleasing you like I am," he whispers, tightening his grip on my throat. "I know your truest desires, the darkest corners of your mind. Remember that next time you seek pleasure, luv."

Then he cuts the power-sharing, leaving me breathless as he turns and strides toward the door.

My mouth drops open, and I'm about to give him a piece of my mind when Dash steps up beside me, looking the worse for wear.

Dash places a hand on my shoulder. "Wait," he calls. Lex stops and slowly turns a murderous gaze on Dash. "I call on thee, Lexyll, God of War, Warmonger, Sama's creation, for aid. I surrender myself to your blessings."

Then, Dash steps forward and drops down to a single knee. He bows his head before Lex.

A sharp, metallic tang fills my nose as the air grows thick around us. Heavy, as if weighed down by magic. Both Lex and Dash spasm briefly, their eyelids fluttering shut for a moment. Then suddenly, the weight lifts as if it was never there at all.

"What was that?" I whisper.

"Fucking Dargan," Lex mutters. He pinches the bridge of his nose and exhales audibly. "Get up."

Dash does so, wearing a cocky grin. "I'm only trying to show you respect."

"This feigned show of respect is null after the downpour of disrespect I've received from you."

"I don't have to show any respect, if you want to get technical," Dash responds. "Per the goddess's law, you can't ignore my request. But I kneeled anyway to try and make amends."

"I should have killed you when I had the chance," Lex growls.

"Too late."

I gape at them.

"What's your request?" Lex grits out. "I'm assuming you require assistance for the war." His nostrils flare. "But you need to specify exactly what it is you desire."

"Request?" I mimic.

Dash steps toward Lex, leans forward, and whispers something in his ear. A strangled laugh bubbles out of me. "Um, please for the love of the goddess, enlighten me. What the hell is going on?"

"Invocation acknowledged," Lex mutters. Then he turns his sights on me. "Watch your back, Aife. It looks like your lover boy hasn't learned his lesson about manipulation." I swear I catch a tinge of sorrow on his face.

My eyes bounce between the two of them, wondering what the hell just happened. A chill crawls over my body. Whatever this is, it can't be good.

"Tell me what the *fuck* is going on." I rub my eyes. What kind of alternate reality did I just enter? "I'm serious. Stop ignoring me."

"Your lover boy here used a centuries-old invocation for bargaining with the gods." Lex's jaw tics. "I am bound to him until the terms of our agreement are completed or terminated. And unfortunately for me, I always keep my word." To Dash he says, "You are a fool. I had already agreed to help with your war. Now, you've made an enemy of me, Dashiel Dargan."

"We've been enemies, Lexyll—I don't know your last name— *Warmonger*."

My jaw goes slack, and I shift my attention to Dash. "Dash, what the hell—why would you do that?"

Dash at least has the decency to look sheepish as he rubs the back of his neck. "I swear this has nothing to do with you, Astrid. This is between Lexyll and me."

I shake my head. "Unbelievable. And what's to stop you from using that little magic trick on me?"

"I would never use it on you. I only used it on him because I don't want him murdering me in my sleep."

"What about once it ends, huh?"

He runs a hand through his hair. "I'll figure something out. I'm sorry for this, but I only wanted to protect myself from him." He side-eyes Lex.

I glare at Lex. "You"—I point a finger at him—"are *not* allowed to harm Dash in any way! Before, during, or after this stupid little invocation thing." I shift my pointer finger to Dash. "And *you* need to stop with the sneaky bullshit, or I will personally end you. It's not Lex you should fear; it's me."

I storm between the two of them, knocking both their shoulders as I pass.

Behind me, Dash says, "Well, that went well."

"Shut the fuck up, Dargan," Lex growls.

"We've regressed to last names now? Oh come on, Sexy Lexy, let's be friends."

"I can't wait to disembowel you."

Goddess above, their bickering is annoying. I rub my temples.

"You two better get your shit together and make amends or I'm not getting on that ship with you!" I yell without looking back.

But little do they know, it's not an empty threat. I have no intention of joining them. In fact, I'm more determined than ever to leave Hakran with Ilona.

We don't need these two bastards getting in our way.

CHAPTER TWENTY

DASH

The day breezes by, and although the daylight fades, my self-satisfied grin doesn't. Every time I replay pleasuring Astrid on the throne, my chest swells.

What a fucking surprise it was that Lexyll happened to wander in. His obvious conflict in that moment—he appeared both violently outraged and violently turned on—only feeds my arrogance.

It felt better than punching him.

The only thing that eventually dampens my confidence is the realization that Astrid is, once again, pissed at me. Even worse, I'm still waiting for the right moment to tell her about my father and his mission to hunt and kill the gods. I don't want to keep the truth from her. I meant to tell her earlier, but my dick got in the way, and then Lexyll showed up.

I can't let him find out before I tell Astrid. At least with him bound to me and committed to serving Stellaris, he cannot harm me or my family.

The afternoon and much of the evening are consumed by making arrangements for our journey to the mainland. The island must be able to run efficiently in my absence, and the number of trustworthy people in the palace is still rather small for my liking.

We are leaving soon—in the middle of the night, when the tide is highest.

I enter my quarters, cleaning up as quickly as possible before throwing on a fresh pair of brown slacks, some boots, and a white tunic.

When I enter the throne room a few minutes later, hair still wet from my shower, Lexyll and his blonde companion are already there, standing amidst my wary guards.

Lexyll's eyes immediately drop to my shirt, and his lip curls in disgust.

"Try to contain your excitement," I say sarcastically. "I know, I'm your favorite person."

"That is a terrible color choice," he drawls, inspecting my shirt.

"You are a terrible color choice." The lame insult slips out before I can stop it.

The woman next to Lex—tall and lithe, with dark, upturned eyes and a platinum braid down her back—looses a lilting laugh. "Really? Mature."

Meanwhile, the god of war himself looks far less amused. "Where is Aife?"

"Astrid is coming." I cock my head, and my eyes crinkle with humor. I lower my voice so only Lexyll can hear. "Oh wait, she already did."

His sharp green eyes penetrate me as he stares. He doesn't blink once. When I wink, we both know I'm testing his patience and the limits of our new oathed bond.

Lexyll grits his teeth. "Have you seen her since our conversation earlier?"

"You mean since I made her cry out my name and—"

"Dargan," he growls. "Answer the question."

I open my mouth to respond, then close it, shaking my head. Up until my shower, I'd been too busy to even take a piss, let alone seek out Astrid. "No. She was with Ilona last I heard."

"She's fleeing." Lexyll's voice is monotone. His eyes narrow into slits. "Likely at this exact moment."

"No. She wouldn't—" Oh… She would. "Fuck."

I push my fingers through my hair as Lex continues to glare at me.

Damn unnerving bastard.

I try to use my power and read his thoughts, only to be met with silence. Of course. The gods are particularly adept with their barriers.

Which is why it was almost impossible for me to believe Astrid is a goddess. Her mental barriers have always been awful. It was much too easy for me to peer into her thoughts.

"Where would she even go?" I ask. "Back to Nevaris?"

Lexyll rubs a hand over his jaw. "For now."

"Then what?"

"She'll find a way to Vespyn."

"Why the hell would she go there?" She can't go there. We're about to be at war with them. He gives me a look that makes me feel two inches tall. It's a talent of his—making me feel like a bumbling fool.

"She has a house there." It's all he offers, but at least it's said neutrally and without the hostile tone he seems to reserve especially for me.

"In Vespyn?"

A frown tugs at his lips. He closes his eyes for a minute, almost like he's gathering his strength, before meeting my gaze once again. "Imbecile," he mutters. "Lo," he then says to the blonde woman, breaking our stare-off. He nods at her, a silent command of sorts.

The room goes quiet as Lo stares off into the empty space above Lexyll's head. Her eyes glaze over, and she goes eerily still.

When I try to invade her thoughts, I'm met with a block. She quirks a brow at me, as if she can tell I'm trying to read her thoughts. Which, of course, should be impossible. That's unnerving.

"Callan and I have a connection," she says after a beat passes, giving me a pitying smile. I almost expect Lexyll to shush her, to ban her from speaking with me, but he remains silent and impassive. Clearly, he doesn't view me as that big of a threat if he's letting her reveal secrets. "We can communicate telepathically across distances."

Callan.

The guy with dark blond hair and the gap-toothed grin. He must be keeping tabs on Astrid.

I hate to admit it, but it's smart of Lexyll to keep an eye on her. Especially after what I told him.

"She's," Lo says after a moment, "still here. Callan says they're in Ilona's room."

"Is he certain?" I ask. "Astrid is crafty. She wouldn't take the door. She'd take a window." Lexyll's brows knit together as he studies me. "What? Surprised I know her?"

He doesn't respond to me. "Did he check the room? The windows?" he asks Lo, repeating my concerns.

A tickle of satisfaction rises in me at Lexyll's realization that I do know Astrid.

She smiles and shrugs. "Cal says he can hear them chuckling in the room. They're there. You two can relax."

"I am the epitome of relaxed," I say.

She chuckles. "It's hilarious how both your priorities line up, yet your attitudes don't." She points at Lexyll and me.

He scowls harder at me. "We are nothing alike."

"What he said." I jerk my thumb toward him.

"Mm-hmm." She gives us a coy look. "I need to finish my discussion with Fatima. She's prepping me on Hakran's emergency protocols."

I nod, letting her step away to find Fatima. I like Lo. I'm relieved Lexyll assigned her to look over Hakran during our time away and not his broody minion. In fact, it's a relief he's not around for once. I can't say I miss his incredibly sunny disposition.

I chuckle to myself.

"Come on, buddy." I nudge Lexyll with my elbow. "Let's get the ships ready."

CHAPTER TWENTY-ONE

ASTRID

I drag a half-asleep Ilona through the jungle as we make our way to the tunnel. The air is muggy and rich, thick in my throat.

"Are you sure they won't know we left?"

"Nope, we're in the clear." I chuckle to myself. If someone comes looking for us, Charity and Abigail, two of the kitchen girls, are posing as Ilona and me in her room. The door is locked, and they were explicitly instructed not to let anyone in.

I bribed them with some of Enira's jewels. They'd been more than happy to help us out for free, but their eyes lit up at the offering.

I instructed them to fake cry and throw a tantrum if someone tries to come in. With my reputation, it should do the trick and successfully scare most people off.

Hopefully by the time Dash and Lex figure out we've left, it will be too late. Dash can't back out of his trip to the mainland, and Lex will be forced to accompany him thanks to the invocation. As long as we get a head start, we should make it to Nevaris on our own just fine.

Ilona and I navigate through the shrubs and palm trees of the forest, careful to avoid any dangling vines. The night sky is clear, and a full moon is out. The overhead canopy is thick enough to act as a roof above us, barely allowing the moonlight to filter through. A flame glows in the fire orb in my hand, guiding us.

"I can't believe Dash would pull that shit," I mutter to Ilona once we've made it a good distance away from the palace. "Invocation? Who even knew that was a thing."

"Well—"

"And what if someone tries to invoke *me*? I'll just become their puppet?"

"Actually—"

"I can't believe I thought he changed. He's still the same manipulative little—"

"Astrid!" Ilona screeches. My head whips toward her. Her eyes are wide, her mouth open in a little circle.

"Alert the whole palace that we've left, why don't ya?"

"Sorry," she whispers. "I didn't mean to yell, but you're not listening."

I nudge her with my elbow. "Sorry, Lonnie. What were you saying?"

We continue walking as she talks. "Dash had me searching for information on invoking the gods. We'd thought it to be a myth. I had no idea he was planning to—well, you know." She sighs. "He really means well. He's left his entire family to take care of Hakran. And Lex isn't as innocent as you think."

My blood pounds in my head. "What does that mean?"

"According to my research, whoever invokes a god must offer something in return. The god can decline or agree. As shady as you think Dash is being, Lex could've declined."

My irritation lessens, giving way to curiosity. "What the hell did Dash offer?"

"I don't know. Honest. Ask him." Ilona stifles a yawn. She trips over a rock and squeaks as she grabs my shoulder to steady herself.

"Careful," I say with a frown. "Keep an ear out for rustling."

"Yeah, snakes. Great"

"They're as afraid of you as you are of them."

"I grew up here too, you know." From anyone else, those words would sound rude, but from her, they simply sound matter-of-fact. "But I would prefer not to be traipsing through snake territory at night."

"Better than being on a ship with those two pains in my ass."

She snorts. "You know, maybe Dash was smart to invoke Lex. I mean, wouldn't you do the same? He's afraid the guy will throw him overboard."

"Honestly?" I sigh. "It's not even the invocation that pisses me off. I'm mostly annoyed that he didn't discuss it with me first. It feels like he's always doing sneaky things behind my back."

"Or maybe it's because he hasn't seen you in months? And he owes you absolutely nothing? Maybe you're just taking it too personally?"

I bite my lip, a little stunned at her blunt retort. "When the hell did you get so feisty?" But she isn't wrong. I do take it personally.

"Sorry," she whispers.

"Stop apologizing."

We move in silence for a few minutes until she restarts the conversation. "Do you think Dash meant what he said?" she asks.

"About loving me?"

"About *sharing* you." She giggles.

"I think that he'd say anything to win me over right now."

"Maybe. But didn't he offer to share you with Zale once?"

"What—no!"

"That's what you told me. That one time after your breakfast with the Vannyks you said he—"

"I remember what he said." I scowl as I hold the fire orb high and continue to lead Ilona along the winding footpath through the shrubbery. Dash had mentioned something along the lines of *combining forces* with Zale to *please me*. "I also told you he likely said it to unsettle me. I doubt it was a true offer."

"What if it was?" she asks sincerely. "Would you take him up on his offer?"

Now it's my turn to blush. "I'm not interested in Zale."

She playfully swats my shoulder. "You know what I mean. *Lex* and *Dash*."

My face blazes at the simple thought of being sandwiched between those two. "I'm swearing off lovers. Plus, Lex would never go for it."

"I didn't ask about him. I asked about *you*."

I don't respond. We continue walking, leaves crunching beneath our feet. The soft buzzing of cicadas fills the air.

"I thought you didn't like Dash," I say, "and I definitely thought you would *hate* Lex after what he did."

"It's not that simple," she says quietly. "I don't dislike Dash. I think he could make better decisions, but I can also tell he really cares about you. I've gotten to know him over the past few months, and he's a good guy. And I don't know anything about Lex. There could be more to both of their stories."

"Maybe."

"You've done a lot of things you're not proud of, but you're not heartless. You're the kindest, strongest, best person I know." She takes a deep breath. "I tell you this not to make you upset but to remind you that maybe Dash and Lex had reasons for their actions too. I see the way they both look at you, the way they fight for you. They have both gone tremendously out of their way to protect and help you, even if you're too stubborn to admit it."

Her words strike something deep inside of me. "I know."

"But you certainly have a thing for arrogant men."

"I know."

She chuckles.

"Everything is so complicated," I mumble. "I feel like the last thing I should be focused on is my love life—*two* failed romances, at that."

"Why though? Love is the best part of life. It's what gives us hope when everything else seems hopeless. It's what gives us tingles even when we're numb to the world. It's what makes us see the best in ourselves and the best in others, even through our imperfections."

"For fuck's sake." I groan. "You *do* sound just like Dash." We stop walking, and she places a hand on my shoulder. I reach up, giving it a gentle squeeze. "Thanks though. You're right, Lonnie."

"I'm glad you agree. Now stop calling me that," she scolds.

"Thanks for forgiving me and still being my friend through everything."

"Always. We're more than friends. We're family. Maybe recycle some of that forgiveness I've given you and pass it on to the other people in your life. Love is complicated, and if you're lucky enough to find it, you should hold onto it and never let it go."

Her words remind me of the discussion Dash and I had yesterday about Ayana. If it had been anyone else, I would have found the declaration of love to be too soon and too strong.

But it's Dash.

He's loved and lost before. Maybe he's afraid of waiting to tell me how he feels in case he never gets another chance. He knows better than anyone what it's like to lose someone he loved, yet instead of recoiling into himself and hardening to the world, he continues to spread his joy and share his heart freely.

It's admirable.

And Ilona is right; love is complicated, and we are all imperfect. Maybe *I* am the one with the sharp edges and cold heart, not the people around me.

It's in this moment, weighed down by the salty, citrusy air of the jungle, with Ilona at my side and a renewed purpose in my heart, that I realize I can forgive Dash. I do forgive him.

And maybe, just maybe, I can figure out why Lex made the decision he did and can find it in me to forgive him too.

Unlikely, but not impossible.

"You should totally make them share," Ilona says with a nefarious grin. "Talk about payback."

"Okay, seriously, who are you and what have you done with my sweet, innocent friend?"

"After you left, I explored the romance shelves a little more… intimately, and I learned some things."

"Oh?" I side-eye her, intrigued.

"I wanted to feel closer to you and figured if I read the things you like, it might work."

My chest squeezes at the thought of Ilona in the library alone, missing me and our normal routine. "Don't worry. I—of all people—am not judging you. I'm just surprised, that's all. And I feel even worse now about leaving you alone."

"Don't feel bad. We all needed some space. It helped us, I think."

"I like to hope it did."

We walk for a few paces as the conversation lulls.

"So, what did you read while I was gone?"

"So much! I've read books that would make even you blush, A."

I laugh. "I doubt that."

She grabs my arm, stopping me to level a serious gaze at me. "One girl. Five guys."

"Ouch."

"Right?" She giggles. "They take turns."

"That sounds like an orgy."

"Kind of, but not. When it's only one girl and three or more lovers surrounding her, it's called a reverse harem. Their main focus is pleasuring *her*. But that's not the wildest part." She pauses for dramatic effect, waiting for me to encourage her to continue. I wave for her to go on. "Get this: in one of the books I read, two of the men hate each other. Absolutely, disgustingly despise one another. But they put their own feelings aside and learn to share, in hopes of satisfying her."

"That sounds incredible, but it also sounds like fiction."

"It could be your reality. You have the makings of a reverse harem."

I snort a laugh. "I thought you said three or more lovers are required for a harem?"

"There's room for potential."

"That would *never* happen. I like sex, but I like being able to walk more. Plus, who has time for that?"

Her light laughter fills the air, like bells tinkling. "You do know that it's in your nature as a goddess to be polyamorous, right?" I frown. Does this mean Lex sees other people? I couldn't imagine him being okay with me taking anyone other than him as my lover, and I was definitely not okay seeing him with Ana, even though nothing happened between them. "I read about it in a lore book. The gods and goddesses are known for being sexually fluid and taking multiple lovers. They can certainly be monogamous, but many desire open or polyamorous relationships."

"I mean, it makes sense considering Enira's knack for hosting orgies. But I really cannot imagine Lex being a sharing type of guy."

"You never know."

"Dash would never do it either. They're both too...alpha." I roll my eyes.

"I wouldn't say *never*." The pitch in her voice rises, emphasizing the last word. "Zale and I stayed in touch—we write to each other—and he's mentioned how he and Dash have shared—"

"Nuh-uh." I wave a hand. "Nope. I do *not* want to hear about Dash's other exploits." Yep, I am definitely too jealous to hear about him having fun with other people. "How about we talk about you and Zale though?" I waggle my brows at her.

She swats my shoulder in return. "We are very much just friends."

"Suuuuure."

"I mean it, A."

"Okay, what about you and Marnie then? What happened there?"

Ilona sighs. "Honestly?"

"Always honestly."

"We had a lot of different views on important things."

"That's nothing to be ashamed of. It happens. That's kind of the point of dating—to figure out if we're a good fit with someone."

"I wish I could sleep around with ease. Like how you do—or how you used to. No offense or anything, of course."

"None taken. But that's a beautiful thing, you know—to need a connection first. It's better that way."

"I had that connection with Marnie, but honestly, as time went on, we just weren't a good match. She's still amazing, and I wish her the best, but she definitely isn't my fated or anything."

"Did you kiss under the falls and find out?"

She knocks into my shoulder with her own. "Absolutely not. And after seeing you and Dash, I don't think I'll be kissing anyone under the falls anytime soon. Probably never, really."

"Can people without magic even have a fated?"

She shrugs. "I really don't know. I would think only those with magic can be fated, since the whole connection revolves around a matching magic signature. Everything I've read talked about power-sharing and magic."

"I wish I could remember Lex and how we met. And how we ended up kissing under the falls." I wish I could remember the good parts.

Why can I only remember one little thing? Why *that* memory?

A sharp inhale comes from Ilona, and she fidgets with her hair.

"So, speaking of forgiveness and all that...I have to admit something to you," she whispers. "Please, please don't be mad at me. We just made up and everything, and I can't stand it when we're not talking."

I scrunch my nose. "What is it?"

"Please promise you won't be mad."

"You know I can't promise that." My heart begins to race. "But I can promise that I will try my best not to react poorly."

She exhales a steady stream of air before whispering, "My memories returned."

"What?" I whip around in shock, nearly stumbling over a rock. "What do you mean they *returned*?"

"I haven't told Dash or Fatima or anyone yet," she says quickly, pausing to take a deep breath. "I wanted to talk to you first. The memories came back after you killed Enira. I was coming to see what all the ruckus was that night in the servant's wing, when I saw you take out Dash's guards. I was terrified. It was just like in my dream. But then I ran through the corridors, heading back to my room, and then a sharp pain drove through my skull, and I nearly passed out from it.

"When the pain cleared, I remembered. I don't know why your memories haven't come back too, but I didn't want to tell anyone until I talked to you about what I remembered."

My eyes are so dry from not blinking that they start to burn. "What did you remember, Ilona? Did I—"

I'm terrified to ask if I was the one responsible for her mother's death, if that was true or if it was a false memory implanted by Enira.

She sighs, glancing at the ground. "I didn't want to say anything to anyone because I didn't want them to stop looking for a way to return *your* memories. I figured if they thought I still didn't remember, it would add to the urgency."

Her logic is understandable, in a sense. If multiple people were missing their memories, there might be a more pressing inclination to search for them.

"If you have yours back, then what about Cedrik?"

"Mine returned immediately. As did most of the villagers'. When Cedrik left on the ship a few days later, he hadn't mentioned anything about—"

"But if *you* lied about having your memories back"—she flinches—"he very well could have too."

But why? It's more imperative than ever that we find Cedrik. As Enira's former confidant, he *must* know something. If Lex and Dash knew Ilona's memories were back, they surely wouldn't have waited to visit Cedrik. If all the villagers got their memories back, they must've assumed that only those closest to Enira were still affected. If Ilona, and maybe even Cedrik, lied about not getting them back, then that would leave just me with gaps in my mind.

"Why didn't you come find me? Why didn't you tell me sooner?" I yell. When Ilona winces, I sigh. "How could you keep this to yourself?"

"I just told you why," she says in a small voice. "I also didn't want anything to change with our friendship."

"For the goddess's sake, Ilona, you should know that we are friends for life. Nothing will change that."

"It might if you remember," she whispers.

"No it won't. Not with us." I grab her hand, giving it a squeeze to let her know she's not alone. "Wait—did it change for you?"

She squeezes back before speaking. "Do you know how long you were with Enira?"

"Yes," I whisper, pained at the thought.

"She had you under her thumb for seventeen years." Her eyes fill with apology. "You're immortal. I'm not."

"So, what does that have to do with us being friends?"

"Think about it, A. I was young when you got here—barely six years old—but you...you were exactly as you are now."

A pang of agony hits my chest as her words sink in. I inhale sharply.

We were never children at the same time. Never actually grew up together. At least not in the way I thought. Does that make me more of a mother figure than a sister to Ilona? I squirm, discomfited.

"Was any of it real?" I ask, searching for a glimmer of light in the darkness. "Our life together?"

I'm almost afraid of hearing the answer.

"Of course it was." She nods. "Everything, really. My entire life—it's the same. The only difference is, in my memories it's like a cloud has been lifted and I see you in your true form. Like the time we picked out our horses, Pancake and Aife." She gives a soft, sad chuckle. "Everything about that day is the same. I remember you picking Aife because even though everyone called her a useless runt, you knew she had a warrior's heart.

"I was only seven," she continues, "but *you* weren't. I remember you as an adult now. It's weird. Enira definitely distorted my memories, but from what I can tell, she didn't outright change the memories of anything that happened to me. It seems like the manipulation was mostly to hide you and your identity. I know my mother died shortly before I met you, but I don't remember her. Nor do I remember my father. I only remember you and Enira taking me in."

"Wow," I breathe out, trying to process her words.

I hate the relief that comes when I learn she doesn't remember her mother. If Enira didn't change our histories, I fear it means I *am* the one responsible for Ilona's mother's death. That isn't something I'm ready to face.

"I'm sorry for not telling you right away. I don't even know what to make of it myself, and I couldn't lose you." Tears stream down her cheeks, and it breaks my heart.

"None of that matters," I whisper. "It doesn't change our friendship."

So what if we met at different ages? I already knew Enira manipulated my entire life, and I figured my entire past was fabricated. But if Ilona and I truly spent so many years together and made so many true memories, then the reality is better than I could've hoped for. Our bond *is* real.

She's always been a sister to me, and it doesn't matter if we're a year apart or a thousand years apart; she's my family.

I would burn the world for that girl.

CHAPTER TWENTY-TWO

LEX

Despite Callan reassuring me that Aife is in Ilona's room with her, a nagging instinct says she isn't. As Dashiel and a slew of his guards stomp through the jungle to South Sands, toward the ship awaiting just offshore, I veer away from them and go off on my own. I stride back to the palace, my pulse pounding in my temples.

I'm neither disappointed nor shocked when I kick down Ilona's door and two unfamiliar girls, perched atop a lavish, purple four-poster bed jump up and scream in terror. One starts blubbering, crying and screaming.

"Knock it off," the other girl says, elbowing the crying one. "He's already seen us. The fake crying won't work."

"It's not fake!" she wails.

"Where is she?" I rub my forehead, eyeing them impatiently.

The taller, composed girl crosses her arms, giving me a sassy look. "We don't know."

"They gave us jewels…" The other girl sniffles. "And said to stay here. And if anyone knocked, to tell them to go away…and to pretend to have a meltdown if they won't leave."

"Yeah, we were only doing—"

I curse under my breath and spin on my heel just as a couple of guards fly in, demanding to know what's going on. Leaving them to sort out their own mess, I dart down the hallway.

My best bet is that Aife is headed to the tunnel—back to Nevaris. At least for now. Where else could she possibly go? She doesn't know *how* to get to Vespyn yet. Her redheaded friend is a bookworm, I've heard, *and* the boy-king's advisor. No doubt she's as smart and resourceful as Aife.

The two of them are dangerous together. They will certainly discover a way to get to Vespyn. It's only a matter of time. While I'm a fan of letting Aife live her own life, trying to go *alone* to Vespyn—my current enemy of war—is far from wise.

It's dangerous.

Grabbing a lit fire orb from a sconce as I pass, I clutch it in my grip and bolt from the palace. I step into the jungle and head toward the tunnel. The night air slaps me in the face like a damp rag. It's slightly cooler now than it is during the day, but Hakran is still far too humid for my liking.

"Lex, I fucked up." I don't stop when I hear Callan's voice behind me. "I thought they were in there."

I grunt, gaining speed. None of my anger is directed at him, nor is it directed toward Aife. It's simply the situation. I would tell him to fly ahead, find her and detain her until I catch up, but the vegetation is too dense for him to use his wings.

"I should've known better," Callan continues as he catches up to me, keeping pace. We move as quickly as we can, but it's too dark, too thick with plant life for us to go much faster than a jog. "This is like the time I snuck her into Harmony House—before you two met. I convinced her you'd be gone, and…well, you got home early." He chuckles. "I told her to wait in my room, that I would get rid of you." He sucks in a big breath. "But of course, she didn't listen. She tried to sneak out of a window and fell straight into the lake." He laughs breathlessly. "Her stubborn ass swam—*swam*—all the way back to the shore. Didn't want you to see her. That's how badly she refused to meet you."

His words almost stop me in my tracks. Annoyance buzzes within me, like an angry swarm of bees. "You brought her to Harmony House," I drawl.

"We were only there a few minutes before you got back. She refused to visit again after. Well, until you guys became an item, of course."

She never told me that story. Neither of them did. I was under the impression her first time at the house was with *me*. *After* we met. Frowning, I wonder what other secrets she kept from me over the years.

My cheek twitches. "Did you fuck her?"

"What? No!" He stumbles over an exposed root but quickly recovers. "Never. You know that."

A layer of irritation lifts from me, and I relax my jaw. Breathing in through my nose and out through my mouth, I jog a few more paces before responding. "I saw her swimming away." I glance at him briefly, catching his profile in the golden glow of the fire orb. He keeps his focus on the dark jungle ahead. "Didn't know it was her at the time."

I had thought it was a conquest of his or Lo's trying to escape.

He hoots a laugh. "No way."

"There was a scream, followed by a splash. It was hard to miss," I deadpan. I remember finding humor in the fact there was a brunette head bobbing in the water, sloppily swimming to shore.

Now, knowing it was Aife trying to avoid me before even meeting me, the memory has a whole new interpretation. I shake my head, and a small chuckle escapes.

"She told me not to say anything. Guess we both forgot about it. Well—" He waits an awkward beat before continuing. "*She* definitely forgot about it."

I grind my teeth, hating that she doesn't remember.

If that healer in Stellaris is hiding anything that has to do with Aife's memories, we *will* find out. If he refuses to cooperate, well, I will personally ensure he enters an early grave. Then, after quickly concluding this war business, I will escort Aife myself to the cottage she so dearly misses in Vespyn.

She's ready to remember, and I am tired of holding back.

"There!" Callan points.

Up ahead is a faint glow, illuminating what must be Aife and Ilona's silhouettes.

"Aife!" he calls as we draw nearer.

The shorter, curvier silhouette turns.

"What the hell? Callan?" Aife says. Shock mars her face as she holds up her orb to get a better look. "*Lex?*" She groans. "For fuck's sake."

"I knew this was a bad idea," Ilona mutters.

"You better not have done anything to Charity and Abigail," Aife warns.

My brows draw together.

Who?

Oh, the crying-screaming duo.

"The gals are fine," I say. "You're going to Nevaris." Not a question. "You want to find a way to Vespyn."

She scowls. "And I will."

"Not like this, Aife. Come with us to Stellaris. Let me accompany you to Vespyn, once we're certain it's safe."

She perks up. "You— Of *course* you know where my cottage is."

Ilona tucks a loose curl behind her ear, offering Callan and me a polite smile before turning to Aife. "Maybe we should go with them, Astrid. Nevaris isn't going to bring us any closer to Vespyn. Plus—you said it yourself—the village library in Nevaris is pathetically lacking. We could do better research somewhere else. Dash says Stellaris has a massive—" Her eyes widen as she glances at me. "No offense, Lex, sir."

My lips press together in a tight line, even though I find her words humorous. Of course Aife finds the village library lackluster. It certainly is. It's rarely used.

Her library—the one I assembled for her in Harmony House—is in the turret above my piano room. She loves it there because the music carries up to the second and third floors, allowing her to read and listen all at once.

I don't attempt to remind her of this. Not right now. There's no point in forcing memories that won't come yet.

"Aife, luv. I believe the healer might have answers. If you can be patient a little while longer—"

"Fine," she concedes.

My brows rise, and I tilt my head. "Oh?"

"Ilona said we should, so let's go."

I squint at her, then at Ilona, wondering why that was so easy. Not wanting to question my luck, I nod at the red-haired gal in solidarity. This might be one of Aife's better friends. Perhaps we will get along well, when we are able to truly get to know one another.

"I like you," Callan says as he puts an arm around Ilona's shoulders.

She blushes, but she doesn't push him off.

"We should go before your lover boy has a coronary," I say, stepping aside and extending an arm for Aife to pass.

Dashiel doesn't know that Aife and Ilona tried to escape. He mistakenly believed they were having a bonding session.

Fool.

If he hasn't already, he will soon discover that *I* abandoned him too.

But I have it under control, so we need to return before he tries to fix the situation and ends up making it worse.

We trample through the jungle, filling the air with our clumsy footsteps and loud breathing as we head south, where the ship awaits us.

CHAPTER TWENTY-THREE

ASTRID

We've been on the ship for less than ten minutes, and I'm already certain I despise sailing. My stomach rocks along with the ship as we make our way out into the Insipid Sea.

As stunning as this savage sea is, I would much prefer to keep my feet in the sand, waves lapping at my calves, than to float in the middle of a liquid abyss with no land in sight.

With every dip and swell of the sea, my guts lurch.

Though storm season is over, the treacherous navigation is best left in the hands of skilled sailors. The waters near Hakran are especially dangerous, with jutting rocks, sandbars, and tides that pull with an often underestimated force. High tide is the safest time to leave, giving us an opportunity to avoid the worst of the obstacles.

I'm trusting Dash to get us safely into open waters, then safely to Thysia.

Pushing away from the railing on the main deck, I head to the cabin I share with Ilona down below, ignoring everyone I pass along the way.

I try to rest despite my roiling stomach. Eventually, I doze off into a fitful sleep.

The next day, I stay in bed well into the day. Ilona comes

to check on me, and we catch up on the minor happenings of Hakran. It gives me a great sense of pride to know she's so beautifully embracing her role as Dash's advisor. With her love for knowledge and her level-headed demeanor, she was born for it.

"Come up to the top deck with us," Ilona says when she checks on me in the early evening. "Even Lex and Dash are up there, getting along." She wiggles her eyebrows at me, and I groan, shoving my face into my pillow. "Just saying."

It reminds me of our conversation from last night, and I'm overwhelmed with an onslaught of nerves. My chest pounds. I'm as unsteady as the sea during a storm.

"Come," Ilona stands, yanking me up from the cot. "Please? Callan mentioned he has something that will help your seasickness."

"Okay, fine." I roll my eyes, though I secretly adore her persistence. She seems much more confident than she did before I left her, and I guess I have Dash and Fatima to thank for coaxing her out of her shell.

Or perhaps she's simply growing through the trauma she's faced. I'm not the only one who's been challenged by these past few months.

"Let me change and brush my hair." I run my fingers through it. The lengths almost reach my chin now.

"Yes!" She claps her hands together and does a silly little dance. "Let's get you cute for your men."

"Let's get *you* cute for Fatima," I tease.

Her cheeks redden. "I don't know what you're talking about."

"Mm-hmm."

A small smile plays at her lips, and this time I'm the one waggling my brows at her.

We make it to the top deck as the sun is setting.

"Wow," Ilona says breathlessly. "It's gorgeous."

"Terrifying is more like it." I grip the rail to steady myself as I stare into the endless blue glass. It's vibrant, crystalline, as it reaches for the horizon.

The sea *is* stunning—there's no doubt about it—but it is a beast.

"How much magic do you think is down there?" Ilona asks, leaning over the railing and gesturing toward the water.

I shrug. It's impossible to know. The storms that blow through in late summer, dredging up the magic that rests on the seafloor are unruly. Dangerous. They probably don't uncover anywhere near the full extent of the magic lying beneath.

In silent wonder, we behold the setting sun as it kisses the sea. The sight fills me with a sense of insignificance. It's all so grand that it makes me and my problems seem small.

A few guards I don't recognize work the sails. I'm relieved Dash safely navigated us into open waters while I slept and we're free from the jutting, rocky obstacles near the Hakranian shore.

As we round the main deck, toward the back of the ship, I spy Dash, Fatima, and Callan sitting on a couple of the wooden benches arranged in a semicircle around a fire orb that illuminates them in a soft glow as the daylight fades away.

Dash and Callan, who share a bench, are laughing together at something as Fatima shakes her head from the bench across from them.

She spots us coming and says, "Hello, ladies." Her eyes shift to Ilona, quickly scanning her, and her smile widens.

"Fatima," Ilona responds with a grin. She tucks her loose curls behind her ear.

Ilona grabs the seat beside Fatima, and I sit beside Dash, with Callan on his other side.

I greet them with a forced smile, trying not to let them see how nauseated I am. The bile in my stomach swirls, threatening to rise. I grip the bench so tightly, my knuckles ache.

As the conversation picks back up, Dash continues to stare at me. I duck my chin, hoping to hide my discomfort. He leans toward me, playfully bumping me with his shoulder.

"Hey," he whispers. "Are you doing okay?"

"Perfect. Why?" I lie.

"Lexyll mentioned you have an—eh, an *aversion* to ships."

"He did, huh? And where is he?"

I glance up, scanning what I can see of the deck, but I don't spot him. It's a massive ship. He's likely by the bow, or down below in one of the cabins.

"I can't believe you tried to run." Dash laughs. When I turn back to him, he's watching me carefully. "Maybe it was good you did, because it spurred an...interesting conversation with him."

My heart picks up its pace. They talked while I napped? "Oh?"

His brows draw together, and he sighs. "I can't compete with him."

"What?" I lean forward, careful to keep my voice low so the others won't hear us.

"I see the way you look at him. The way he looks at you. I can't compete with that." He runs a hand over his face. "I want to hate him so badly. But how can I hate the man who cares for you so fiercely?"

"Why are you bringing this up now?" I wrap my arms around

my stomach, leaning forward and willing it to settle down. The last thing I want to do is puke in front of everybody.

"He said I bring a *light* out of you, Astrid. One he hasn't seen in a long time."

"Dash—I don't know what to say to that." Acid burns my throat as I try to quell my stomach while focusing on his words.

"How the hell can I hate the bastard after that?"

Damn it, Lex.

Just like Dash said, I *want* to hate the guy. I should hate him for what he's done. But I can't. He makes it impossible.

Before I can respond, my stomach makes a gurgling noise and I dry heave.

"You all right, Aife?" Callan calls from the other end of the bench, having paused his conversation with the others.

"Yep."

"Oh no! Don't lie," Ilona admonishes. She directs her attention to Callan. "She's seasick."

Dash rubs soft circles on my back. "You're okay, sweetheart. I was trying to distract you by talking. Guess it didn't work." He sighs with defeat.

"Keep massaging her," Callan tells him. "I have something that'll help."

A weird nostalgia washes over me. Another memory that's just out of reach. It's like my fingertips can graze it, but I can't quite grasp it. Unexplainably, I ache for Lex.

I *need* him.

My skin grows clammy and gross, and I'm on the verge of hurling. I keep my mouth clamped shut.

"Callan," Dash calls. "Can you get Lex? Please?"

Callan's golden eyes bounce between me and Dash curiously before he nods and darts away.

If I wasn't ill, I'd be more annoyed that Dash clearly listened to my thoughts.

"I'm sorry," he whispers to me. "I was only checking to make sure you're okay."

I grunt in response. *Fuck off.*

He smiles. "I will once you're feeling better." He kisses my temple.

A few minutes later, Callan returns with Lex at his side.

Lex's expression is unreadable as he strides toward me. When he reaches my end of the bench, he kneels, and when he reaches up to cup my face, I lean into his touch.

I don't miss the irony that I've had not one but two powerful men on their knees before me over the past couple days. I almost giggle, but another wave of nausea washes over me, and I clutch my stomach.

"I told you she gets seasick," Lex growls at Dash, giving him a dark look.

"Well, we could have *all* taken the tunnel had you not decided to be such a secretive bastard."

Lex grimaces. "How the hell do you know about that?"

Dash's eyes flash with humor and he taps his temple. "Sora."

I groan, shaking my head at them. "There are etheryn routes to Stellaris, and you put me on a ship?"

"I'm sorry, luv." Lex's fingers caress my cheek while Dash's palm rubs circles on my back. Their touch soothes me. "We can discuss that later."

"Ass," I hiss. Dash chuckles, and I glare at him next. "You too. You're both asscheeks."

Dash's laughter builds. "If we're asscheeks, then you're the crack that keeps us together."

"Wouldn't a crack keep you apart?" I mutter.

"Not in our case." He kisses my forehead.

I exhale a half-laugh, grateful for his piss-poor humor and attempt to distract me.

"I brought something that might help," Callan says, rejoining us. "Moonberries."

"What the hell is a moonberry?" I grip my stomach.

"They're from my realm. They help with pain, sickness, nausea. You'll feel quite delighted after."

"They're safe?" I ask.

Lex's body goes rigid. "They are. But there are also...side effects to be wary of."

"I've never heard of moonberries," Ilona says. "And did you say they're from another *realm*? What do you mean, from another—" She peers at me from behind Lex and bites her lip to stop talking. "Not important. We'll catch up when you're feeling better."

"Come on," Fatima says, pulling Ilona to her feet. "Let's give Astrid some space."

I want to thank her for thinking of me, but my stomach protests with gurgles.

"What are the side effects?" Dash asks, rubbing my shoulders as Fatima and Ilona trek toward the bow. Ilona looks over her shoulder at me, lips pinched into a frown, but I offer her a small smile to let her know I'm fine.

Callan gives us a lopsided grin. "Nothing too bad. The berries are quite fun, actually. They're typically used in rituals and festivities to...enhance one's experience."

Dash scowls. "I'm not sure she needs an *enhanced* experience right now."

"It will help her nausea."

"It will also enhance her desires and her honesty, as well as lower her inhibitions," Lex drawls.

"But she's safe here, with all of us." Callan quickly adds. "It'll be a good time."

"I'd much prefer a finger of whiskey," Lex mutters. His slender fingers tap out a rhythm against my thigh. I focus on that instead of my upset stomach.

"Alcohol is much more dangerous than these. Think about it. Alcohol and ships don't mix. Why do you think so many pirates are missing teeth and limbs? Give them a small space on the wide-open sea, plenty of liquor, a few weapons—"

"Give me the damn berries." I dry heave, and Callan pauses.

"Oh shit." He opens a worn, leather satchel, and pops out a few small, iridescent, crescent-shaped berries. "Here."

Desperate to escape the intense seasickness, I reach out and accept them. I plop the fruit into my mouth, and a delicious, citrusy taste caresses my tastebuds. Callan pops a couple into his mouth too.

"Want some?" He offers the berries to Lex and Dash, who both shake their heads.

"If I'm doing this, you two are too." I glower at them. "And stop bickering."

Without breaking eye contact, Lex plucks a couple of berries from the satchel and places them in his mouth.

It warms me that he does what I ask without any hesitation or resistance. And when Dash follows suit, eating some of his own, I smile smugly to myself.

"I'm going to go find the gals," Callan says. "You three have fun." He winks before sauntering off toward Fatima and Ilona.

"Why do I feel like that was a setup?" I ask.

"Because there are many other options for seasickness," Lex says, scowling at Callan's retreating form. "Many that are easier to come by and don't require leaving the realm."

Exhaling heavily, I close my eyes. I try to relax and let the berries work.

At first, nothing happens. Then, after a couple of minutes have passed, my body grows lighter. A warm tingle swarms my skin. The nausea subsides, leaving behind a giddiness.

Dash chuckles, and his hand slides from my shoulders down to my waist, giving me a squeeze. I give him a surprised look, bursting out into giggles. I lean toward his touch, growing pliable.

"Lightweights." Lex sighs, running a hand through his luscious dark waves. An urge to do the same hits me.

I reach out, running my fingers through Lex's hair. He watches me with an inferno blazing in his jade eyes. When I'm finished, my fingers trail along his jaw, grazing the stubble there. It tickles the pads of my fingers.

"You are so incredibly handsome," I whisper breathlessly. More giggles bubble up, spilling out of my mouth. "I think the berries are working."

Dash's fingers dig into my side, and I turn to him. My breath catches in my throat at the sight of his face. His honey-brown eyes are so filled with love. He's sweet and soft, where Lex is all sharp edges and danger.

"Hey," he says with a smirk. "I'm dangerous too."

I swat his shoulder. "Stop listening to my thoughts."

"I can't help it. I swear! I think it's the berries."

"Liar!"

"Hey—no. Lex said the berries inspire honesty."

I snort.

Lex stands and pulls me to my feet, then spins around and sits on the bench where I just was, drawing me into his lap. I settle into him, leaning my head on his shoulder as he trails his fingers along my side.

Dash watches us eagerly, without any jealousy or annoyance. "I'm glad you're feeling better," he says. "You two are so beautiful that it hurts."

"You're definitely high. Since when do you consider Lex *beautiful*?"

"His looks were never in question. It was his personality I complained about."

Lex mumbles something under his breath. My shoulders shake with laughter.

"What on earth did Callan give us?" My head is buzzy and light, and I'm filled with nothing but positivity and…lust. Burning lust for the two men in my proximity.

Beneath me, the floor is soft and squishy. I pat the wood, giggling. "It's like a sponge."

Dash chuckles. "It's wood. It's not a sponge." He moves to the floor, lying back with a sigh. Then his eyes flick open, and he jolts up. "Holy shit. It *is* spongy. So soft. Is it possible to be soft and hard at the same time?"

"Of course. Lex is soft and hard." I mumble something about a soft heart with hard edges.

"And here I was thinking you were referring to his dick."

Lex exhales heavily. "You're partial to referencing my manhood, Dargan. I can't say I appreciate it."

Dash snorts. "Who the fuck says *manhood*?" Dash mimics Lex's low tone, and we both burst out laughing. "Well, shit." Dash nudges Lex with his foot. "I am high with the god of war." He gives Lex a sly grin. "And how are *you* feeling?"

"Fantastic," Lex says without his usual sarcastic tone.

"Did you forget about *me*?" I wave a hand in Dash's face. "Goddess here? Arguably superior. Death outranks war."

"Never, sweetheart," Dash says, leaning over to plant a kiss on my cheek. He's slow to pull away. The heat from his breath causes me to squirm.

Lex's arm wraps around my waist, holding me in place on his lap as we slide to the floor. "Stop moving like that," he hisses in my ear. "*Please.*"

"I like it when you beg." A wry grin settles on my face, and I wiggle again, making Lex groan.

He shifts beneath me.

"I don't mean any offense," Dash says, stealing our attention, "but when I was young, I heard so many stories about Lexyll." He gazes off into the distance contemplatively. "I wanted to be just like him when I grew up, you know. Lexyll—so strong and unyielding." He turns to me. "People think he started wars, but from what I learned, he *stopped* wars. I thought he was a good man, even though the cost was high. Am I rambling? I think I'm rambling."

"You're also talking as if I'm not a foot away from you, Dashiel."

A spark lights in his eyes as he focuses on Lex. "Is it true?"

"Did *you* call on me to *start* a war, or *end* one?"

"Good point."

I squirm again, brushing against Lex's length. He hisses, gripping me tighter.

"It's ironic," Dash says, sitting before me with crossed legs. "You are God of War, yet you *end* wars." He grabs my hand in his, interlacing our fingers. "And you are Goddess of Death, yet you *give* life."

"Sometimes I kill too," I say. It comes out so matter-of-fact, so devoid of negative emotion, that I chuckle. It doesn't hurt to say. At least not right now. It's as easy as ever. "You are very talkative right now, Dash."

"Isn't he always?" Lex asks.

"And you're funny." I tilt my head back, licking Lex's jaw.

Dash laughs. "Hey, if you want to lick something, come over here."

"Shut up, Dash!" I shake my head.

Lex clears his throat. "I've been called many things, and *funny* doesn't usually make the list."

I snort. "Unsurprising. Dash is the funny one."

"Thank you, sweetheart."

Lex grunts. "I'm aware."

I jolt up, turning to look at Lex. "You admitted it."

"Admitted what?"

"That Dash is funny."

"No. I—"

"Do you think he's funny?" I lean in close, invading his space as I press him for an answer. Our breaths morph into one, only millimeters separating us.

He grits his teeth and looks away. "On occasion."

I clap my hands and squeal. "I knew it! You two will be best friends in no time."

That gives me an idea—to ask all the questions that have been burning inside of me for too long, driving me insane. I sit all the way up, hopping off Lex's lap and reclaiming the bench, leaving the men on the floor.

"I was thinking that we could ta— Hey!" I point at Lex's crotch. "You have a boner." I double over in laughter.

"What do you expect? You were grinding into me. I very nicely asked you to stop." He adjusts his pants, trying to hide the visible proof of his arousal.

Dash's eyes travel down to where Lex's pants are tented.

"That thing is huge."

Lex's brow furrows, and he and Dash share an awkwardly long moment of eye contact. "Twice now you've commented on my erection."

"It's not my fault you keep getting boners around me," Dash says.

"*Boy*, if you don't watch yourself," Lex growls.

"I want to see it," I whisper.

"Color me curious too," Dash adds. I laugh, clutching my stomach. He looks down at his own crotch with a contemplative look, as if he's trying to make a comparison.

"Don't do that." I cup his chin and force him to look up at me. "You're both perfect. And I care more about the size of your hearts than the size of your cocks. Plus, it's about how you utilize what you have."

"I assure you, luv, I wield all my weapons with great skill."

I squirm at Lex's words, my skin ablaze with temptation. "Wait, wait, I'm getting too horny, but we need to talk first."

"She loves to talk before sex," Dash whispers to Lex.

Lex's brow rises, and he glances at Dash. "I should want to punch you in the mouth for that, but luckily for you, I don't. Thank Callan later for that."

"I like these manipulative berries."

"Manipulation," I mutter. Knowing he can't lie, I say, "Speaking of manipulation, Dash—"

"I know. I fucked up. But I *promise* I have never intended to hurt you." He runs a hand through his hair. "I've been attracted to you since we first met, but I fell for you that day at the falls. You are a warrior with a big heart, Astrid, and I am in awe of you."

I smile at him, my head buzzing with his sweet words, at

the confirmation that he's truly harmless to me. "That's what I needed. Thanks." Why was I so upset again? It seems like an incredible waste of energy.

Next I turn my sights on Lex. His green eyes are filled with tenderness, instead of their normal detachment. "Why did you kill my sister?"

"Aife, luv," he says softly. He strokes his stubbled chin, watching me intently. "Invidia meant to harm you."

If I wasn't floating so high from the berries, I probably would've panicked at those words.

"Tell me more," I whisper. Dash and I sit quietly as we listen to Lex's story of how he found Invidia—of her and Enira working together.

"What were their intentions?" I ask.

Lex scratches his jaw. "I had wanted Enira alive for questioning, but I suppose your vengeance burned too brightly."

Whoops. I killed Enira before he could learn anything from her.

"And what does it mean that Dash invoked you?"

Lex scowls at him. "That he clearly isn't done with manipulation."

"I didn't even expect it to work." Dash grins. "But honestly? I was afraid you might murder me either way, so I figured it was worth a shot."

"You make it impossible for me to *not* want to murder you."

"We're having a good time," I whine. "Can we not talk about murdering each other? Plus, Dash said he looks up to you. Cut him some slack. It's cute."

"I said I *used* to look up to him," Dash says. "Before I met him. It's complicated now."

"How does the invocation work though?"

Ilona told me the basics, but I want to know more about how invocations work in practice.

Lex's fingers drum on his thigh, and I wonder if he's missing his normal glass of whiskey to keep his hands busy as he talks. "Long ago, when the humans still worshiped the goddesses and gods, they could call on them for assistance. If we were called upon in good faith and offered a good bargain, we would often accept."

"But you're not often called upon anymore?" I ask. I wonder what would happen if someone called upon *me*.

"No," Lex says. "It's been a while since the invocations were used. Many gods found other ways to utilize their talents. And those who didn't, well, they create chaos out of boredom."

"Like Enira," I mutter.

"Precisely."

"What do you do to not stay bored?" I ask. "Other than play piano and drink whiskey?"

"You play piano?" Dash asks, but Lex ignores him.

"I protect Nevaris and its people. The village was formed as a safe haven long, long ago when humans were persecuted for having magic. I've watched over many generations of families there, people from many realms."

No wonder they love him. "What does it mean exactly when you're invoked?"

"It means that I am bound to help Dashiel with his intention to end the war in Stellaris and protect his family. I cannot bring harm to him. I must protect him."

I laugh so hard I double over. "Holy shit."

"My sentiments exactly."

"I told you. I was afraid you'd kill me," Dash says.

"Perhaps if you'd stop engaging with my woman, that desire

might subside on its own."

"Maybe she likes *engaging with me*," Dash says, mimicking Lex. "Or maybe you need to learn to share."

"Never," Lex mutters.

My thoughts quickly shift back to the conversation Ilona and I had yesterday. I wonder if he seriously would share me with Lex.

"I would," Dash replies to my thoughts.

"Get out of my head!" I shake a fist at him, and he smirks.

"*Your* woman might be happier if you stop being so selfish," he tells Lex.

"Ilona says the gods are known for being polyamorous," I say. "Have you ever...shared before?"

Lex grips his knee so tightly that I fear he'll shatter his own bones. Clearly he's not a fan of this conversation. "I have been with many men and women before you, Aife. Just as you have been with many before me. But I cannot fathom sharing *you*. Pleasure and lust are separate entities from love."

"Pleasure and lust are better when combined with love," Dash says.

"What do you know about love, boy?" Lex asks him.

Dash absentmindedly touches the spot on his bicep where his tattoo of Ayana's words are. "Enough to know it's the most precious thing we have."

"You have a bicep tattoo too!" I point to Lex, remembering the words on Lex's inner arm. "What does it say? And what do the swords on your chest mean?"

In a surprising move, Lex lifts his shirt over his head and whips it completely off, baring his body to us. He's chiseled, much more muscular and filled out now that he's been out of the pit for a few months.

My breath catches in my throat as I eye the old scars criss-crossing his chest. He points to the swords on his pec. "The swords near my heart represent that I am a warrior at heart. They point down to represent the end of conflict, rather than pointing up, which would signify being on guard."

"Ha! I knew it," Dash says, pumping a fist into the air. "You do end wars."

Lex shrugs. "And this"—he points to the words on his bicep—"says *amor vincit omnia*, which means 'love conquers all,' in the old language."

"Holy shit." I exhale loudly. "You both have tattoos about love. What a fucking coincidence!" My insides flutter with giddy delight, courtesy of the lingering effects of the berries. "You two stubborn brutes are both romantics."

I laugh so hard, tears form.

"No wonder you're interested in us both then, eh?" Dash asks with a chuckle. "I guess we have more in common than we thought."

Lex's face darkens as he glances at Dash. "I'm not sure I like the thought of having things in common with you, lover boy."

But *I* like the thought of them having things in common. Especially when that commonality is *me*.

CHAPTER TWENTY-FOUR

ASTRID

As time passes, I expect the effects of the berries to wear off, but instead, they only grow stronger.

"The water is so pretty," I whisper, pointing out into the dark abyss. The full moon glitters off the sea like broken glass. My problems are a million miles away from me. In fact, they seem laughable now. "I can't believe I tried to run away again." I snort with laughter.

"I certainly can," Lex says. His lips tighten, but his eyes crinkle at the edges.

The three of us have been laughing—well, mostly Dash and I have—and chatting about the silliest of topics.

"What do you think Callan and the girls are doing?" I ask.

"Probably playing cards," Lex says. He sighs, a strange vulnerability taking over his features. "Callan is a good man. I don't deserve his loyalty."

"Oh, Lex." He sits on the deck floor, with his back against the bench. I slide onto his lap, cupping his jaw in my hand. Dash sits adjacent to us. I stretch my legs out onto Dash's lap, and he begins massaging my calves. A tickle skates up my spine at his touch. "Goddess, that feels so good." I stare into Lex's eyes, barely able to make out their bright coloring in the dim moonlight and soft glow of the fire orb nearby.

Wrapping my arms around his neck, I lean in and whisper, "You deserve all the loyalty and love, Lex. *You* are a good man."

Lex says, "I want nothing more than to kiss you, luv."

"Then kiss me."

"It won't be sweet or soft. It won't be anything like what you get from Dashiel," he warns.

I glance at Dash, but he only leans his head back and shuts his eyes. He continues to massage my legs, swaying to an invisible tune.

"I don't want you to give me what he gives me. I want you to give me what you have to offer." I love them both for different reasons.

Love.

Do I love them?

Dash squeezes my feet in his calloused hands, and then his eyes whip open. "I love you too, Astrid."

I giggle—a delirious, high-pitched sound. "I didn't say that, Dash."

Lex's eyes narrow as he moves the hair out of my face.

"Don't worry, old man, she loves you too," Dash says.

"Get out of my head," I say, but my words lack vigor.

"I love you more than I can put into words," Lex says. His tenderness undoes me, and I lean toward him, kissing him softly. Just as he promised, it quickly turns demanding.

One of his big hands palms the back of my head, holding me in place as his lips devour mine. Dash's hands skim up my legs, tickling the insides of my thighs through the thin fabric of my pants.

I can't help the breathy moan that escapes me. Lex growls in response, gripping my hair and tilting my head back, baring my neck to him. He nibbles there, just enough to mix pain with pleasure, and my legs open to give Dash's hand access.

There's a slapping sound, and my eyes whip open to see Lex glaring at Dash.

"Did you just slap my hand away?" Dash asks, humor dancing on his lips.

"Mine," Lex growls.

"Are you a god or a caveman? Learn to share." Dash nods at me. "It's what she wants."

"Get out of her head." To me, Lex says, "I thought I told you to keep your barriers up."

"Yeah?" I tease. "And what are you going to do about it if I don't listen?"

His strong fingers crawl up my exposed neck, squeezing slightly. "Then I'll punish you, luv."

"Yes," I gasp, enjoying the thrill of his domination. I spin around to straddle Lex, pressing my lips to his throat. I trail kisses up to his lips, and his mouth opens immediately. Our tongues dance together as I grind against his lap.

I lean back, pulling my shirt off and baring my chest to him. Lex wastes no time leaning down and taking a nipple in his mouth. He clamps down ever so slightly on my peak.

At first, it's a weird sensation, and I cry out, squirming on his lap. But when Lex says, "Be a good girl for me, Aife," I want nothing more than to please him. As he sucks and nips on my bud, mixing pain and pleasure, I rock against his erection, desperate for the friction.

Glancing over at Dash, I see he's whipped his cock out and is slowly rubbing it as he watches us. His eyes are hooded with desire.

It spurs me on.

I want more.

Need more from them.

I stand, sliding my pants off rather ungracefully. Now I'm fully nude, swaying with the ship and moonberries. Both men watch me attentively, as if I'm the most enticing creature they've ever seen.

"Take your pants off," I tell Lex.

Despite how dominant he is, he readily accepts my instruction. And when he springs free, my mouth waters at the sight of him.

"Stay," I demand as I get into position.

Dropping down to my knees on the deck between them, I angle my bare ass toward Lex and turn my face toward Dash's lap.

"I want you both," I tell them. "Now."

I lower my head to Dash's lap, licking the velvety soft head of his cock. He hisses, and I smile as I take him deeper into my mouth, desperate to return the favor he so generously granted me in the throne room the other day.

"Fuck," Lex growls from behind me. His hand lashes out and lands on my bare ass.

A gasp bursts from me, and I choke on Dash.

I didn't expect that.

And I didn't expect to enjoy it so much.

I whimper, wiggling toward him as he lands another strike. It hurts in the best way. He strikes me just hard enough for it to sting but not hard enough to actually harm me. Afterward, he massages the spot he struck, and moisture gathers between my thighs.

"*Fuck*," Dash says. "It feels so good when you take me that deep." He's slightly aggressive with the way he pushes my head down, forcing me to take him whole, but I like it. "Who would've thought you liked to be such a bad girl?" he whispers to me, running his fingers through my hair as I continue to tease his cock with my tongue.

"You know nothing about what she likes," Lex says, his tone lethal.

I whimper, spreading my legs wider and begging for him to fill me. "Stop talking and show me, Lex."

"Holy fucking shit," Dash says with a hint of amusement. "Lex *likes* this. He likes watching us together."

"Watch yourself, Dargan."

"*Your* barriers slipped, and I heard it myself. You're a fucking masochist."

Lex grips my hips so tightly that I swear his fingers will leave a mark. When the head of his cock nudges my slick entrance, I whimper on Dash's cock.

Lex presses against my folds and uses his velvety head to spread my slickness around. He pauses at my clit, rubbing himself against it. I moan again, and the vibrations of my throat cause Dash to lean back and groan. He grips my hair tightly with both hands.

"I'm not gonna last long," Dash says breathlessly.

"You don't come until my girl does," Lex commands. Then, inch by inch, he slowly slides into me. I stretch around him in the most deliciously painful way. He gives me a moment to adjust, and I feel so full with Dash in my mouth and Lex between my legs.

He begins moving. It's slow at first, as he works in and out of me. Then he picks up the pace, thrusting against me with an unhinged desperation.

The sound of skin slapping fills the space, and with each thrust, I take Dash deeper into my throat.

"I'm going to come," Dash mutters. "Swallow all of me,

sweetheart." He holds my head down as he shoots a salty stream down my throat, and my eyes water as I gag.

Lex slows his pace and pulls out of me, giving me a moment to wipe my mouth and catch my breath.

"Holy fuck," Dash says. "That was—wow."

"Pull yourself together," Lex demands. "This is about her, not you."

"Yes, sir," Dash says with a wicked grin.

Without needing further direction, and with me still on all fours between them, Dash slides his head underneath my hips, right as Lex presses back into me. And when his tongue meets my clit in time with Lex's pounding, I gasp in pleasure.

Lex jerks. "I don't need you licking my balls, boy."

Dash's mouth leaves my clit, and he chuckles. "It's kind of impossible not to down here."

"Shut up and keep going," I whimper.

"Your pussy was made for me, luv," Lex whispers in my ear. He groans, and it's the sound of danger and pleasure mixed into one. "I'm going to fill you up with my cum until you're dripping with it."

I press my hips back, meeting him thrust for thrust. Dash's tongue continues to work between us, and I can't help but think that Lex secretly likes it.

Lex wraps one hand around my throat, squeezing just enough to send a zing of adrenaline through me. "But I need you to be a good girl first, and come for me."

Goddess knows his dirty talk drives me nuts.

My inner muscles clench around him. The pleasure builds, and I try to hold on for as long as I can, buying myself time to enjoy this experience. But with Dash's tongue working me into a frenzy and Lex's hot breath on my ear as he whispers dirty words, I can't hold it off.

I cry out as ecstasy drowns me.

"Just like that," he says. "That's my good girl."

Dash slides free from under me, sitting up and wiping the wetness from his lips with a smug grin.

Lex pulls out of me, and before I can protest at the loss of his warmth, he turns me around so I'm straddling him, both of us sitting up. He wraps his arms around me, holding me tight and cuddling me in an unexpected show of intimacy as I slowly lower back onto his hardness.

My body shudders as he fills me back up, and we slowly move together at a calmer pace. He keeps one hand on my hip, guiding me, and lifts the other to my cheek. Brushing the hair out of my face, his brow softens, and he looks at me with so much tenderness that my heart nearly bursts.

"You are everything to me, Aife," he says quietly. "I would do anything to bring you pleasure and happiness. I would bring war to the whole world if it meant protecting you."

He kisses me softly, our lips moving together lazily as I ride him. He pulls back just enough to whisper against my lips. "I love you with everything I am, my angel of death."

He initiates power-sharing between us, and our energy cycles freely between us both.

As much as I loved his roughness and dirty talk, nothing beats the intimacy of this moment. Lex kisses my neck, and my body burns with pleasure. We stay that way, gently rocking into each other until I feel my core throbbing with another release. And when I moan his name in his ear, he grunts, finding his own release inside of me.

When we finish, I turn to find Dash watching us with a lustful gaze. He strokes his cock, giving it a few final tugs before spilling all over his lap.

"Like what you see?" Dash teases Lex as he cleans up.

Lex grunts, looking away, and I chuckle, still floating from the berries.

"Astrid does." Dash smirks. "And you would do *anything* for her. But this was also for you. You get off on the pain. You like being hurt."

I glance at Lex curiously, waiting to see what he'll say, knowing he can't lie.

He grunts. "Stay the fuck out of my head."

"Keep your barriers up," Dash mimics.

Lex's jaw tics. "It's the berries."

I giggle as Lex mutters something under his breath about *never talking about this again.*

The three of us lie back on the deck, side by side, with me in between my two warriors. I take their hands, interlacing my fingers with them both, and smile.

Only the stars overhead have witnessed our pleasure, winking down at us as if promising to keep our secret.

I'm dirty, spent, and sated.

But most of all, complete.

CHAPTER TWENTY-FIVE

ASTRID

As we dock in Cerulea, my chest tightens with apprehension. Now that reality is settling in, the time I spent with Astrid and Lex seems like a distant dream. But I hold onto the memory, using the ghost of that high to carry me forward.

I exhale a long breath, shaking off my nerves. Being back in Stellaris, where my family is, brings me comfort. Judging by the broad, toothy smile Fatima wears, it's the same for her.

But it also stirs up some unease.

Once the ship is secured at the dock—and tied tightly to the posts, thanks to the assistance of the dockhands—we descend the rickety gangplank and venture out into the city.

"Thank the goddess," Astrid says, glancing up at the deep blue sky with a relieved grin.

I chuckle, half-expecting her to drop to her knees and kiss the ground.

The thought of her on her knees again warms my cheeks. I smirk, shaking my head and willing the image away before my lust can consume me.

Donkeys clomp by, their hooves striking up small clouds of dust with each step as they lug their goods along. The chatter of city-folk surrounds us. Coins jangle as customers exchange them for goods. Children squeal as they chase each other along the docks. Nostalgia washes over me as I'm assaulted by the comforts of home.

The aroma of sea salt and rich, tangy spices wafts past me. There's a hint of something fishy in the air too, but luckily, the fish market is further south, away from the main docks and streets, sparing us the full assault of unpleasant odors.

We've docked near the middle of the city—near the spice market.

Up north is the military port and training posts, with a smattering of beaches in between.

As far as the eye can see are sandstone buildings in various shades of beige and eggshell. It's a practical choice; lighter colors reflect the heat of the day. The climate here is similar to Hakran, but during this time of year it's hotter during the day and a chilly breeze comes from the sea in the evening. It's more arid than tropical.

The sun begins to set beyond the city, melting into the distant sand dunes and heralding the coming of cooler night air. We'll have to hurry to get to the palace before night falls.

I take a moment to observe the various people bustling around, a sense of awe filling me. Their king recently died, and Stellaris faces war, but that hasn't stopped Cerulea's heart from beating. At this moment, I know my homeland will overcome the adversity it faces.

Had we docked with one of my family's ships—one waving the navy and gold royal colors and displaying the Vannyk crescent moon crest—the people would have been clamoring to greet us. But having arrived in a plain, wooden ship with no visible markings, flags, or crests by which to identify it, we're only getting a few curious looks and cautious side-eyes.

Astrid steps up beside me. "Holy shit." She squints against the bright sun as she observes the sprawling city. "This is—wow. Hakran and Nevaris seem so tiny in comparison."

"Welcome to Cerulea, sweetheart." I try to chuckle, but it comes out flat. I end up clearing my throat and staring at my boots.

"Hey," she says, her words barely audible over the commotion of the dock. Slowly, I glance up to meet her concerned teal eyes. "I know you're not okay right now, but you're not alone." She reaches for my hand, interlacing our fingers together and giving me a squeeze. Her small hand tucked into mine brings me a warm sense of relief. I smile down at her, and this time it's genuine.

Lex seems acutely aware of our interaction, but he says nothing. He keeps his gaze locked ahead. Like a predator, he's constantly scanning the area for any signs of a threat. As a trained soldier myself, I recognize and appreciate that proactiveness. Especially considering how overstimulating the city can be.

His attention shifts to me, as if he's aware of my staring. His lips stiffen, but the twinkle of understanding in his eyes speaks volumes. On instinct, I lower my mental barriers, trying to draw his thoughts to me. I'm surprised when I'm met with his low voice, loud and clear. He's purposely letting me into his thoughts.

You're not in Hakran—you're not a king today. Nor are you Stellaris's prince or even an on-duty guard. You are a son mourning a loss. A friend in need. His eyes quickly shift to Astrid before returning to me. *I do not like you, but I* will *protect you and your family. Not because of your childish invocation, but for her.*

His words shock me. It takes me a few seconds to fully process them. I finally smile and open my mouth to tease the old man for having a heart, but his voice floods my mind again.

If you repeat this, I will find a way to kill you. Oath or not.

Don't be a fool, boy.

Then my mind goes silent as he slips his barriers back into place with skillful control. I snap my mouth shut, but it's impossible to wipe the smirk off my face.

He narrows his eyes, gives me a brief, sharp nod, and resumes scanning the cobblestone streets that are saturated with evening patrons. People bustle by as we wait for the rest of our crew to catch up.

Astrid, seemingly unaware of the interaction between Lex and me, turns and says, "Your city is stunning, Dash. Thank you for letting me accompany you." She leans up, ghosting her lips over my cheek.

For a second, I wonder if Lex gets these tender moments with Astrid too. But I don't care. They can have their passion—their anger and fire. Astrid and I will always be connected through our emotions, our grief, and our insecurities. We are two hearts begging to love and be loved.

Lex might cause her heart to pound faster, but I help her heart beat stronger.

We follow the streets deeper into the city, weaving through the congestion. Fatima, ever the leader, walks ahead with a group of guards. Callan and Ilona trail behind us, and Lex lingers near Astrid's side. I glance over my shoulder. Ilona is taking in the sights with wide eyes while Callan sniffs the air.

A blend of cardamom and cinnamon greets us as we pass a restaurant that has its doors wide open. A wooden A-frame sign advertises buttered chicken and eggplant dishes.

Callan groans. "I'm definitely getting lunch there later."

Stands and booths with bright-colored fabric roofs display woven baskets filled with a variety of vibrant powdered spices. Some vendors sell rugs, flags, or handmade crafts, but most are peddling spices and vegetables.

"I like all the colors. It's so bright and cheery," Astrid says. "I thought Hakran was filled with color, but this is something else." She points to the higher levels of the buildings, where flags and blankets hang out of open windows in a vibrant display.

"It's a sign of mourning," I say. "In Stellaris, when someone dies, they're sent off into the ocean in a funeral pyre." Their ashes return to the sea, honoring Sama—the original goddess. They say Sama and her magic was born from the Inspid Sea. That's probably why some lore says she's from Hakran. And it's probably why Hakran has unique magic of its own, like the falls. "Afterward, everyone wears their brightest and best to negate the darkness of loss. It's common courtesy to hang bright flags and colorful paintings."

"That's beautiful," she says, squeezing my hand again.

"Much of our culture is rooted in art, in appreciation for life, experiences, and the senses. Instead of mourning death in darkness and solemnity like some might, we celebrate the beauty of living."

"That explains a lot," Astrid murmurs as we weave through another group of patrons.

"Turmeric tea?" a man with a broad smile and several missing teeth calls to us from a wooden-wheeled cart on the side of the street. "Turmeric tea?"

He grips a mug in his hand, his fingertips stained orange from crushing the herb.

Aife slows to a stop, looking back at Ilona and then me. "Can we stop really quick?" she asks softly. "Ilona loves tea."

For some stupid reason, I look to Lex for confirmation. He nods his approval, and I quickly purchase some tea for Ilona and Callan. Lex, Astrid, and Fatima decline, still full from this morning's breakfast of fresh salmon on the ship, and I can't stomach anything because of my nerves.

"This is spicy." Ilona hiccups. "Sorry—spicy things give me hiccups."

"Turmeric is *not* spicy at all!" Fatima chuckles, glancing over her shoulder at Ilona, who flushes as we continue to maneuver through the bodies.

"Neither of you is *wrong*, per se. It does have a little kick to it." Callan tilts his mug back, chugging it to the dregs. "Delectable though. What do I do with the cup?"

"Toss it in the street," I tell him. "It's made by earth aethyns—from clay. Squeeze it. It'll crumble and blow away with the wind."

"Neat." He does as I say, crushing the mug in his grip. It disintegrates, and the barely-there breeze carries the dusty remains away. "You know, I've been to Cerulea a few times, but I've never stopped to enjoy the streets. Only flew through. I've been missing out." He inhales noisily, practically salivating as we pass another restaurant. He leans in toward me conspiratorially and lowers his voice. "Did you know that some realms don't have magic? None at all." He scratches his chin. "I've been to a realm once that had 'technology' though, which is its own kind of magic, and—oh, they had something called 'electricity.' There were these things just like fire orbs. They called them lights too. *Light bulbs*. But instead of being magic-powered by aethyns, they were powered by—" He shakes his head and smiles sheepishly at me. "Never mind. I like understanding how things work, and I could talk all day."

If I hadn't already learned on the ship that Callan was from another realm, that he could *fly*, I'd never take his goofy gap-toothed smile and stories seriously.

"You and Ilona might enjoy spending time together."

He jumps out of the way of a child bolting past us, bumping shoulders with me. "Sorry. You think so? We haven't talked much."

"She likes to read."

A laugh escapes him. "I'm not much of a reader. More of a hands-on guy. I gotta see it, touch it, to understand it."

"I get that," I say with a brow waggle. "I'm more of a hands-on guy too." I mimic squeezing boobs while Callan bursts into laughter. When it subsides, I continue in a more serious tone: "No, but Ilona has to *read* it to understand it. But you both like knowledge, facts, and history. Sounds like you two could have great conversations."

"Are you trying to pawn me off on her? Not partial to my company?"

"If I didn't like you, I would never dump you on Ilona. She's much too kind for that torture." I cock a brow at him. "So, when exactly have you been to Stellaris? I often received the diplomats. I'd have remembered you."

"Indeed. It's impossible to forget my handsome face." He chuckles. "I've passed through more than a few times, but a diplomat I am not. I'm a *harbinger*. You know? One of the god of war's harbingers of death?"

I shrug. "That wasn't in the history lessons." Not that we talked much about the gods outside of occasional story swaps. In fact, it was my biological mother and father who taught me the most lore through bedtime stories. Though, after the Paramour Falls situation went awry, I'm not sure I can believe the stories fully. They were inevitably imbued with a sprinkle of fiction. Or perhaps I'm misremembering.

Sweat beads on the back of my neck as the last vestiges of the day's heat fade away.

"What the hell *is* a harbinger?" I ask.

"Harbingers lead Lex's legions. If Lex has escalated the situation to a group activity and you meet us on the battlefield, you
can expect a swift death."

I frown.

Legions.

Being home and hearing about Lex's legions brings back
memories of running with the Stellari soldiers, training the
sailors in the navy, accompanying Zale on royal meetings with
Father, and being privy to the political happenings without
having to make the difficult decisions. My gut churns, and I
realize I miss that.

I miss being a guard. A soldier.

It's more *me* than ruling is.

"Remind me not to piss Lex off," I mumble, wondering what
it would be like to train with him and his armies.

"Too late for that." Callan laughs. "Aife wouldn't let him kill
you though. He's too loyal to hurt someone she loves."

If that's the case, why would he kill her sister? I frown,
wondering what the hell happened there.

We meander through the city, opting for narrower side streets
rather than the main road, which is jam-packed with vendors,
booths, and people. The smaller streets are still wide enough that
three of us can walk abreast, with room enough for passersby.

An old lady with black braids, selling rugs woven with vibrant
threads, smiles widely at us, showcasing her missing teeth. She
grabs a golden tassel, lifting it up and waving it toward us as if
to snag our attention.

I smile back, continuing to move with the group.

Unfortunately, I have no spare change with me. I make a
mental note to return another day, to support my city's artisans.
They are the backbone of Cerulea—of Stellaris—after all. Our

fish and spice trades do quite well, but it's the local art and crafted goods that breathe life into the streets.

"Why does it surprise you that I've been through here before?" Callan asks, drawing my attention back to him. "You can't possibly think I sit around Nevaris doing nothing all day?"

I clear my throat. "I'm surprised you've been to my home city, is all."

"*Through* it, not technically *to* it. It's stunning from above. Maybe I'll take you for a flight sometime so you can experience it from the air." He winks.

It's surprising how the easygoing Callan is so close with the brutish Lex.

"Anyway. When I'm not training the second legion—that's mine, by the way. The second line in defense. Lo has the first legion, and Sora, the third. I act as a spy. It's part of my job description to keep an eye on things. I'm pretty great at it."

"Cocky, eh?" I tease Callan.

Astrid, catching wind of the conversation, whirls around, a teasing glint in her eye. "No, Dash. *You're* cocky. *Callan's* confident. There's a difference."

Callan grins at me, shrugging, and I laugh.

"Okay then. If *I'm* the cocky one, what does that make old Sexy Lexy?"

A rumble of laughter goes through the group. Like a good soldier, Lex ignores us all, keeping alert.

The only reason I'm able to relax a bit is because of his presence. He might not be my favorite person, but he's a beneficial guy to have around. Anyone would be a fool to cross us.

"He's Daddy Lex," Callan says. At this, Lex grunts.

I try to hide my humor, but Astrid openly shakes with laughter.

"What?" Callan asks, all wide-eyed with innocence. "He

takes us all in like a father figure."

"I think *daddy* and *father* have two different meanings," Astrid supplies. "Grumpy Daddy Lex." She snorts.

"I read a book once where the main character called the love interest *Daddy*," Ilona adds. "She would act up just so he would spank her to tame…" Her voice fades, and she flushes a deep red when she realizes we're all gaping at her. "Never mind."

Ever so quietly, Astrid leans in and mutters to Lex, "You can spank me all you want, but don't *ever* expect to tame me, Lexyll."

"I wouldn't dream of it, luv."

Astrid smirks at Lex, who, much to my surprise, actually smiles back at her. I'll be damned.

Lust flares through me, and a swell of comfort fills my chest seeing them interact. She brings out a softer side of him, and he brings out her sharp edges.

"You can tame *me*, Daddy Lex," I tease.

He shakes his head, but his jaw relaxes, and a hint of humor plays on his lips. Did I just make Lex laugh? Maybe not audibly, but on the inside?

Astrid's eyes coyly dart between us. "I would give up a kidney to see that."

"I would give up both kidneys to see the entire dynamic between you three." Callan's grin grows. "You are all stubborn as mules. How does that work? I bet it's hot as—"

"We all *heard* how it worked." Fatima glances at us over her shoulder.

Astrid's cheeks pinken, and Ilona giggles, covering her mouth with a hand.

"Then you'll have heard everyone ended the night quite pleased." I place a hand on Lex's shoulder. "Even this old man."

He shrugs me off, scowling at me. "Astrid, do tame your lover boy before I must do so myself."

"Don't you mean *our* lover boy?" I smirk. "I know you liked that trick I did with my tongue and your—"

"Unless you want your innards staining these pristine streets, I suggest closing your mouth, *boy*."

"We both know you like my mouth better open." I wink at him.

"You two are fucking annoying." Astrid rolls her eyes, linking arms with Ilona and joining Fatima a few paces ahead. "Maybe you should spank him, Lex."

Everyone but Lex laughs. He curses under his breath and rubs his temples.

After a few minutes of walking in comfortable silence, I use my myndox power to poke around and see what everyone's thinking. Old habit. It's my way of staying ahead of any potential threats.

Callan's mind is focused on food. *Damn, that smells good. Honey-glazed chicken? Or lamb? Maybe it's lamb. Do they eat lamb here?*

I sniff the air, grinning to myself. Immediately, my mouth waters for grilled eggplant curry—made with a tomato and coconut base and an assortment of herbs. It's my *favorite*.

Lex has his barriers up, and I have no need to peek into Fatima's mind, so I try Ilona next. *Oh my goodness. So many people and sounds and—it's so much. Fatima and Dash actually grew up here. And Zale too. Do they ever get a moment of peace? I hope he has people to look after him. Poor thing. Maybe—*

Next, despite it being a less-than-honorable idea, I try Astrid's.

As I prod around her mind, I'm filled with guilt, but not enough to keep me from doing it.

Does no one recognize Dash? He's still royalty here after all—even if he's a guard and not technically a prince. Right? Maybe it's because of how big the city is. Everyone seemed to know Lex in Nevaris—but that's such a small village in comparison. And are there no carriages to take us to his home?

My verbal response bubbles up, but I choke it down, not wanting her to know I listened to her thoughts. I want to tell her that the streets are too congested for a carriage, that the palace isn't much farther. I want to explain that my people likely don't recognize me in these plain clothes. They would expect me to be mourning my father's—the king's—loss traditionally, in brightly colored garb. It was a strategic choice to dress blandly; I didn't want to draw extra attention to myself.

Her next thought cracks my heart a little. *Where would I live if I chose them both? Nevaris? Hakran? Stellaris? My cottage? I don't even know where that is. I don't belong anywhere. I don't have a home. I could never make it work with both; neither would agree to give up their own home for the other.*

I stop listening in, not wanting to disrespect her any more than I already have. It thrills me to know she still considers a life with me. But it pains me to know she feels like an outsider everywhere she goes. Hopefully I can make Cerulea feel like home while we're here.

And hopefully one day I can show her that I'd go anywhere she is. I only settled in Hakran for her—so she could rest easy knowing the people she worries about are safe after Enira uprooted their lives. But I would go anywhere with Astrid, even if that meant dealing with Lex. Even if it meant handing Hakran off to someone more capable.

In fact, it would be a relief to step away from Hakran. My long-dead ancestors might've been Hakranian, but I was never meant to rule the island. It's confirmed in the way my chest lightens with relief at being away, in how my heart swells with love and duty by simply being around the people who matter to me.

I'm starting to think home isn't a place but a group of people.

CHAPTER TWENTY-SIX

LEX

The sight of the Cerulean palace is certainly remarkable. And by the look on Aife's face, she's equally as impressed. Her jaw drops open, and she alternates between staring at the palace and at Dashiel as if she's shocked *this* is where he's from.

I must say, I'm in agreement with her.

The palace stretches tall and wide, with round edges and multiple stories. A massive dome is centered between two man-made ponds with rows of palm trees on either side.

I'm tempted to snark about how Enira's excessive palace is *nothing* compared to this monster estate, but once we climb the stone staircase and enter through a hand-painted cerulean archway—escorted by a couple of friendly guardsmen—the remark dies on my lips.

If Enira's palace was made of bones and marrow, the Vannyks' is made of flesh, blood, and a beating heart.

Beautiful multicolored murals, rugs, and furnishings fill the space, all tied together through cobalt, gold, and maroon accents. Artifacts perched on pedestals sit prominently around the foyer, as if placed there to draw the eye and induce awe. There are several golden oil lamps, a marble elephant statue, ceramic pottery with intricate patterns, and more.

Dashiel steps up by my side, a proud grin on his face. He claps me on the shoulder. "These are gifts from our most famous artisans throughout the years."

I cock my head, taking it all in. "And the ceiling?" I point above us. A magnificent painting of the sun setting behind the ocean waves takes up the entire domed ceiling.

"Painted by Mariabella Marachini. The one and only."

Never heard of her. But I don't care to ruin the boy's pride. This *is* his home, after all. The palace interior is a hodgepodge of art, color, and culture. That is something worth being proud of.

"It smells so good." Aife inhales deeply beside me. "Even better than the city, if that's possible."

"Sandalwood," I mutter at the same time as Dash.

He chuckles, shooting me an amused look.

"Really?" Aife asks. "No wonder I like it." She gives Dash a sly smile. "It smells like *you*."

A handful of courtiers wearing baggy navy-blue clothing with gilded accents and brightly patterned shawls—the palace uniform, I surmise—greet us. They inform us that King Zale took an early rest and that the queen mother is to not be disturbed. Although Dashiel's face hardens in displeasure, he refuses to wake his brother.

The courtiers offer to show us to our rooms. Aife and Ilona, tired from the journey, eagerly accept. They request rooms near each other, say their goodnights, and part from us, following one of the courtiers up the grandiose staircase and out of sight.

Dashiel turns to a servant and requests that supper be brought to our rooms. He promises me a tour in the morning before taking off with Fatima down a side hallway.

Callan and I exchange a look and immediately get to work exploring on our own.

Hours later, I stand in the vestibule, carefully memorizing where each of the four hallways leads. Having walked each one from end to end, I've mentally mapped out the general layout. It'll take time to investigate the other wings in more detail later.

I must admit, the Vannyks have taste. Their palace is elaborate and rich in style, constructed mainly out of local stone. Gleaming fixtures and painted murals decorate the hallways, with colorful mosaics set into the floors. Fountains and plants bring life inside. It demonstrates the opulence of Hakran's palace but has comforts similar to those of Harmony House. It's ten times the size of my house, however.

Personal vendetta aside, I'm quite relieved Aife has Dashiel *and* me looking after her. He is fairly qualified to keep an eye on her and would do anything to keep her safe.

It's in my nature to constantly scout and be on high alert, especially outside of Nevaris, where there are no wards in place to protect us. Knowing Dashiel is by Aife's side gives me a small sense of comfort. I failed to protect her before—from Enira.

Aife having Dash by her side will also allow me to do my job more efficiently.

Two guards stand nearby, tracking me with distrust. Ignoring their cautious gazes, I stroll across the mosaic floor and gaze up at the portraits lining the wall. A variety of men and women stare back vacantly, all clad in hues of navy and gold. Royalty, no doubt.

Curiously, in the center of the room is a grand statue—a woman with soft curves and warm features carved of chalky stone. She's draped in fabric, and real desert marigolds sprout up in the flowerbed at her feet.

"And this is—?" I ask aloud, waving toward the statue. When no one answers, I turn to the nearest guard. "You there. Who is she?"

The guard's face morphs into an expression of shock, then disgust. He clears his throat. "Sama."

"Sama," I mimic. *Interesting.* I chuckle to myself. Surely they can't believe that this plain, insignificant woman is meant to be Sama, the Mother of all mothers, the creator, *the* original goddess.

The guard mumbles, "Ignorant."

"Yes. I agree. The rendering of Sama here is quite ignorant in nature. Perhaps we owe it to an ignorant perception?" I cock a brow at the guard.

He scoffs, leveling a glare at me. He pulls a black stick from a holder at his side and takes an aggressive step toward me.

"Do you plan to strike me with that?"

"Berris," another guard hisses from across the room. "Stand down. He's a friend of King Zale's brother."

"Well, I wouldn't call us *friends.* Though I suppose we're in an alliance of sorts."

"He disrespected Sama." Berris wipes his sweaty brow with the back of his hand. "That's treason as far as the king is concerned."

"The *late* king, Berris," the other guard warns. "We serve King Zale now."

"This is quite tiresome." I turn my back on Berris and his pal, adjusting my cuffs. "I had expected a city with such renowned culture to possess more intelligence." I take three steps before Berris brings his club down on the back of my head. It stings something fierce, but I work to keep the displeasure off my face.

"Like I said"—I slowly turn back around to face Berris, my fingers flexing at my sides—"ignorant." Before he can react, I unleash a sample of my power, drawing Berris's life-force energy toward me. "Apologies," I tell the other guard as I do the same to him before he can run and get *help*.

The guards topple to the floor. Their heads meet the tile with sickening *thuds*.

I'll need to explain this to Dashiel, unfortunately. That should be fun. His invocation protects his *family*, not his family's idiotic guards, however.

"You sure know how to make friends," Callan calls as he steps into the room. His boots clack against the mosaic tiles as he joins me and presses a crystal glass into my hand.

I grunt a thanks, reveling in the smell of oaky whiskey. The liquid meets my lips and slides down my throat with a burn, but my tense muscles unravel slightly.

"Not quite what I'm used to, but it'll do."

"You sound like a spoiled brat." Callan chuckles.

"When you've been around as long as I have, you develop a taste for the finer things in life. There's nothing wrong with knowing what you like."

"Yeah, and there's nothing wrong with appreciating what you have, either."

A tentative smile creeps onto my face. He's been wise for as long as I've known him. "And I do appreciate this whiskey. For tasting of horse piss and reminding me of how decadent ours is back home."

Callan loses it, releasing a laugh that echoes through the domed space.

"The grounds are secure," he finally says when his laughter subsides. "I caught up with Fatima. She introduced me to a few key soldiers. Did you know Dashiel was not a regular guard but a *captain*? The new woman in his place seems competent enough. She was receptive to our concerns." He scratches his chin. "Though I had expected them to have taken more caution prior to our arrival, given the situation. She was tight-lipped, reluctant to give us any information. I'd like to talk to Zale and see what information he's given his soldiers so we're cohesive."

I sip my whiskey.

Lack of precautions.

A resistant captain.

A sleeping king not here to greet us upon arrival.

These are not things I would expect from a king who begged for assistance. Something is off here. Perhaps it's nothing, but my instinct is rarely wrong.

"Find the healer. Ensure he's on the grounds. Then rest. In the morning, follow Zale, Dashiel, or anyone else of import to ensure there's nothing they're keeping from us."

"What about them?" Callan nods at one of the unconscious guards at my feet.

"They're fine."

Callan nods. "And Aife?"

"I'll keep an eye on her tonight."

I don't bother asking about Lo and Hakran. If there was anything to report, Callan would have done so already.

He gives me a sly look before fading into transparency.

I hand my empty glass off to a passing servant, and head to Aife's room to check on her. My hand is poised to knock, to see if she's up, when I hear a soft whimper followed by mumbling.

Who in the goddess's name could be in there with her at this hour?

When she cries out again, my body goes rigid. Forgoing the knock, I barge into the room.

"You should really—" *lock the door*, I finish mentally. Aife is alone, tangled up in gold sheets as she writhes. Her wispy hair sticks to her sweaty cheeks.

"Oh, Aife," I whisper.

She was crying out not in pleasure but torment.

An iron vise grips my heart and squeezes as I witness my fated struggling in her sleep. Whatever demons haunt her, they come for her at night, when she's alone.

Not wanting to startle her by waking her, I sit at the edge of the bed. Carefully, I untangle the sheets from between her legs. She doesn't wake as I push her hair out of her face and tuck her back in properly.

Suddenly, I'm transported back to when it was just Aife and me. When I would soothe her with my voice, gifting her the relaxation she was unable to find elsewhere.

Gripping her hand gently, I begin singing to her. It's an old lullaby, one she favored. I learned it some centuries ago, and it's sung in a language that has since died out and been forgotten.

It's a beautiful language, one that rolls off the tongue like a sweet caress.

The words pour out of me, barely above a soft whisper, as I sing to her. It does the trick, and slowly, Aife's whimpering dies out and her breathing steadies. Her body relaxes.

When I finish, I kiss the back of her hand and stand. I want to curl up beside her, tuck her body into my own and hold her. I want to plant my kisses along the soft skin of her collarbone. I want to see those sleepy teal eyes of hers when she wakes. I want to see the soft, coy smile she gives me in the mornings before swatting me out of her space so she can start her day in peace.

I miss her. All of her.

But if this is all I can have for now, I will take it. Like Callan said, there's nothing wrong with appreciating what I have. Especially if it's all I might get.

CHAPTER TWENTY-SEVEN

DASH

As soon as I wake, I search for Zale.

When a courtier informs me he's holding council, I immediately make my way to the council chamber.

The guards don't stop me as I open the doors, entering in the midst of Zale's speech to the dozen people seated before him.

"Brother," he says. His eyes light up. He wears a bright gold-and-navy ensemble, with a purple sash slung across his chest to indicate his state of mourning. His hair is impeccably styled—longer on the top than the sides. He stands tall and confident at the front of the room, with his hands clasped behind his back. "Leave us, please," he says to the councilors gathered at the table.

The people gather their belongings, scurrying out the door in a wave of color. A few eager eyes and smiles shift my way, and I recognize most everyone from my time in the guard. It's been only a few months since I left, after all. I'll greet them later, but now is not the time.

Once Zale and I are left alone in the room, he strides over to me and pulls me into a big hug. "I've missed you, brother."

"Me too. Me too."

We hold each other tightly for a minute. His familiar coconut scent fills my nose, and it makes me ache for our father.

"You're about six weeks late." He's referring to the resting ceremony.

I hang my head in shame. I wish I had been by my father's side. I'll never have a real chance to say goodbye. "How's Mother?

"She's...struggling." Zale picks at his sash, removing some lint. "The healer has been giving her something to help her sleep."

He lifts his eyes to mine, and I see a flash of anger there. Disappointment. My guilt deepens. I should've been here. For Joccelyn. For Zale. For my people. It seems like all I do is fuck up. I try to do the right thing, always thinking of those around me, but it's never the *right* thing for everyone. I'm bound to disappoint someone.

I swallow the pressure in my throat, summoning my inner warrior. "I'm sorry it took war to get us here."

Zale goes rigid, his eyes narrowing into slits. "War?"

"Yes. I got your letter about the missing aethyns... Vespyn."

He regards me with a puzzled frown. "What about Vespyn?"

My gut drops. I reach into my pocket, presenting the last letter Zale sent me—the one about potential conflict.

His eyes flick across the page. The edges begin to crinkle as he grips it angrily. "I did *not* write this." His voice is grim. "I would never send something so...*sloppy*. It's disturbing."

"Fuck." That's what I said. I had thought the handwriting looked a little crummier than usual, but I chalked it up to stress. It had the official seal and was written on the same parchment as the rest of his letters. "Who is your courier? Who has access to your stationery?"

He gently sets the letter on the table. Even when stressed, he's regal and poised, his posture strict. He's demonstrating qualities of a great king—unlike me, with my scuffed boots, disheveled hair, and ill-concealed anger.

"No one." He shakes his head, deep in thought. "I've moved Mother into my room because it faces east. You know how much she loves the sun. I'm hoping that waking with the sun every morning will bring back her hope. Her joy. I've sent away the maids so they won't bother her. Only our healer is allowed in—to care for her."

I swipe a hand through my hair as I pace the room. "Jules?" She's been our primary healer for as long as I can remember, but she does oversee a small staff, so it's possible Zale is referring to one of them.

"No. The man. Mother's friend."

"Cedrik," I mutter. "Why would *he* write a letter pretending to be you? Lying about threats from Vespyn?" I think aloud, but the answer is immediately obvious. "He wanted to get me here. But why?"

The irony is that we were already planning to come soon—to speak with him.

"Perhaps because Mother needs you? *A potential war* clearly brings you home, even when our father's death does not," he says dryly.

"Zale—" I stop pacing to face my brother. I clear my throat and keep my voice steady as I say, "Hakran might only be a single small village on a remote island, but it doesn't make my responsibility any less important than yours."

Admittedly, I find being a ruler incredibly displeasing and less satisfactory than being a guard.

"No." He sighs, placing a hand on my shoulder. "It doesn't. I apologize for letting my emotions get the best of me. I, of all people, know that duty comes first, and I'm proud of you for honoring that. Father was proud of you. He even said so near the end, Dash." His voice breaks. "He wanted you to know."

"Let's leave the hostility out of this then."

I pull him to me in a tight hug. Neither of us make a move to break free right away. Guilt chokes me.

When we finally do pull away, I ask, "Where is Cedrik?"

"Either in the infirmary or with Mother."

"There haven't been any invasions, any aethyns missing, anything even seemingly insignificant?"

"No, and I would be the first to know. I haven't heard from Empress Rania since I ascended the throne. Our previous correspondence was cordial—pleasantly uneventful."

The notoriously quiet empress of Vespyn. I've never met her in person, despite her country's proximity to our own.

"Are the borders secure?"

"Undoubtedly."

"So it's entirely a farce."

I run a hand over my face, heaving a heavy sigh.

"You brought Astrid here. Why?" I slow-blink, forgoing a reply, and his face contorts. "Damn it, Dash."

I cock my head at him. "You liked her when you first met her. She's the same person, Zale. Don't start this. We'll both end up pissed off. We need to stick together more than ever right now."

"It's just, you know how the Stellari folk feel about the—"

"They won't find out what she is."

"And Lexyll?"

"Same with him." If we didn't know who he was when we saw him, no one else will either. There are no portraits of the gods or goddesses in any of our history books. And hell, those books are stuffed away in the Bibliotheca's basement, out of sight, anyway. Right now, that works in our favor. It's their power that gives them away. So long as they keep quiet about it, they'll be fine. "Neither of them are attention-seeking. It won't be hard to hide. I'll talk to them."

Zale pinches the bridge of his nose. "I'm trusting you with this, Dash. I loved Father, and he was right to be cautious about the gods. You of all people know this. And I absolutely do not condone genocide, but this is risky. Keep them quiet, or *this* could truly start a war." He clasps his hands behind his back and paces the length of the council table. The prospect of harboring gods in his home city stresses him out, but *he* is the king now. *He* can set a new standard for our people. I'll work on him. "Don't let your feelings blind you."

"Fine," I say through gritted teeth.

"And don't let them power-share."

I avert my eyes. I should be immune to vygora magic. The only reason Lex's power was able to knock me out in the throne room the night of the storm was because he had power-shared with Astrid—something we didn't understand until much later.

A flash of our activities on the ship after eating moonberries zips through my mind, and I ache to be back in that moment. I don't bother telling Zale that it's too late. That they power-shared. That Lex and I shared Astrid. That we *all* enjoyed it and I'd gladly do it again.

He doesn't need to know that I'm currently vulnerable to their power.

"You tell her *why* you're immune to her power?"

"No."

Zale grunts. "You said you'd come clean. When she came back."

"Yeah, well…" *Fuck*, he's right. I've discussed Astrid with him plenty during our correspondence over the past few months. At least *he* got my letters, and they weren't intercepted by someone else. The last thing I need is someone else reading the words I wrote to my brother about the woman I crave. "She *just* came back."

"She doesn't know a single thing, does she? About Father? Ayana? Your tattoo?" Zale steps forward and pokes me in the chest. "When are you going to change? Stop acting like an immature little boy and own up to your shit."

Boy.

That's the same thing Lex calls me when he's being derogatory. Hearing my own brother call me that stings sharper.

"It's not like that.

"It *is* like that, and you need to hear it."

"I just don't want—"

"I get it. You're afraid of telling her the truth and hurting her. You're afraid she'll leave. Based on what I know of the girl, she'll leave you for pleasant lies quicker than she will for harsh truths."

I grip the back of my neck. "You're right."

He points to the tattoo on my bicep. "You tell her about that yet? How the ink works?"

I bristle. "Soon."

He sighs.

How do I tell her about the reason for getting that tattoo? The full truth behind Ayana's death? I never meant for these lies to grow so large, become so tangled. They were meant to protect Astrid's feelings. And perhaps even protect myself from losing her.

"I can't lose her," I whisper.

"She's smart, Dash. Tell her before she figures it out herself."

My head spins. I hate that Astrid is caught up in this mess. I love her—I do. If she ever finds out, it will cause her pain she doesn't deserve. Which is why I need to tell her myself.

I clench my teeth. "Can we focus on the more pressing issue? Perhaps forget about Astrid…and Lexyll for a while?" I say that, but we both know it's impossible for me to actually do so. "Let's confirm that it *was* Cedrik who swayed me here, for Mother."

Something doesn't sit right with me about the situation. Even if he had good intentions, he stole the king's parchment and forged his signature and seal. That's a highly punishable offense. Some might even view it as treason.

Why would he risk that? Behind Zale's back?

"I am inclined to agree." He tugs on his collar and clears his throat. "And if it was not Cedrik—"

"Whoever did this will pay, brother. I promise you that. Their intentions be damned."

The irony isn't lost on me. My intentions toward Astrid might be pure, but the longer I wait to tell her everything, the more I will hurt her.

Intentions, I'm starting to learn, don't matter nearly as much as actions—and the subsequent perceptions of those actions.

CHAPTER TWENTY-EIGHT

ASTRID

When I wake around midday, I'm oddly refreshed despite spending the night in an unfamiliar place. I had one nightmare, but I only vaguely remember it. Mainly, I dreamt of Lex—heard his voice in my dreams. Maybe sleeping somewhere new was actually good for me, after all.

The room I'm staying in is gorgeous. Situated on the second floor, it boasts an incredible, oversized balcony that overlooks a large pond. It gives me a good view of the city center in the distance. The blue and gold accented furnishings are tasteful yet luxurious. It's refreshingly different than the bland palace I spent the last seventeen years in.

I dress in my favorite billowy pants and take a moment to step onto the balcony and gaze out at the city.

At first glance, Cerulea is pale and sandy. It's a conglomerate of rectangles and jutting angles. But yesterday, when we navigated through the streets and alleyways, it came to life in a whirlwind of color, spices, and cheer—even in the wake of King Emman's death and even with the country on the brink of war.

The not-so-distant waters are as blue as Hakran's, but the sprawling white-sand beaches are free of jungle and rocks. It's also way busier than any place I've seen before. Hordes of people bustle around the city center, even at this hour, with the sun itself barely awake. They move about like ants.

My heart aches for the brothers, for Joccelyn. Emman was nothing but kind to me when I met him. I want to be there for Dash, to offer him support, but I'm sure he will be kept busy while we're here.

Zale wasn't available to greet us last night when we arrived, so surely Lex and Dash will need to meet with him and his advisors to discuss war tactics today.

That's something I have little interest in enduring.

Instead, I head straight to Ilona's room. She's up when I arrive, already devouring a cup of tea.

Peering into her cup, I take a whiff. It's not lemon, ginger, or honey. None of her usuals.

She laughs. "Chai."

"Is it good?"

"It's black tea." She crinkles her nose. "Stronger than what I'm used to."

"Smells like it." She offers the mug to me, so I take a quick sip. Hints of cinnamon and cardamom wash over my tongue, leaving a slightly spicy, bitter aftertaste. "Wait—this is actually delightful."

Her eyes pop open, and she waves a hand at me. "By all means, finish it. It's all yours."

I thank her and wrap my hands around the mug, finishing the tea off as she dresses. Luckily the weather here is similar to that of Hakran, even in the almost-winter season.

"Have you had any more strange dreams?"

"Not really," she says, shrugging. She refuses to meet my eye, turning away from me fully.

I suppose she's still not ready to discuss it with me. My shoulders slump at the thought that I might have alienated her.

"Will you let me know if you have any? Even if you think they're small or silly? I promise not to laugh or tease or roll my eyes."

She turns toward me with a forced smile. "Of course."

I laughed at her the first time she shared her dreams with me and tried to warn me of impending danger, but I'm learning to listen. Her dreams seem important. Twice now, she's dreamt of events before they happened. Oddly, both dreams were about Enira.

"Maybe it was a weird side effect of Enira's manipulation?" I prod.

"Maybe."

It's clear neither of us truly believes that. If it were anyone else claiming to see the future in their dreams, I would never believe them, but Ilona is one of the few people I trust with my life. She would never fib about such a thing.

I take a deep breath, hesitant to bring up a sore subject between us. "Do you remember *anything* about your mother or father?"

She glances at her bare feet, toeing the area rug, then shakes her head.

"Too bad." I hate that her answer brings me a semblance of relief. "Maybe they were seers? Etheryn?"

"I don't think so. I don't have any magic. Just weird dreams."

"Dreams that come true... Seems like magic to me."

Her lips form a tight line, which is unusual for the normally talkative woman, so I let it go. If anyone knows what it's like to have an identity crisis, it's me. She probably doesn't know what to make of it.

"Come on," I tell her. "Lex and Dash are busy today. Let's

go visit the library."

Hopefully they end this conflict with Vespyn quickly so I can visit my cottage. Otherwise, Ilona and I will keep ourselves busy with books.

At that, she gives me a wide, toothy grin. "Deal, but I'm reading about the gods."

As much as I'd like to investigate the type of romance novels the Stellari folk like, Ilona's plan sounds better. Maybe it's time I learn more about my origins.

According to the palace bookkeeper, the library to see is located in the heart of Cerulea.

She informs us of Stellaris's "shared knowledge" policy—how their culture believes in making education and information accessible to all. Copies of the best reading material are kept public at Mirage Bibliotheca.

We waste no time exiting the palace and making our way into the city.

A few guards see us, and they smile and wave as we pass. Although the clothing and culture of Stellaris and Hakran are similar, the attitudes of the people are quite different. Emman and Joccelyn were both warm toward me, and the workers and citizens appear friendly too.

I grip Ilona's hand and pull her along, moving quickly out of the palace's sight.

Lex knows I have zero interest in politics or planning wars. Once they take action, I'll join in. But for now, if he needs me, we have the celestite necklaces. All he has to do is rub his stone, and mine will heat in response, alerting me to his need.

After traversing the winding alleys and squeezing through the bustling bodies, Ilona and I find the massive library. I fan myself, sticky and sweaty from the dry heat. The sun is scalding, but at least the air isn't humid.

Outside, the library stands like a grand cathedral—all pillars and carved edges. Inside, it has soaring ceilings and skylights, mosaic art on the floor, and endless rows of mahogany shelves reaching up so high that rolling ladders are required to reach the tops. It's awe-inspiring.

"Oh my goddess!" Ilona squeals. A few heads turn her way, and I bump her with my elbow. When she looks at me, I bring a finger to my lips and mouth, "Shush."

"Sorry," she mouths back.

It's quiet, save for a few hushed whispers, an occasional throat clearing, and the comforting sound of pages carving the air. Dozens of readers are spread out around the room.

Ilona grabs my hand and pulls me toward a mahogany counter in the center of the room, where an older woman greets us warmly.

"Welcome to Mirage Bibliotheca," she whispers. "How may I assist you ladies today?" Her keen eyes narrow curiously, roaming over us. In our Hakranian clothing—loose black pants and a crop top for me and a forest-green dress for Ilona—we're not dressed too differently from the natives. Many patrons are wearing similar billowy pants and flowing dresses. But where ours are plain and simple, theirs are filled with patterns and designs and colors.

I realize my mistake was wearing all black during a time of mourning.

My cheeks flush, and I mentally apologize for the unintentional disrespect. When we return to the palace, I'll have to see if Dash has a bright scarf or shawl I can borrow.

"Hi," Ilona says. "Can you please direct us to your section on goddesses?"

"Sama?" She smiles wider. "Of course."

"Yes. And her lesser gods and goddesses, please."

"Oh?" The librarian's face melts into a frown before she catches herself and slips on a forced smile. "That section doesn't get much action these days. Follow me."

Ilona and I share a perplexed look, but we follow the woman as she takes us through the back of the library. After pushing open a door that leads to a dark, narrow staircase, she flicks a switch. The large room at the bottom of the stairs is illuminated by evenly spaced fire orbs.

"Right down here," she says.

Ilona raises her brows. "Weird," she mouths.

"Why do you keep your books on gods in a *dungeon*?" I ask, peering down the stairs. After my experience with the pit, I'm hesitant to trust anyone leading me down a stone staircase.

The woman barks a laugh. "It's not a dungeon, dear. It's storage. Ever since the incident at the palace, we don't get many requests for these types of reads, so they've been bumped from the shelves."

"Disrespectful to the original goddess and her creations, no?" I ask.

"Hear me," the librarian says, her smile melting away. "It's clear you're not from around here, but we do not take kindly to god sympathizers." I swear my heart stops beating for a second. The librarian's smile returns, but this time it's forced. "You dears seem nice, so I will give you a piece of advice: you'll be wise to keep this chatter to yourself. Certain parts won't tolerate that kind of talk. Best case, you run into someone who ignores you.

Worst case? You run into someone who still believes."

My nose scrunches. "Why would it be bad to run into someone who is devout?"

She shakes her head. "I never said they were devout. I said *someone who still believes*. There's a difference. Those around here who still believe in the gods and goddesses hunt them out of fear and hatred."

Hunt them.

Blood pounds in my head. I swipe my clammy hands on my pants. I'm too stunned to speak. Why would Dash not tell me that his home city—maybe even his entire country—loathes my very being? This is not something you simply forget to mention.

"Thanks for the information," Ilona says when I don't reply. "We're just doing research though. *Not* worshiping the—"

"What do you mean, 'incident at the palace'?" I ask.

The librarian sighs, sorrow overtaking her features.

"We don't talk much about it." She glances around and beckons us closer. "The late King Emman—may he rest with Sama—denounced the lessers and banned all worship, save for Sama."

My brow furrows. Yes, this is definitely something Dash should've mentioned. "Why? What happened?"

"It's only a rumor, one I cannot verify, but they say there was a young woman close to the royal family. She had a secret relationship with a god. A powerful vygora, capable of influencing emotion." Ilona and I share a glance. "He could influence emotion—make people *feel* a certain way. Rumor says he made the woman fall in love with him, that he toyed with her emotions, eventually driving her to death by suicide."

Ilona sucks in a sharp breath. "She must've been important to King Emman—if it propelled him into such rage."

The woman stares past us, deep in thought. "It was his poor son's fiancée."

"Zale?" I never knew he was engaged. "Sorry—*King* Zale?" I amend, not wanting to disrespect anyone further.

The librarian's eyes lock onto mine. "The spare heir. The captain."

"Dash," I whisper, my heartbeat crashing in my ears. The lady continues to speak, but I can't hear anything over the roaring sound of disbelief.

Ayana.

She's talking about Ayana.

A shudder runs through my body.

They were *engaged*?

She died because of a god she was two-timing Dash with? And Dash's father had a personal vendetta against gods all this time?

The shock is layered, soul-crushingly deep. None of it makes sense, knowing the version of Dash I know. Yet, somehow, it *all* makes sense. In between the shock and betrayal lingers a deep sympathy for Dash. It shatters my heart.

Was anything Dash and I had between us real? If it *was* real, best case scenario, it must've destroyed him to see me lose myself to my own vygora magic before running away.

Worst case scenario… I don't want to imagine that right now. My power pulses beneath my skin, heightened after power-sharing with Lex on the ship. It pushes and pulls at me, begging to be released.

If he lied to get Lex and me here—

"*Fuuuuuck.*" I groan, unable to focus on anything.

"Are you all right, dearie?" Concern mars the woman's face as she pulls me back to the moment. "That's quite a tongue for such an otherwise lovely—"

"She's fine. Forgive her," Ilona says. She grabs my arm, pulling me down the stairs. "Thank you for your help."

The woman calls after us, "Cerulea is a very safe, very kind city. We accept all who enter our borders. Just keep that chatter to a minimum and you'll be safe."

Ilona and I scamper down the stairs into the storage area. It's fairly clean and well-lit. A wooden table sits in the center of the room. Books are stored along the stone walls, encased in protective glass bookshelves.

I stare at the shelves for a long moment, not knowing what to say.

"Holy sugar," Ilona says. "That was—I guess they don't like you, A." She snorts.

I frown at her, not finding the situation nearly as humorous. "Why would Dash bring Lex and me here, knowing we could potentially be in danger? Why would he keep this from me?"

"He wouldn't," she says confidently. "Maybe that lady was confused. Or maybe she's telling stories. That's sort of her profession—dealing with stories." She gestures toward the books. "Maybe she likes to scare foreigners?"

"I don't know, Lonnie." My stomach twists itself into knots, and I have a bad feeling in my gut. "I need to find Dash."

"We're already here. Let's just check out some of these books and head back to the palace."

I don't want to wait to talk to him. But my notorious impulsivity tends to make things worse. "Okay." I nod my head, reluctant to agree. "Only because I don't know how to feel, and I don't want to explode on him."

She frowns. "I thought your connection to him was broken. Aren't your emotions fixed?"

"Yes, but—" How do I explain that I still don't trust myself or my decision making? My magic, on its own, is dangerous. With Lex's power coursing through me, I'm stronger. Deadlier.

The last thing I would want is for something to happen because I lost control of my emotions.

We start gathering books, eager for more insights on the gods.

After sifting through the shelves for over an hour, I'm still distracted and perplexed by the conversation with the librarian. I can't get it out of my head.

"Dash is the one who told me that all people with magic are descendants of the gods. He knew about the magic in Paramour Falls. He knew about Davvinia and Anwyr," I say, referencing the goddess and her mortal lover who are associated with the Fall's lore. "He said they were his ancestors."

"He also butchered that lore, according to Lex," she says.

"But I don't think it was intentional. He learned most of his stories from his birth parents, before the Vannyks adopted him."

"How did his parents die?" she asks. "Not that it matters."

I actually don't know how Dash's parents died. I chew my lip, embarrassed that I never asked. "Aren't you the one close with him and Fatima now?" They've spent months together, with her working as his advisor.

"Yes, but we don't talk about painful topics...or deep things. It's mostly been about Hakran."

Same for Dash and me. Does he ever let anyone in?

Except that...he has. He's tried, many times, to discuss his past, and I've been the one to shut it down.

"And nothing weird has ever come up in your dreams?"

She bites her lip. "Not that I can remember. I also write Zale often. I don't think there's anything nefarious going on with them. I really, really don't think we have anything to worry about. I know Dash is...a lot, but he, Fatima, and Zale are good people. I believe he cares for you, A."

I nod, but I'm still unsettled.

Unlike Hakran's library, which houses mostly books of lore and myth, Mirage Bibliotheca has copies of original religious texts.

"Look at this," Ilona says. She shows me a brick of a book called *Story of The Mother.* She has it open to a page midway through the book. "It says: *Sama and Osiris watched over the humans from the heavens, using their power sparingly, only interfering when humans faced events of extinction.*" She stops reading and scans further down the page. "Oh! Here—*Sama grew lonely, sick of sitting in the clouds with nothing but magic to keep her company. Osiris's companionship grew old quickly, as the two disagreed on boundaries with the humans. In an attempt to placate Osiris and curb her lonely heart, Sama sacrificed much of her power to create the lesser gods and goddesses. Her magic was scattered into thousands of human-like creations, her deities. She divvied her power up, careful to give them specific roles with relevant magic, to prevent them from facing boredom. She gave them human-like forms so they could roam the realms discreetly. Finally, she paired them off, giving each one a sibling so they would never be as lonely as she.*"

"Who the fuck is Osiris?" I ask, perplexed.

She shrugs. "I've heard of him before. In a book of lore back in Hakran. Something about the Amoral, the fallen deity..." She bites her lip. "Do you think this is true?"

"I don't know, but it makes more sense the more I learn." It matches the bits and pieces I've heard about the original goddess and her creations. I lean in, rereading the passage she read aloud. "This would mean Lex has a sibling. And Enira. I wonder what they're like."

"Or if they're still alive."

"Or if they're dangerous." My heart squeezes at the thought of Invidia. If she truly wanted to harm me—like Lex said that night on the ship—then there's no guarantee that any of the other sibling pairs are inherently close.

We glance at the pages, skimming over some of the religious text. "This is interesting," I say, pointing to a paragraph.

Ilona begins reading. "*Osiris abhorred Sama's creations. His ego prevented him from seeing the new deities in the same light as Sama. He professed only the two of them were worthy of power, claiming the new gods and goddesses were imposters. Over the years, he grew increasingly volatile, threatening humanity instead of protecting them. Sama fought against Osiris, clashing in the skies. Their violence brought destruction to the earth in the form of earthquakes and storms. But with much of her power poured into her creations, she was growing weaker.*" Ilona pauses. "*As the gods began to procreate with humans and the magic began to multiply and spread, passed down through bloodlines, creating demigods, Osiris grew irate. The humans—equipped with their own magic—began to ignore the gods, calling on them less and less. Worse, he and Sama were no longer acknowledged. No longer worshiped. He jumped from the clouds and fell to earth, with the intention of earning back his adoration through force. He began slaughtering the humans with magic, starting with the etheryns, as they posed the biggest threat.*"

She pauses. "It doesn't say much more about etheryn magic here; we'll have to look that up separately."

I barely register her words, caught up on the term *demigods*—the humans with magic, like Dash, Zale, Cedrik…

"Keep reading," I say breathlessly. I need to know what happened next. What happened to Osiris, the humans. The bit about etheryns can wait.

"Okay." She clears her throat and takes a sip of water from the pouch at her hip. "*Osiris strived to eliminate all those with magic, humans and lesser gods alike, so only he and Sama would be worshiped once again. Sama could not stand by and let Osiris's corrupted ego ruin the realm, end humanity; she could not let him murder her children. As many were massacred, their magic did not simply disappear. Instead, it was recycled into the earth. Sama drew on this recycled magic, dredging it up from where it had settled on the seafloor, using it to curse Osiris, banishing him to the Underworld where he would pose no threat. She died with the effort, her last remnants of magic sinking back into the seas.*"

"Holy shit." I exhale heavily and lean back in my chair. My hands rest on my head as I try to absorb everything. "The wild magic—the storms in Hakran—it truly is recycled magic."

"That explains what I read about Osiris being a fallen god. He literally fell from the heavens to the earth."

"Yeah, to murder everyone."

"At least he's in the Underworld. Wherever the hell that is. I've read many things on etheryn portals to various realms—places where different types of beings live. Sort of like mirror worlds. Similar but different. We should ask Callan about his realm and how he travels among different realms."

"He has wings. Maybe that's how?"

"I don't think you can *fly* to another realm."

"Never say never," I mutter. I glance back at the worn pages of the book. "This also explains why etheryns are thought to be extinct—they truly were massacred." By Osiris. My heart aches for all the people murdered, simply for being born with magic flowing through their veins.

I shudder. "Being a goddess is fucking exhausting. Why does

it seem like everyone wants to kill me all of a sudden?"

Ilona laughs. "No one wants to kill you. Even if they did, you're too tough for them."

"You know, I went months without using my power. It felt... unnatural." I don't tell her that sometimes my blood feels as if it's boiling beneath my skin, like my vygora magic is begging to be used. That I work twice as hard now to keep my emotions in check, and it only irritates my magic.

"Okay, I can't wait anymore." I start putting the books back. "I need to talk to Dash."

When Dash first betrayed me, I was devastated. Crushed. Even after understanding his intentions were good. For some reason, as upset as I am at these new revelations, part of me isn't surprised. Dash and I barely know each other, and we've had practically no time to discuss our lives. We moved too quickly, our expectations for one another rising past our reality. On top of that, his moral compass tends to point him in the wrong direction. He has a pure heart with flawed logic.

There's a chance—and goddess, I hope it's true—that he had a good reason for keeping this from me.

This time, no matter the truth I face, I'm not running.

CHAPTER TWENTY-NINE

LEX

My fingers bounce on my thigh as I count to ten in my head. When I'm sure my face is neutral and my rage is carefully tucked away, I barge into the room.

"Occupied!" A gruff voice calls out from behind a door on the other side of the chamber.

I burst through that one too.

"What in the—" Cedrik looks up at me from the toilet, his pants around his ankles, shock marring his features. "Can't a man defecate in peace?"

"You lied about the war," I growl. "Why?"

"What—I have no idea what you're talking about." He curls in on himself, embarrassed by the situation. "Please. Let me finish, and we can talk."

I grip his wispy hair, yanking his head back. He screeches, and his wrinkled face contorts in alarm. "Do you have any idea what you've done?"

Before I sent Callan to keep an eye on Aife, who apparently thought it wise to go on an excursion, he listened in on Dashiel and Zale's conversation. He informed me of every sordid detail. And although I have many bones to pick with the boy, we will have plenty of opportunity to *chat* later.

I'll find him soon enough. I needed to first locate the healer—ensure he was on the grounds. Had he never forged the letter and lied about the Vespyn threat, we would not have rushed to come to Stellaris's aid. Dashiel would have never bound me to him.

And you and Aife might never have been this close. I curse the little voice of reason, centering my controlled fury on Cedrik.

"Please—please." He starts to cry, tears streaming down his face.

Based on Callan's information, the brothers aren't positive it was Cedrik who sent the letters, but there's no one else who has access to the king's stationery other than his mother, and she's been in and out of a grief coma. Even *if* it wasn't the healer, I feel no remorse. Something about him turns my gut sour.

"Why," I repeat, drawing out my words, "did you lie about the war? Why did you call upon Dashiel?"

"I have no idea what you're on about! I swear."

I use the underrated aspect of my power to get a read on his emotions. It's terror—pure and simple. No remorse, regret, or concern. Only terror. As much as I don't trust him, my instinct tells me he's being honest about this.

"Nevertheless, there's another conversation we need to have, healer," I growl. Gas rips from him, echoing in the toilet, and I step back, disgusted. "We'll save it for later."

I'll be paying him a visit about Enira once I sort out this mess.

If there's no threat to Stellaris, there's no oath binding me to Dashiel. I'm done here, done with him. Vespyn is perfectly safe, and I can take Aife to her cottage.

"*Dargan!*" I find Dashiel exactly where Callan said he was:

in the council chamber.

His brother, a lean man with stylish clothing and flawlessly styled hair, steps forward. I recognize him from the pit.

King Zale.

"Hello," I say sardonically. "Pretend I've bowed and given you my respects. Let's skip ahead to the meat of things." I glance past Zale at Dashiel, whose face has gone pale.

"How did you get past—" Zale trails off when he peeks out the door to see his guards sprawled out on the floor. Instead of unleashing his anger at me, he turns to his brother. "Not attention-drawing?"

Dashiel scratches the scruff on his chin. "I said not attention-*seeking*."

Zale smoothes a hand down his shirt and sash. He shakes his head in disappointment.

Any other day, I'd smirk at the hilarity of the boy being shunned by his own brother. But today, I'm a bit ticked off.

"There's no war," I say. "No war means no oath. Answer me with honesty, and I might let you live. Don't tempt me, boy."

The king of Stellaris sighs and pulls out a chair. "Might as well sit." He gestures toward the table.

I oblige—not out of obedience but to unsettle them with my outward indifference toward the situation.

Dashiel slumps into a chair in front of me, with his brother to our left at the head of the table. "There is no war," he admits. "The letter—"

"Was forged. Yes. I know as much as you."

"Unless you also know *who* wrote that letter to get me here, there's still a potential threat to my family. That means you still need to assist me."

"No *war*. No assistance."

Dash smirks and leans back. "We never agreed on your help for a *war* against Stellaris. We agreed on your help for the *threat* against my family. Someone stole the king's seal to lure us here. It was a setup, and as far as I'm concerned, whoever did it is a threat to my family until proven otherwise."

Fucking specifics.

He's right.

Until we know who forged the letter and why, I'm bound to help him.

I ignore him, getting to the unanswered question plaguing me. "Vygora power doesn't affect you. Why?"

Dashiel glances at Zale, then back at me. "I'm excusing myself," Zale says, standing. "I've an expansive list of tasks to attend to, unfortunately." He cocks a brow at me as he passes. "If you lay a finger on my brother, I'll have you hanged for treason."

Resting my hands on the table, I steeple my fingers. "And here I was thinking we were in an alliance against your idiot brother."

"Family always comes first." He narrows his eyes at me and exits the room.

Zale seems to be a formidable man with a self-assured air to him. It's a shame Aife fell for the messy brother. Perhaps I'd hate him all the same if he were the one who caught her eye instead.

"Speak," I command.

Dashiel scrubs a hand over his face. "It was never meant to be a secret from Astrid."

"I'm not asking about *Aife*." But we both know that's a lie. Of course she's the reason we're having this conversation.

As if he's drawn the same conclusion, he takes a deep breath and dumps it all on me. "How do I tell the woman I love, a goddess, that my father's late life mission was to hunt gods? That it was because of another god with vygora power that my first love died? It's all connected, Lex—the catalyst being the god who manipulated Ayana's feelings, leading her to suicide. It was what spurred Emman into action, causing him to publicly denounce all gods save for Sama, the original goddess."

Suddenly, it's much too warm in the room. My skin prickles. Even without using my power to draw his emotions out, I know he's not lying. There's a lot to unpack in his admission, but for a brief moment, all thoughts of Aife, or Dashiel, or Stellaris's false war fall to the wayside.

This god he speaks of, with the power of manipulation as he described... No. It can't be.

He's *dead*. Been dead a long time.

I lean forward, my voice barely above a whisper. "Are you certain it was a god she was involved with?"

"Ayana never spoke of him...but there were rumors among the palace staff. A few who recognized his power. He bragged about it, allegedly. I never knew she was—" His voice cracked. "She was *not* seeing him behind my back. She would never. It had to have been a god, someone with the power to deceive her. She loved me, Lex."

He looks up at me, his face contorted with pain, and there's no animosity in his expression. No hatred toward me—another god with vygora powers—despite what he's gone through.

I curse under my breath. Unfortunately, this bit of information cracks open my cold heart, and out trickles empathy for Dashiel.

The bit about his father hunting the gods worries me little. "It's ironic your family wants the gods dead when it seems humans cause as much drama, if not *more,* than the gods. I clean up wars after humans—not gods. I help humans with their conflicts—not gods." I press my lips into a thin line.

He has the decency to avert his eyes in embarrassment. I'm slightly taken aback when he says, "I know. You're right."

The gods and goddesses have been ostracized, hunted, ridiculed for decades. It has little bearing on me. And clearly, Dashiel does not follow in his father's footsteps. The boy has been consumed by running Hakran and helping me search for Aife's missing memories. I imagine that is not something he'd do if he felt the way his late father did about the gods.

It's rather pathetic, almost heartbreaking, actually. What the hell does he do for *fun*? For himself?

I clear my throat. "I'm sorry for your loss." And I mean it.

"Thank you." He nods curtly. "I don't agree with my father's mission. Not after meeting Astrid...and *you*, I guess. But if I could seek vengeance for Ayana, I would."

If the god who drove her to suicide was who I think it is—despite the impossibility of his death—more ironic words have never been spoken.

The air in the room grows thick; guilt weighs me down. I quickly keep the conversation moving forward. "How exactly are you immune to vygora power?"

Dash's hand mindlessly hovers over his bicep.

My jaw slackens. His tattoo. Of course. Only a special kind of etheryn can infuse magic into ink. "Etherink," I mutter, rubbing my forehead.

His eyes widen. "You've heard of it?" He chuckles, running a hand through his hair. "Of course you have. You're old as shit. You've been around for like a million years."

If Aife were here, she'd roll her eyes so hard at that.

"Yes," I confirm. "I've heard of it." Etherink can be infused with all sorts of spells—protective, anti-aging, appearance-altering, and many more. The ink is incredibly rare, and the price is sky-high. We were lucky to find someone to do Sora's tattoo—the one keeping him permanently young, despite his humanity. "Where exactly did you find your artist?"

"North, in Korchek," he admits. "I snuck across the border on a rumor and found her." He gives me a sheepish look. "She runs a regular tattoo shop as a front. It's called—"

"Cloak and Dagger," we both say at the same time.

He cocks his head, and I scowl. "It explains why Aife only got mind-reading capabilities when you..." I clear my throat. "When you..."

He smirks when I can't get the words out. "Kissed under the falls?" I clench my jaw. "I'm surprised you're being so understanding about this. I thought you'd surely try and murder me."

"Murder is exhausting, and I'm old," I deadpan.

"Are you sure you're not growing soft?" he teases. "Maybe you and I should kiss under the falls too, so you won't feel left out."

"I'd rather kiss bull testicles."

At this, he breaks out into full-blown laughter. "That was funny. You're actually funny." He shakes his head, his eyes crinkling at the corners. "You know, you're really not as bad as I thought. No wonder Aife is partial to you." Then he grows serious. "I'll be gone one day. Dead. It's my fate as a human. Your fate is the goddess of death, but mine is death itself. It's the only promise life ever makes. The years of my life will pass like only seconds of yours, and you two will be together. Alone. Again. Man to man, I ask you to spare a few of your seconds for me. Let me bring her joy and love. *You* will be the one to comfort her when I'm long gone."

For the second time during this meeting, Dashiel catches me off guard. There's genuine respect in his voice, and for the first time, he's acknowledging me as Aife's fated—her destiny. Stripped of his cocky attitude and awful sense of humor, he comes across as honorable.

I cock my head, waiting for a quip or barb.

Instead, he says, "Have you ever thought about letting Astrid just be herself—love without boundary and without pressure?"

Yes.

She's alive. She's freed from Enira. It's more than I ever wished for when I slept on the pit's cold floor.

Dashiel could offer extra protection and love for her. I can't always be with her or watch her—not that she needs or wants that—but at least with the two of us, she will always have someone around to look out for her.

She's emotional, irrational, and impulsive, and she certainly has a big enough personality to handle two men.

I give a sharp nod. "If Aife truly cares for you, it will be impossible for her to let you go." Like Dash, she's lost her family. She's lost everything.

"For what it's worth, I'm sorry for falling in love with your fated. It wasn't intentional. I didn't think I'd fall for her. I thought we would just fuck a few times and—"

"*Dargan.*" I glower at him.

"Sorry. Sorry." He holds his hands up, grinning nervously. "If it's any consolation, before the ship, we only fucked once, and—"

"You need to learn when to keep your mouth shut."

"Mouths are more fun when they're open." He winks at me.

"Grant me strength," I mutter. Sighing dramatically, I pinch the bridge of my nose. "I still don't like you, Dashiel. But you keep her safe. You protect her. You do right by her, and we won't have any problems."

A smile lights up his face. "Yeah?"

"We'll see if she even wants anything to do with you when she hears all the bullshit you've kept to yourself."

"I'll worry about that. I've won her over twice now. I'll do it again."

"Playing with your luck there, boy," I warn. But I know Aife's heart is far too forgiving for her to turn her back on someone she's let in. "You're on your own. Don't expect me to actively try to assist your...*relationship*."

"It's *our* relationship now." He winks again.

I clench my teeth together, wondering why the hell I agreed to this.

It wasn't only my desire to please Aife that swayed me. It was also the story of how Dash's first love died. The god who influenced her emotions seems all too familiar, and it puts me on edge. Much to my dismay, it makes me empathize with him.

CHAPTER THIRTY

ASTRID

When Ilona and I return to the palace from our visit to the library, Dash and Lex are nowhere to be found.

We run into Zale, however, which surprises me, considering the recent threats to the city. I'd expect him to have more guards around him, or for him to be with Dash and Lex. After a particularly vague exchange of platitudes, I'm left feeling uninterested in more conversation with him. The guy is a walking, talking biscuit—dry, tasteless, and disappointing. When I ask him how the war stuff is going, he doesn't reply but merely gives me a weird look and asks Ilona to join him in the gardens. Ilona seems particularly excited to see him though, so I leave them to it.

Exhausted from exploring Cerulea and the library, I head up to my room. Callan appears out of nowhere as I approach my door, and I give a start.

"You were following me, weren't you?" Fucking invisibility.

A smile and lazy shrug is the only response I get. He pulls an apple out of his pocket and takes a juicy bite. "Off to bed so early?"

On cue, a yawn escapes me. "If you're going to be creepy and spy on me, at least do me a favor and stay out of my room while I'm sleeping." At least I have the comfort of knowing he can't walk through walls.

He agrees, chuckling as I slam the door behind me. My irritation, however, is not toward him. It's toward Dash and today's new information. I'm itching to hunt him down and interrogate him, but I don't have the energy to go raging around the enormous palace searching for him.

There's a chance I might lose myself—lose control of the magic squirming beneath my skin, begging to be released—if I see him. Though I've decided not to run away from my problems again, I *have* decided that spending time on my own to cool down will serve me well. Perhaps it's best I rest in my room tonight, to let the shock subside, and then I can find him tomorrow when I'm more levelheaded.

Luxurious sheets wrap their arms around me as I sink into the plush bed. With a sigh, I stare at the ceiling overhead, barely able to make out the intricate, hand-painted mural in the dim light. The palace bleeds art, and it's phenomenal. Eventually, I flick off the fire orb beside my bed and submerge myself fully in darkness.

Only, tonight, sleep doesn't come.

The blue cottage flits into my mind, followed by my memory of Lex and Invidia. Despite Lex's harsh admission of murdering my sister, the more time I spend with him, the more positive I am that there's another layer to the story. When I first arrived at Nevaris as Astrid, Fara mentioned that Lex's *guests* normally arrived in chains or without heads.

A fact I found disturbing.

I've experienced the depth of his power firsthand, but he isn't a savage by any stretch of the imagination. I've come to realize he relies on his reputation to intimidate others, likely so he doesn't have to get his hands dirty. Though it seems like he certainly would if he needed to.

The god of war is nothing but a big fucking softy with an adopted family of misfits, a lethal scowl, and a drinking problem.

All bark and...a bite only when provoked.

And Dash...goddess help me with him. I'm trying my damndest to stay positive, but this man has tangled me so deeply in his web of bullshit without ever offering me a picture of the full truth. He's not all to blame though. Perhaps if I hadn't run and had faced him, he would've fessed up. I'll give him one chance, and one chance only, to come clean about everything before I decide how I feel about him.

Not that I get to *choose* who my heart grows fond of.

For all his faults, he has a lot to offer. His proximity puts me at ease. His jokes and smiles lighten the shadows in my mind.

With Lex, I dive deep into the depths of my soul. With Dash, I splash in the shallow end. But they balance out one another. Lex challenges me to go deeper when I need *more*, and Dash pulls me back to the shore before I drown.

The edges of my love for them have melted together, merging into something beautiful and inexplicable.

I pray to the original goddess that my heart does not lead me astray.

After ruminating for a while, I decide to go find Cedrik and procure a sleeping draught. The last thing I need is to get riled up by my chaotic emotions.

I've been waiting until Lex and Dash are ready to accost Cedrik about Enira, but I'm a big girl. I can handle an old healer myself.

I'm not sure where exactly his clinic is located, but I've no doubt I can ask a guard or servant where to find it.

Sure enough, I run into a servant in the corridor outside my room, and he offers to take me there. He yawns the whole time, giving me curious looks when he thinks I'm not looking. Neither of us bother to make conversation.

We end up in the far-north wing of the palace—on the complete opposite side from where my temporary room is. The end of the hallway has no doors, just an archway that opens up into a large room. The aroma of dried eucalyptus and lavender greets my nose, reminding me of Cedrik's chamber back at Hakran.

His clinic here is much larger than anything back on the island—it's an entire infirmary. The space is gigantic, with rows of beds separated by white curtains. I pass a nursemaid, who smiles at me as she rocks a baby, and walk past a few cots with sleeping forms in them until I reach the back wall, where rows of drying herbs hang.

"He's normally in here at this time." The sleepy servant gestures to the single door in the wall of herbs and gives me one last nosey glance.

"Thanks," I say. When he doesn't move, I give him an awkward wave. "Good night."

He retreats, and I turn to the door, giving it a couple of quick knocks.

When no one answers, I knock again. After a minute passes, I try the handle. It's unlocked, so I push the door open and peek inside. A couple of candles flicker around the room, filling the space with a soft light, but Cedrik is nowhere to be found.

The walls are filled with shelves of potions, tonics, and salves—more than I've ever seen before. No wonder he was so quick to return to Stellaris with the Vannyks. The resources here must be a dream.

After years of using it on and off, I know exactly what the sleeping draught looks like. It's a light brown liquid and can normally be found in a slender vial with a dropper. I draw near to the shelves, scanning the hundreds of apothecary jars and herbal mixes. Finally, I spot what I'm looking for up on a higher shelf.

Reaching up, I stand on my tiptoes and stretch for the tube. In the process, my hip bumps a table beside me, sending a glass jar tumbling to the ground. It shatters, splashing dark liquid on my feet.

"Dammit!" I curse.

Suddenly, a painful stabbing resonates through my skull. I screech, falling to my knees beside the mess of broken glass.

Just like when I killed Enira, a memory comes rushing back.

Nevaris is dark; moonlight glimmers off the lake like glass. I scurry to my apartment, frantic about what I just witnessed.

Lex killing Invidia.

Someone grabs my shoulders, jerking me backward against their body. Breasts press into my back, and an unusual citrusy, floral scent wafts into my nose.

"You will not use your vygora powers on me," a sharp voice whispers in my ear as something cold is pressed against my throat. "You will not fight me. You will not move."

Immediately attuned to the threat, I ignore the demand and try to pull the woman's life force out.

Except, something stops me.

Myndox power.

I...don't want to pull her life force out. I can't.

After witnessing Lex murder my sister, I apparently went into shock and left my mental barriers down.

This woman must be the myndox who can alter free will. The one tormenting Nevaris. The one Lex has been searching for. I never saw the sketches Sora made of her, but I don't need to in order to know it's her. I can feel it in my bones. Her power is too great for any old myndox. She's bending a goddess to her will right now, so she must be a goddess herself.

Only someone with tremendous power could cast a net of magic this wide, inhibiting the majority of villagers, challenging other gods.

"You are a lot shorter than I had expected." Her breath smells sour. "Curvier, but shorter. I do see your sister in you though."

"Who are you?" I whisper. My skin prickles. I'm horrified at having been caught off guard, and for a moment I wonder if Lex is a traitor. If he is the one working with this woman. Is this a setup? Perhaps he let her into Nevaris and they've been working together, and that's why we've not found any true leads. Or maybe she got beneath his barriers and influenced him to kill my sister. Maybe he's working against his own will?

Except that is utterly impossible. Lex is the strongest person I've ever met, mentally and physically. He has mastered his barriers. He never lets them down, not even for a second. He would never make the same mistake I just did—allow his emotions to weaken him.

He would never betray Nevaris.

Never.

It hits me that this woman is an incredible threat if she has managed to be here this long without alerting us to her presence, if she's managed to catch me unawares. But it's my own fault for not paying attention and guarding my mind. I should've followed Lex's advice to always keep my barriers up.

"Your sister had wanted you disposed of properly." The woman's nails rake through my hair viciously, scraping my skull. "Care to know the truth? I am quite pleased she failed. I have much use for you, Aife."

What does she mean she has use for me? And that my sister

wanted me disposed of? My sister has—had—no idea who this woman is—I'm positive. Invidia told me everything, and I would know if she made friends with another goddess. There are many gods and goddesses, but we're spread out around the world. Most live quiet, modest lives, fulfilling their duties without drawing much attention to themselves. It's rare that we cross paths with one another.

But it's the worst ones that make the most noise.

I try to will myself to jerk my head out of her grasp, but I can't move. Her order not to fight her is keeping me docile. Although my insides burn with rage, I'm paralyzed in place.

"It appears things have not gone according to plan," she says with a sigh. The statement breaks through my cloud of confusion.

"What are you talking about?" I grit my teeth and ball my hands into fists, mentally begging for someone to find us. Lex, Callan, Lo…even Sora. Anyone who can help.

"We have every right to free our true natures and dominate the peasants of this world," she says. I have no clue what she's talking about, but it's apparent she's not of sound mind. Her use of the word "peasants" in a derogatory manner makes my stomach churn. "Invidia should have listened when I told her my plan. Instead, her envy got the best of her."

"What the hell do you want with me?" It's such a cliché question, and I know Lex would be disappointed if he were here to see me collude with an enemy, but I have no other choice right now.

"I have what I desire—a game of my creation. A means to rise above you all with a man of endless power at my side. I only need your help, and your lover out of the way, before I lose it all." She lowers the blade from my throat and licks the beads of red that line it. It barely broke the skin—there's not a lot

of blood—but I hadn't even felt it. My high levels of adrenaline and shock are blocking out the sting of the cut. Her other hand continues to run through my hair. "Your sister believed you will lead us all to an early grave. How wrong she was. No, Aife. You are the key to rising from the grave."

My face twists in confusion, and a boulder drops into my stomach. "You've lost your damn mind."

"Since your lover killed my companion, I shall return the favor, use you to get him out of the way."

"No!" The word flies out of my mouth before I can stop it. "Please. I will do anything. Leave Nevaris and Lex alone. Anything you want at all, name it, and I will make it happen. We can make a deal." I'm ashamed that I'm begging, but she has the upper hand. It's clear I've lost this battle. Lex killed Invidia, and I will never forgive him for that, but I don't want him harmed by this woman's hand.

"A deal?" She finally releases her claws from my hair, stepping in front of me. The woman is lithe and graceful, with pale skin and dark hair like mine, but her eyes are truly terrifying. Her pupils and irises blend into one shade of midnight, and the smile she wears on her blood-red lips makes wicked promises. "I do love a good deal. What do you have in mind, dear?"

My mind works rapidly, trying to untangle her motives. If I can figure out what she wants, I can try and make a deal that appeals to her more than killing me or Lex. It should buy us time to figure out a plan.

She said something about being her true self, freeing her nature and dominating peasants... A game of creation... And if she's manipulating free will and causing chaos, that means she has a deep-seated need to control others. My guess is that she wants to take Lex out and rule Nevaris.

"I can help you get a throne," I spit out. *"A real throne. Nevaris has no throne. Lex is no king. But I know a place that does have one, and I can help you become queen."*

Her smile grows, her eyes shining with interest. "What is the name of this place?"

I think back to the lovely jungle island tucked away in the Insipid Sea. To my favorite place to visit with Lex—Paramour Falls. The place where we kissed on a whim, testing a legend and sealing our fates to one another.

"Hakran," I whisper. *My eyes squeeze shut, and tears stream down my face. I don't want to harm the Hakranians, but I refuse to let her have Nevaris. Lex has worked too hard to protect the village. It's not just anyone he protects either. He takes in refugees from various realms. People who have no other place to go. After what many of them or their ancestors have been through, it's much too cruel to subject them to another horror. Lex would protect them until his last breath, and I shall do the same.*

"It's beautiful," I continue, my voice cracking. *"It's a small island that stays warm year-round. It is as isolated as Nevaris, and it has many people to rule. Many...peasants."* I wince inside as I say the word, only trying to play her game and appeal to her using her own terms.

Wickedness glints in her eyes. She gives me a coy look. "Perhaps there is something else you can offer me? Think hard. Choose wisely. Your sister wanted you dead, and I am inclined to follow through with her wishes to honor her memory."

Her eyes flash with sorrow, and I realize she genuinely cared about my sister.

Invidia never mentioned a lover in her letters. Not even a friend. What else did she leave out? And why?

I don't plan on going anywhere with this woman, but if I can distract her a little longer, I can come up with something better.

What can I offer? What would be believable enough?

My eyes scan her gaudy gold jewelry and revealing dress... her fully made-up face and sharpened claws. She likes games, but she also takes pride in her appearance. She wants to rule and calls anyone beneath her a peasant. It's clear she's vain. What do I have that might be of interest to—

"My power," I say. "I can transfer life force to you. I can make you stronger, more beautiful." She's a goddess, and therefore immortal, so she doesn't need the life force to remain young or beautiful, but it will make her more powerful as a myndox. It's quite possible she's power-hungry enough to accept the deal.

"Now that is exactly what I was hoping you would offer." She's breathless as she leans in and gives me a haunting smile. Goose bumps erupt across my skin, and I immediately regret the offer. There's something dark in her pleasure. "I was almost wondering if I had the right girl after all. I had never expected the goddess of death to grovel and cry at my feet. Metaphorically speaking, of course." Her eyes sparkle, and she tilts her head. "It seems your sister did not die in vain, after all. Here we are, together at last. You have yourself a deal." She chuckles quietly. "Nevaris will remain unharmed. I will not kill Lex. And you will help me acquire Hakran's throne and lend me your power."

I go over her words quickly in my mind, looking for any way she could possibly fuck me over. "You will not hurt Lex, me, or anyone from or in Nevaris. You will release the village from your power and never return."

"In exchange for your power, Deathbringer? It is a deal."

Terror and adrenaline cloud my judgment, and in the heat of the moment, I agree, wanting to protect Lex—protect Nevaris, the people who deserve a second chance at life. I can't let this *woman take that from them.*

She grabs my palm, slicing it with the blade before repeating the action on her own hand. It's then I realize I'm not getting out of this. No one is coming, and it's too late. Blood wells in our palms. Then she clasps our hands together.

Blood pacts between gods and goddess are a sacred thing— it's not the blood necessarily, but the magic that flows within that seals the pact.

"Let Sama bless this pact."

"Let Sama bless this pact," I mumble reluctantly. Everything inside of me screams that this is a terrible idea, but I don't see any other options. I've lost my sister. I can't lose Lex too. Or Callan—my best friend. Or Lo. Or even Sora.

At least this will keep Nevaris safe, keep me and Lex alive.

A sense of foreboding grabs hold of me as I realize the implication of this pact. I'm bound to this woman, this terrible woman, and must help her assume control of another country—a small island with a single village. A village filled with happy, innocent folk.

I must help her remove the Hakranian queen—Queen Zena, a very kind and just ruler. A woman I've met. A woman who does not deserve any ill will. I'm uneasy at the thought until I remind myself that this is all to protect Nevaris and my fated. Lex will get me out of this blood-oath. Hakran will be fine. It has to be.

"We shall leave at once," she says.

"What? No!" I haven't spoken with Lex yet. I haven't seen him since I witnessed him in my garden, killing Invidia. I haven't laid her to rest, or even begun processing her death. "I need to inform my fated I'm leaving." I need to figure out a way out of this.

"His spy can tell him." She waves her hand toward the row of arborvitae shrubs behind me. "Show yourself!"

The bushes rustle, and then a figure steps out. I squint, trying to make out who it is.

He steps forward cautiously, and once he's under the lamppost's fire orb, an orange glow washes over his cruel features.

Sora.

Thank the goddess.

"Sora!" I quickly call, trying to tell him what happened before the woman orders me to shut up. "I need you to get Lex. She's trying to take me to—"

"Shush," the woman whispers in my ear. My voice dries up. "Take this blade and slit his throat."

I try to scream, but it's useless. My hand reaches out of its own accord, accepting the blade from the woman. I step closer to Sora. My heart drops into my stomach. Sora and I have never gotten along. He's made it clear that he thinks I make Lex weak.

But he doesn't deserve this.

"Run," I whisper to him, my hand shaking. "Run."

He stares at me with anger, then confusion, jumping back right as I slice the blade across his throat. He moves quickly enough to prevent the slice from killing him immediately, but based on the amount of blood seeping from his neck, it's a severe wound.

I turn my sights on the smirking woman beside me. "Help him! You can't hurt him! You can't! That was part of our deal."

She laughs, and it's a cold sound. "We made a blood-oath. It would never allow me to disobey the terms. However, the wound was created at your hand."

Shaking my head, I stare at the bloodied blade in my trembling hand. When I meet Sora's eyes, they're wide with shock. I mouth, "I'm sorry" to him, but he continues to glower at me with unveiled rage.

"Come, dear. You must take me to Hakran now." I follow the woman's voice as if I'm in a trance. I have no choice now.

What did I do? Oh no, no, no. What did I do?

How could my sister have been allies—or worse, lovers—with such a monster? How could she have never mentioned her? I'm crushed that she left me out of such a big part of her life.

Worse is the realization that Lex must have discovered this. There is no other plausible reason for him killing Invidia. He knew she was working with this cruel woman and intended to bring us harm, so he ended her life to protect me.

Her betrayal is hard to wrap my head around.

But the thing that hurts the most is the way I've betrayed myself and everyone I love by agreeing to this bargain. I've made a mistake, and now I'm stuck with it. Nevaris will be safe, at least, but now I'm a slave to this woman's desires. I fear what I will have to do to make her wishes come true.

The woman turns, a cruel smile on her face as she reaches out to pet my hair. "Such gorgeous hair you have, dear. No wonder your sister envied you so."

Her words pierce the last remaining piece of my heart. I wish my faith in my sister wasn't broken. I wish Lex had never killed her. I wish Invidia had never shut me out. I wish I hadn't been so weak when confronted, but I was distracted—emotional and desperate.

Invidia always said my heart is my biggest weakness. She said it would get us all killed one day.

I finally understand what she meant.

"Make me forget," I whisper to the woman. "Please. I know it's not part of our bargain, but I don't want to remember."

It hurts too much, and I don't think I can live with the pain.

She inches closer to me as she scrutinizes my face. "Again your sister was right." She frowns. "Your time empathizing with humans has made you much too weak for a goddess. So be it."

A pain pierces my skull as I come back to reality with a start, and bile rises in my throat. I grit my teeth to keep from crying out or puking.

It's been months, and I haven't had any other memories return. My mind replays the new memory obsessively. It's too much, and the stress of it tightens my chest.

How could I have done that? I've made many mistakes in my life, but how could I have made so many poor decisions at one time? Grief can make people do stupid things, but I should've been wiser than that.

I should've listened when Lex told me to keep my barriers up. No wonder he's so adamant about it.

Looking back, without the pressure of the moment weighing me down, I realize it was all a con. All a game to Enira. She *used* Invidia to get to me. She manipulated me into agreeing to exactly what she wanted. Whether Enira and Invidia truly felt something for one another, it doesn't matter. Enira was more concerned with finding me, getting her hands on my power, than she was mourning the loss of her supposed companion. That speaks volumes.

But why?

Why was Enira searching for me?

Why did she need my power?

What am I missing?

It had to have been more than a simple craving for power or an expansion of ego. There was something devious there. I could feel it.

My stomach roils with disgust at myself. I'm not sure I want to remember these wicked truths.

CHAPTER THIRTY-ONE

ASTRID

Bolting from the room, I race back through the main infirmary, intent on finding Lex.

"Hey, are you all right?" The nursemaid's voice is filled with worry as I flee, but I don't bother stopping.

I don't know why or how that memory returned, but it shifted some pieces into place for me. Acceptance of what happened with Lex and Invidia, even without knowing all the details, washes over me.

I understand small things now—like why Sora hates me. He likely saw me make the blood-oath with Enira—and leave with her. He blames me for Lex's imprisonment on top of that. If I were him, I'd find my actions unforgivable as well.

But he doesn't know all the details, and like Callan said, context matters.

Despite what Sora's perception of that night is, Lex still came looking for me after I disappeared with Enira. He still waits beside me, ready to give me the love I don't deserve. When he told me that Invidia meant me harm, he wasn't lying.

I still don't remember how I helped Enira assume the throne. It's plausible I killed Queen Zena to remove her, and if that is the case, it would mean I was never eligible to assume the Hakranian throne. Per the goddess's law, killing the rightful leader would have prevented me from ever becoming queen. In that case, without Dash, the people would have had no leader. It was never meant to be *me*.

It softens me toward Dash further, though I've already forgiven him for *those* transgressions.

Tonight, every beat of my heart pumps forgiveness through my veins.

It's late.

But after that new memory, I need to see Lex. I pray to the goddess he's around.

My legs tremble as my bare feet slap across the colored tile. A few guards watch me as I hurry through the infirmary, none of them making a move to deter me. My hair sticks to the back of my neck with sweat. I push it out of my face, take a deep breath, and exit the room.

My hands fiddle with my silk nightgown as I find the courage to knock on Lex's door—a few rooms down from my own.

A moment later, the door swings open.

There's a deep crease in Lex's forehead, but it smooths out when he sees me. "Aife."

Without hesitation, I launch myself into his arms. He catches me with ease, and I wrap my legs around his waist, clinging to him like a sloth.

"Callan said you went to bed early. "His words tickle my shoulder. He holds me tight to him. Kicking the door shut, he leads me to the bed in the center of the room.

"I couldn't sleep."

He places me on the edge of bed and kneels between my legs, squinting up at me.

"You're crying." His voice is hard, his eyes dark with anger.

"Who made you cry, luv? We'll maim them."

When he reaches up to wipe the moisture away from my cheeks, I lean into his hand. Something about the way he says *we* instead of *I* makes my body buzz with excitement.

Lex has always wanted us to be equals.

Not wanting to rehash the painful memory sitting heavily on my chest, I aim for a distraction. "You used to sing for me."

Surprise flickers across his face, and he doesn't bother to hide it. "Yes."

"You were playing piano." I grasp his hand, pulling it away from my cheek and squeezing it tight. "Months ago, when I barged into Harmony House as Astrid. That was our song. You wrote it for me." Though I don't have a direct memory of it, I can feel it in my soul. Shadows of memories and moments linger in my mind, right below the surface, bringing waves of nostalgia.

"Yes."

The fire orb beside the bed bathes his features in a soft, orange glow, and for the first time, he doesn't look so sharp and dangerous. There's a tenderness in his gaze.

"I remember, Lex." His eyes snap to mine, and the air between us thickens. A longing warms my insides, and I offer him a small smile. "I don't remember everything, but I—I almost remember the song. It's like I know things that happened, but I can't fully pull up the specific memories. Something happened tonight. I knocked down a potion in the infirmary, and—" Lex's head tilts, and his eyes narrow. "Never mind. I remember. That's what matters."

"Aife…" He reaches up, gently cupping my cheeks in his strong hands. "I—"

"Please don't say anything else." I don't want him to ruin this moment. I'm finally warming up to him, and I'm scared that if he pushes too much too soon, I'll get the urge to flee again.

"I knew you would remember." He brushes the bangs back from my face and rises, planting a gentle kiss on my forehead before slowly pulling back. The ghost of his lips linger on my skin, and I want to draw him back to me.

"I won't push you. I don't expect anything from you, Aife." Lex sighs.

His words sit heavily on my chest. He never pushes, never asks me for anything I can't give. "Sometimes I run," I tell him. "When things get hard, I mean. When I'm emotional, I overthink things and doubt myself. It feels like the worst side of me comes out. And when that happens, I fear no one will understand me, and I run."

A rare smile crosses his lips. "I know."

"But I don't want to run from you anymore, Lex."

"Then don't, luv. Don't run from me. Stay with me."

Scooting to the middle of the bed, I pat the mattress and beckon for him to join. He crawls onto the bed, resting his back against the headboard in front of me so we can face each other. It reminds me of all the nights Ilona and I stayed up late to chat.

It's familiar…but new.

I inhale until my lungs can no longer expand, then slowly blow it out, thinking about how to word my question. "When I left—when Enira took me to Hakran—Sora saw."

He nods slowly.

"I don't what he saw, or what he told you, but I never—"

"Aife," he cocks his head with a frown, "I know. I know you better than that. I went over it a thousand times in the pit. It's no coincidence Nevaris settled into peace after you left. I figured you had made a deal to protect our people."

"Invidia was—" I chew my lip. He reaches forward and pries

it from my teeth. "She deserved it, didn't she?"

He nods again. "I'm sorry, luv."

"You have nothing to apologize for."

"Does this mean you've come back to me, my Aife? Do I have you back?"

"You might not have me *back*, but you can have me again, Lex."

"That's enough for me."

"Even if I can't promise you're the only one who has me?"

His eyes grow stormy, and I shudder beneath his intense gaze. "The worst torture of all is missing you while you're standing next me. You are only ten inches away, but there might as well be ten thousand miles of ocean between us. If sharing you with another man is the price I must pay to keep you, I'll pay up."

"Ten thousand miles is nothing when you have etheryn tunnels to traverse." I extend my leg, nudging him in the thigh with my foot. He surprises me by grabbing my foot and kneading it with his strong fingers. "Oh my goddess." My muscles relax, and I sigh at how good it feels, and he chuckles, gesturing for me to give him my other foot.

I extend my other leg, placing it on his lap. He leans his head back and leisurely rubs my tired feet.

"If a *tunnel* could have brought you back to me Aife, I would've had you in my bed long ago."

I playfully kick him in the thigh. "Great. Now I know what you really want from me."

He pauses his massage and smirks at me. "I meant like *this*— as we are now. I want to hold you. Touch you. Make you feel good." He squeezes my feet to emphasize his point. "You have no idea how hard it is to keep my hands and lips to myself when you're around."

"Even though I piss you off?"

"*Especially* when you piss me off."

I laugh and pull my legs back under me as I sit up and scoot closer to him. It's not lost on me how easy it feels to be with Lex. How *normal* we are together. When I glance up at him, his eyes are moist.

I feign shock. "Are you telling me the god of war cries?"

"If you say anything to Dash, I swear to the goddess, Aife—"

I shoot upright. "What did you call him?" He scowls. I clap my hands together excitedly. "You called him *Dash*! Plain ol' Dash!" My heart drops for a moment when I remember what I discovered at the library—my revelations about Dash and his family. Not wanting to lose this precious moment with Lex, I shake my head. "We'll talk about this later. But for now, I relish this moment. It feels like a small miracle—Lex has a heart after all. And he *can* cry."

"Why are we so focused on *me*? I am certain the goddess of death cries at kittens." He smirks. "And romance books."

"I don't—"

"And love songs."

He isn't wrong, but it's almost frightening how well he knows me. My cheeks heat, and I think about the song he wrote for me on piano—one of many, I'm sure.

With a sigh, I ask, "Can you just...sing to me, Lex?"

"My songs are meant to be accompanied by pianoforte."

"Please?" I jut out my lower lip, giving him a pouty face.

"All right, luv." He runs a thumb over my dramatic bottom lip, and I smile. "Anything for you."

I crawl toward him, lying down perpendicular to him with my head on his lap. He begins stroking my hair, and it's so comforting. So natural. I hadn't meant to get so close to him like this, but my body craves his touch.

Lex clears his throat and hums a few soft tunes, running through a small warm-up.

When he begins singing, his voice is low and decadent. My skin prickles with awareness of his proximity, of his words and lovely voice.

He begins to sing beautiful lyrics about fighting for the one he loves. When he gets to the chorus, his voice deepens, taking on a sexy rasp.

My insides buzz with satisfaction as Lex continues to sing to me. My eyes shut, and I let his voice carry me to sleep.

For the second night in a row, it's a tranquil slumber.

CHAPTER THIRTY-TWO

DASH

The purple-pink rays of dawn wash over me as I stand on the balcony overlooking one of two identical reflecting pools on the property. The narrow pool runs parallel to the palace's main walkway, with its twin sitting on the opposite side, mirroring it. The water in the pool sparkles an almost unnatural cyan color, not only because it reflects the vibrant sky but because of its blue-green mosaic flooring. The pools and palm trees help break up the monotony of the mundane desert landscape.

Hints of spices—rich, sharp, and savory—float past me on the barely-there breeze, mixed with ocean salt. It's an aroma that settles my bones. This will always be *home*.

Pale, packed sand stretches around the property, all the way down to the city. Most of the buildings appear as if they've risen from the dirt itself, built of similar-colored stone.

Perhaps that's why our city is thirsty for art. For color. It brings life to an otherwise barren land. Cerulea is special because it's one of the few places on the mainland where desert meets ocean. There's something spectacular about that fact; it's almost representative of the unique relationship between life—the ocean—and death—the desert.

The ocean is brimming with life, yet it is where we send our deceased to rest. The desert is harsh, barren, and challenges survival, yet it's where we choose to live.

The two are opposing yet symbiotic.

Sort of like Lex and me when it comes to Astrid.

Shit. Shit. *Shit.*

Zale and Lex are right. I need to talk to Astrid as soon as possible. It's time to give her the full story, before it's too late.

But first, I need to see my mother.

I don't bother to knock on my brother's door. According to Zale, my mother has been in and out of consciousness since my father died, all those weeks ago.

"Ma?" I call as I step inside the dark room. "You up?"

It's dark. Only the pale glow of a bedside orb light washes over her. I take a seat at her side and gently grip one of her frail hands in my own. Her skin is ashy, her hair hidden beneath a silky wrap.

"Hey, Ma," I whisper. "Sorry I didn't come sooner."

My chin trembles, and I suck in a lungful of air. Seeing her like this—without her usual spark and warm smile—is haunting.

"My boy."

My spine straightens at the sound of her voice. "You're awake, Ma?"

"I am." She chuckles and tries to sit up, but her arms give out, and she sighs, slumping back into her pillows. "I'm tired. Sometimes can't sleep. Cedrik helps."

I frown at her broken sentences. Her pupils are wide, her eyes glassy. I glance at the empty vial on her bedside table. Picking it up, I give it a sniff. It smells bitter. Unfamiliar.

"What is this?" I hold up the vial. Her eyelids sink, and she doesn't respond. My stomach roils with nausea. "Where's Cedrik?"

At this, she perks up. "You just missed him. Just left." She chuckles again. "My boy. My boy. You're here."

"I'm here." I lift her limp hand up, planting a tender kiss on the back of it. Tears well in my eyes. "You don't need to take this shit, Ma. It isn't good for you."

"*Language.*"

For a moment, she almost sounds like her vibrant self again. A laugh breaks free from my throat. "Sorry. You shouldn't take this *stuff.*"

"Cedrik helps."

I swipe a hand across my jaw. "Do you know where he went?"

"They're not coming back. Tani and Nial have gone to rest for good, my love." Her eyes shut.

My skin grows cold, and I almost drop my mother's hand.

Tani.

Nial.

My biological parents.

We've rarely spoken of them since I came to live in the palace, but I do remember her saying the same thing—"Tani and Nial have found eternal rest"—the day my house burned to the ground and my parents died.

She and Emman said it wasn't my time to rest yet. That my life had a purpose.

I was too young to remember much of my parents. Joccelyn and Emman filled that void for me.

I swallow the lump in my throat.

"No, Ma. *Cedrik.* Do you know where Cedrik went?" I speak slowly, as if conversing with a child.

"Tani." Her voice is weak. "So very like her. You." I run a hand through my hair, not knowing how to respond. "She would be proud." My heart skips a beat, and her eyes open, meeting mine. "I am proud of you."

"Thanks, Ma." I sigh. "It'll be okay. You'll be okay. Just go to sleep." It might be best that she sleeps off whatever medicine Cedrik gave her. Whatever he's using, it's keeping her partially sedated—she's wavering in and out of consciousness.

"Emman never told you," she mutters, her eyes fluttering shut. "He wanted to tell you before he—"

I pause, waiting for her to continue. "Tell me what?" I whisper. "Ma?"

"Emman and Tani—they. He—Nial was not your father." Her eyes slowly open. They're filled with tears. "Emman was."

My heart squeezes inside my chest, and I lose my breath. I scan her face, searching for lucidity. The implication of her words is heavy. Hurtful. If it's true, it would mean Emman and Tani had an affair. And lied about it.

It would mean Zale and I are half brothers.

It would explain why the fucking *king* took an orphan in off the streets—something I never fully comprehended. It would also explain why my myndox power is the same as his and Zale's. A coincidence, Joccelyn has always told me, that proved we were meant to be together as a family.

Not a coincidence at all, it seems.

"Fucking hell." I pinch my eyes shut, swiping a hand over my face.

This is *not* something we should be discussing right now, with my mother in this state. I can't be sure there's any truth to it. If there *is*, I doubt she would have wanted me to find out like this.

I clear the lump in my throat, trying to swallow down my anger and confusion. "Go to sleep, Ma. You need some rest."

I pull the sheet up to her neck to tuck her in, but she grips the corner weakly, trying to tug it back down. Her strength isn't all there.

She shakes her head. "No. Lift."

"What do you want, Ma?"

"Look."

At first I'm confused, but then I pull the sheet back, revealing a wet spot on the bed beside her. I'd have thought she soiled herself, except the location of the wet spot is near her chest, right below her pillow.

"What is that?" I lean down to take a whiff.

Bitter.

Like whatever was in the vial.

"It makes me sleepy. Don't like it. I spit it," she murmurs. "He didn't see." What the fuck is going on? "Cedrik's friends are nice too." She stares past me, her eyes glassy. "The one in the shadows."

"What friends? What did they give you?" My voice rises in panic. I want to shake her, to snap her out of whatever fog she's in. If she spit out the sleeping draught, why is she still so out of it? Did Cedrik give her something else? "What shadows, Ma? Tell me!"

"I'm tired." Her eyelids grow heavy once again, her head tilting to the side. "The shadow man."

"Mother?"

The back of my neck prickles. I reach for her wrist, searching for a pulse. It's there—faint, slow, but there. I exhale heavily, only slightly reassured that she's merely unconscious. This doesn't sit right with me.

Not at all.

"Guards!" I bellow.

The two guards standing outside her room barge in, and I scrutinize them with narrowed eyes. I'm not certain I can trust them. Not if they let Cedrik's *friends* in earlier.

"Fetch Fatima and whichever healer is on the grounds—now!"

I might not be the king, nor the crown prince but, apparently registering the urgency in my voice, they bolt from the room.

"You'll be okay, Ma. I won't let anything happen to you."

I'll have Fatima watch over her when I can't personally do so myself.

I'm not leaving Cerulea until my mother has recovered. Until we figure out what the hell Cedrik is up to.

"She's in a coma," a voice rasps. My eyes flick toward the sound. A moment later, the man himself steps out from behind the velvet curtains.

I lunge toward him, gripping him by the lapels and thrusting him against the wall with a force that makes him yelp. "What the fuck did you do, old man?"

"Easy now, son. Joccelyn is an old friend of mine. I don't want to see her hurt."

My heartbeat is erratic as I work to control my anger. A hysterical laugh bursts out of me. She didn't take the draught. She'll be fine. She outsmarted the healer.

Something clatters to the ground beside me. I glance down and notice a syringe and needle rolling on the floor beside my foot. My breath catches in my throat.

"I had to," Cedrik whispers. "She spit out the tonic. This wasn't ideal for me either."

Slowly, I drag my eyes up to meet his. Instead of pride or triumph, I spot sorrow. My grip tightens on his shirt.

"Why?" My voice cracks, and I clear my throat. "What the fuck are you playing at, you son of a—"

"Without the remedy, she won't wake."

"I'll kill you. When she wakes, I *am* going to kill you," I grit out. I'll have Lex do it for me, maybe, but either way, Cedrik will cease to walk this earth.

I slam him against the wall again, and his head cracks against the stone. He winces, sputtering a few times before choking out, "I need—I need the deathbringer. We can make a trade."

Astrid? What the hell for? "*Trade* my ass. I'm not trading you shit."

"Listen to me, Dash." His eyes are bloodshot, and more wrinkles line his aged face than the last time I saw him. "You have time, but very little. Over the next few days, your mother's brain will begin to shut down, followed by her organs. Death will be painless, but it is inevitable."

I glance over my shoulder at my mother's still form, my heart shattering into a thousand pieces. I've lost too many people—my parents, Ayana, Emman. I can't lose her too. *Zale* can't lose her. "Fix it," I croak out. "FIX HER!"

Tears well in my eyes, and when I turn to Cedrik, his face is pinched with remorse, as if this pains him too. He has no right to wear that expression.

My knuckles go white as I grip his shirt tighter. I shake him, causing him to cry out. Rage vibrates through me.

"This is your fault. Fix this, or I will end you."

"Send Aife—Astrid—to find me. Alone. At her cottage—she knows where. And I will give you the antidote for your mother." He coughs. "Only I can fix Joccelyn, Dash. Only I know what she needs. Make a wise decision."

Using my power, I peer into his thoughts, only to be met with confirmation that the antidote is not here—it's at Astrid's cottage. I don't have time to sift through his thoughts and uncover his motives.

I release the healer, and he slumps to the ground. I pace the floor, running both hands through my hair. If what he's saying is true, I need him in order to revive my mother.

And we're in a time crunch.

Fuck.

Cedrik rises from the floor, pocketing his syringe and wiping his hands on his pants. "Be wise, son."

I raise a trembling finger at him, jamming it into his chest. "I am not your fucking *son.*" He's not my father.

Emman was.

My mother's admission burns in my brain.

"I know you're not. But you have to understand, all I want is *my* family back." He squeezes his eyes shut. "Sorry about this."

He jams something sharp into my arm, and my body goes limp as the world around me fades away.

CHAPTER THIRTY-THREE

LEX

Leaving Aife in the morning, after finally getting her back, is a new form of torture. Pressing my lips to her forehead, I tuck her in as she sighs and snuggles deeper into the bed.

In record time, I make it to the infirmary. Aife mentioned something about knocking a potion down before her memory returned. I'm certain Cedrik has answers.

I barge into the infirmary, going straight to the healer's herbal room. A couple of nursemaids call after me, but I ignore them.

I kick the door open.

My heart sinks.

On the wall are several shelves of potions, tonics, and salves, but one shelf sits bare. As if it was recently cleared. Beneath it, on the floor, is a scattered mess of glass and dried liquid.

That must've been the potion Aife broke last night.

My mind whirls with questions. When Enira died, the magic that held Aife's mind should've released her.

"Unless Enira's magic still lingers," I mutter to myself.

I have a haunting suspicion the healer was somehow siphoning off Enira's magic for himself. Bottling it up. But why? And is he purposely trying to prevent Aife's memories from returning? Or does he need her magic for another use?

I turn to find a sleepy-eyed Aife staring at me. Her hair sticks up adorably around her head. Not wanting to fight the urge to touch her, I reach for her.

When she steps forward into my arms, my entire body sighs with relief. "Aife, luv."

I crush her to me, smoothing her hair down gently. "Where'd they go, Lex?" she mumbles into my chest. After a moment, she pulls back, giving me a serious look. "That's why my memory came back, isn't it? Cedrik has something to do with it."

"I can't say for sure, but I do think so, yes."

"Where'd they go?" Her eyes narrow into slits as she peers at the empty shelf, her fire rising now that she's waking fully.

My jaw tics, and I shake my head. "We'll find him."

"Was he working with Enira?"

Doubtful. But at this point, anything is possible. I give another shake of my head. Aife's teal eyes burn into me, filled with fury and sorrow. It steals the breath from my lungs. I'd do anything to replace that pain with a smile.

Without a second thought, I stride over to a shelf and swipe everything onto the floor in one motion. The bottles clatter to the floor, smashing and spilling their contents. I glance at Aife hopefully, but she sighs and shakes her head.

"That didn't work," she mutters.

She joins me, and together we knock everything onto the floor, ruining all of the healing paraphernalia. By the time we're done, Aife is red in the face, her features scrunched up in anger.

"We should—"

A shout from the main corridor cuts me off, followed by the rapid pounding of boots echoing through the hallway.

Aife grabs my hand, pulling me out of Cedrik's office, through the infirmary, and out the door. We catch sight of a few people bolting down the corridor, but only a single guard remains in the hallway, appearing flustered.

"What's going on?" Aife asks the lone guard.

He stares past her, toward the commotion, not giving her the courtesy of a response. Without second thought, I release a wave of my vygora power, pulling enough life force out that it brings the guard to his knees without rendering him unconscious.

He squeals, an inhuman noise. "Please…" He gasps. "Don't."

I release Aife's hand and step forward, rolling my sleeves up unhurriedly. When I reach the guard, I place a foot on his chest and knock him backwards.

"I do believe the lady asked you a question."

"He's knocked them out—the queen mother and her son, Dashiel—they're searching for—"

Without giving him a chance to finish, I link my fingers with Aife's once again, and we rush through the corridors toward the main stairwell and up to the royal wing on the second floor, where Joccelyn currently resides.

Memorizing the layouts when visiting a new place *always* comes in handy.

When we reach the chambers, there's a flurry of movement from the guards lining the hallway. They try to stop us. As I'm about to knock them to their knees, my palm tingles.

A pale shimmer of gold surrounds my hand where it links to Aife's. Energy pulses between us. I watch as she knocks them to their knees, one by one, executing an impressively careful control over her power.

They lose consciousness, slumping to the ground like sacks of flour.

"Holy shit," she whispers. She stares up at me, her eyes wide.

I can't stop the proud smile that appears on my face. "Very

impressive, my little vygora."

"I figured we might need them later," she whispers back. "Plus, it's a lot better than going around killing people."

I chuckle as she yanks me into Zale's room. The queen mother lies unconscious in bed. A mousy lady with a mess of gray waves holds Joccelyn's mouth open as she tips a small vial of liquid between her lips.

But what catches my eye is the crumpled form on the floor by the windows.

A teary-eyed Fatima sniffles, pushing her curls behind an ear. She stands from beside the body. "He's breathing."

Aife gasps at my side. "Dash!" She drops my hand, rushing to where he lies on the floor. "What happened to him?"

She brushes the stray hairs off his forehead, cupping his cheek tenderly. My chest tightens, but not in the way I might have expected it to.

Not with jealousy.

Not with anger toward Dash.

But with fear.

I rub at it absentmindedly, wondering when the hell I started caring for the damn boy.

"Pardon me." The gray-haired lady gently pushes Fatima aside. "Didn't work on the queen," she mutters. "Worth trying on him."

Zale bursts into the room just as the lady forces her concoction down Dash's throat. "Jules," he barks, coming to kneel beside his brother. "What happened?"

She shakes her head.

Zale's eyes bounce from his brother, to Fatima, to Aife before finally landing on me. "*You.*"

"I had absolutely nothing to do with this," I say, arching a brow. I find it irritating that his first instinct is to place the blame on me.

"Seriously?" Aife hisses at Zale. "He didn't do this to Dash, and you know it."

Fatima glares at Aife. "Don't talk to my king like that."

"Don't tell me what to do."

A groan comes from the floor. "Nice to know my pain is unifying," Dash mutters sarcastically. He clears his throat, rubbing his temple as he sits up.

"Dash!" Aife yells. "Thank the fucking goddess."

Everyone swarms him, but I stand back, carefully observing the scene.

"Believe it or not, this was the work of Cedrik, the old wrinkly bastard, *not* this cranky bastard." Dash juts a thumb in my direction, giving me a half-grin. There's a heaviness to his demeanor, a stress line running through his forehead.

I stare him down, unamused, but my muscles loosen in relief.

Zale claps his brother affectionately on the shoulder, then stands, immediately spewing orders at Fatima to send for the captain. She nods, taking his instructions with grim seriousness, and the two exit the room.

Aife wraps her arms around Dash, burrowing her face into his neck and mumbling something inaudible.

"If this is all it took to get your attention, I would've knocked myself out much sooner," he says.

She pulls back, rolling her eyes. "Not funny."

A look of alarm crosses Dash's face. "My mother." He stumbles as he tries to stand.

"Careful," Jules tells him. "Might take a moment for your system to absorb the medicine. Didn't work on the queen, unfortunately. Whatever she took, she's not responding to my—"

"She didn't *take* anything." With Aife's help, Dash stands. He looks directly at me. "We need to talk."

He excuses Jules, who scurries from the room, and a few minutes later, Aife and I are informed of everything that happened with Cedrik.

Including how he tried to barter with my fated's life.

My hands clench into fists at my sides. "He is absolutely *not* getting anywhere near Aife."

"It's not up to you, Lex." She crosses her arms and glares at me in a way that sends heat to my groin. *Oh sassy, fiery Death-bringer.* "I'm not letting Joccelyn *die!* I can handle whatever the hell he wants from me."

My jaw aches from clenching my teeth. She's right. The woman I love would never let an innocent die over something she could prevent.

But I'm too selfish to risk *her* life over anyone else's.

"One more thing," Dash says sheepishly. "Cedrik visited the caves before he left the island—"

"Enira was using vimstones to collect the storms' aethyn magic," I remind Aife. I'm about to ask how that's relevant, but then it strikes me: what if the stones were somehow drawing out *Enira's* magic too?

One thing I've learned in my many years is to *never* underestimate the enemy.

Dash confirms my fear. "He took stones with aethyn magic when he left. Quite a large quantity. He said he used them to extract the magic for healing potions. I didn't think much of it..."

"Even after Enira's death, Aife's memories are still befuddled because Enira's *magic* still exists," I mutter. Aife and Dash appear confused, so I explain before they can ask. "Aife knocked a potion down last night, and a memory came back. My theory is that Cedrik was collecting Enira's magic in the vimstone. It's likely she didn't notice, and perhaps he was collecting it under the guise of needing aethyn magic for his healing potions. If Enira's magic still exists, regardless of whether it's in potions, stones, or flesh, Aife's memories might not return until every last drop is destroyed."

Aife perks up. "So, if we find Cedrik's missing stash, we could find my memories?"

I purse my lips. "It's possible."

"Then that's that." Aife glances at Jocelyn, then back at Dash. "I need to find Cedrik."

"*We* need to find Cedrik," Dash says.

"Good," I growl. "I'm in the mood to wrap his intestines around his throat."

Dash grins. "I was hoping you might say that." But when his eyes flicker to his mother's unconscious form, his humor fades. "But Cedrik could be much more dangerous than we expect if he has Enira's power."

"Can he *use* it like that?"

Dash shrugs. "I'm not sure. Most of his tonics and potions are of the herbal variety. But it's quite possible, considering the way aethyn and etheryn magic are harnessed and infused into objects—fire orbs, ice walls, ink—"

"But I don't get it," Aife mutters. "He's been at the palace with me since I was a young—since I arrived, I mean. At least I *thought* he was there the entire time. Maybe it was a false memory..." She goes silent for a moment. "But Ilona said the memories weren't false. She—" Her eyes dart guiltily between Dash and me.

"What is it, sweetheart?" he asks at the same time I say, "It's okay, luv."

Dash and I exchange a glance. He smirks. I scowl back.

Aife chews her lip. Dash does exactly what I want to do—reaches up and pries it from her teeth.

"Tell us," he coaxes.

"Ilona's memories came back. They've *been* back."

"Which means Cedrik likely remembers too. *Fuck!*" Dash slams his fist into the wall, immediately wincing in pain.

I quirk a brow. "He very well could've had his wits the entire time." I cross my arms, leaning against the writing desk. The boy's outburst is amusing yet warranted. I turn to Aife. "Where is your little redheaded friend anyway?" I'd expected the gals to be inseparable after making up.

"She's sleeping," Aife says. "Actually—" Her eyes dart toward the window, where the curtains lay wide open to let in the bright sun. "Ilona doesn't sleep in like this," she mutters.

Her eyes widen in alarm.

CHAPTER THIRTY-FOUR

ASTRID

"Ilona!" My heart beats against my ribcage as I burst into her room. "Ilona! Wake up!"

I flick on the overhead fire orbs and jerk to a stop. Her blankets are thrown aside, the bed unmade. So very unlike her.

I circle the room, scanning her few belongings, which are strewn about. Her room in Hakran was in disarray, but not like this. Ilona wouldn't leave her bed unmade—and she definitely wouldn't leave without telling me.

Or maybe she would, considering the freshly-stitched rift between us. But she definitely would have told Fatima or Dash or Zale at the very least. But they're here with me, and it's clear none of them know where she is.

"Where the hell is she?" Dash mutters behind me.

"Something's wrong." I spot her flats beside the door and hurry over to snag them and hold them up. "Her bed's unmade, and her shoes are here."

"Maybe she's wearing boots?" Dash offers.

Lex scowls at him, a line forming in his forehead. Then he turns to me, softening a fraction. "Is she connected to the healer in any way?"

"Other than living in Hakran? You think Cedrik kidnapped

Ilona? No way."

It's ludicrous.

Even if Cedrik has nefarious intentions, the old man is much too fragile to kidnap a whole woman and escape a palace full of guards so quickly.

"I wouldn't put it past him, luv," Lex says before he and Dash look at each other. "We don't know what kind of concoctions he was creating with his magic. If perhaps he has a way to tap into other powers."

"My mother said his *friends* were nice," Dash mutters, tapping his chin. "He has inside help."

"But what the hell does he want? With Ilona? With *me*?" I raise my arms up in defeat. "I'm going to go find him. Whether you two like it or not." Lex opens his mouth, but I cut him off. "Nuh-uh. Joccelyn's life is on the line. He might have my best friend. I'm not letting anything happen to them."

"She's got a point." Dash scratches his neck, trying to avoid Lex's eyes.

Lex's jaw tics. "I was *not* going to stop her," he grits out. "We're all going."

Shaking my head, I frown. "Cedrik said I have to go alone."

"You're not," Lex and Dash say together. They both give me a stern look.

"I have an idea."

"Do tell, luv."

"Callan." I pause, letting it sink in. "He can go with me and remain invisible. Cedrik won't know."

"No," both men say at the same time.

I roll my eyes. "Cedrik has a head start—"

Dash's cheeks flush. "Hey, I didn't plan to be knocked out!"

"—and Callan can make up for lost time by *flying*. He can

get me to the meeting point. The quicker we meet Cedrik, the quicker we move on with all of this nonsense."

Lex glares at Dash.

Dash groans. "I feel like you're blaming me for this. I thought we made progress, old man."

"And *I* thought Aife would be safer with you around," Lex says. He meticulously adjusts his sleeves, turning from Dash to level me with a stern look that sends a shiver down my spine. "Fine. If I can't be there with you, Callan is the next best option. The healer won't know he's there."

Dash clears his throat. "If *we* can't be there for her." He nudges Lex with his elbow. "We're a package deal now. The three of us. Stop trying to exclude me."

Dash's honey-colored eyes lock onto mine, and my stomach melts beneath the sincerity in his gaze. "I am so fucking sorry for this, Astrid. So sorry—" He runs a hand through his messy waves. "Once we get Ilona back and secure the antidote for my mother, we need to talk. But I hope you know that I will spend the rest of my life making this up to you."

We stand, staring into each other's eyes for a moment, unspoken words fluttering between us. Our relationship is a constant cycle of secrets and apologies, so this isn't new territory for me. Deep down, I feel like there's more to this situation than what's on the surface.

Just as there is with Lex.

I look back and forth between Dash—warm and inviting—to Lex—cool and intense.

The two are so opposite. So different, yet so synergistic.

Fire and ice.

Desert sand and ocean water.

Summer and winter.

And I'm the bridge connecting them, bringing them into perfect harmony.

My heart skips a beat at the realization that the three of us are in this together.

Whatever Dash has to tell me can wait. It can't be worse than what I learned at the library already. My focus right now is on my best friend and Joccelyn.

I sigh. Cedrik asked me to meet him at my cottage. The one place I've been desperately yearning for. Except there's one small problem.

"Guys, I don't know *where* my cottage is."

"Callan does," Lex says softly, reaching out and caressing my face tenderly. "And *I* do. I never forget, Aife."

I close my eyes and lean into his hand, letting his touch infuse warmth into my skin. When he finally pulls back, I glance at Dash.

There's no envy or anger there. A soft smile sits on his lips. "We won't let anything happen to you, sweetheart."

Aife narrows her eyes. "I thought we agreed neither of you is coming."

The men share a long look, and Dash nods. I realize Dash is listening to Lex's thoughts—that Lex is *letting* him. It's an odd thing, seeing them working together. It sends a tingle through my body.

"We won't let you go unarmed, luv."

"I know you remember me as Aife, some badass warrior, but I still don't remember how to fight." I cross my arms. "I can barely use a dagger. Definitely can't grapple, let alone use weapons. Just ask this one." I jerk my chin at Dash, who chuckles.

"Goddess knows it's the truth." He waggles his brows. "But I sure do miss practicing with you."

Lex shakes his head. His eyes blaze and his nostrils flare. "I'm not talking about using weapons," he whispers, stepping toward me slowly. "*You* are the weapon. I'm referring to power-sharing. To make you stronger."

We've already done that a few times. I don't understand the sly look on his face, but something must click for Dash, because a grin lights up his face. Once again, the two men share an unspoken conversation.

The gaze they both give me is predatory in nature, and a thrill shoots through me.

"Sexual energy is the most potent for absorption. Is it not, luv?"

Dash reaches out, trailing his fingers down my arm. "We can help with that."

"You—you're immune to my power," I sputter. I can't draw energy from him.

He leans in, whispering in my ear. I shudder as his warm breath caresses my lobe. "Not if you and Lex power-share first."

Power-sharing would grant me extra strength, yes, but it would also leave them weaker. "I can't leave you vulnerable."

"You won't." Dash smirks. "You have two of us—take a little from each, and we'll be fine."

"Come." Lex reaches for me, and I interlace my fingers with his, while Dash takes my other hand.

But my feet don't move. I'm frozen in disbelief.

We're not under the influence of moonberries, so there's no way Lex is going to willingly share me with Dash. And now is *not* the time to get frisky—with lives on the line—but they're right. If I can absorb some of their energy—a little from each—I'll have extra life force coursing through me.

Sexual energy *is* the most potent of all. Meaning, if they're aroused when I take their energy, I can take less and reap the same rewards. They'll be left unharmed, and I will thrive.

Something about the adrenaline coursing through my veins heightens my own arousal, and I wonder if it's the same for them.

I don't know what Cedrik is up to, or who he's working with.

But I need to save Ilona. Need to awaken Joccelyn. All the same, I must protect and prepare myself.

And when I take in the decadent sight of the two powerful men before me, the decision is easy.

CHAPTER THIRTY-FIVE

DASH

As we step into Astrid's room, Lex calls out, "We do not require your spy services; thank you very much."

I spin around to see who he's talking to just as Callan, wearing a sheepish grin, materializes with a shimmer.

"What the fuck?" I blink a few times, trying to make sense of his appearance. "Where the hell did you come from?"

His broad, gap-toothed smile makes him appear harmless. It's hard to reconcile his looks with the man known as Lex's second spy—a harbinger of death—and apparently, an *invisible* man with a voyeur kink.

Not that I blame him. We're a hot trio.

"What the hell, *Callan*!" Astrid takes off one of her shoes and chucks it at him. He ducks, but not fast enough, and it hits him in the shoulder.

He laughs harder and puts up his hands in surrender. "Shit, Aife. Ow! I'm just doing my job."

"He was fucking invisible?" I mutter, causing Callan to laugh even harder. "Does he do that often?"

"Callan," Lex warns.

Astrid crosses her arms. "Time crunch, hello?"

"*Invisible*?" I repeat.

"Callan—out!"

"Let him watch if he wants." I shrug.

All three of them turn toward me. Lex rubs his forehead. His nostrils flare. He shares a long look with Callan, who finally salutes us all and leaves the room. The heavy wooden door groans shut, cutting the three of us off from the chaos of the world beyond.

The gravity of the situation hits me.

My mother is unconscious down the hallway.

Ilona is missing.

Cedrik is a rogue.

And somehow, the woman I love is tied to it all. I nervously run a hand through my hair.

Relax. Shut everything out and enjoy the moment, Dashiel. Lex's voice floods my mind, and I jerk, my eyes widening. He can't read my mind, but he sure as hell can read body language. I take a deep breath, letting my arms relax at my sides.

He doesn't say anything else, choosing to inspect his nails instead, but I keep my mental barriers down all the same, just in case.

Astrid grabs my hand and leads me to the oversized bed. She pauses, pushing the excess of pillows onto the floor, then climbs atop the sheets. Crooking a finger at me, she leans forward seductively. The neckline of her nightgown dips down, allowing me a glimpse of her tantalizing cleavage.

A smile crosses my face. Quickly, I pull my shirt over my head, unbuckle my pants, and slide them off along with my boots. Everything falls into a heap onto the painted tile beneath me. When I'm standing fully naked in front of her, I climb onto the bed, prowling toward her.

When I reach her, she lies back against the pillows, and I

plant a knee on either side of her, hovering. She gently grabs my face, her lust-filled eyes connecting with mine.

"Right now, Dash, nothing outside of these walls matters. Focus on me. On us. Enjoy this moment. We don't know how many we're promised, after all."

She's right.

We're not promised *anything* in life. She smirks, tugging her shirt over her head and baring her breasts to me. When her eyes flick over my shoulder, I follow her line of sight. I catch Lex leaning against the wall, watching with narrowed eyes.

Astrid grips my chin and forces my focus back to her. "He likes to watch, remember?" She gives me a coy look that sends a blaze of heat through my spine.

"So let's give him something good to watch, sweetheart."

Leaning forward, I capture her lips beneath my own. She tastes sweet, with a hint of spice. Fitting. Our mouths move in tandem. It's a tender kiss, one I hope shows her how I feel about her. How much I love her.

Hints of her floral scent and Lex's earthy one mix in the air, and suddenly, this has become incredibly intimate. Much more intimate than it was on the ship.

We're in bed.

We're sober.

Breaking the kiss, I move down her body and take one of her dark nipples into my mouth, toying with it until it's a hard peak and she leans her head back with a moan. I switch, ensuring neither breast is neglected.

It's soft. Sensual.

Slowly, I slide down her body, hooking my fingers in the waistband of her pants. Her hips lift, allowing me to slide her pants down her olive skin. When she's fully naked beneath me, I take a moment to sit back on my knees and observe her.

She's gorgeous with her full breasts and curvy hips, the soft skin of her stomach. The way her oceanic eyes widen with wonder as she watches me is enough to steal the air from my lungs.

I run my hands up her thighs and over her waist, grabbing onto the curves there with a groan. "You are fucking decadent, Astrid. And you are all *mine*."

Lex clears his throat beside me, and I turn to see he's naked, his thick cock in his hand. "Mine," he growls, narrowing his eyes at me.

I chuckle darkly, but before I can retort, Astrid wiggles and sighs. "Will you two shut up? I am not a toy for you to fight over. Get over here and fuck me, Lex."

My smile widens, and I pull back to the edge of the bed, sitting on my heels and giving Lex room to crawl over to Astrid. She needs to take *him* first so they can share their power. So she can grow strong enough with his life force coursing through her veins that she can also take some of mine.

Unlike Callan, I'm not normally a voyeur, but something about the way Lex grips Astrid's throat, stealing her kisses like a possessed man, makes me hard as steel.

One hand stays around her throat as he kisses her, the other trailing its way down to the apex of her thighs. She gasps when his fingers connect with her, sliding through her folds.

My dick aches to be stroked, to fill her, but I refrain from touching it. I'll finish too early.

He doesn't fuck her—not yet. Instead, a soft, gilded glow forms where their skin connects, and they moan together. After a few minutes of kissing, fingering, and power-sharing, she breaks away with a gasp.

He kisses down her body, stopping at her center. I almost

burst at the sight of Lex's dark hair between Astrid's legs, at the way she throws back her head in unbridled passion as their bodies shimmer gold.

"Lex, oh, *fuck*!" she screams.

He keeps going until her whole body shudders and she's begging for him. I expect him to be brutal, to flip her over and pound into her from the back, but he doesn't. Climbing over her, he lines up his cock with her pussy and takes his time pressing into her. She squirms, aching and moaning beneath him.

He cradles her head, propped up on his elbows as he stares into her eyes. He whispers something to her, and she nods, offering a sweet smile. She wraps her legs around him, holding him close as he slowly rocks into her. She mutters his name, and he groans. After a few minutes, he shudders, and they pull apart.

He exhales heavily as he leans back onto the pillows beside her, spent. Reaching for her hand, he lifts her knuckles to his lips and plants a tender kiss there. She runs her fingers over his jaw lightly in return, eyes full of reverence, before turning to me.

Her eyes hood as they lock onto mine, and before I can ask what she wants next or if she needs a minute, she's lunging for me. Her palms connect with my chest, knocking me back onto the mattress with a light bounce.

I grin, letting her push me around. "All right, sweetheart. I'm all yours. Take what you need from me."

She straddles me, slick from both of their pleasures. She slowly lowers down onto my cock, inch by inch. I groan, my eyes fluttering shut for a moment before I rip them back open, not wanting to miss the bliss that fills her eyes.

Her warm heat devours me.

Lex comes up behind her, wrapping his hand around her throat as he nibbles on her lobe. She whimpers softly.

"That's my good girl," he mutters. "Ride his cock like you mean it, luv."

Her walls clench around me, and I'll be damned if his words don't send a burst of desire through me too.

The sight of her riding me, with Lex behind her, doing nothing but whispering in her ear and kissing her neck, is a thing of beauty. Her breasts bounce invitingly, but I can't rip my eyes from her beautiful face.

"Are you gonna take him too?" I murmur, fascinated.

"Too much," she pants, continuing to bounce on me. "I'm not ready for—*that*."

"Soon, luv," Lex whispers in her ear. "We will warm you up for that. Soon."

The prospect of us both filling her at once causes pressure to build in my spine. My impending release.

"I'm—close," I whisper.

She nods, leaning forward to kiss me. I'm fully open to her as she begins to draw out my energy. It starts with a slow simmer of pleasure where our skin touches and expands to a feeling of pure ecstasy.

"Astrid," I groan.

Fuck.

My body vibrates, raptured, as I fill her up in more ways than one, coming inside of her as she draws my life force into her body—as if I was meant to be consumed by her. It's utterly indescribable, and I know without a doubt that I will never find pleasure anywhere else, with anyone else, ever again.

And the fact Lex and I have both filled her is savagely sexy. It makes me wild. Based on the feral look on Lex's face—the way his pupils are so blown there is almost no green left—I can tell it does the same to him.

I don't need to listen to his thoughts for confirmation.

"*You're* mine, Dash," Astrid whispers so quietly I almost miss it. "And *you* are mine, Lex," she says to him, with me still inside of her.

My body goes limp. I'm spent, complete, and shocked in the best way.

When she climbs off me, my body mourns the loss of her heat. Before she can get too far, I jerk forward, running my hands through her hair as I kiss her with every last bit of energy I have.

Her eyes glow a luminous teal—so clear, so bright—ringed with gold. I wonder if it's a side effect from the extra life force she carries from us. Sweat dots her brow, and her cheeks are flushed.

"How do you feel, luv?" Lex asks her.

She sighs happily. "Like I can do anything with you two filling the hole in my heart."

"That's not the only hole we'll fill," I tease.

Astrid groans, and Lex smacks me in the face with a pillow.

I slam back into the mattress with a chuckle, drained from sharing my life force with her but not regretting spending a single ounce. I would gladly give our girl *all* my life force just to see that smile on her lips.

CHAPTER THIRTY-SIX

ASTRID

Twenty minutes after cleaning up and kissing my men goodbye, I'm wrapped around Callan, clutching onto him for dear life as we soar over Cerulea and the rest of Stellaris.

As in *flying*.

My heart wants to replay the sensual moments with Lex and Dash—live in those moments as long as possible—but my brain and stomach have other ideas, forcing my focus to unapologetically remain in the moment.

"We're fucking flying," I mutter breathlessly, my teeth chattering against the breeze. My bangs flutter across my forehead and eyes, which is fine, considering I'm currently refusing to open my eyes and look down.

My stomach feels as if it's about to fall out of my ass.

"We sure are," Callan says. I can hear the grin in his voice.

His wings *whoosh* gently as the breeze whips past my face.

With my legs around Callan's torso and my arms around his neck, I feel like the sloth on that tree branch—the one Lo was afraid of.

Knowing she, as an angelli, is afraid of a harmless animal is comical enough to relax my body a bit. My curiosity wins out, and I slowly peel my eyes open. It's so bright I have to squint.

Enormous white, feathered wings with gilded veins protrude from Callan's back, beating the air around us as we sail through the sky. The endless, clear blue sky offers a stunning backdrop; it's like sailing across a smooth sea.

"Where the heck do you hide those things?" I mutter.

"Magic, baby." Of course Callan appreciates an opportunity to explain how things work. "I can will them away, like they were never even there. It's what allows us to walk among humans unknown."

Interesting.

Carefully, I crane my neck to the side and look down.

"Holy mother of goddess shit balls and goats." Bile rises in my throat, and I squeeze my eyes shut again.

"That's a colorful vocabulary you've picked up there, Aife." Even with the steady motion of zooming through the air, I can still feel the rumbling laughter pour out of him.

"I don't like this." I gag, and Callan groans.

"You're going to ruin someone's day if you vomit from up here."

"And if I shit myself?"

He laughs so hard I fear we might crash. "That'll definitely ruin their day."

I take a few deep breaths, my body trembling. "Then get us down."

"Shhh," he says. "Just go to sleep or something. We'll be there in no time."

"Go to—*sleep*?" I screech incredulously. My fingers dig into his back.

"Ouch! I'm not going to drop you. Stop scratching me up."

I try to will myself to ease up, but I can't. My body is paralyzed with terror.

"If you have to puke—or shit yourself, which is very unattractive to say the least—please give me another thirty seconds to clear the city. There's a forest over there. You can fertilize the trees."

"Shut up," I croak.

"You're in a good mood."

"Callan, I swear to the goddess—"

He laughs again. "I'd rather you spew curses at me than spew chunks of—"

"No." I groan. "Please, please just shut up."

"You're missing the view. It's really something, you know."

"I'm sure."

His tone softens. "You used to love flying."

Doubtful. How could anyone *enjoy* this? "I hate boats, and this is basically the same."

"No way."

"It's the motion. The great wide expanse of the unknown."

He's silent for a moment. "So it's not the falling you're afraid of? But the *unknown*?"

"Maybe if I had my own wings I would like it, but..."

"You don't trust me. I get it." There's a pause. "I hope one day you trust me again, Aife."

My heart aches for the friendship I don't remember. Instead of replying, I keep my eyes and mouth shut and continue to battle the motion sickness.

A while later, Callan changes direction and shoots us downward at a dizzying speed.

We land softly in a small meadow, and Callan places me on my feet. The sudden stillness throws me off-balance. I wobble a few steps before my stomach heaves and I bend over and let it all out—partly because the adrenaline of flying has worn off and the motion sickness has caught up with me in a delayed manner, and partly due to fearful anticipation of what will happen once I make it to my cottage.

Behind me, Callan chuckles. He pulls a few small green leaves out of his pocket and hands them to me. "Here. At least this time I don't have to hold your hair back."

"Perks of short hair," I mutter as I sniff the leaves. *Mint.* "Thanks." I pop them into my mouth and chew. "I really hope I didn't have a habit of throwing up in front of you."

He stands beside me, rubbing my back with small, circular motions. "Nah. But as much as you loved flying, you definitely lost your lunch a few times." He pauses, as if he's lost in thought. "And there were a few times with Lex. Like when he brought that decapitated head to Harmony House after—"

"He *what*?" I make a disgusted noise.

Callan shakes his head and claps me on the shoulder. "Come on. Let's take care of that damn healer so you can get your memories back and remember for yourself."

I'm more worried about Ilona—and Joccelyn—than I am about my memories. But I nod, wiping my mouth on the hem of my shirt and shaking away the unsteadiness.

Around me, the sunflowers and plum blossoms sway gently in the breeze. It smells sweet and earthy. Something stirs in my chest. I know without a doubt that I'll find a small blue cottage on the other side of the hill before us.

CHAPTER THIRTY-SEVEN

LEX

After Aife leaves, Dash turns to me. "You're not seriously letting her go alone, are you?"

My lips tighten into a frown. "Of course I'm not."

"What's your plan?"

"Be patient, boy."

"Back to that?" He clutches his chest. "Always wounding me, old man. I thought we were finally friends."

I grunt, not in the mood for his jesting.

He lowers his voice scandalously and says, "I know what your balls taste like. If that doesn't classify us as friends, I don't know what does."

I close my eyes and massage my temples in slow, circular motions. "The urge to punch you has lessened, but anytime your mouth opens, it flares up again."

He chuckles and shrugs. "What can I say? I get a thrill out of riling you up."

"I'm amazed you find humor in the current circumstance."

"It's part of why Astrid digs me," he says. "My life is much too short to take seriously."

"Your mother's life is at stake."

"And I have you and Astrid helping me. She'll be fine."

I study him, wondering where his blind faith comes from. "You truly believe that?"

"Yes."

"Why?"

"Because I trust you guys."

The admission tightens my chest. It's a strange feeling, and it makes me uncomfortable.

I clear my throat, turning away from him. "Back to what matters. What about your mother and brother?"

"What about them?" His tone hardens, so I tread carefully.

The Vannyks are myndoxes with the ability to resist myndox influence. Dash is unable to hear their thoughts.

"Are you absolutely certain they have nothing to do with this?"

He recoils, hurt flickering on his face. "You think my mother poisoned herself to, what, set us up?"

"Considering your late father's history, it's a fair question."

"You think my mother—and Zale—and, hell, probably me too, have some cruel, elaborate plan to *murder* you and Astrid?" He scoffs. "As if we couldn't have done it a much easier way if we wanted to?"

"I am not assuming anything," I grit out, ignoring his latter comment for both of our sakes. "I am simply *asking* you." Holding onto my composure for dear life, I take a deep breath and slowly let it out. "I am...*trusting* your word."

His brows fly up. "Ahh. And why didn't you just say that, old man?"

I mutter, "Sama, grant me grace." My eyes flick to the sky and back to Dash. "Just answer me, boy. Are you certain they have nothing to do with this?"

"I'm positive, Lex."

"All right." I let it go, giving him a nod.

If he believes they are innocent, I won't pursue the line of questioning any further. I'm surprised to find that I genuinely trust his judgment on this. I can't pinpoint when exactly things changed between us. During the last few months, my river of dislike slowly trickled away into a minuscule stream, and I've started to treat him like I do my closest pals. I *care* about the boy.

He's one of us now. Even if I want to punch him.

It's infuriating.

"Speaking of family"—he gives me a long look—"I heard the gods were created in pairs. I thought it might be a myth, but Astrid has a—*had*—a sister. I figured you might have a sibling too? Maybe they can help."

My skin grows cold. For a moment, I don't know how to respond. I shove any lingering guilt deep into the shadows. My brother has been gone a very long time. There's no reason for it to haunt me.

I straighten my sleeves, not meeting Dash's eye. "I had a brother. He's dead."

"Oh. I'm sorry—"

"Don't be." I wave him off. "If you think *I'm* a bastard, you would've despised—"

Knock. Knock. Knock.

My shoulders sag in relief. I open the door to reveal Lo and a tall Black man with warm, knowing eyes.

Vince.

One of the angelli warriors from her legion.

"Ah, right on time, Lo." I glance at Dash, then jerk my head toward the door. "Let's go."

"Where the hell did you come from?" Dash asks, confused. "I thought you were— Who's watching Hakran?" Panic flits across his face, his eyes widening.

"Relax." I had every confidence Callan would summon Lo earlier, via their mental connection, the moment we hatched the plan for Aife to meet Cedrik. The harbingers are splendidly competent for many reasons, one of them being their ability to read and anticipate each other and my commands.

And once again, Callan did not let me down.

Lo gives Dash a saccharine smile. "Vince and I flew here as soon as we could. Hakran is fine. Sora's there. We have legions planted in the Nevarian mountains and the Hakranian coast." She gives me a sharp nod. "Ready?"

"Yes. They just left." I'm sure Callan flew to the cottage more slowly than he's capable of—not only to accommodate Aife's motion sickness but also to give us an opportunity to catch up.

Dash's eyes bulge. "I've never...flown. Is that safe?"

"Yes," I say. "May we move forward now, or do you need more time to gape like a fool?"

A short while later, we're in the air. I'm being transported by Lo, while a very concerned, very green Dash clings to Vince.

Aife will be pissed when we show up right behind her, but I'd rather she be angry and alive than—

No.

I refuse to consider any alternatives.

She'll be angry, alive, and stubborn as always. I—*we*—will make sure of it.

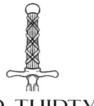

CHAPTER THIRTY-EIGHT

ASTRID

As we descend from the hill and make our way through the overgrown gardens around the cottage, Callan remains invisible. Cedrik can't know he's here. I can't risk the old healer reneging because I didn't come alone.

"Keep your barriers down so I can feel your emotions if I need to," I tell Callan. It's a power I rarely rely on these days. I don't want to feel others' emotions when I can barely handle my own. But it could be handy to know what Callan is feeling, if he notices something I don't and can't speak aloud to warn me.

Based on what I've observed, he's normally relaxed and controlled, so any alarm from him could give me an advantage. I have no idea what to expect.

The cottage comes into sight, and my stomach somersaults. It's like it was in my memory, albeit slightly rundown.

It's a stout, two-story abode straight out of a storybook. The white paint around the windows is chipping in places. Weeds and tall grass mingle with the sunflowers, tulips, and blue daisies. The blue-green coloring has faded slightly, as if it has battled the elements alone over time. The grounds are overgrown, neglected. It's a beautiful disaster.

My chest collapses as I take it in.

"Callan…" I exhale a heavy breath, looking toward him and seeing nothing. "It's—"

"Beautiful?"

"—been a long time." Like my knowledge of Lex, the recollection of my cottage sits hidden somewhere in the wrinkles of my brain.

It's like having a word on the tip of my tongue—so close, yet so out of reach. Something I can't remember fully until it comes back to me on its own.

Tears well in my eyes at the realness of this moment. I had a life. A house. A sister. An entire history.

Erased.

In the blink of an eye.

The moment of sorrowful nostalgia gives way to rage. Cedrik is likely in there. With my best friend. And the cure for Dash's mother.

I ball up my fists at my sides and work to quell my simmering rage before it boils over and burns us all.

"Are we sure he's here?" I ask.

"No," he whispers. "But it's where he said he'd be."

Cautiously, I scan the property. The hair on the back of my neck stands up. Why the hell did Cedrik want to meet here? Did he somehow know I've been wanting to come back here?

We step onto the dirt footpath that's half-hidden by overgrowth and unruly weeds. I hesitate at the wooden door before carefully pushing it open.

We step inside, greeted by musty air that reeks of mildew and unwashed clothes, along with a hint of something spoiled.

"Hello?" I call out into the living space.

It's too dim to see much. I walk over to a curtain and push it aside to bring in some natural light. A tsunami of dust rises up, and I cough, choking on it. An overstuffed beige chair and matching worn sofa sit in front of a fireplace, with crocheted blankets draped over them. Empty vases are scattered around the room—on the mantel, on a side table, and near the front door. A small shelf full of books with yellowing pages sits in a corner next to a staircase.

If it weren't for the layer of dust and dirt, it would be clean and tidy.

It's simple.

Comfortable.

Not exactly what I was expecting, but then again, my memories are muddled. I mostly remember a life of opulence with Enira in Hakran. This cottage is much more in line with my apartment in Nevaris.

"Hello?" I try again. "Ilona? Are you here?"

My hands tremble. Not with fear but with anticipation. I still don't know what Cedrik is playing at. And after all I've learned about Enira, my past, and my identity, anything is possible. There are precious few people I trust in this world, and Cedrik certainly isn't one of them.

I head toward the kitchen. There are rocks everywhere. On the table. The countertops. Scattered across the breakfast booth off to the side.

"What the hell is this?" I mutter.

I take a second to reach for my magic, letting it flow out of me. When it stirs inside my veins, my body relaxes. But when I don't succeed at pulling Callan's emotions toward me, I tense up again.

My magic is there, and I can reach it—I can send it out—but I can't call it back.

"Silenxstone?" I frown in confusion.

"Not silenxstone." Cedrik steps out of what must be a pantry, between the breakfast nook and kitchen counters. "Vimstone." He sighs, shaking his head. There are purple bags beneath his eyes. He watches me warily, almost apologetically. I expected gloating. Triumph. Maybe pride. I did not expect the sag in his shoulders or the grim set to his lips.

Vimstone.

From the caves where Enira was gathering magic.

It's even worse than silenxstone, because instead of *silencing* the magic, it *absorbs* it.

"What is all this, Cedrik?" I gesture to the stones of various sizes around the room. My eyes bounce from him to the pantry beside him before landing on the back door. I need to be prepared, should I need an out. "We've known each other long enough. Give it to me straight. What the hell do you want with me?"

I peer past him, trying to see if Ilona is in the pantry. I catch a glimpse of empty shelves, but I can't tell if she's there or not. Two thoughts strike me at once.

First, it's clear that he's been stockpiling vimstone here, so this location was *not* chosen on a whim. He was preparing—but for what? And why?

Second, I can't figure out *how* exactly Cedrik got here so quickly, or how he got all this stone here, for that matter.

"Ilona?" I call out.

I move to rush past him, but alarm washes over Cedrik's face. "Wait."

It's his fear that gives me pause. For a kidnapper, perhaps even a murderer, and someone who's decided to challenge the gods, he's awfully lacking in confidence. I would use my power to feel him out, but the vimstone is absorbing it quite thoroughly.

"It wasn't supposed to be like this, Aife. But you showed up.

With Lexyll." He takes a deep breath, his eyes shuttering. "And Ilona." He says her name with an unexpected tenderness.

None of this makes sense, so I wait to hear what he has to say. I sigh. "Can we skip the villain speech?"

"Villain...?" He hesitates. "Of course you see me as a villain." He wrings his hands in front of him. "I suppose we are all a villain in some way or another."

I cross my arms, narrowing my eyes at him.

"*You've* taken countless lives," he says. "Enira manipulated an entire island. Lexyll has cut down armies and severed realms. Even your sweet Dashiel is not so innocent. He came to Hakran specifically to hunt Enira. To take her life. I'm sure he's explained it all by now though. Or maybe he hasn't because he plans to take you and your fated out together." He pauses, scrutinizing my face.

I swallow the thick ball in my throat and try to ignore the way my skin burns hot at his gibes. Angry bile overwhelms my taste buds.

That is between me and Dash. And it's not something I'm hashing out now, with Cedrik. I'm sick of being played. I'm choosing to trust that Dash had his reasons, and I'm *not* going to let it affect my emotions.

Mindlessly, I finger the celestite necklace around my neck. Lex and Dash will come immediately if I call them. They might not arrive soon enough, but they'd come. If anything happened to me, they'd burn this realm to the ground to avenge me.

That thought brings me a sense of peace.

"You murdered Ilona's mother," he says.

My body tenses, and I try to keep the shock off my face. The confirmation of one of my worst fears punches me in the gut. Ilona is going to hate me.

My fingers release the necklace, my hands falling limp at my sides.

"You see, Aife?" He widens his arms. "We are *all* somebody else's villain. A hero to some, but a villain to many."

"I get it." I grit my teeth, waiting for the melodramatic spiel to end. "And?"

"I'm sure you've forgiven them all. But have *they* forgiven you?" I roll my eyes, wondering how this is relevant. "No one came to visit you when you left. No one begged for you to come back. If it wasn't for you, Lexyll would not have wasted years in the pit. Enira would never have taken over Hakran—"

My heart pounds erratically in my chest. "I know what you're trying to do, Cedrik." I'm just not sure *why* exactly he's doing it. "You're riling me up. Trying to get me to lose control of my power, because it can't hurt you." I kick a small rock toward him. "These stones will eat it all up, leaving me dry. But *why?*"

I'll play this game a few moments longer to obtain a solid answer. If he doesn't give me one, well, I know how to kill a man with my hands. It's not my favorite thing to do, and I'll probably cry afterward, but hell, I'm not letting an old man take me down.

Plus, Callan is at my side listening to all of this. Luckily, the vimstones seem to have no effect on his magic—perhaps since he's from another realm? Either way, it's a huge advantage.

"Your memories are back," I say. "Or you never lost them?"

He opens his mouth and hesitates, seeming to weigh his words for a moment, before saying, "Vimstone is native to the caves around Hakran." He takes a deep breath. *Okay, villain speech it is.* I fight the urge to roll my eyes. "It was my idea to harness the wild magic. I told her we could both use it—me for my experimental healing potions, and her for whatever struck her fancy. She agreed—for her ego. She was desperate for more power in any form."

That confirms Enira's mission to collect magic *was* purely selfish. Not at all in the people's interest. It doesn't surprise me.

He continues, "Enira was too narcissistic to realize the stone was taking a bit of her power and *your* power each time a storm blew in."

"*My* power?"

He nods. "It was coursing through her veins after transference. Dormant. Unusable. But it was still *your* vygora magic nevertheless."

I blink slowly, wondering where he's going with this.

A realization pops into my head. When I got sick from transference, he recommended I take *more* lives, lest I get sick and die. Was it a farce? Or was he hoping I'd harness more magic, thereby transferring more to Enira so he could take it from her through the vimstones?

My head spins as I try to put it all together.

"Was this all a ploy to steal my magic? This whole time? *That* is what you want?"

"Not initially. I truly did experiment with the magic from the wild storms. It's how I learned to extract it. You can do many wonderful things with—" He drops his eyes for a moment and slumps. "I'm a healer. I wanted to help others, and I did. I experimented on myself with my creations before ever using them on anyone else. That's how I discovered the stones were absorbing both your magic and Enira's magic too."

"So you drank our magic...and what? You turned into a vygora-

myndox hybrid and decided you wanted *more* power? You wanted to take over the island yourself? Maybe Stellaris too?" My voice rises as I consider the absurdity of that theory, but

Cedrik makes a strangled sound and shakes his head.

"That's not what happened." His voice cracks. "Each magic has its own signature, and when I extract the magic, mixing it with a neutral base, it changes color. I was able to separate the magic. At first, drinking the potions with Enira's magic broke the mental hold she had on me. My memories returned. Subsequent doses prevented her from further affecting my mind. And as for your magic—" He shifts his weight between his feet, glancing around nervously.

Paranoid, I look over my shoulder to make sure we're still alone. A warm, invisible hand brushes my arm gently—a reminder that Callan is here. He's with me. My stomach settles slightly.

"Why? Why do you want *my* power, Cedrik? What does it do?"

"It's death magic," he whispers.

At this, I do roll my eyes. "No shit."

"But your magic is so much more than that." His eyes widen, a bit of excitement bringing life back into him. "After watching what Enira was doing in those caves, with your magic... She—*I* can use it to access the Underworld."

"The—excuse me? The fucking *Underworld*?" I scoff, holding up my hand, palm facing him. "Wait. You wrote fake letters to Dash to get me to Cerulea so you could lure me here to my old cottage? All to steal my magic using a bunch of pebbles"—I pick up a fist-sized rock from the table and chuck it at the wall by Cedrik's head—"to talk to ghosts or some shit?"

A weird urge to laugh bubbles up.

It's the stupidest thing I've heard.

"What letters?" His brow furrows.

"The ones you—forget it. Am I close here or not? Because I'm dying for this spiel to end. I came for Ilona and a remedy for Joccelyn. Give both of those things to me and we can move on from whatever strange, makeshift magic project you have going on here."

He shakes his head. "Preserving Enira's magic after her death was a gamble I took. I theorized that with the amount of mental power she held over you, it would take eliminating *all* her magic for you to return to normal. A theory that was proven correct after her death. See, I still hold many samples of her magic."

"Yeah," I say bitterly. "I figured that out when I knocked one of your little concoctions over last night."

"And you never stopped to wonder *why* I didn't want you to remember?"

I scowl. "Of course I did."

His brown eyes soften before growing steely. "You killed the love of my life, Aife."

My spine goes ramrod straight, and I stop breathing for a moment. Something tells me a smile and an apology aren't going to fix whatever happened.

"When I drank Enira's magic and regained my memories, I remembered it all. How *you* brought Enira to Hakran. How *you* murdered the queen and placed Enira on the throne. How *you* took everyone from me." His face tightens. "I might be *your* villain now, but you were mine first."

A trickle of sympathy spreads through me. "Cedrik…"

"Please. Don't." His voice cracks. "Finding out what your magic can do when harnessed was a happy accident. You killing Enira, me making a deal with—never mind. Happy accidents, I tell you." Wait, *deal?* "Life is all about balance. After losing so much, nature was finally giving me a way to gain it all back." Tears fall down his face, but he smiles through them. A sad sort of smile. Then a delirious laugh escapes him.

"I'm not following."

"With your magic, I can visit the Underworld. But unlike you, I cannot restore life to the dead."

"You think I can bring back the dead?" My eyes widen. "You lured me here to bring back your dead lover? Cedrik—that's ridiculous."

Not to mention that she has been dead for a *long* time. Seventeen years.

"It's not, *Deathbringer*." He pauses. "*Lifegiver*. You are capable of both. *He* confirmed it. He promised me that if I bring you here, you can help us both."

"*He* who?" The back of my neck tingles. Having Callan here is suddenly a huge comfort. There's more to this situation than Cedrik has revealed—something is going on that I haven't quite figured out yet. I stare at him, unblinking. "Look, I'm genuinely sorry for anything I did in the past, but I'm not playing necromancer for you. No way. Where the *hell* is Ilona?"

"Please," he begs. "I need you to bring back Zena."

Zena.

Queen Zena.

The woman I killed to help Enira to take over. The woman I killed to protect Lex and Nevaris. But Cedrik wasn't a *king*. I'm certain of it. It's not something I remember; it's intuition—something I *know* deep down. Like how I knew Lex wrote that song for me.

"You were her consort?" I whisper.

"I was more than that, Aife," he says sadly. "I was her *everything*. We were in love."

My skin prickles, a silent warning.

I push the old man out of my way to look into the pantry, and he doesn't fight me.

"I can't let you go, Aife." His voice takes on an apologetic tone. "I made a deal."

I pause. That's the second time he's mentioned it. "A deal with who?"

But the answer comes from a warbly voice in the pantry. "The correct term is *whom*."

When I whip toward the voice, my eyes nearly pop out of my head. Dread fills my core.

A darkness washes over me, and it sends a tingle up my spine. There's a figure in the shadows, but I can't make him out. Whoever it is fills the air with an invisible buzz of power that's different from anything I've felt before. Unlike Lex, who has a magnetic presence, or Dash, who has a charming presence, this man has a vile, cruel energy. I take a step back, wanting to distance myself from the abysmal aura.

"Aife." His voice slices my soul. It reverberates deep in my core. A tremble wracks my body. "I came to offer *you* a deal as well."

CHAPTER THIRTY-NINE

DASH

As soon as we land, I bend over and hurl. Surprisingly, Lex, Lo, and Vince wait patiently for me to finish. None of them make a joke.

"Aife gets sick sometimes too," Lo says in a wistful voice. She and Lex share a look.

A small ball of jealousy builds in my chest, and I will it away. Of course Astrid has friends, a history without me. But it still hurts to see that Lex knows her on a deeper level than I do. That they share friends—a family. Even if she doesn't remember it.

She will soon enough.

And I can't help but wonder—will she still have room for me then? Will she feel the same about me when she remembers her past with Lex?

Behind me, Lo and Lex's muffled voices draw my attention. I wipe my mouth with the back of my hand and stand up straight.

Their faces are grim, and Lex's teeth are clenched. It's his telltale sign of irritation. Callan and Lo can mindspeak with one another, so I surmise she's received an update on the situation.

"What is it? Is Astrid okay?"

"She is fine," Lex says slowly. He glances at Lo. "The situation is under control."

"So what do we do?"

"We wait."

I nod, squaring my shoulders and mentally preparing myself for a confrontation. Despite the situation, I am as calm as I've been in months. The thrill of being a soldier, a warrior, has always completed me. It fuels me while grounding me at the same time.

The adventure. The adrenaline. It's nourishment for my soul.

I hate that the people I love are in peril, but I've missed *this*— being in the middle of the action. I'm not meant to sit on stone and boss people around. I'm meant to participate, to make the moves myself.

Dread fills me as I realize I don't *want* to return to Hakran. I haven't once missed my responsibilities—I've barely even spared the Hakranians a thought, except for when Lo showed up and I was momentarily concerned.

I don't want to be a fucking king. It's not me. And the Hakranians deserve better.

Running a hand through my hair, I push the realization aside to dissect later.

After a few minutes of antsy pacing, I ask Lo, "Where's the cottage?"

Lo points at a small hill to the north. "Close. About a mile past that hill."

"Let's go. We should at least get close enough that I can use my power on Cedrik. If we can get in his head, we'll have the advantage to—"

"Can't," Lo says, shaking her head. "We've a small problem. The place is packed with vimstone. Luckily, it doesn't seem to be affecting Callan at all."

"What the hell does the healer want with vimstone?"

"Callan's listening, so he can't explain it all right now." She pauses, her eyes glossing over for a second. "But don't worry.

His elephant-brain will remember everything. He has a talent for details and information. Sounds like Cedrik wants to use Aife's power to resurrect his deceased lover."

Finally, a hint of emotion spills out of Lex. "What?" he says, leaning toward Lo, as if he didn't hear her right. "Absurd."

"Have they found Ilona or—"

"Shhh." Lo waves a hand at me, successfully shushing me. Her eyes go glossy again, and she blanches. "Someone else is with them. He hasn't seen who it is yet, but he has a bad feeling."

I widen my eyes at Lex, and at that same moment, the pale blue stone around his neck begins to glow. His hand flies up, and he touches it for a millisecond before shooting toward the hill. "Let's go! Now!" he barks out.

The three of us chase after Lex, fear licking at my spine.

Please, please, let Astrid be okay.

CHAPTER FORTY

ASTRID

The hairs on the back of my neck stand up straight. I gape at the wispy, shadowy figure before me. The figure strides closer, but I still can't make him out. He's tall, broad, but missing the features that would make him corporeal. He's nothing but dark wisps and tendrils forming the shape of a man.

"Fuck that," I mutter at the vision before me. I have no interest in any kind of deal. "What the hell *are* you?"

The dark wisp chuckles, and it sounds like he's underwater.

I'm tempted to call for Callan as backup, but I fear alerting Cedrik to the fact that I'm not alone. He still has Ilona, and I can't risk not securing the antidote for Joccelyn.

"Sorry, Aife." Cedrik gives me one last apologetic glance before pulling a mask over his face and chucking a small glass vial onto the floor of the pantry. The glass shatters, sending shards in all directions.

A pale green fog that smells like rotten eggs rises up.

It happens so fast.

I cough as the stench overwhelms my nose. My body starts going numb. I quickly rub my celestite necklace before my fingers go limp and my hand drops uselessly back at my side.

I hope Lex will get the call.

I'm not a damsel in distress. I don't *need* anyone to save me, but I'm not alone anymore. I have friends who will come.

My body becomes rigid, as if I'm paralyzed, though all my senses work fine. Stuck like a statue—frozen in time. I'm hyper-aware of everything.

But I can't move.

Can't talk.

"It won't last long, Aife," Cedrik says, his voice muffled through his mask. "It'll keep you still just long enough to listen to his proposition. You can make this all right by agreeing to help me. And him."

I can't move anything to respond. How the hell am I supposed to agree to anything?

Where the hell is Callan?

Now would be a great time to intervene. Forget about blowing the arbitrary deal we made. I say we kill Cedrik, get Ilona, and get the fuck out of here.

There's a thud from behind me. Cedrik grunts, and then glass shatters.

"You were supposed to come alone." Cedrik sighs. "I don't know where your little blond friend came from, but he can't help you. You need to do this, Aife. No other choices."

Callan.

Shit.

My eyes—forced to remain open and focused on the shadow in front of me—start to water. The shadow wafts closer, and I can vaguely make out strands reminiscent of hair, fuzzy features. Like a man encased in black fog.

"Leave us," the shadow's warbled voice hisses at Cedrik.

The healer stammers a nervous response, clearly afraid of whoever—or whatever—stands before me. I hear him shuffle away, back into the kitchen.

"It feels like eons since I have last seen you, Aife," the shadow says. He reaches for me, but his hand goes through me without connecting. A cool breeze kisses my skin. "Though, unfortunately, we have never had a formal introduction."

Tears leak from the corners of my eyes—partly from rage and fear, and partly because I still can't blink.

"That human man is a fool. He thinks he can pull his lover's spirit from my realm, bring her back from where she rests."

My breath hitches.

He's talking about the *Underworld*, clearly. But *his* realm?

That means he's—

"It has only benefited me that the human used your magic and called upon me. He is a genius in that regard, but he's a fool to assume he can meddle in the affairs of gods, as if we are puppets and he is our master." The shadow chuckles. "We have no master. Especially not a demigod abomination."

The shadow continues to waft around me, pausing and cocking its head at me.

"I came to offer you a deal," he repeats. He makes a clicking sound of dismay. "It's a bit inconvenient that the man froze you, but it should weaken at any moment. You're the goddess of death, and he's a mere mortal. His toxins stand no chance."

A few beats pass. Sure enough, my eyelids soften, and I'm able to blink again. As the rest of my body thaws, I stumble backward.

But when I turn to flee, the shadows are a solid wall around me, caging me in. I try to step through the dark fog, but it's like a wall of ice. Impossibly cold and impassable. I shudder, wrapping my arms around myself and turning back to the man in the shadows.

"What do you want?" I ask, hating how my voice trembles.

"I can return your memories."

"No." He's lying. I'll locate Cedrik's stash, break the remaining potions to free Enira's leftover magic—allowing it to be recycled back into the earth—and I'll remember everything.

"How do you think the healer learned to summon me?" He chuckles darkly. "From Enira, of course—albeit by accident. She and I first made a deal. She was to find you. We searched everywhere for you, Aife. She was to use your magic to free me, and I was to give her anything she desired in her realm."

"No," I repeat, shaking my head. "My memories are returning. Without you." When I find Cedrik's stash, I can break every single one of his potions, all of his tonics, and even eradicate his salves for good measure if I must. My memories *will* return.

"Oh, Aife." He chuckles again. "You might remember tiny moments throughout time, but you have hundreds of years behind you. You don't really believe dumping a human healer's few concoctions will bring that all back? Do you think you received the memories you did by mere coincidence? Perhaps it is what I wanted you to remember. To slowly lure you home."

My lungs deflate. "How?" I whisper.

"Enira was using your magic, harvesting enough to open the gate to my realm and eventually free me." He sighs. "Each week, she grew stronger—closer to succeeding. Unfortunately, you killed her before that was complete. I figured it would be wise to make a deal directly with the source this time."

"No. I mean how are you holding my memo..." I trail off.

So *that's* why Enira agreed to my bargain. It truly was in her favor. That's why she held the weekly bacchanals. Why she had me absorb so many life forces over the years.

What a fucking fool I've been.

"Why only weekly? You said *each week*." Wouldn't it have been quicker to absorb as many lives as possible and harvest larger amounts of magic?

"You're focusing on the wrong things," the man says. "Enira is not a deathbringer like you. Her body can only handle so much life force, so much of your magic at once. When she learned how to use vimstone to harvest the power, to release it from her flesh, we found an opportunity to harness more."

My gratitude for Dash hits me with double the impact now. He had *no* idea what the hell he was actually walking into when he came to Hakran, what he was saving me from.

"Why didn't you just ask *me* for help the first time? Why go through all the trouble of using middlemen?"

"Oh, Aife. Of *course* I tried to make a deal with you first. I had nothing you wanted. Enira, and then Cedrik, were easy to convince. She had an insatiable craving for power; he had a deceased lover he wanted to see again. Both are desires I am able to fulfill. *You*, on the other hand, take what you want. Even if it means storming my realm yourself." He chuckles. "Though I suppose you don't remember that. I digress. This time, I have something more enticing to offer you."

I blink, not understanding what that means. "I don't care. I'm not helping you."

"You don't wish to remember the many years you have walked upon this land? You don't crave the memory of your forgotten sister, your lovers, your *fated*? Your lack of memories causes your loved ones pain."

I hesitate, understanding what he means. Even if *I* don't want my memories, even if *I* am okay with moving forward and forging a new life, there are people who knew me and loved me. People like Lex, who ache with the one-sided loss of our history.

Then there are people like Cedrik and Ilona, whom I've hurt without recollection.

Lex has pointed out that we have many enemies. How many people am I putting at risk by *not* remembering?

"How?" I whisper. The wall of shadows is cold where it meets my back, and I shudder, wrapping my arms around myself.

"I have the power to restore your memories. All I ask for is a bit of assistance in return. You help me, and I will hand over everything you have forgotten."

The last time I made a deal with someone—*Enira*—it turned out downright regrettable.

"Nobody has power that great," I whisper.

The shadows seem to grow in size. A tendril reaches out and caresses my cheek. I flinch, and the shadows shake with a low rumble of laughter all around me.

"I am the original god."

"No." I curse as I shake my head. "Hell no you aren't. Sama was."

"Sama." He laughs. "Sama is long gone. I was Sama's partner before she pushed me from the skies."

"God of the Underworld," I confirm.

"They call me many things, but you can call me Osiris, child."

"You hate us—the *lesser* gods."

"Do I though? Or do your precious humans tell stories for their own advantage and amusement?"

"I won't take that risk either way."

"*You* are the goddess of death. Your power is grand. It is of great use to me, to the dead I oversee. It is a blessing. How could I condemn the very goddess meant to aid me? You, Aife, were meant to be a child to me. A carefully curated gift from my beloved. I only regret our missed chance to connect."

I swallow the knot in my throat, refusing to entertain the idea that I was *made* for him. Not even as a child, but a tool. "Pretty words for a man who won't even show his face."

"*This* is the only way I can appear before you in this realm. Precisely why I need your help." He pauses, contemplating. "I will, in good faith, return some of your memories first too, show you the power I hold in my hand." A hand-shaped shadow reaches out for me. "Come. Let me show you my realm, child— *our* realm."

I stare at Osiris's outstretched hand, wondering if it's worth it. It would be so easy to accept his offer, to remember everything about my life, to feel whole again.

But at what cost?

Despite the cool chill of the sentient shadows enveloping me, my palms sweat. My mind races, trying to weigh the pros and cons of accepting Osiris's deal.

"If you will not accept for *them*, for the people you love, accept my offer for *you*. Be selfish, Aife. Protect yourself and your heart. Do not let others steal from you any longer. Reclaim your memories; reclaim your life. Let them see who you truly are without bounds." The shadows stretch closer.

"I—I can't." The shadows are relentless, closing in tighter around me as I begin to push against them, desperate to escape. "I do not accept your offer!"

"Have you never wondered about that burning sensation in your veins? The way your magic begs to be released? Begs for the kill. It thrills you, taking lives. It is the only time you feel truly alive, when you are taking the lives of others. You are the death-bringer, Aife. Join me in the Underworld, and see the realm you are meant to walk free in. You will thrive. You will see your power works differently, and you will not have to hide your true self."

"I don't *like* killing." Disgust fills me. "And I definitely don't have to hide myself." Lex, Dash, Ilona, and Callan—to name a few—all love me for who I am.

"You are not meant to suppress your powers. You are not meant to be *human*." The shadows crawl around my skin like icy water. A thrum of energy works its way through me. It's as he said—my power begs to be released. I'm on the precipice of exploding, and I need to let it out. "You are a goddess!" His voice booms around me, making my bangs flutter.

I flinch. "What the hell are you doing to me?"

"Showing you the truth of the power that lives inside of you should you choose to explore it fully."

"Stop!"

"Embrace it, child. Experience how blissful it feels."

Once the cold sting subsides, my skin buzzes. He's right. Comfort, pleasure, and strength wash over me all at once. I've never felt so alive, so strong. So filled with power.

My skin prickles with delight, and my magic squirms through my veins.

I wonder if this is what he did to Enira—manipulated her into doing his bidding by showing her what she was meant to be.

Is he right? Is this what I am meant to be? Is there more to my life than simple memories from the human realm?

There is a way I could find out and settle the debate about myself for good. I can accept what he's offering. Perhaps that will allow me some freedom, or at the very least, closure.

"I have one last gift for you. A gift given in goodwill, to convince you my words are not a trick."

CHAPTER FORTY-ONE

ASTRID

Osiris's gift is accompanied by a piercing pain that drives through my skull. A melody of images, visions, and knowledge assaults me. All at once, flashes of my life return.

One specific memory hits me like a bag of marbles, and nostalgia screams deep in my soul.

"Thanks for coming," Callan says. His boyish grin is charming; I can't help but smile back.

"So formal. You say it as if there was a chance I would've said no."

"You could have," he teases. "But you can't say no to me."

"Oh, I can say no to you. It's the villagers I can't resist." I nudge him with my shoulder as we walk together down the cobblestone path.

It's a quiet evening. All the vendors have packed up for the day. The sun has dipped behind the mountains, leaving a cool shadow over Nevaris. I shiver and pull my jacket tighter around me.

"How did it go today?" he asks.

I sigh, gazing off into the distance. "We only executed one today." Only one. Callan knows I don't like to talk about what I do. He never asks for details. It doesn't matter who I was with or where—all that matters is that I do the dirty work. All in exchange for life force.

It's a mutually beneficial arrangement, one that extends far beyond the two of us. On days like today, when my dear friend Callan seeks me out, we're able to save lives.

"Did they deserve it?" he asks.

"I don't know. Did they? I'm not a judge, nor am I a jury. I am simply the executioner."

"If they're murderers, they deserved it."

"You don't find it ironic that I punish killers by killing them? I'm no different than the criminals whose lives I end, yet I am held in high esteem while they rot away, disgraced."

"It's diff—"

"Before you argue that it's different because I'm a goddess, let me remind you that I feel as human as anyone else."

"It's assimilation. You might identify as human, but you are still a goddess. Even if you are as emotional and empathetic as they are." He chuckles, and I frown at him. "That isn't a bad thing. A healthy emotional range is what makes mortal lives rich and full. They feel strongly. I only implore you to be careful. As a vygora, you're susceptible to—"

"I know, Callan. I won't lose myself to my emotions."

"You're an enigma. Most people wish they were a god or goddess, yet you wish you were human."

I roll my eyes. "I never said that."

"You should come by Harmony House today."

"And risk jumping in the lake in these temperatures?" I make a pfft *noise, thinking of the last time—the only time—I visited the house with Callan. "Not a chance."*

"Or you could refrain from jumping out a window and simply meet Lex. Like a normal *person."*

"I told you before; I don't care to meet another god."

"It could help you—being around your own kind. Isn't that why Sama created all the gods in sibling pairs in the first place?"

"Yes. And thanks to her, I have Invidia."

"Invidia is never home. You haven't seen her in—what has it been, two years? Three?"

"Four," I mutter. There's a reason I stay among humans—and Callan and Lo, the angelli cousins. I'm not a fan of the other goddesses and gods. I tend to clash with them. Many view themselves as above the humans, which is recipe for an egotistical disaster. It leads to unnecessary conflict.

"Lex is different," Callan says. "He saved Lo and me. Other than you gals, he's my best friend."

"I get it. He's special. He's not like other gods," I mimic. "I'm glad you adore him. Truly. I still don't care to make his acquaintance."

"He plays the piano."

"Good for him."

"His voice is exquisite—magical. Hearing him sing is an instant erection."

"For the love of the goddess, Callan." I rub my forehead, stifling a chuckle.

"He loves the humans as much as you do. He still looks out for them. Nevaris is his creation, after all."

I snort. "So much common ground. What, are we supposed to bond over our admiration for the mortality we'll never have?"

"Aife, you're being pessimistic."

"I deal in death; what do you expect?"

"That's a matter of perspective. Look at what you're about to do—it's the opposite of death."

With that, we enter a small cottage, crossing through a dingy *kitchen with yellowing counters and horrid floral wallpaper. Inside the only bedroom, a frail woman lies in bed, dressed in long flannels and wrapped up in mismatched crocheted blankets despite the warm air. Her dark skin is slick with sweat, yet she shivers. Her features are sunken, her pupils blown.*

The air smells sour, heavy with the sick stench of impending death.

A baby wails from a bassinet beside her bed. Suddenly it's as if someone has cleaved my chest open. My mouth tightens, and I try to keep my pity from showing.

"Oh, sweet Fara," the woman croaks. "It'll be"—she coughs, and blood splatters onto the back of her hand—"okay, my little blossom."

My lungs squeeze at the sight.

Lo jumps up from where she was sitting in a wooden rocking chair beneath the window. "Good. You're here." She gives my arms a squeeze, leaning in so close I can smell her vanilla-scented hair product. "Zee is much too young to go like this. She's one of the good ones. Her baby is only six months old. The father died a year ago. You're saving them both, Aife."

Lo rounds the bed, reaching into the bassinet and scooping up the baby in her arms. Her upturned eyes crinkle with joy at the wrinkly bundle.

"Shhhh, shhh, it's okay, Fara." Lo is careful to support the baby's head, rocking her gently in her arms. "The lifegiver is here to fix your Ma."

"Don't call me that," I mumble. I swell with emotion, but it's tinged with guilt. In many circles, I am known only as Death-bringer. My face is the last many people see.

But my friends remind me time and time again that I am more than death. To some, I am hope. I am a second chance.

Without wasting any more time, I greet Zee and sit beside her on the bed.

"Close your eyes. Relax. It'll feel good," I promise her. It's not a lie. It will only hurt for me.

Gripping her bony hands in mine, I focus on pushing life force out. Doing this is significantly more challenging than absorbing it. I close my eyes, grit my teeth, and work against the resistance.

The magic fights me, not wanting to relinquish the extra life force. It burns me from the inside, but I don't relent.

Whether or not the criminal I killed tonight deserved it, at this moment it doesn't matter. What's done is done, but at least now I'm saving a life.

Two lives, as Lo pointed out.

Slowly, Zee's breathing becomes stronger. Her grip on my hand tightens. The room is quiet. Even the baby's crying subsides.

By the time I'm finished a few moments later, I'm weak. Dizzy. I relinquished more than I normally do—digging into my own energy reserves, beyond what I took from the criminal.

"Thank you! Thank you!" Zee gasps, squeezing my hands with a newfound strength. She's no longer the sickly woman she was a moment ago. Her cheeks are round with health, her smile strong and sure. She throws the covers off her and sits up in bed. "My baby! Oh, I need my baby."

She cries as Lo hands her Fara. Callan smiles at them, and Zee reaches for him, pulling him down for a hug. "Thank you for bringing her, Callan. Oh, goddess bless you all." She sobs harder, and Callan and Lo sit with her, talking in soft voices.

Nevaris is a tight-knit community, and it's beautiful seeing how close they are here.

My head spins. I blink a few times to clear the black dots. Zee coos over her baby, and I don't regret giving her as much as I did.

She needs that energy more than I do.

I stand, leaving them behind as I head out of the room.

I don't want them to see me so weak.

When I enter the kitchen, I gasp for air, gripping the back of a chair to steady myself.

"You gave too much." Slowly, I turn, latching onto a pair of intense green eyes. I've never seen this man before. His skin is tanned a light brown, and he has thick, wavy hair that reaches down to his shoulders, with dark scruff to match. He's dressed in all black and is rhythmically drumming his slender fingers on the countertop beside him.

My stomach clenches at the way he stares at me unabashedly. "What did you say?"

"You gave too much." His voice is wholly attractive—a sexy, lazy drawl.

"I didn't give her nearly enough." My eyes flick through the doorway to where the mother tends to her baby. "She deserves more."

"Here." The man steps forward, close enough that I must look up to meet his jade eyes.

He's the most stunning man I've ever seen—not because of his sharp features, hypnotic gaze, or muscles, but because of how he stares directly at me, unwaveringly. He's confident yet not arrogant. Perceptive but not judging.

I pick up on all of this during the few moments I hold his gaze.

There's something intimate in the way he holds eye contact with me.

"Here," he repeats.

He offers me his palm. I hesitate before reaching up and linking my fingers with his, entranced.

After a few moments pass, his lips pull up, and humor dances in his eyes. "Not all vygoras can transfer." I'm too flustered and drained to decipher what he means. "You must take it."

"Take it? You want me to—" I realize he's trying to give me his life force. To make up for what I lost. "No."

I try to pull away, but he grips my hand tighter in his. He gently tugs me closer, until our bodies touch. His musky pine scent encompasses me.

"Yes," he whispers.

"Why?"

"Because you deserve more."

I shake my head. "You don't know me."

"I know enough. You come to Nevaris every time someone nears death. If it's their time—old age or natural causes—you ease them peacefully into slumber. If it's not"—he tilts his head toward the other room—"you afford them more time with their loved ones."

"I kill people," I hiss. He chuckles, and his warm breath caresses my cheek. My heart picks up its pace. "The ones who I save, they only live because I take someone else's life first."

"A better man might care, but I'm not a better man." Darkness flashes in his eyes. "Nevaris is my home. These people are my family. Anyone who protects my family is someone worthy of more." He squeezes my hand, and I try to calm my rapid pulse.

His proximity isn't helping my lightheadedness.

"Take it." He leans forward to whisper in my ear, "Take what you need from me."

A beat passes before I slowly begin drawing out his energy. A golden glow appears where our skin connects, and I gasp with pleasure.

Unlike transference, absorption is decadent.

"Take whatever you need," he repeats.

Lust heats my body. I've never absorbed energy from someone I was attracted to before—not like this. It's always been under unfavorable circumstances. A reluctant punishment rather than a gift.

It feels too good as waves of his energy invade my body. I peer up at him through my lashes, noticing his mouth is only inches away from mine.

I'm lost in the bliss of the absorption, utterly enthralled by this mysterious man.

"I knew you would hit it off, but this is better than I expected." Callan's voice cuts in, and I rip free from the stranger.

I take a step back to compose myself. My cheeks flush with embarrassment as I glance at Callan. His eyes are wide, but a smile plays on his lips.

"I didn't mean to interrupt. I was looking for snacks," he says in a too-happy tone. "I'm glad you two finally met."

Slowly, I turn to face the man before me. "You are…"

"Lexyll," the green-eyed man says. "Pleasure to make your acquaintance, Aife."

My spine stiffens as I turn away, catching sight of Callan's grin doubling in size.

"The god of war," I mutter. "Of course." I cross my arms and narrow my eyes at Callan. "I'm leaving." I glance back at Lexyll, trying to ignore the fluttering in my stomach. "Thanks for…that."

Lexyll's eyes twinkle with mischief. "Next time you're in Nevaris, come find me, luv. We have unfinished business."

I gasp, clutching my chest. Tears well in my eyes as I stare at the shadow in front of me.

"That was—so real."

Callan.

Lex.

My head spins with the recollections.

"Do you accept my offer?" Osiris asks as his shadows begin to squeeze me from all sides.

The jumble of memories bounce around my head, competing for space at the forefront of my mind. Tears blur my vision, and my mouth opens to answer, but a loud bang resounds through the cottage.

I jolt, and the shadows rumble before slowly retreating. But I barely register it, stunned still by my memory of meeting Lex.

A tear streaks down my cheek—a mixture of longing and relief.

Osiris's voice is no more than a whisper as he says, "Think about my offer, Aife, if you want the rest of your memories. I'll be ba…" His last word fades into silence as the black smokey shadows around me dissipates into nothingness, as if it was never there at all.

The tears fall faster when I realize, for the first time in as long as I can remember, I *feel* like Aife.

I'm not entirely whole. Not yet.

But I feel immeasurably more like *Aife* than *Astrid*.

As much as I loathe Osiris, he gave me that clarity. And he possesses the power to make me whole again.

CHAPTER FORTY-TWO

LEX

The small blue cottage comes into sight as I race over the hills, and I squeeze my fists at my sides. Knowing my fated is inside and in danger has shifted me straight into war mode. I steel my spine, ready to make someone bleed.

I bolt across the yard, kicking the front door open. It slams against the wall. A plume of dust rises, highlighted by the rays of afternoon sun streaming in.

"Aife?" My voice bounces off the walls. I quickly glance around the living room, then nod to Lo and Vince behind me. "Check upstairs."

They oblige wordlessly, pounding up to the second floor.

I enter the kitchen, immediately spotting Callan unconscious on the floor. Broken glass and liquid lie on the floor around him. There are stones everywhere.

"Check him," I command Dash. Like a good soldier, he immediately does as I ask. He doesn't fight me on it, doesn't demand to find Aife first. He trusts that I know what I'm doing, and he listens when I give orders. My respect for him increases.

A sob from across the room catches my attention. Huddled in the booth of a breakfast nook beneath the window, Cedrik trembles.

"You," I growl. I'm at his side in four quick strides. Fisting his shirt, I yank him up and level my eyes with his. Despite the vibrating rage inside of me, my voice is calm and cool when I speak. "Where is Aife?"

"I—he—I never meant to..." Tears stream down his red, swollen face. "I only wanted my family back! I swear!"

"I will only repeat myself once." I shift a hand to his throat, pressing down where his Adam's apple quivers. "Where. Is. Aife?"

"There," he chokes out. His head flops to the side, and I follow his gaze to the closed pantry door beside us.

"Don't kill him!" Dash calls. "We still need him. Your harbinger is down. Slow heart rate. He's likely been poisoned, like my mother."

I drop Cedrik, and he crumples into a heap.

"Stay," I spit. I'll take care of him in a minute. "Watch him," I order Dash.

The only thing on my mind is Aife.

Something thumps inside the pantry, and I rip the door off its hinges, revealing a wide-eyed Aife standing alone among the bare shelves.

"Lex, darling, I'm so sorry," she whispers, her teal eyes filled with tears. "So sorry."

Everything around us fades away as my body goes slack.

Darling.

My ears ring. She hasn't called me that since—*before.*

"It's okay, luv," I whisper, scared the fragile moment will shatter.

My pulse races as I wait for her to say something, do something, confirm that she *remembers* us.

Neither of us move, both rooted to the spot, so I break the spell first and open my arms. Without hesitation, she rushes to me. I groan with the impact as she collides with my chest. She wraps her arms around me, squeezing with ferocity. Her nose nuzzles my neck, and she shamelessly inhales.

"Sniffing me again, are we?"

She chuckles. "You smell good." A sob rips from her. "Oh, Lex. I've missed you. I'm so sorry."

"I've missed you," I mumble into her hair. "So much."

My Aife is back.

"I remember," she whispers. "Not everything. But enough to know that— To *know*." She pulls away, her eyes boring into mine with unmistakable heat.

Dash steps up beside me, and Aife turns her attention to him, softening. The fire goes out, but her entire body heaves with her exhale. She throws her arms around him, sniffling.

"You came," she mumbles.

"Always." He grips the back of her head, winding his fingers through her hair and holding her tight.

I'll be damned if it doesn't make my heart squeeze with a feeling akin to joy.

"I'm sorry," she mutters.

Dash and I exchange a look over her head.

"You have nothing to be sorry for, sweetheart." He frowns. "When the fuck did Cedrik turn into a supervillain?" he asks, baffled. "I did not see that coming. He's so old and...nice. And a *healer*."

Aife shakes her head, turning to me with desperation in her eyes. "Lex—"

"We found the girl!" Lo's voice snaps us out of our reunion trance, forcing me to focus on the situation.

"Ilona," Aife breathes out. "Where?"

I lean forward, planting a kiss on her cheek. Dash and I follow behind her as she rushes out of the panty to greet her friend. But Ilona is nowhere to be seen.

"Where is she?" Aife cries.

Lo jerks her chin up. "The girl is upstairs in bed. Unconscious. Like Callan." She glances at his prone frame, then back to me, fire in her eyes.

Aife bolts up the stairs.

A moment later, she returns with a mixture of relief and anger on her face. "I can't believe he took Ilona. She doesn't deserve this." She glances at me. "Where the fuck are the antidotes?"

I open my mouth to speak, but Lo beats me there. "I'm going to kill him, Lex," she says, staring at Callan's form. Her hands tremble. "I'm going to kill the healer."

Though their bond is different than a fated bond, I understand the urges flooding her system.

"Get in line," Dash says. "I call dibs."

Aife balks. She shakes her head, pursing her lips. "I thought you were the nonviolent one of the group."

"Not today, sweetheart." A dark expression crosses his face. "He fucked with my mother and my woman."

"Your mother…" Aife grabs his hand.

"Stay with Callan, Lo," I say softly, giving Aife and Dash a moment together. "We'll take care of the healer."

She nods once. "Vince is standing watch outside, just in case."

I turn toward Cedrik, who is currently whimpering pathetically in the corner, but Aife grips my wrist and tugs me back. "Lex."

A look of sorrow decorates her soft, feminine face. She stares at me with trust and longing. I've missed her. I shove my hands deep in my pockets, fighting the urge to grab her and take her away from all this—somewhere I can have her all to myself.

"What is it, luv?"

"As much as he deserves it, you can't kill him," she whispers. She bites her lip, looking from me to Dash. "None of us can. Not yet."

I raise a brow in inquiry.

"Not that I want him dead," Dash whispers back, "but why not?"

"I think—" She takes a deep breath and wrings her hands together. "I think he's Ilona's father."

"Quite an assumption." But not an impossibility. It could explain why he took the girl. He did say he only wanted his family.

Her cheeks redden. "I'll explain everything later, but I've already murdered her mother. I can't be responsible for her father's death too."

"Shit." Dash scrubs a hand over his face. "Shit, Astrid."

"I *know*, Dash," she spits back at him.

"No," he says, opening his arms and beckoning her into them. "I didn't mean it like that. I meant *shit*, I know how badly you didn't want that to be true."

He rubs small circles on her back.

"Whatever's happened, you're not alone, luv."

She gives me a look of gratitude. "Just don't hurt Cedrik until we know for sure, okay? And don't say anything to Ilona until I can talk to her."

I hold her gaze, letting the truth of my words embed themselves in her as I say, "Anything for you."

CHAPTER FORTY-THREE

AIFE

Dash and Vince work to clear out the vimstone—storing it in a shed out back until we can figure out what to do with it. If it contains magic like we assume it does, we can't risk destroying it until we know what will happen.

Lex ties up Cedrik as I watch. My eyes continuously flick out the window, to where Dash and Vince are lugging the rocks to the storage shed, before returning to Lex and Cedrik.

"Where the hell are the antidotes to the poison?" I cross my arms, inclining my head toward the old healer. I might not be open to killing him yet, but I'm certainly not above torturing him for answers. His utterly defeated demeanor tells me I likely won't need to.

I refuse to pity him. This is his fault after all.

"Answer the lady," Lex drawls, inspecting his nails as if he's bored. A muscle in his cheek twitches, and I know that, like me, he is working to keep his anger in check.

"They're…they're…" Cedrik sputters, his leathery face turning red. His eyes dart around the room.

"Look at me, asshole." I lean down, close enough to smell his sour breath. "Where. Are. They?"

He winces, his eyes slamming shut. "In the cupboard.

Above—above the sink."

I run to the sink, standing on my tiptoes to reach the small cupboard above the window overlooking the garden. Tugging open the door, I find five small, corked vials of clear liquid. They're out of reach, so I glance around for a stool.

Was he planning on drugging someone else?

"They're here," I call to Lex.

"Wonderful," he replies.

There's a shuffling, and then Cedrik calls out, "No, no, no! Please! Don't hurt me—"

Glancing over my shoulder, I catch Lex shoving Cedrik into the pantry. "Stay there, and perhaps I'll let you keep your limbs, today. We'll see what Aife thinks."

Lo appears beside me. She reaches up, her height working to her advantage, and she snags two vials, passing them to me.

"Thanks."

She snags a third vial, stuffing it into her pocket. "I'll fly to Cerulea and give this to the queen mother. When Callan wakes, I'll send word with her updates."

I nod, and she darts out of the cottage.

Lex takes one of the vials from me. "I got Callan. Go to your friend."

It's the only nudge I need to bolt up the stairs. I'm desperate to wake Ilona. Stumbling over my own feet, I'm out of breath by the time I make it to her side. Quickly, I uncork the vial, part her lips, and carefully pour the clear liquid into her mouth and tilt her head back. A little bit spills out of the corner of her lips due to my trembling hands.

My heart thuds in my chest as I wait for her to stir. She lies on her back, looking as peaceful as ever, her porcelain skin dusted with freckles. Her unruly, fiery curls fan out beneath her.

She looks like a princess.

I intake a sharp breath at the sight of her. If my suspicions are confirmed, she more than *looks* like one.

She *is* one—the daughter of the late Queen Zena Palmetta and her consort, Cedrik the healer. It takes considerable effort to keep myself from panicking as I work to rouse her.

"Ilona," I whisper as she makes a soft groaning noise. "I'm so sorry. This is all my fault. All of it."

From the very beginning.

If only I had done things differently. There are so many *ifs*. If I had never gone to Hakran with Enira, if I had never made that deal with Enira, if I had never murdered Queen Zena—she would still be ruling Hakran, and Ilona would have—

"What's your fault, exactly?" Ilona croaks, squinting at me. "Goddess above." She coughs. "My mouth is drier than the Stellari desert. I'm *thirsty*."

"Oh, Lonnie!" I wrap my arms around her neck, squeezing her tightly as she tries to sit up.

"Where are we?"

I laugh through my tears, a hiccup bubbling up. "Vespyn. My cottage. Can you believe we made it?"

She blinks, her emerald eyes widening. "Well, shit."

My mouth drops open, and a hysterical laugh pours out of me. Ilona *never* curses. "How the hell did Cedrik get you here?"

"Cedrik?" Her lips twist with confusion. "I don't know. I was walking to your room. Then something sharp pricked my neck"—her hand flies up to the back of her neck—"and then I woke up here. Cedrik drugged me? Why?"

I chew my lip, not sure what to say. I don't want to keep anything from her, but I also don't want to tell her about her parents' identities until I know for certain what I've worked out is true.

"I'm not entirely positive, Ilona." My lips flatten together.

After she shakes out her limbs and regains her steadiness, we head downstairs. Callan's awake, talking urgently with Lex in a low voice beside the pantry.

I get him and Ilona some water—despite the disarray, the cottage has running water that looks and smells good enough to drink—and I lead Ilona to the table.

We sit in silence as she chugs the entire glass. Outside, Dash and Vince continue working to move the vimstone, grunting with the effort and occasionally slamming stones together as they stack them. Ilona glances toward the window nervously but doesn't ask what the noises are about.

"It's just Dash." I'm not sure where to start, how to explain the vimstone, Cedrik, Osiris, and everything that's happened. Based on the pallor of Ilona's skin and the way her eyes shift around the room, I'm not sure she's in the right state of mind to hear it all right now.

I reach out, placing my hand over hers. It trembles beneath me. "You're okay now, Ilona. You're safe."

"I had a dream," she whispers. "While I was unconscious. One of—" She glances at Callan and Lex. I follow her gaze, my eyes connecting with Lex's. His face softens, and he gives me a small smile that sends a flicker of warmth through me. "It was one of *those* dreams."

My attention snaps back to her, and I keep my voice low as I ask, "What about?"

"I—I don't know how to explain." She bites her lip, tilting her head down toward the table. "There's a man—with a scar on his eyebrow. I don't think you like him, but you need his help. He can—"

"Whoop!" Callan yells, darting over to us and interrupting

Ilona. "Lo sent word. Joccelyn is okay!" He gives us a thumbs-up, then opens the back door. "Heard that, Dash? You mom is good. Awake."

Dash bolts into the kitchen, sweat dotting his brow. He uses the back of his hand to clear it, a big smile filling his face.

Relief sweeps through me. I jump up, wrapping my arms around Dash. "Oh thank the goddess."

"And I found these stashed in another cupboard." Callan hands me a leather bag when Dash and I break apart. I open it to reveal a variety of vials and tubes filled with different-colored liquids. "What do you want to do with them?"

I glance around. All my friends are up and conscious. Ilona is safe. Joccelyn is okay.

This shit with Cedrik? It's over.

I tie the bag closed. Ilona shrinks down, tucking her knees into her chest and wrapping her arms around them.

Fuck Cedrik. Healer or not, he's brought nothing but pain and hurt to everyone.

He's traumatized Ilona.

He threatened the queen mother of Stellaris.

He tried to manipulate me into doing his bidding.

My vision goes spotty, red with rage as I cock my arm back, ready to slam the bag straight onto the ground.

"Wait." Callan places his hand on my arm, stopping me. "There might be more toxins in there."

Squeezing the leather strap so tightly it bites into my skin, I nod at Dash. "You're up, myndox," I grit out. "Ask him if there's anything dangerous in here. Make sure he's not lying."

Dash nods, striding into the pantry to fulfill my wish. All the vimstone is cleared out of the house, safely tucked away in the shed out back, so extracting the truth should be a simple matter.

Cedrik whimpers and Dash calls, "Nope. Nothing toxic."

With that, I swing the bag up over my head, slamming it down against the counter. The sound of crushing glass fills the room, and I grunt as I hit the bag on the counter again and again, pulverizing Cedrik's handiwork.

From the pantry, Cedrik moans. He begs me to stop. Lex barks out a threat, and the old man grows quiet.

I continue shattering the potions until the bag sloshes around—a mess of broken glass and liquid.

"Astrid—" Dash calls, but it only spurs me on, and I keep slamming it down.

I'm *not* Astrid. Osiris made sure I remember *who* I am, giving me just enough to hook me with snapshots of random memories.

Astrid was a lie.

A farce.

I think of Enira, of Cedrik, of Osiris—all the people who've manipulated me.

I keep going.

Slamming the bag again.

And again.

My ears ring with the sharp clatter of broken glass. I mentally plead for the best of my memories to return. Begging Osiris's words to be a lie.

Until my face is flushed and my breath comes in ragged pants.

But no memories come.

Tilting my head toward the ceiling, I bellow in frustration.

"Aife, Luv." Lex's warm hand slides up the back of my neck. "I think you've brutalized them plenty."

"But—" I take a few steadying breaths. My head is fine. No sharp pain. No memories. "It didn't work," I mutter. "It didn't work."

Osiris wasn't lying. *He* is the one blocking my memories. He has the power to restore them.

But why?

How?

"Maybe we need to destroy the vimstone?" Dash offers. He charges into the pantry, advancing on Cedrik, and then yanks him out and tosses him onto the kitchen floor.

Ilona gasps, scooting deeper into the booth as Dash bends at the waist, getting right in the old healer's face.

"How do you get the magic out of the stones?" he demands. "I know you know how!"

"You—that bag," Cedrik says, lifting a shaky finger toward the sopping mess of leather, glass, and liquid at my feet. "It contained my bases. They're neutral agents that work like a magnet."

Callan steps forward. "How *exactly*?"

"The magic favors the base, scurrying away from the rock. I can use them to attract the magic from the stones—draw it out—but now, they're ruined." He sniffles.

Dash curses under his breath. "These bases work on *our* magic too?"

Cedrik shakes his head. "No. It can't draw magic directly from flesh. Only—only from nature. Like the stones."

"How do we get the magic out of the fucking rocks?" Dash demands.

Lex leans against the wall, a flicker of amusement on his face as he watches Dash interrogate Cedrik.

"You—you can't. Without the base—you can smash them and release the magic back into the earth. Recycle it—but—"

"Shut up." Dash runs a hand over his face. "My head fucking hurts from all this sciencey shit."

"It's not even that complicated. He explained it in layman's terms." Callan frowns. "It sounds like the flesh might act as a rebuffing—" He takes one look at Dash's face and shuts his mouth. He mimics locking it and throwing a key over his shoulder.

Dash glares at the sad excuse of a bag containing the ruined bases. I shrug, unbothered. I *know* I'm not getting the rest of my memories back with the bases.

Not if what Osiris said is true. He's personally holding them hostage. He achieved exactly what he set out to do—he gave me a big enough taste to tempt me.

"Why did you write to me? Lie about the war?" Dash growls at Cedrik.

"Write to... War?" Cedrik trembles, eyes wide. "I swear to you, son, I have no idea what you're referring to. I told Lexyll the same."

Dash scowls. Lex cocks a brow, muttering something under his breath.

Callan mimics unlocking his mouth, then raises his hand. "Can I speak?"

"You just did," I mutter.

"Apparently, your mother wrote the letter, Dash."

We all freeze.

"What?"

He shrugs. "Lo said your mother woke up. First thing she said was that she needed to talk to you, apologize for forging letters to get you here. She said she was desperate, and Zale was busy, and she needed you—"

"Please, don't." Dash holds up a hand toward Callan. "I need to speak with her myself." His eyes flick to me, overflowing with regret and apology. "Actually, Astrid, I need to start with you."

Stop calling me that! I want to scream, but I don't. Because they won't get it. And I haven't had a chance to explain how Osiris—in those few moments—changed me.

How he gave me hope and took it away at the same time.

Unease prods at my gut. I glance at Ilona, then Cedrik, and I open my mouth to tell Dash it's not the time, but surprisingly, Lex speaks up first.

"Go," he says, giving me a sharp nod. "Cedrik isn't going anywhere. Lo is on her way back. We have time."

Ilona whispers, "I'll be fine. I'm okay." She gives me a forced smile.

Something gnaws at the pit of my stomach, telling me not to go. Not to leave her.

But there's nothing else we can do at the moment, until we figure out how we're getting back to Cerulea—if we're even heading back tonight.

And Dash and I *need* to talk.

So I nod and nervously follow Dash outside. The bright sun blinds me temporarily, and I squint, letting my eyes adjust. The air smells floral—fresh and sweet at the same time—stirring something in me.

We head into the shed where they put the vimstone, and I'm slightly relieved to know Dash won't be able to use his power to hear my thoughts. Perhaps he brought me here on purpose, to reassure me that he won't try and listen in.

Or perhaps he's going to tell me something he knows will unsettle me and he's protecting himself from *my* power.

That thought heats my skin up, and I nervously wring my hands in front of me. I'm already on edge, distraught by the day's events and revelations. I eye the piles of pale rock.

"We only put it here to keep it away from everyone. We'll smash it as soon as possible, sweetheart." His expression morphs into something somber. "I don't know where to start with this."

He scratches his neck and glances out the shed's window, toward the unkempt garden. The garden where Lex killed Invidia. My chest squeezes, and I plop down on one of the larger rocks to mitigate the onslaught of nostalgia and heartache.

"I know you hate when I bring up Ayana—"

"I don't hate it. I just hate feeling like you're comparing our relationships."

He sighs. "I'm really sorry if I ever made you feel like that. I never meant to. It's impossible to compare you. You're both very different women. But there is more to the story that we haven't discussed. More to it that haunts me."

I already *know* where he's going with this—thanks to the librarian at the Mirage Bibliotheca.

"Dash." I sigh. "Now is not the time for this."

"It's never the fucking time," he says. "I've waited for the right time, and it never came. The longer I wait, the more pissed you'll be at me when I finally tell you. Please—just let me get it out."

I chew my lip and nod. Despite suspecting what he's about to reveal, I'm relieved to know he never meant to keep it hidden away. It seems genuinely important to him to explain his story, and that alone means a lot.

He sucks in a deep breath and begins. "My parents and Ayana's parents were friends. We grew up together—Ayana, Fatima, Zale, and me. Our relationship was easy. Looking back, I think it was always more of a best-friend type of love. It wasn't as passionate as it is with you and me, but I couldn't imagine life without her. Anyway, like I said, I'm not here to compare relationships. They're different, wholly incomparable.

"Our parents expected us to marry one day. Not in an

arranged-marriage manner, but in a 'those two are meant to be' way. We were inseparable; we never had eyes for anyone else. I didn't propose to her—not officially—but we were talking openly about getting married. It seemed like the natural next step. But then…she died." He squeezes his eyes shut. "I know it's not my fault, but it sure feels like it is."

His distress moves me deeply. I reach out, rubbing his arm and letting him know I'm here for him.

"Technically, she died by suicide. But it's not that simple. Mutual friends who worked in the palace alleged that she was seeing someone behind my back—a vygora with the ability to influence emotion, a strong power only a god could possess. Everyone was livid. My dad—a king with resources at his disposal—led an investigation into the man she was seeing, this supposed god."

I swallow the thick ball of emotion in my throat, patiently waiting for him to finish.

"It spurred my father onto a path of—" He looks away from me, shaking his head. "Emman was a good man, Astrid. I swear to you. He was always kind and fair, and the people loved him. But he wasn't perfect. He…"

When Dash doesn't continue, I finish for him. "He hunted gods." It comes out bland, monotone.

His eyes flick to mine, wide with surprise. "Yes," he whispers, and I squeeze my eyes shut, flinching at the confirmation. "I never meant to keep it from you. I promise. I never questioned his intentions after seeing what happened to Ayana. We were all hurting, and we had no reason to trust the gods. It wasn't until I met you— and Lex—that I realized it's not that simple. Gods are as complex as humans, if not *more* complicated." He waves his arms in the air. "I didn't know how to tell you, and then this happened."

He steps forward, gripping my hands in his own. His eyes explore my face, trying to read my reaction. I work to keep a natural expression, despite the simmering anger and hurt inside of me.

"There's one more thing," he says. I sigh, but I don't pull my hands away. "Emman might be my biological dad."

I gape at him. I was prepared for almost everything he said, but *this* is an unexpected piece of news. I exhale slowly. "*Might* be?"

"Joccelyn wasn't exactly in the right frame of mind when she dumped it on me."

I frown, conflicted. Dash is going through a lot right now. Fatima was right before—when she said I'm not the only one going through shit.

Releasing Dash's hands, I rub my eyes and groan. "Well...it could be worse. At least you already considered him a father." Under my breath I add, "And at least you liked the asshole."

"You're not mad?" He pulls back, reading my face.

"Oh, I am *pissed* at you, Dash."

"But you're not..."

"Throwing a fit and murdering people out of rage?" I narrow my eyes at him.

"Well, you do have a history of—"

"Dashiel Dargan!" I punch his shoulder. "Do you *want* me to have a meltdown?"

His cheeks darken. "I'm sorry. I had to." He chuckles.

"Poor timing for jokes."

"We just talked about this. It's *always* poor timing for every-thing—conversations, jokes, *sex*." He clears his throat and smirks. "Plus, you love my jokes."

I roll my eyes. Normally, his humor and lightheartedness even at the worst of times brings me a sense of calm. Right now, it only aggravates me.

"Do you or Zale plan to continue hunting gods?"

His brows pinch together, and he flinches. "Wha—of course not."

My shoulders relax. Dash might keep things from me, but he doesn't typically lie to my face. There's relief in knowing Zale doesn't plan to continue his father's previous agenda.

He swipes a hand over his face, avoiding eye contact. "But…"

Any minor relief I felt quickly leaves, and my heart drops. I scrunch my nose. "But *what*?"

He chews his bottom lip. "Many of the people in Stellaris— Cerulea especially—followed my father blindly. They respected him. Trusted him. They harbor their own vendettas against the gods."

The librarian's words come back to me, her warnings about openly discussing the gods.

"You see how this could be an issue, Dash, yeah?"

He sighs. "Yes, but it's an issue for another day."

That line erodes a bit of my resolve. "You can't just put things off because they're *hard*, Dash." I stand, my face heating. "I've been trying extremely hard to be patient with you, to *trust* you. You had no idea I knew all of this already, did you?"

His body goes rigid, panic flaring in his eyes.

"No. You didn't," I say.

The surprise gives way to irritation as he invades my space. "That's my business, nobody else's. It's my job to tell you, and I'm telling you now. When the hell else could I have told you? We haven't exactly had time to chitchat. We haven't had the luxury of dating or having conversations."

"When it's important, you make time, Dash. You don't put it off."

"What do you think I'm doing now?" he growls, raising his

arms angrily.

I step back, squaring my shoulders and taking a deep breath. Osiris's offer, the memories he restored, float to the front of my mind. Suddenly, Dash calling me *Astrid* doesn't work for me anymore.

"And I'm *Aife*. I'm not Astrid."

He jerks back as if I've slapped him. "Since when? What does that mean?"

"Since always. It means that I *know* who I am now." I have the potential to retrieve all my memories. My entire life. If I say yes to Osiris's offer...

"Why does that sound like a threat?"

"It's not, but it means I'm finding myself. My confidence. I'm not wavering or lost. I don't need to rely on you or anyone else. If you keep shit from me again, Dash, I swear to the goddess—"

"Fucking Lex," he mutters.

"What does Lex have to do with this?" I throw my arms up, exasperated. "This is between you and me."

"He had no right to tell you this."

My body freezes. Slowly, I drag my narrowed gaze to him. "He knew?" I pause, inclining my chin. "Lex *knew* your dad hunted gods, that you were keeping this from me?"

Dash groans, running a hand through his hair. "For fuck's sake."

Red spots fill my vision. "You told *him* but not me?"

"I told him because I had the opportunity to, because it was never meant to be a secret from you—or him! If he didn't tell you, who did?"

"A librarian."

Confusion washes over his features. "When?"

I ignore his question. "I can't believe neither of you assholes told me."

"Listen, Ast—Aife. Why don't we calm down and talk about this—"

"Don't fucking tell me to *calm down*," I mimic, scoffing.

"I'm sorry for keeping things from you…Aife." He hesitates before saying my name, as if it pains him. "It doesn't change the way I feel about you, and I hope it doesn't change how you feel about me."

"Damn you, Dash."

"Come here." He opens his arms.

My chest heaves, my heart racing. The magic in my veins begs to be released, simmering to a slow boil. If the vimstone weren't here, it would be so easy to let it out.

Too easy.

Too easy to fall victim to my anger—to my lethal emotions. Is Osiris right? Am I *meant* to let my power rule me? Am I destined to submit to it?

No.

I don't want to be like him—like Enira. Or Invidia, for that matter.

Instead, I close my eyes and silently count to ten. Dash says nothing, but I can feel his gaze boring into me.

When I'm slightly calmer, I open my eyes and blink up at him, stepping forward and letting him embrace me. I force myself to swallow my anger and try to forgive him—right here, right now, without running.

"I'm so fucking annoyed at you," I mutter.

"I know." He chuckles into my hair, holding my head tight to his chest. His heart thumps against my cheek. His familiar sandalwood scent softens me. "You have the mouth of a sailor when you're pissed off."

"I don't fucking care."

His body rumbles with laughter. "I hope you know how sorry I am for upsetting you." He sighs. "I'd never let anything happen to you. Neither would Lex." I incline my head, nuzzling his neck. "You're—I don't know, stronger somehow. More resilient. I would never have thought that possible. But you handle everybody else's shit with so much ease. We don't deserve you."

I snort, glancing up at him through my lashes. "You're damn right you don't."

He kisses my nose, and I giggle, heat rising in my core.

"Do you know the name of the god who—" *murdered your ex-fiancée.* I swallow thickly, not wanting to say it.

His body stiffens. "I do," he whispers. "Gedeon, God of—"

"Vengeance," I finish, and he goes eerily still.

I pull away.

"You know him?"

My brow furrows. His name seems so familiar. Deep down somewhere, I know it. I've heard of it. But the memory, like so many others, is just out of reach.

A collage of images, faces, and places passes through my mind. None of it makes sense. I'll have to sit down and process all of this at some point, dive deep into my subconscious and see if I can remember something.

Anything.

For Dash's sake.

"I'm sorry I didn't tell you about this sooner," he says.

"You let me—and Lex—come to Stellaris, *knowing* we'd be in danger."

He shakes his head adamantly. "I would've never let anything happen to you."

"The road to hell is paved with good intentions," I mutter.

An image flickers through my mind—*a bitter, bone-chilling*

cold. A darkness that seeps into my skin, consumes me. A silence so loud it pierces my skull.

Sucking in a breath, I blink it away.

What *was* that?

Death.

Goose bumps line my arms, and a sickening feeling slithers beneath my skin.

"I wanted to tell you sooner but never had the chance, Aife. You have to understand that. You also have to realize that is exactly *why* I'm telling you now. I don't want any more secrets between us. No more hidden truths. No more miscommunications."

I nod automatically, but there's a hollow space in my mind. The leftover chill haunts me.

"You deserve to know everything. And you should know that—"

A bloodcurdling scream pierces the air.

Ilona.

CHAPTER FORTY-FOUR

AIFE

I burst through the kitchen door, Dash hot on my heels. Immediately, I spot the wisps of smoke from earlier—Osiris—in the shape of a shadowy man, with a wall of darkness surrounding him.

Lex's hair is mussed, his shirt ruffled. With a wild, unhinged fury, he throws powerful punches at the shadow, only to hit air. Callan is beside him, winged sword drawn, slicing uselessly at the smoke.

"Stop!" Cedrik wails. "Stop! This wasn't our deal."

The shadow chuckles, and it's a haunting sound. "You brought Aife to me. Thank you. I promised to reunite you with your family. A deal that death can eventually uphold."

"No—" Cedrik croaks. "That's not what I—leave her alone. Leave my daughter alone. Please."

He drops to his knees, wailing desperately beside Osiris.

My heart skips a beat, the blood whooshing in my ears.

Daughter.

Ilona.

He has confirmed my theory, but I have no time to give it more thought.

I surge toward the shadow, shoving through the blindingly dark fog and breaking free to the other side. Ilona lies on the ground, bug-eyed and blue-faced.

"ILONA!" I scream, clawing at the shadowy tendrils around her throat.

Dash drops to his knees beside me, and we desperately grasp at the air, trying to release Ilona from the hold Osriris's shadows have on her.

"She can't breathe!" I wail, panic consuming me. "She can't breathe... Help. Someone, help—" Tears stream down my face. "Ilona, you'll be okay. I won't let anything happen to you. It can't, okay?" Her eyes begin to roll into the back of her head, her face turning an unnatural purple color. "Hold on, Ilona."

Moments with Ilona flash in and out of my mind: the two of us picking out Pancake and Aife together, swimming in the falls, laughing over tea, me making her blush with descriptions of smutty books, all the times she sat with me in the tent during bacchanals, never abandoning me even though her heart was too big, too soft for what I was doing.

I close my eyes and hear her voice in my head:

"I love you, I do, but I just find it hard to believe so many people willingly show up each week, knowing they might die."

"It's their choice," I tell her.

"Are you sure your mother doesn't...you know, influence them?"

My chest tightens, and I can't breathe. Ilona is the only reason I found myself. Dash and the Vannyks came to the island to hunt Enira, but it was *Ilona* who made me realize something was... *wrong.*

She doesn't deserve this. Not her.

My power—fueled by power-sharing with Lex and having consumed a bit of Dash's life force—bursts out of me unbridled. I let it out, trying to suck the life force from Osiris.

Only…he has none.

Osiris and his shadows laugh again, the sound coming from all directions and reverberating through my body. "You should know better, Aife. I am of the Underworld. I have no life. None for this realm, at least. You see why I need you now."

I have no time for another monologue. No time to ask *how* he appears before us or *why* he's able to harm Ilona. He isn't corporeal. This shouldn't be happening.

I jump to my feet, facing Osiris. My fists aim for his face, bursting through the shadows with an icy chill.

"Leave her alone! I'll do anything." Now, I realize why I agreed to assist Enira in order to protect Lex and Nevaris. Desperation makes you crazy. And when you love someone, you'd give up anything for their safety. "I'll agree to your bargain. I'll help you. Just please—leave Ilona alone."

"Aife, no!" Lex bellows, and it's the first time I've heard him truly fearful.

Ignoring everyone else, I continue to stare at the subtle, eerie shape of a face lingering in the shadows.

"Take me instead." My voice cracks. "Leave her alone."

"I will leave her alone, as you wish." The tone is taunting, not obliging. I tremble. "But you will come to me of your own accord."

I drop back to my knees beside Ilona, desperately clawing at the shadows to no avail. Her eyes flit back to mine, wide and fearful as she continues choking. A single tear streaks down her cheek, and I hear her voice in my head again—the words she said to me so many times, at so many bacchanals: "*I'll see you later. Remember who you are. The most incredibly strong woman I know.*"

My tears blind me as I reach for her hand, clutching it tight.

The shadows begin to retreat, recoiling from Ilona's body.

I release her hand, shaking her shoulder. "Ilona. You're okay. You're okay now. It's over."

"You know what you must do, Aife," Osiris says, his voice growing distant. "Come find me when you are ready."

Without sparing him a glance, I lean down and put my head to Ilona's chest. I wait a few seconds for the *thump-thump*, but nothing comes.

Reaching for her, I press two fingers against the tender spot on her wrist, hoping to find a pulse but feeling nothing.

A haunting silence fills my head.

"She's not—" Tears fall so heavily, I can barely see through the blur. Lex drops onto his knees beside me, immediately beginning compressions on her limp body. My best friend's body. My *Ilona*. "Bring her back! Now! Please!" My voice grows hoarse as I scream at the barely-there shadows that are fading away into nothingness. "Bring her back!"

"Sorry, Aife. You know it's not possible for me." And with that, the shadows disappear entirely.

I cup Ilona's warm, freckled cheeks in my hands.

I'll see you later. Remember who you are. The most incredibly strong woman I know.

"It's later, Ilona," I whisper as my voice breaks. "I remember who I am now." I choke down a sob. "Thanks to you." My breath comes out unsteady as I try not to hyperventilate. "You can't go now. You can't leave me." Sobs shake my body. "We just got back to each other—you can't go now!"

This isn't happening.

This isn't happening.

Not to Ilona.

"Please wake up," I whisper. "*You* are the most incredibly

strong person I know."

I close my eyes and focus until the surge of life force stirs inside me. But instead of flowing into her body, it continues to circulate in my veins without release.

"Why isn't it working?" I scream, desperate. My eyes rip open to see Lex on the other side of Ilona. He's no longer doing compressions. "Help me, damn it!"

"Aife, it won't work. She's already gone. She has nothing left for the life force to latch onto. It won't work, luv."

"Fuck you, Lex! I remember the day I met you—I helped Fara's mother. I *cured* her!"

One of his strong hands covers mine atop Ilona's cheek. "Aife," he says. The pity there shatters my already broken heart. I can't look at him, don't have time to care that I revealed I remember how we met. It's not important.

"I can do it. I can do it. I *need* to save her." My voice is rabid, hysterical.

"You were able to give Zee life force because she was still alive. Ilona is—"

"Don't you fucking say it, Lex!" I screech, my face scrunching up as I glare at him. "You help me right now!"

He shares a pitying look with Dash, who sits down beside me and pulls me to his chest. I push him away, slapping him. "Fuck you too! Help me!"

A deep sob echoes from across the room.

Cedrik.

He's slumped on the floor with his head in his hands.

"You!" I bellow. I drag myself across the floor to him, wrapping my hands around his wrists and gripping so tightly that my nails dig in. "This is all your fault."

"No. No. I never meant for this—"

It's too easy to draw his energy toward me. Sucking out his life force only makes me angrier, reminds me that *he* is here, alive, while his daughter's light fades away.

"Aife, don't do this. This isn't what she wanted," Lex says.

Firm hands are on me, pulling me away from Cedrik.

It doesn't stop me.

I don't need to touch him to take his life force. Not after power-sharing with my fated.

Giving Cedrik a predatory smile, I let out a guttural screech and continue drawing his life force into me.

Violent noises leave his throat as he drops to the ground, thrashing about. Those whose life force I've consumed previously have always experienced pleasure. Until now. Somehow, now, it's hurting him, and I'm viciously thrilled about it. I slow down the process, dragging out his pain.

Is that what I can do with *more*?

It makes me...powerful.

Dangerous.

The thought propels me onward, and my crazed smile grows.

"Aife—"

"Sweetheart, please."

Ignoring the men trying to hold me back, I consume Cedrik's energy until his thrashes slow and his eyes begin to glaze over.

"Let me," Lex whispers in my ear, no longer fighting me. "Let me finish this for you, Aife. For Ilona."

Her name washes over me like a wave, clearing my mind enough to agree. I nod, ceasing my energy pull.

Cedrik slumps over, barely alive, gasping desperately for air.

Air Ilona didn't get in her last few minutes.

Air Ilona deserved.

Not Cedrik.

But I've already taken Ilona's mother from her. I don't want to be responsible for taking her father too. Can't. It feels like letting Ilona down, betraying her even in death.

This isn't what she would want for me.

"How is Osiris able to appear?" I ask Cedrik, sneering down at him.

He sucks in a few lungfuls of air, his weathered face sunken and pale. "He—I—he never could touch us before."

"Not what I asked," I growl. Cedrik's eyes flit to Lex, then back to me. "Answer me!"

"I theorize it's because of...your life force...from Enira. Years of transference have powered him. He is almost corporeal. Almost free. It's why...why he needs you. To finish what they started."

"All this time, and you *knew*," I spit. "You *knew*." I wipe a stray tear and nod at Lex. "Make it hurt."

Pushing Dash and Callan out of the way, I bolt back to Ilona's body. Planting my hands on her, I try to force Cedrik's life force into her body. I have Lex, Dash, *and* Cedrik's energy coursing through me...but it's still not enough.

It's as if her body is rejecting it.

Lex already said it, but I don't want to believe it.

I slump over her body, wrapping my arms around her and sobbing into her chest. "I'm so sorry, Lonnie. So—so fucking sorry." I hiccup between sobs. "I can't— You didn't—"

"Shhhh." Dash is by my side again, stroking my hair. "We're here. It'll be okay, sweetheart."

No it won't. I made that same promise to Ilona.

I lied to her.

She's gone.

She's *dead*.

Grunts fill the air, followed by the sound of meat being tenderized.

A bitter, metallic scent fills my nose. I glance at Lex, who is pummeling Cedrik's face. Punch after relentless punch, brutalizing the man until he is completely unrecognizable.

Blood pours from Cedrik's nose and mouth, and he's wavering in and out of consciousness. When Lex finally drops Cedrik to the ground, he's too weak to ask him to stop. Too on the brink of death to move.

Lex wraps his hands around the old healer's throat and squeezes. A look of violence mars his features. Lethal hatred contorts his handsome features into something ruthless, almost unrecognizable. His hair hangs loose around his shoulders in messy waves. Blood is splattered on his cheeks.

Lex's eyes lift to mine. A flicker of sorrow crosses his face, and he loosens his grip, pausing, as if waiting for my permission.

I give an almost imperceptible nod, and he returns it.

"This is for Ilona," Lex says. His voice sends goose bumps up my arms.

With one final effort, Lex resumes his grip and squeezes so hard that a brutal crack cuts through the air.

And Cedrik breathes no more.

EPILOGUE

AIFE

Everything is a blur.

Cedrik's death brings me no relief. No regrets, either.

Another memory flashes through my mind, and I swear I hear the echo of Osiris's laughter alongside it.

It's incohesive.

Bits and pieces.

It's cold—dark. The mountains around me are bare and endless. There's no life. No plants, no beating hearts.

Only bleakness.

The Underworld.

A sour scent fills my nose, and I try not to gag. I need to get in and out. Find him before Osiris finds me. He knows I'm here. I've breached his wards. It's only a matter of time.

Searching.

Finding the man I came for—

My boyfriend—square jaw, sheared hair, dark green eyes. A scar runs through his left eyebrow, and there's a small mole on his right cheek, beneath his eye. He's handsome, in a too-severe sort of way, with a pointed nose, arched brows, and day-old stubble.

I need to find him.

Breathe life into him.

Bring him back to the realm.

I blink and lose touch with the memory. Who was the man I saw? I knew him...intimately. Long, long ago. But I felt nothing romantic when I saw his face.

There was no lust, no longing, no warmth coursing through my skin like there is when I see Lex and Dash. Only...a deep-seated anger.

Disgust.

His face brought a deeper chill to the already cold air of my memory. It was...haunting. I try to gather further context, but nothing comes to me. It's there...but just out of my grasp.

My lungs constrict when his image conjures up something Ilona said to me in our last full conversation, when she was telling me about a dream she had. She said, *"There's a man— with a scar on his eyebrow. I don't think you like him, but you need his help."*

I gasp as his name fills my mind like an ancient whisper, long forgotten.

Gedeon.

God of Vengeance.

He was in the Underworld. And I...got him out? Which means he lives.

And he's the one Dash thinks is responsible for Ayana's death.

But that memory is so old. I can't explain how I know that. It's a feeling in my bones. Ayana died not too long ago. Which means either Gedeon didn't kill Ayana...or I succeeded in finding him and bringing him back to life.

If he is alive, I need to find him, need to figure out how it's possible I visited the Underworld and brought him back.

"I'll see you later, Ilona," I whisper up at the stars, my hand on my heart. "I remember who I am, and I am nothing without you."

To be continued...

Stay tuned for book 3, *These Wicked Gods*, coming soon.

In the meantime, be sure to check out *A Curse of Malice and Mercy*, book one in my all-new Courts of Malice series, coming soon!

ACKNOWLEDGEMENTS

Writing a book is such a strange phenomenon. It's pure magic. Writers start with a single blank page—the fleeting whisper of an idea—and end with hundreds of pages of words that bring characters, places, and ideas to life. No matter how fictional my stories are, they carry a piece of my heart and soul with them.

It's a complicated task, even on its best days, and I could not fathom doing it alone. So, thank you to everyone who has assisted me in some way along my journey.

First, my husband gets my biggest thanks. Thank you, Bryam, for enduring my chaos, encouraging my passions, and loving my flaws. You're the best dog dad a gal could ask for, and doing life is better with you by my side.

Next, big thanks to Charity and Abigail for being my earliest alpha readers. Thank you both for being my soundboard and brainstorming partners when this book was in its primitive stages. You both kept me grounded, were honest when I needed it, and truly understood my vision for these characters. I can't believe you've read this book almost as many times as I have and still want to read more. You two are a true blessing, and I am grateful to call you my friends.

Another big thank you goes out to Sam and Becky for

being my last minute, early ARC readers to ensure the story was indeed ready to go out. Imposter syndrome and artist panic are real things, and your enthusiasm for this story helped move it forward.

My bestie Alex gets a huge thank you for so many reasons. Thanks for being a fantastic friend and the best accountability partner a gal could ask for. You are incredibly intelligent and kind, and it's amazing talking craft and story with you.

My amazing editor Emily deserves all the thanks for being the most patient, thorough, and thoughtful editor around. Thanks for not quitting on me even when I mix metaphors and can't get "me and you" straight to save my life. You are a true gem.

Thank you to my wonderfully creative cover designer, Fran, for bringing my cover vision to life and making it gorgeous.

Thank you to Lindsay for formatting my book while lugging around a whole mini-human in your stomach. You are going to be a super-mom—I just know it! Thanks for making TWT pretty.

And last but not least, thank YOU! Yes, you. Without my readers, this book would not be here. Thank you for sharing your time with me. Thank you for giving my stories a chance. And thank you for rooting for Astrid as much as I do.

ABOUT THE AUTHOR

Miranda is a fan of all things magical and romantic. She believes some of the best heroes come from dark pasts, and family is more than blood. She loves writing about strong characters who overcome unpleasant situations and find love along the way. She holds a BA in English and is currently pursuing an MFA. When she's not scratching out notes for her next story or devouring a book, she's petting her dogs. Bookstagram is a huge part of her life (@readwritejoy) and she loves to connect about all things bookish!

Follow Miranda on Instagram, Twitter, or TikTok @ readwritejoy, and online at www.authormirandajoy.com

Ingram Content Group UK Ltd.
Milton Keynes UK
UKHW040947240323
419106UK00004B/413